Last

To

Know

By: Lindsey Marie Abraham

A Spun Yarn Publishing 6890 Baystone Road | Fayetteville, NC 28314

Last To Know

(2nd Edition)

10 Digit ISBN: 0-615-31725-1

13 Digit EAN: 978-0-615-31725-0

Check out the following website for order information:

www.lasttoknow.webs.com

or send comments, questions or orders for autographed copies to:

lindseymarieabraham@nc.rr.com

Acknowledgment…..I want to thank all of those that were not only inspiration for the book but supportive. There are so many that I am afraid to mention them for fear of forgetting someone. But…I will try…Thanks go to Sheri T., Graham C., Allan D., and Anne C., for their encouragement. Thanks to Tarek and Josh for fan and blog pages. Thanks to Jeff P. and Karen, and also to Ken K. and Steve J. for their work on the cover. To Steve J. for the final cover. To Melissa K., Lori L. and Pam J. for their help with editing. And to the many, many more that read and gave me critiques of what they read.

To the famous author Stephanie Meyer who unintentionally inspired me to add the next 100,000 or so words to it. I was lost in my own pain and stupor until I read her books. Then as if the floodgates opened, my life changed. She inspired much more than the completion of this book. She inspired a reconnecting with God. Because of one small part in her book, I finally began to believe that God still loved me in spite of my faults and finally I give my thanks to God for sticking by me through all of those horribly bad times and personal doubt.

And finally, thanks so much to my family for their support. My daughters, who lived through some of the events in this book in our real lives, but thankfully have all managed to come through it with more strength than I.

May this story, truth woven into fiction, inspire others to just hold on to who you are, no matter what changes may come and what you don't know you don't know.

Bria's journey through every up and down may not be anything like your own journey, but if God is willing, you too will discover that there is always a way to survive.

"He wasn't in love with me like I thought. What I'm trying to say is; I understand feeling as small and insignificant as humanly possible. And how it can actually ache in places that you didn't know you had inside you. And it doesn't matter how many new hair cuts you get or gyms you join or how many glasses of chardonnay you drink with your girlfriends, you still go to bed every night going over every detail and wonder what you did wrong or how you could have misunderstood. And how in hell for that brief moment you could think that you were that happy. And sometimes you can even convince yourself that he'll see the light and show up at your door. And after all that, however long all that may be, you'll go somewhere new, and you'll meet people who make you feel worthwhile again, and little pieces of your soul will finally come back; and all that fuzzy stuff, those years of your life that you wasted will eventually begin to fade." Iris (Kate Winslet) in conversation with Miles (Jack Black) in "The Holiday" 2006

"I can't do this anymore. It hurts so badly. Why?" I cried. "Why?" I slid to the floor and my face fell into my lap. I was sobbing now, my body shaking. My heart was breaking with every thought of what Warren had meant to me. James knelt in front of me, his hands on my shaking shoulders. I looked up at James from my position "Why can't I just die? Maybe if my heart stops beating, it will stop hurting." I felt so broken. Like the glass of my snow globes, my heart had shattered into so many pieces I couldn't see how it could be mended.

CONTENTS

"Once upon a time…" is always a fairy tale. Never let that stop you from telling your own story. Each and every word is worth the telling.

Preface

When a friend of a friend tells Bria that she has the perfect match for her, Bria files it in the back of her brain with all the other "perfect matches" that never were.

When Bria meets Warren however, his goofy charm and good looks persuade her to take a chance on a date with him. Romance was not in her plan but when a surprise proposal comes a year later, she believes that she has finally found love.

After almost two years of blissful marriage, Bria is somehow thrown into a world that lends itself to secrets when Warren shows a different and much more violent side to him. She has no choice but to turn to strangers for help so that she can thwart his attempts to kill her.

Her new found attorney, James Laughton becomes a friend and comes readily to her rescue when every move she makes on her own seems to bring her to the brink of death.

Bria decides to leave her safe haven in the hopes that it will alleviate the danger to her friends. Mistakenly believing that by leaving she will no longer be a burden to them, she will come to know that she is more of a burden to them as they fear for her safety.

While absent from those who love her, two young would be rescuers decide she needs their help. They label her with the unsettling title of "damsel in distress". It seems all in fun at first but turns deadly serious as her declining health puts death on her doorstep. Their involvement helps her to understand that sometimes letting others take over can knock down the barriers that will allow her to finally be free of the physical and emotional turmoil.

As they join Mr. Laughton and friends in a combined effort to protect frail Bria, their own life lessons begin.

Reflecting on the death of his wife three years before leaves Mr. Laughton's emotions raw. He sees in Bria the same frailty that he saw in his wife and his need to protect her leads the two of them down a path that neither of them are ready to embark on. As their relationship changes it catches Bria off guard, she begins to wonder how she can possibly love or trust anyone else when she can't even trust herself.

Throughout her whole journey, trial drugs poison her body and bring vivid nightmares that keep her body and mind weak and needy.

The haunting words spoken by Warren just before his first attempt to kill her play over and over again in her mind.

"I will never love any one or any thing much as I love you. And no matter how many fights we may have, promise me that you will always remember that I love you. Please Bria; promise me that you will remember that one thing." He had said.

How could words so very tender hurt her so much? They were now only a reminder of how her love for him had placed her in danger and of Warren's continued attempts to kill her. It is a lesson of just how thin the line between love and hate can be.

*These first few chapters are exactly as it was, please ignore the boredom as the story begins....

Chapter One
Reflecting

The bench I was seated on was hard. There was way too much varnish on it. I looked down at it as my nails dug unintentionally into the sheen. I could almost feel the different layers as my nail continued to scrape away that varnish. I wasn't sure exactly why I was doing it, but I suspected that I just wanted to see anything that looked as scarred and damaged as I felt.

I was wishing that I would be strong enough to meet Warren head on, but I knew I couldn't. Just how hard this would be for me, I didn't have a clue, but I hoped that in the end that I would at least be standing on my own two feet.

Was that too much to hope for?

Many emotions raced through me as they jumped from one extreme to another. Every possible emotion seemed to be fighting amongst themselves in an attempt to be the one that would surface next. All would show the world my heartache.

I tried to analyze those emotions. Give reason to them. Ticking them off I started. First, I was reflective. Looking back over everything; I tried to play the part of an outsider. I was nervous because I was afraid to stand before strangers and tell them my story.

Anger too was right there on top. Why was I angry? Just who was I angry at? I had those answers. I was angry because it had come to this. Even though I was angry at Warren, I was angrier at myself, and, angry that I was sitting here in a local courthouse waiting for my divorce attorney.

Disappointment was another strong emotion. I had been so sure that Warren was truly in love with me. There had been no doubt or else I wouldn't have allowed myself to fall in love with him. So yes, I was disappointed in myself that I had let my heart rule my head.

Hurt. I was terribly hurt. Because…well because my broken heart did actually physically hurt me. I had taken to crossing my arms across my chest and curling into a near fetal position in my attempt to ease the crushing pain. I didn't know if my heart or I, would ever recover from the damage Warren had caused.

It was there on the courthouse bench that I discovered that there was a huge hole in my heart. Warren had once filled my heart so completely, and now that place was missing.

There was also another emotion that had suddenly come into mind. It was the hardest emotion to get a handle on. That emotion was grief. I wanted to grieve for what might have been.

I sat alone with my emotions trying to keep them from surfacing and showing on my face. As it was, my face had become a canvas and all of my emotions were being painted there, painted by my broken heart.

I was mourning for all of my losses. Not only my losses in love but in life. I had heard it said that when your heart is broken, you have to grieve just as you would with the death of a loved one. Thus far, I hadn't had time to grieve for any of it, and it swept over me now in waves so deep that I couldn't control them.

The dam had burst and those emotions would soon overflow. Until now they had all taken a back seat to fear. Fear had taken over.

I looked around, trying not to think of anything. Then suddenly I had this bizarre thought. I had been so in control of my life just a couple of years ago. And yet here I was sitting in this lobby waiting on *someone else* to tell me what my future would hold. I sighed. While I waited, I realized that I could do nothing but try and figure out where my life had gone off of my carefully planned track.

Too many questions kept my mind busy, but I didn't have any answers. I wanted one. No! I needed one. How does any life come to this place? Hadn't I followed all the rules? Was it possible to look back and find the little clues that I had missed along the way? Would noticing them have kept me on the right road?

The lobby was quickly filling up with strangers as I sat reflecting on my life. A young blind woman walked in with her hand on the arm of another person and suddenly it hit me. That was the explanation for the reason that I was in this situation. I was blind. I could suddenly see it clearly in that all important twenty-twenty hindsight. Blind to all of Warren's hidden faults and though I could try to make myself believe that I had seen the signs, I honestly hadn't. I wanted to believe that I hadn't just chosen to ignore the signs before.

Every part of my marriage seemed to be shrouded in mystery. For some reason, I needed to feel the things I had missed in the palm of my hands to make them real. I wanted to know them, to hold them, to understand them so that I would know for the next time. *If,* there was a next time.

Most importantly, as with all lessons, I needed to remember them. Always. I needed to let the lessons I would learn be a guide to my future. Something that I could tangibly point to that would say, "Don't go down that path again."

Self reflection is a brutal thing that taunts you when you blame yourself for everything. And now, I had to keep reminding myself that none of it, no matter how many 'signs' I had missed, was my fault. I had always been naïve and extremely gullible. I believed the best in people. Even bums on the street could come up to me with unbelievable stories and I would readily hand over cash believing their every word.

Where Warren was concerned, I had believed everything. Every excuse and every single word that Warren had said to me, I believed. I believed it all. I closed my eyes remembering them. "I'll be late at work." "I'll be out of the country for the next few days." Were they real excuses? How many times he had said those things and I always took them to be honest words. I shook my head remembering, was any of it true? When he would return from wherever he had been, I could see the wear and tear on him and he would say; "I just need to have some down time, love." I would leave him be and let him recover. I was so in love with him that being in love had led me to believe our love was one for the ages. Correction, what I had believed was our love and his devotion for me. I couldn't change what I was rapidly finding out. This was all one big deception.

I was indeed a victim of the "Love is blind" adage. I was just as mistaken as the rest of those "poor unfortunate souls" that everyone described abused women as. No one could have pointed it out to me, the error of his ways were normal for me. I would not have believed them anyway. No! Instead it had to be a very public display of his contempt for me and his harsh anger.

I leaned my head back against the high back of the bench and dissolved into a quiet peaceful world. It was what I had to do lately, a trick I had learned in college yoga classes. It seemed to be the only way to quiet the questions of my own existence. It was a great way to just wash away my worries if only for a just a few minutes at a time.

The noise level increased and I couldn't bear to look at the people around me shuffling from one side of the foyer to another. They too looked as if they were trapped in their own little worlds. I assumed that they may have been having the same problems with their emotions that I was with mine. I didn't think I could bear to see. I didn't want to read their worries. I also didn't want them to read my face either.

As the foyer got more and more crowded with the people waiting on that nine o'clock opening of the courtrooms, the anxiety in the room grew as thick as fog on an early summer morning after rain.

I thought about all the women I had heard about in the news or through friends and family that had similar circumstances. They too were often taken by surprise just like I had been. These women, who, like me, had had their lives torn apart by a husband, were living in the same sad sphere that I was in now. Husbands, whose offenses against those wives, didn't really matter. The point was that the men in their lives had abandoned their chief responsibility as a husband and in some cases a father and even more than that, they had shirked their responsibility as a human being.

From cheating to gambling or even drugs and alcohol, something caused them to change. The thing that hurt the most to think about was the abuse. Physical and emotional abuse. I had fallen prey to it just as so many others had.

How stupidly we allow ourselves not to give up on what we think is love. How could we not know what was going on? I used to be sure. I used to think that if something like that were happening in my world, I would know it; after all it was sure easy to pick out the signs in others.

I was surprised to find that I had been fooled. I was more than surprised, I was shocked. I knew that I was wrong and that was so unsettling.

It had only been two years ago that I believed Warren to be the perfect man for me and I had agreed to marry him. Now, however, I sat here with the awful knowledge that he wasn't what I had supposed him to be.

Before Warren, I had been a very strong independent woman making a good living doing what I loved. I had plans on buying my first house in the not to distant future. I had a new car. I had loved my life! I suddenly hated what I knew love could do to a person. What love had done to me.

Laughter interrupted my thoughts and my self loathing. Its shrill brightness brought me quickly from my thoughts. It annoyed me. Someone was obviously not here for the same unhappy reason that I was. I slowly leaned forward and put my head in my hands, my fingers going inconspicuously in my ears to block the sound. I did not want to hear any happiness today.

Where was Mr. Laughton? He was my attorney and he should have been here on time. This was too frustrating! I bit my lower lip and I realized that I was feeling the tension in the air from all those around me. I was sure that they didn't appreciate the interruption to their thoughts by the laughter either. We all seemed to be reliving our dilemmas while we waited for the courtroom doors to open. I just wanted everything to be over with.

An unexpected door slam caused me to notice all sorts of people were here. I checked the door for the umpteenth time for my attorney, but I looked around at the people. Some of them, sure, were in some kind of trouble. You could tell by their faces. Their emotions were indeed shown on their facial canvases. For that's what faces truly were, canvases for the soul. Why hadn't I been able to see Warren's canvas for what it really was?

Ugh! Being in this crowd was so difficult. It was becoming more and more unbearable. The only good thing I could find about it was that I was able to hide among the strangers. Sitting here dressed in my disguise, I was just a face among the crowd. These strangers unknowingly were protecting me from the one someone that I did not really want to see. Not one of them actually cared about me, or knew one way or the other, but I had decided that they were performing a blessed service just by being there. Even if it was hard for me, their presence allowed me to hide in plain sight.

Laughter again! Stupid, bright, happy laughter. Couldn't they go somewhere else and be happy? I was already too aware of the sadness in my heart and I wanted her to shut up! I could feel my heart beating all too fast as it continued to overwhelm me. I was taking deep breaths to try and slow down the much too fast pace that was sure to cause it to pound out of my chest. "Please" I pleaded with my heart, "let this work." I didn't want the world to know of my suffering. But I didn't want the rest of the world to be so blasted happy either.

Some of the other people that were milling around me looked up in disgust trying to find the laughter's source as well. It was then that I realized that each person seemed to have someone by their side. For the first time, I felt alone. I realized that each person had a support system with them. Someone was there that commiserated with them during their time of need. Whether they were family or friends I couldn't tell but at least they were there. I didn't see anyone alone.

Everyone had someone.

Everyone… but me.

Chapter Two
Frustration!

It was the first time since this turn in my life began that I began to think about my own system of support. More importantly, the lack of. Most of my family was unavailable to come with me as they were busy with their own lives. Others bluntly said that they didn't want to be involved and therefore wouldn't come to stand by my side.

My parents were out of the country. And even though I had told them that they didn't need to come home for this, I wished they had. Of course I hadn't let them know that Warren was trying to kill me. I didn't want them to know about how bad it had gotten and besides, they were heartbroken already for me.

Even close friends that I thought would have surrounded me in my time of need were no where to be found. I made the comparison between myself and all those around me. I was left severely lacking. Envy suddenly added itself to my tally of emotions.

The people joining me in the foyer of the courthouse made me wish for more. Much, much, more. I had to acknowledge just how empty I felt.

Yes my family and most of my friends had all been too busy in their own lives. But I didn't really want them involved. The fact that they didn't even take the time to know just how much I needed them, nevertheless, hurt me deeply. In fact, thinking about the recent past, most of my friends seemed to be more distant now than the ever were before. I surmised that they simply couldn't believe everything that I had told them about Warren and what he had done to me.

After all, my story now was completely different from what I had regaled them with early on in our relationship. I had introduced him as this great guy and he quickly become fast friends with everyone that was my friend. Looking at it now, I was sure that this trait had helped him tremendously in his work and it served him well in life too.

My friends had become his friends. I understood that their loyalty was divided. I had to step out of my little bubble and think about it for a moment. The conclusion I reached was; I really couldn't blame them. I was having the same difficulty believing everything myself and it was happening to me.

Family members were a different story. They in the beginning said things like, "it couldn't have been that bad" and I knew that they thought that I had made more of it than it could possibly be. "You're turning a mole hill into a mountain."

Their aloofness at my circumstances changed only when the abuse finally affected their lives. It took a major event for them to see clearly what I was going through.

The night at the party was just the beginning. Warren had tailed me from work one day and when I saw him, he passed me and pulled in front of me. I was frightened and was going to turn off at the next street, whatever street it was, just to escape him. No matter how lost I would become it was better than knowing he was near. I was too late. I was almost to the next street, when he slammed on the brakes and my little car crashed into the back of his Escalade.

My car crumpled. My head went forward onto the steering wheel. He wasn't thinking clearly either though, because too many witnesses were around, thank goodness, and they called 911 to tell them not only to hurry, but what had happened and how it had happened.

I was taken to the hospital and even though there were no permanent injuries, I was kept there. I had to call on family to come and pick me up and take me home. The change of heart was immediate when they were able to hear from the doctors the report of how everything happened.

The side effect of that was; now they believed me but they didn't want to have anything to do with me while "my situation" was going on. They had spouses and children and didn't want them exposed to the violence or involved in any way. I had to agree with them and I knew it was too much to ask them to.

It had taken almost a week to get my new Mustang. A replacement that was "just as good" as the original, but as soon as that was over with, I was back to being alone. Just as I was here in the foyer. Alone amongst the masses.

I leaned forward even more to look past the person now seated beside me and looked around one last time for Mr. Laughton before I put my head back into my hands. I couldn't help but quietly wish I was as far away from here as possible.

Behind my closed eyes my mind again closed to the sounds around me so intently that I found myself daydreaming again. It was becoming a habit in my effort to examine my life and pick up on some of those missing clues I was sure that would lead me to answers.

It was over two years ago when I had spread the news to everyone about how perfect Warren was. I gladly shared every happy moment with all of my friends and family. I bubbled over with that giddy school girl type of enthusiasm that such a wonderful man like Warren could possibly be in love with me.

Tears suddenly flowed. Guess I was wrong on both counts. He wasn't in love with me, and he wasn't so wonderful. Instead of living a happy life, I was caught in the middle of a very messy divorce fraught with troubles beyond even my most vivid imaginings. Because of his threats to me, I had entered some new and unfamiliar world of disguise and clandestine behavior. His world. It was a world that he was as comfortable with as I was uncomfortable with. I knew he had an advantage.

This was now my window into Warren's world. What his "normal" was. I had this vision of what Warren's normal life must have been like. Or what it still was like. In fact, this behavior had now become a part of my normal every day life, so I knew it was hard on your soul. I could no longer leave my home without peering over my shoulder and looking out the windows to make sure that he wasn't waiting to attack me again.

Nothing that was part of my life now, was at all like I had envisioned my future with Warren. What a waist of energy it was to be worried all of the time. I shook my head bringing me back to the present and to the fact that I was here as a direct result of Warren's actions and that someone else would decide the fate of our marriage. It sucked. I wanted to run out on it all. I couldn't but that didn't mean I didn't want to.

Warren had given me no choice now but to listen to those others. Others, who until recently, didn't know I even existed. Others, who were familiar with this type of life in some way or another, and I knew I had to do what they asked of me. If I didn't, well, I didn't want to think about that. I knew it would not be good.

My dad used to say: "You have to learn to hit the curve balls, or learn to be happy with striking out." Of course, no one is truly happy about striking out so I decided right then that I would learn to hit the curve balls. I was standing at the plate and no matter what else happened, striking out wasn't an option.

Laughter again interrupted my thoughts and I was drawn back into the lives of those standing or sitting around me. Where was my stupid attorney? I was to meet him here, right? I knew that I would spot him immediately but would he recognize me? "Dress in a disguise," he had said, "For your own safety", he had said. Ugh!

I really did like him, but I had thought that this was a bit much. His secretary had said that he really did have my safety in mind and I knew that he had, especially given everything that we had already been through. He had paid for and kept me pretty much safe since our very first meeting.

That and everything that had happened *in* our first meeting together made him an easy man to like. He was the most intimidating man I had ever met. I smiled at that thought. Sure that was in my favor where Warren was concerned.

He was a nice man. I was glad now that one of my friends, a fellow co-worker, had recommended him to me. "He's fabulous." She had explained. "I've used him several times." I smiled. In her past, he had represented her very well. She had said when she was going through her divorce that he really did care about what she was going through. It did not take much of her convincing for me to tell her to make an appointment for me to see him.

That day, I had stood outside of a brown brick building and looked at the nameplate on the door. The doors were ornate with frosted designs in their glass plated insets. "James Aaron Laughton, Attorney at Law", was stenciled on the nameplate just below the glass. I have to admit that I was afraid to walk through the door. It meant that I was indeed putting an end to my marriage. I also had an irrational fear that a male lawyer would not be as sympathetic to me or to what had happened to me. I really wanted to turn around and find myself a female attorney that might be more compassionate towards me.

I was still standing in front of the closed door when I finally decided that I would at least have to walk in and listen to what he had to say. That way, I didn't disappoint my friend. I knew that it would be my decision to hire him or not. After all this initial consultation cost me nothing but time. I could walk out and feel good about looking for a female lawyer on my own if I felt any bad vibe from him.

I took a deep breath and blew it out. I was just about to reach out to open the door to walk in when I heard a voice from behind me say: "Let me get that door for you." I was startled by the sound of his voice and so I jumped a little, bumping into him. I didn't think that I had been standing at the door for so long. I had been so involved in my own thoughts that I had not heard him walk up. It had become a very bad habit in recent months.

He had apparently been there for at least a couple of minutes watching me before deciding that I was not going to open the door immediately. It was at that exact moment that he spoke and decided to open the door for me that I too reached for it. Like I said, I jumped back, bumping into him as he opened the door. What must he think of me? He must think something is terribly wrong with me. I nodded my head at him and whispered a soft "thank you' as he pulled the door open in front of me. He crossed his arm above my head as he held it open and I walked underneath his arm to enter the building.

Actually making it across the threshold and into the office was a big step for me so I couldn't look back at him or I might not continue on. I could see a tall reception desk in front of me and I proceeded to walk as fast as I dared without running to the desk.

I watched him as he walked past me. He was a very tall and imposing man and even though his face seemed kind, I felt embarrassed that I had been so afraid to just walk in the door. Just before he was to disappear down a hallway, his big long strides had covered the distance quickly, I called awkwardly after him and thanked him a second time.

I smiled but his "You're welcome" was lost to me. I had not expected it. Instead I turned, flustered, to the secretary that was waiting behind the tall counter of the reception desk at which she sat.

Barely glancing up at me, she asked: "How can I help you?" I briefly pondered asking her to give me directions to the local Pizza Hut because I knew that my cheeks were flushed with embarrassment. I looked to my left and watched as the gentleman walked down the hallway and disappeared from view, waiting to tell her my name and reason for being there.

She looked up at me again and said, "Ma'am? Can I help you?" I cleared my throat, "I'm here to see Mr. Laughton. I'm Bria Stone." I watched as she ran her finger down her list of appointments for the day. I thought. I'm the first one, why are you checking the list. But then she said, "Yes, I see you here." And I waited on her directions.

Instead she stood and walked around the desk to the hallway. "Follow me, Mrs. Stone." I silently followed her down the same hallway that the gentleman from the door had disappeared down. In just a minute she had led me into a luxuriously dark and rich office.

One whole wall was nothing but books and there was a couch as well as several chairs. I thought briefly that it was more like a library than an office, filled with nice furniture and end tables with books and lamps on them.

In front of a large ornate cherry wood desk were two large comfortable dark burgundy chairs. If it wasn't for all the electronics in the room, you might think you had stepped back in time to where these kinds of offices were the norm.

"Please take a seat, Mr. Laughton will be with you in a moment or two."

"Thank you." I said as I sank into the chair on the right. She turned then and walked out of the office leaving me to ponder over just what the heck I was doing here. I was very nervous as I waited on him to return to his office.

Moments passed.

When he walked in, I started to stand, but he reached out and took my offered hand and quickly waved me back into my seat. He held my hand while chuckling as he introduced himself. "If I had realized you were Mrs. Stone, I would have walked you back myself." I blushed at my earlier behavior. "I'm sorry." I mumbled, but I wasn't sure why I was saying it.

He walked to his chair behind that very large desk and sat down. He clasped his hands in front of him and then as if he had gathered his thoughts, cleared his throat. I lowered my head and began to watch my hands as I clasped and unclasped them over and over again.

The awkward few seconds of silence left me sufficiently intimidated by the man. I was afraid to just begin telling him why I was here to see him so I waited and hoped that he would ask me instead.

Finally, he stood up. The noise from the wheels on the chair was a deafening interruption to the silence that filled up the space between us. He walked back around to the front of his desk and then sat on the front edge of it. It reminded me of a professor in front of a classroom as he taught his students or a principal intimidating a misbehaving student.

There was another few seconds of silence before he quietly said: "Mrs. Stone, I know the basics from Leslie, but tell me exactly what you need from me?"

If only he knew how much I wanted to unburden myself of everything that I was feeling as well as how frightened I was of my own husband. I was so overwhelmed by his presence in the room that I couldn't find my voice immediately.

I tried to blink back the tears that were ever present in my eyes and they fell onto my cheeks unwillingly. I knew I couldn't speak. He reached back onto his desk and grabbed a tissue box and presented it to me. I took two of them and cleared my throat while dabbing my eyes.

I swallowed hard but continued to look at my hands. Finally I tried again, "I," but I couldn't go on, the tears were now in my voice and I wasn't ready to be this emotional with a complete stranger.

Once more it was the noise that interrupted the silence. He moved from the front of his desk and sat down in the chair beside me, the leather squeaking, announcing his presence and waited. I found myself wondering why he was such a patient person.

His close proximity to me was even more intimidating. I didn't dare raise my eyes yet to look at him. It felt as if he was genuinely interested in what I might have to say. It was not helping me to be at ease at all.

I finally opened my mouth to speak, but again our minds were in sync with each other and he began at the same time.

Silence.

We both stopped again. Finally he cleared his throat and he spoke very tenderly as if he really could understand my pain. "I know that it hurts to speak of it, but I need to know everything you can give me. That's the only way for me to know just how much I can help you or if I even can help you at all."

That shocked me into action. I raised my eyes to meet his and I locked my eyes on his. I tried to focus on the details of his face as the memories I needed to tell him about, crowded my mind. I looked away for a moment, sighed and then back to his eyes. I could see he really did have a look of concern for my well being etched in the deep blue pools of his eyes.

I thought; that's a great thing to do, like the good bedside manner of your doctor that helps you to become calm in the face of bad information.

Even so, my voice still cracked with tears and I asked: "What do you know already?" He answered, "I only know that Leslie thinks that you have need of my services. I also know that because your husband became abusive at a Christmas Party, you were rushed to the hospital. I have indeed confirmed that with the hospital."

Okay so he knew only the very basic information. I looked up at him again, cleared my own throat and continued. "I have a restraining order in place, but it hasn't stopped him. He has stalked me continually since and I seem to see him everywhere."

He was nodding his head as if he knew exactly what I was referring to. "I haven't asked yet for police reports or witness statements, but through only minor investigation, my PI Daniel said that you were choked to unconsciousness in front of hundreds at this Christmas Party."

The memories flooded me instantly as fresh as ever, but I held it in check. I took a deep breath and I sniffed. I looked back at him but it was too much and I put my hands to my face.

"Why don't I just ask you some questions?" Without waiting he continued. "Several men had to pull him off of you, is that correct?" I nodded my head. "Was he trying to kill you?" Again I nodded. My tears were flowing freely into my hands and onto the wadded up tissue that was now of no use.

He waited as I tried to slow down the tears. He grabbed the tissue box again and then held them in front of me. He patted my shoulder so that I could see the offered box. I grabbed several more tissues. I had not expected to be this out of control.

"May I call you Bria?" he asked. "Yes" I answered through the muffling of the tissues.

"Bria, I know this is hard for you, but I have decided to take your case if you want me to. The decision is up to you, but I want to."

He paused, seeming to choose his words carefully so as to make me feel more at ease. "I know you must be scared, terrified even. I understand that all of this had been completely unexpected. But I can assure you that Leslie would not have recommended your case to me if she didn't think it was worth my time."

He continued as I looked up at him. "On a second and much more personal note, I believe that women should be treated with respect and dignity. They are not possessions that you can use and abuse, nor are they toys to be played with."

He said the words with such a vehement conviction that I felt sure that he meant them. It was a relief and I knew then that he was quite possibly the right lawyer for me. Once more he continued though much slower and more business like. "Also, I must tell you that I also represent the pharmaceutical companies that support the research program you work with. I can halt any question that might interfere with the proprietary knowledge that you might have about your work. I will know what must be kept out of the public knowledge."

I stared up at him,understanding that he had taken into consideration everything. It had been a little while since I had seen such chivalry at work. Other than Warren, that is. The fact that any modern man believed women were to be treated with gentleness and respect these days was always a very nice surprise.

Like I said, it was only an instant, but in that instant, I knew by the tone of his voice that I had assumed correctly. He did believe the words that he spoke and I had no doubt that he lived them. It was in that same instant that my decision had been made for me. He would represent me and it looked like he was honestly upset at my ordeal so that meant to me that he was very much on my side.

I began to slowly tell him bits and pieces of my story. Just the bits and pieces that I felt I could share about the incident that led me to him. I watched as his face reacted in response to my rushed words. He listened intently to each and every one of them.

When I had finished my short tale of that evening and the subsequent events, his eyes were shining with emotion of his own. Anger or sorrow, I couldn't tell. He took a deep breath and shook his head. I stopped. I did not know what else to say and so I waited for him. His opinion was suddenly very important to me. It would mean that I had some sort of validation to everything that I had suffered through and I wanted him to represent me well in court. I wanted him there. I needed that strength that he embodied. I felt for the first time that this decision was the right one and that he really was the one to help me get through all the legalities of whatever I would soon have to go through.

Chapter Three
Hired Help?

I waited patiently as he got to his feet and walked to his chair at the back of his desk. Without saying a word he began writing notes on a notepad. I looked back down at my hands again. My head was still trying to wrap itself around all of the things that were happening.

Hearing my own words, I knew that it sounded more like some made for TV movie than real life. I began to question, was any of this real? Had I been just making things out to be worse than they were?

And so, as I sat there in front of his massive desk I began to have doubts. Not of him as a lawyer, but of the whole thing. I began to fight the urge to hire him. It felt like I was fighting back and forth like that character from the "Lord of the Rings." One voice giving me confidence in him, and the other giving me all the reasons not to hire him.

There I was sitting right in front of him and trying to find a reason not to hire him, any reason at all, and yet, I knew that he was exactly what I needed. I truly wanted him to take my case. What was wrong with me? It was a very strange feeling. I wondered why I was even struggling with it. Why was I so confused?

The fog cleared and suddenly I knew the answer. He was a man and I was having trust issues with people just now, more especially, with men.

When I glanced up at him, a unique thought crept in my head. Especially given my circumstances.   He was extremely attractive!

How could I be thinking this? I found him attractive. Astonished at that thought I realized that not since Warren had I even noticed men at all.

I looked at him with a more critical eye. His deep piercing blue eyes could penetrate any soul and his imposing height and his well proportioned physique came together to make him a very attractive male specimen. I giggled internally. It didn't change the fact that I was very intimidated by him.

A small part of me, very small now, still felt that it might be nice to have a woman by my side representing me in court but I quickly pushed that thought away, knowing it was silly to even think about.

This time I laughed a little. I could feel that a small smile had crept across my face. It was a relief. One thought was now giving me a great deal of confidence and assurance. I hoped that Warren would also easily be intimidated by Mr. Laughton, who stood at least six inches taller. I started thinking just how easily Mr. Laughton would put Warren in his place.

I was reasonably sure that Warren would not be intimidated by any female, attorney or not. In fact, his friendly nature and incredible good looks would probably sweep her off of her feet. I smiled again, completely at ease with my decision to hire Mr. Laughton and now amazingly completely at ease in a man's company.

My head had just stopped having its own private conversation when he reached over and pressed a button on the phone. I heard his secretary answer. "Yes sir, Mr. Laughton."

He answered, "Please get me the transcripts of the protection order hearing for Mrs. Stone." He pressed the button ending his conversation with Kim and walked again to the front of the desk. He sat again on the front of it. He put his hands in that familiar teepee pose in front of his mouth and nose. I waited on his next words but they surprised me when he finally spoke.

"Okay, Mrs. Stone," he paused, looking down at me, "I will be your representation but you must do whatever I may ask of you in order to stay safe. I don't want to end up hearing that you have been killed because you let him in your front door. Many women change their minds because they believe the lies they are told. All I ask is that you not be that kind of woman. Can you do that?"

My mouth had dropped open. I couldn't stop the argument in my head. "How bold you are?" I thought. "I haven't even asked you yet and I make all my own decisions. I don't need anyone to tell me what to believe or how to behave." My mouth suddenly snapped closed. Even though I had already made the decision myself to hire him, I wanted to rebel against him. I really did. I couldn't speak those thoughts out loud because I knew deep down that he was right.

In reality, the decision to hire him was probably made from the second that I realized that the kind man that had held the office door open for me was the same man that I had come to see.

I realized that the fact that Mr. Laughton thought he would be the best representation for me meant so much more than I could have imagined. It meant that I could feel safe and that was something… given my recent circumstances.

In fact, not being safe was what had brought me to his office in the first place so I decided to ignore the feelings that someone else was again in control of my life.

The next few minutes we talked about what other information I would need to get him, finances and legal ownership papers and of course when we would be meeting next. It was all the regular stuff that you take for granted when you are setting up an appointment for divorce.

I was emotionally drained and it had felt good just to talk about the business part of everything. It appeared that our meeting was about to be done with and Mr. Laughton extended his hand once again but this time taking mine in his in a farewell handshake. I looked up at him and spoke easily for the first time.

"Thank you." I paused. "I wanted to find a sympathetic woman to represent me, be on my side and do a little hand holding so that I didn't feel so alone." His eyes brightened as if he could understand, so I continued. "Instead I find you. You seem very sympathetic." I let that thought sink in.

He smiled and I went on. "But… you are also a very imposingly large man." I laughed softly to myself. "I truly hope that Warren is as intimidated as I am." He laughed out loud at this point. Again I interjected. "I really didn't want to like you." At this his eyebrows rose, I suppose he was expecting the worst, so I finished speaking quickly. "I am glad that I do."

We had stopped our walking and he had continued to hold my hand while I spoke. He looked straight in my eyes and said. "Then let me intimidate you just a little more." He leaned in and down towards me like a father to a child. My own eyes must have taken on a look of fear for he laughed again but this time at my expression and then added more seriously.

"It's really important for you to know that I will have no secrets. Secrets in a case like this can get you killed. This means that I need to become as "intimate", pardon the use of the word, with your relationship and your life as anyone can be. I don't want to find out that something is missing from your history together that will cause a failure in this case. In your situation, I am afraid it really could kill you. Are you up for giving up that much of your private life?"

I did not look at him. That old insecurity took over and I looked instead down at the floor. I nodded my head and I could feel the tears begin to flow again. I knew that this would be very difficult. I had only given him the barest of details and I was an emotional wreck, I wasn't sure how I would get through it all, but I would try.

I had been very naïve where Warren was concerned. From the money that he made to the job he did, to the people he knew and worked with. I realized that I was not really a part of very much of Warren's life at all. I was very pained at that realization.

I knew that telling all I knew would mean not only sharing all of my personal life with Warren, but all of my fears and all of my happiness, all my joy and all my pain as well. It would mean reliving every moment of our relationship. I swallowed back the choking sob I could easily have made. This was the first step in my quest to find out the reasons for all the things that had been happening to me. To both of us. Warren and me and to our marriage.

I knew that my next conversation with Mr. Laughton would be damaging to me; like raking myself over hot coals with each and every word. But, that would be better than sitting in the courtroom and retelling everything completely unprepared and with the raw emotions that took over every time I opened my mouth now. How could I build up my resistance to those very raw emotions by the time I had my next meeting with Mr. Laughton?

We walked together out to the foyer of his office; he stopped at the secretary's desk. She wrote my next appointment down in her book. She looked up at me and smiled. "Are you a little more at ease at least?" I smiled. She had understood my feelings in that short minute or so with her. "Yes," I answered.

"Thank you both for your kindness." Even though she wasn't really who the words were for, I could tell that she too, was sympathetic to my needs.

Mr. Laughton had been so kind and concerned and I was thankful that he warned me about being careful with my situation. He spoke again softly as I turned towards the door. "Don't take chances. Play everything as safe as you can."

I looked towards the door. Walking out felt so much better than walking in. So as I began walking towards the door again, I responded. "I will be as careful as I can be." With that, I walked out of the building feeling like I had accomplished all I had come here to do.

I stood outside the front door again. Happy. My first meeting was over! I breathed a deep sigh of relief. I was on that first very difficult step back to my former life or forward to an even better one.

How it had all changed in just two or three years. Feeling the sunshine as it hit my skin, I felt firm resolve steel over me and my whole body about my situation. I not only could, but I would fight back. I would not let Warren get away with hurting me again.

By the time I stepped off the sidewalk and started towards my car, I was already feeling stronger. Physically and mentally stronger yes it was true, but, more importantly, emotionally, I felt ready to conquer my fears. My mind raced along the path of "now, what should I do next?" The words of that old song, "I am woman, hear me roar," rang in my head. I smiled to myself. It was a very deep secure satisfying smile that said that I was on my way and I would be okay.

The feeling that I had accomplished the first step in where my life must now be headed felt great! It was almost euphoric. I reached in my purse and pulled out my keys as I drew closer to my newest Mustang. The sky seemed clearer, the sun seemed brighter. Everything felt wonderful.

Suddenly the door of my car swung open as I came within about 15 feet of it. I screamed and fell backwards at the shock of seeing the door swing open. I didn't even realize just who had opened it. As I fell hard onto the pavement, I looked up and I saw Warren as he stepped out of my car. He slammed the door behind him and started to walk toward me, the grin on his face was sufficient to make me panic.

All I could do was scream. And scream I did. That powerful feeling that had me smiling vanished in a single skipped heartbeat and was now pouring out of me in a state of sheer terror.

He sneered at me, his lips curling into a vicious tight shape. "Shut up! What do you think you're doing?" It was not a question that needed a reply and yet I began to stammer. "I – I – I was" I couldn't move nor could I speak. I was frozen to the ground.

I heard the office door open behind me. Warren stopped instantly as Kimberly stepped out. He just glared at her when Kimberly asked, "Are you okay?"

I did not answer as she ran over to where I sat on the ground and helped me to my feet. I was shaking violently and tears had filled my eyes before she realized that I was staring at Warren completely terrified.

Again she asked, "Are you okay, Mrs. Stone?" When I didn't answer her, it dawned on her what was happening. She looked over at him. By instinct she was aware that this situation was not a good one and she turned me towards the door.

She could only know that he was someone I was frightened of. Her hand pulled on my arm and she placed her other arm around my shoulders steadily guiding me back to the door. She calmly looked back at him. I looked only at her as her eyes met his. She said, "I think you should get off of this property." She paused, waiting on a response, but Warren just stood where he was.

She continued, "Or better yet, stay right there and I'll call the police to escort you off."

He laughed and walked nonchalantly over to his big Cadillac Escalade and climbed in. When we got inside the office door, Kimberly turned instantly and looked back at him through the glass. When she did so, I moved to the side, wanting more than anything to be out of his line of sight. I stood in the shadows watching him.

He sat behind the steering wheel of the big vehicle and watched the door, staring at Kimberly. She reached down and turned the lock on the door. She slipped the small placard in that reported to the public that the office was closed.

She took my arm again and began pulling me further back into the building away from the glass of the door. She walked quickly back to the front desk and reaching over the front ledge she paged Mr. Laughton to come up front. She did not give him details.

It seemed like forever, but only a few seconds passed before Mr. Laughton walked back into the foyer of his office. He looked at me and turned questioningly to Kimberly. Kimberly said, "I heard a scream and went to the front door to find out what was happening." Her words were tumbling out fast. "When I opened the door I saw a man a few feet away from Mrs. Stone and she was on the ground." Mr. Laughton looked at me, "Warren?" I nodded yes. Tears were streaming down my face now, the floodgates that were all too frequently and easily opened were not enough to hold them back. I could not speak. Looking back at Kimberly he asked: "Where is he now?"

"I don't know. When I locked the front door he was sitting behind the wheel of his car. I grabbed Mrs. Stone and pulled her back into the building. I told him that I would call the police but I locked the door, just in case that didn't deter him. He was sitting in a dark grey to black SUV."

At that, he moved towards the door. He stood for just a second or two while he reached down to unlock the door. He stepped outside and disappeared from sight. I couldn't help but think that he was confronting Warren and I didn't want to see it. In fact I was sure that I couldn't see it. I had seen Warren angry and I didn't want to see it again. It probably wouldn't have mattered because I couldn't make my legs move and get up to see for myself anyway. I was as terrified now as I had been confident just a few minutes before.

Chapter Four
Running

The door opened and Mr. Laughton walked in, turned and locked the door again. He was already on the phone with someone, speaking quickly and angrily. They were getting an earful and were quickly learning that Warren had followed me to his office. "I'm sure that this is a direct violation of the protective order already in place. Not that that has ever stopped a desperate man." He stopped speaking and it appeared that he was either on hold or listening intently to someone on the phone.

When Kimberly started to ask a question, he held up his hand to prevent her from speaking. He then covered the phone and said, "Please help Mrs. Stone to get cleaned up. There are bandages in my office." That was the first time I noticed that the palms of my hands were scraped up and bleeding from my fall to the asphalt.

Kimberly stood and left the room only to return with a well stocked first aid kit. We worked on cleaning me up and bandaging my scrapes while we waited for Mr. Laughton to complete his call. My mind was racing but I had no choice but to continue to sit and wait for him to finish his call. It seemed to go on forever but it in reality was only a few minutes. Time and space seemed to be changing for me. I couldn't get a handle on just how much time had passed from one minute to the next, let alone one day to the next.

When Mr. Laughton finally finished with his conversation, he knelt down in front of the two of us, making sure that I would look directly in his eyes. I was still shaking. I had not been ready for another frightening and possible dangerous situation.

"Do you have anywhere you can stay locally that Warren doesn't know about?" I shook my head. I had been completely open with Warren about my friends and family members. He knew as much about me as I knew little about him. It was a very discouraging thought. Were my family and friends in danger now also? I didn't know so I asked.

"Do you think my family and friends are in any danger?" He answered thoughtfully, shaking his head. "No." He paused and I could tell that he was thinking, planning, trying to come up with a solution. "You can't take chances like this again. It is just really important that you stay safe. Too many times this kind of thing has gone very bad."

He turned to Kim and continued to talk about me. What was the best answer? Where *could* I be safe? They were trying to come up with an answer to my problem while I searched my mind for any safe place that I could go.

"I'll take you to your home." Mr. Laughton directed his words to me. I looked up at his face. I knew he was serious.

"Kim," he said looking back at his secretary, "Let's go on a little field trip." She instantly stood, ready to go. In no time she had rescheduled his appointments for the rest of the day and left the closed sign on the front door of the office.

We, or rather they, had decided that I had to leave my car. Kimberly, or Kim, as Mr. Laughton had called her, would get it to me

44

at another time. She and I then walked to the back of the office building. Mr. Laughton left through the front to get his own car. Kim and I waited by the back door of the building while he got in his own SUV, a Honda Pilot, and drove out of the parking lot. He must have driven around for about twenty minutes before we heard him pull up outside the back door of the building.

Immediately we got in and he told us to get down as far as we could. I felt foolish, but we both did what he asked. "This way it looks like I am the only one that has left the building." While we exited the back parking lot he kept looking over his shoulder and around him for any sign of Warren. We drove for another ten to fifteen minutes before he would let us get up.

The words were left unspoken but we were all still quite aware that Warren might be watching. In fact, I was sure that Warren was already wise to the ruse. After all, this is what he did for a living. I knew that he was good at it, and knowing that he had apparently led a double life throughout our entire marriage, I was positive that he was lurking not far behind. He was really too good at living in the shadows of life.

We traveled for just over an hour when I found myself standing at my front door with my two new 'best' friends. I couldn't get the keys to work as I fumbled, my hands shaking as I attempted to open the front door. I was trembling so badly that Mr. Laughton took the keys from me and swiftly turned both the locks.

We entered my home as fast as we could and Mr. Laughton told me that I should get some of my things to last for a significant stay in a hotel. Kim offered her help to me and together we made our way to my bedroom upstairs. Mr. Laughton stayed below looking out the windows for signs that we had been followed by Warren.

I packed lightly, in spite of his warning to pack for a "significant stay". I was confident that I would be back in my home soon. When we finally made our way back to the living room, he asked us to wait until he flashed his lights to come running to his car.

Once more, that feeling that I was in a world that I didn't belong overcame me. We waited for several minutes while he drove around on several streets before pulling back into my driveway. The lights flashed and we both ran to the car hoping against hope that Warren was not watching from somewhere nearby.

Once more we were on the road. We drove to a hotel that he had arranged while we were upstairs packing. The drive was nerve wracking even though it was quite uneventful.

Even so I kept looking out the back window to make sure I did not see Warren anywhere.

The hotel was not one that I had ever been to before but it looked from the outside like a very luxurious one, an Embassy Suites Hotel. Mr. Laughton left both Kim and I in the running car with instructions to Kim that she should drive off without him if we saw any sign of Warren or his vehicle.

Kim began to explain as if she needed to talk. "Mr. Laughton would check you into the hotel. He will have told them that he was providing safe housing for a client." It was obvious that they had done business for Mr. Laughton before. "They won't even ask for any of your information. It is a security measure he will say to them." She stopped as he stepped out of the building.

When he came back to the car, we drove around to another side of the building. Both Kim and Mr. Laughton got out of the car, and while they grabbed my things, I started towards the door. We walked together through the doors and to the elevator.

The elevator ride seemed very slow as we rode it to one of the higher floors. No one spoke as we listened to the movement of the elevator.

Breaking the silence, my cell phone rang sharply. I looked at the screen and I could see that Warren's name and number were lit up for the world to see. I dropped it and leaned back against the back of the elevator, sliding down to the floor, hands over my face. I couldn't believe his nerve.

Mr. Laughton bent down and grabbed my cell, opened it and closed it, and then opened it again to add both his and Kim's numbers into its memory. He was clearly worried for my safety. I tried to pull myself together as he handed the bag he held in his hand to Kim and squatted down to where I sat on the floor.

I was trying to breathe but I couldn't get a deep breath in my lungs. He pulled me slowly to my feet and put his arm around me. I swallowed hard as we walked out of the opening doors and down the hall to my room. I was grateful that he had put their numbers in my phone. At least they would be there if I needed them. They were two strangers at the beginning of the day and I was now inexplicably in their debt and dependant on them.

We reached the room fairly quickly from that point but I was still overwhelmed with fear. I locked the doors as they carried my things in. I closed the thick curtains but just to be on the safe side, I pushed one of the kitchenette chairs under the handle of the door. They both watched me move mechanically through those steps and they both knew that I must have been doing these same things at my home. This was the only way I knew that I could get some measure of sleep at night. And maybe, just maybe I could come up with a plan that would put me back in charge of my own life.

We talked for a few minutes and Mr. Laughton told me that going to work would not be a good idea. I had just started an important phase of my work not two months ago. I was actually receiving the trial drug injections for the study I had been working on. It was an attempt to see what side affects there were for people who had any genetic link to cancer but not active cancer. It was important to me and I started to protest. I was already aware of how weak the injections had made me but, I knew that in the end, my sufferings might very well lead to a cure. I needed to participate.

He stopped me with one raised hand. "I promise that I'll take care of everything. I'll make sure that you can still do your job and participate in the trial but it has to be done discretely and definitely away from your office."

He paused; looking in my eyes, "You may have to put a hold on the injections"

I stopped him. "You can't interrupt the injections, it might affect the results."

He continued then, but much more slowly, thinking and planning as he spoke. "I'll ask the physicians to make sure, if not, then we'll figure it out when the time comes." I knew I should agree because I was sure that I couldn't talk to anyone at work without becoming emotional. They were all too likely to ask personal questions that I would not be able to answer.

I nodded my head and he said that he would arrange for a paid leave if at all possible. That way I could keep my house by continuing to pay my bills. He had no idea yet that I didn't make the payments on the house. Warren did.

He reached into his pocket and pulled out a large sum of cash for me. There was about five hundred or so that he pressed into my hand. He pulled out his wallet and handed me a credit card. I was taken aback and once more protested his actions.

"Look, Warren knows how to trace the use of your credit cards or checks you might cash. Don't use them. Use this cash and this card. We'll get it back from him later." He smiled. "Warren will just have to pay in more ways than one."

I placed all of it on the dresser, understanding sweeping over me so that I had to sit down on the edge of the bed. It was all so...so wrong. Everything was just wrong. This was just another one of those things that I hadn't yet thought about.

Mr. Laughton reached over to me, towering over me as I sat on the edge of the bed. "Be smart about things. Be safe about things. We'll get through this together."

Somehow, I believed him.

Kimberly put her arms around me and hugged me good-bye. She whispered. "Call me if you need to talk and please be careful." It was sweet of her given that we had only met a few hours before.

When they finally walked out the door, I felt more at ease but I repeated my process of "battening down the hatches" as they say just to give myself some level of comfort. I was stuck here with no transportation and I wasn't sure I liked that at all.

The rest of the day and the evening were uneventful. I finally ordered take out and had it delivered to the room. As I used his credit card, I felt guilty for the first time. Why was he taking all of these steps for me? Did I really seem all that frail? Who was I kidding? I was frail. Both in mind and body and spirit. In fact, for the first time in my life I wasn't in charge of my life.

Someone else had taken over and I was afraid of him and the things that his actions had caused me to do. I had stopped being that strong woman that I was before. Why didn't I feel that power any more? Part of it was because I was so physically weak. And I would be for a long time yet. I had steeled myself for that before, but now, I was emotionally weak and that made my physical weakness all the more apparent.

I pondered over the situation for several hours and the only conclusion was that Warren had changed me. He had made me vulnerable. He had always played the role of the protector. I let him do it. I let him take over.

And as for the cash and the credit card, I finally took in what he had said. "Warren will pay in more ways than one. He could include all of these expenses in a request for Warren to pay "all related expenses". I laughed when I reached that conclusion. Wouldn't that just be a kick in the pants? I intended on requesting spousal support as well and in an amount that would cover the house payments if he was still paying for it. I knew that he was taking care of it all before without any of my income. So he could continue to do so.

The night continued to be uneventful and long. I found myself falling asleep totally exhausted but waking up occasionally to the TV still being on just a short while later. I could no longer sleep a normal night's sleep. I had stopped that from the night of the party. Nightmares would overcome me as I relived his attack the night of the Christmas party.

I was also uncomfortable here. I wanted to be at my own home but deep down I knew that I had already been doing the same thing there.

Warren knew how to get into our home. He still had keys but I also knew that he didn't need keys, so I hadn't even bothered to change the locks I had just changed the password on the alarm system. Suddenly, I was sure that that wasn't enough either. Finally sleep came. I was able to close my eyes and not see the nightmare my life had become.

The sound of my cell phone ringing startled me early the next morning. It was only shortly after seven in the morning if the clock on the TV was right. Hesitantly I got out of bed to get to the phone on the table. Fear wrenched through me. The ringing continued. I picked up the phone and slowly looked at the screen, afraid of what I might see. With relief, I answered the call: "Hello Kim."

She asked me if I was okay. I lied and told her that I was just tired. Little did anyone realize that sleep was a rare commodity these days.

"Mr. Laughton is having your car towed. We will be bringing you another car."

"Why? Did something happen to my car?"

She quickly answered my worry. "No, no, Mr. Laughton says that he thinks that Warren may have put in a GPS or other tracking system in your car. Maybe even a theft detection device that lets him know where you are."

I didn't say a word. I didn't know what to say. This too was another thing that I hadn't thought of. It would explain how he seemed to pop up every where I went. I shook my head. What next?

Finally she broke my silence. "Mrs. Stone." I interrupted her. "Call me Bria. Leave off the Mrs. Stone until I can change it, would you please?" "Sure. I'll let James know. Bria, we'll be dropping a car by the hotel at eight this morning. Mr. Laughton wants to check in on you and still be at the office by nine. I would get dressed if I were you." She laughed.

"I guess so. Thanks for the warning call." I replied. "See you in a few."

I got dressed and contemplated the conversation. Could Warren really be tracking me? If so, how could we fix that? I just didn't know. I loved my car. I had worked hard to pay cash for my dream car. I had wanted a Mustang all of my life. From the time I had first gotten my drivers license I had dreamed of getting one. I had seen too many friends buy expensive cars or SUV's and not be able to keep up with payments. I had driven a little used Honda for years just to save up. He had already hurt me once when the accident happened. This replacement was a much better model and I loved it as much as I had my first one.

Warren was doing one more thing that hurt me. He knew how I felt about my car. It was disturbing as if he was pulling out all stops to hurt me.

I sat on the edge of the bed twiddling my thumbs. I kept looking at the motion. I never really knew that people actually did this. Now I knew that when there is nothing left to do, you do this.

The room phone rang loudly. I jumped off the bed and answered it. "Your party is waiting in the lobby, would you like them to come up?" "No, I'll be down in a minute." I replied and I grabbed my purse, phone and keys and locked the door behind me. I knew that I would not be going anywhere for a little while.

Downstairs, I was relieved to see the two of them sitting in the lobby. I walked over to them and sat down. Mr. Laughton began:

"We have a car for you to use for a little while. I also want you to follow me to my second office. It's quite a ways away, are you up for a ride?"

"Yes" I answered quickly as I rose and began to walk to the door. I waited for Kim to see where she would walk to. I recognized Mr. Laughton's Pilot and saw immediately another SUV beside it. I recognized the Nissan Pathfinder. I had a co-worker that owned one and raved about it. I liked it.

I noticed almost immediately that it did not have rental tags on it, but she pointed to it and handed me the keys. I instinctively went to the driver's side and climbed in. It was quite nice and I locked the doors and waited for them to pull out of their parking space. I followed them as closely as I dared. I didn't however want it to look like I was following someone. I didn't want to be a mouse in a game of cat and mouse either. I kept them in my sight at all times.

An hour or so later we finally pulled into an office on the Virginia side of the bridge. We parked side by side and we all got out of the cars. Immediately, I looked over my shoulder to see if Warren was around. I was grateful that he was not. I could breathe a little easier.

We walked into a much smaller and less grand office than the one outside of D.C. It was a quaint office and looked much more like a home office than the other one actually did. I could tell that great care had been used in setting up both offices.

"Are you ready, Mrs. Stone?" I looked at Kim. He asked me again. I knew I wasn't. Instead I said, "Could you please call me Bria instead of Mrs. Stone. I just can't take that right now."

I couldn't bear to hear the name anymore without wanting to cry. I looked around the outer office and stood there. Again his voice interrupted my private thoughts. "If you're not up for this today, we can postpone it. After all it will be spring before we are in court. You don't have to do this today."

I quietly answered, "Yes, let's get this over with." He turned and I followed him into a smaller but just as elegantly furnished private office. He motioned to the couch that sat against an opposite wall. "I sometimes take power naps at work. We can sit here while you tell me everything."

We both sat down and I struggled to begin, so I finally just blurted out. "I want to go back to work. I need to go back to work. It's the normal everyday things that I miss and I think that I'll be able to focus on other things instead of this." He nodded. "I know. Sometimes normal is all that we can hope for." I was sure he understood exactly what I meant.

Finally he said. "Just begin with how you met." He turned on a recorder that was in his front shirt pocket. "The good and the bad, let me get to know both of you..."

I nodded and as I began to tell my story, pictures filled my mind of my life. I could see that from beginning it was filled with extreme joy. But towards the end it was filled only with extreme sorrow. There seemed to be little in between the two extremes.

My heart skipped beats as I told of every first that we experienced together. It fell hard with every sad detail that began when he choked me at the party. Every detail of his following me, and even the court appearances for the protection order was so painful that it was at times hard to continue.

Chapter Five
A Tell All Story

I began, closing my eyes and just talking as if no one were really listening.

We met quite by accident. Everyone knows how that goes. A friend of a friend of a friend kept saying that she knew the perfect man for me. Even though she and I were barely more than acquaintances, only together in groups of common friends, I felt flattered that someone would think of me when matching up a friend.

Over the years many friends had tried to set me up with the "perfect guy". I was always just a little bit disappointed when it didn't work out. That we weren't the perfect match was never a surprise really. And I wasn't really looking for someone anyway. What I was looking for, was what would come next in my life. If it was a man, then great and if it wasn't, then I was fine with that also. I was still young. I remembered someone telling me long ago, that you should always move forward in life. If you aren't moving forward there were only two ways left to go.

Sideways or backwards. Sideways was like living in a stagnant pool of water, it eventually got smelly and had to be thrown out. Backwards could be dangerous. You eventually repeat mistakes that you made before and should have learned from already. So I had made a vow to always move forward in life.

Moving forward I had discovered was the best strategy for success in both love and life. So even when I had failures, as long as I moved forward and learned from them, I was successful.

So in this case, I decided that moving forward meant that I would agree to meet him. No matter how disastrous the results might be. I didn't know at the time just how important that decision would be.

Kaye had meant to introduce him to me properly, but when he walked into the book store coffee shop, it seemed like the perfect accidental opportunity for a quick introduction from the moment she realized it was him.

There were six of us all crowded around a small table, laughing and having a great time. We were sipping hot cocoa and eating an array of fruit and cheese pastries along with various muffins or bagels. We were discussing the latest books and what we were going to be buying next.

Kaye noticed him and as her eyes followed him we all began to follow him too. He was a very handsome man. Not too young, and not too old. He was in his late twenties or perhaps even thirty. He was dreamy, as they used to call it, and we were all immediately captivated by his smile. He walked into the shop and ordered orange juice and a muffin.

As he turned around, he caught sight of Camille and Kaye. These were the two friends of a friend twosome that had told me about him. They were the two acquaintances that we had in common. Kaye waved him over and you could see the charming and yet goofy little qualities that made him almost irresistible.

He did all the right things in that first few moments and so I was ready when Kaye said that I was the girl that she had told him about. "Really?" he asked. "Well then, how about a movie? After all, we're," he paused and looked at Kaye and quoted her, "perfect for each other." We all laughed and I blushed as he reached behind him and pulled up another chair to crowd next to me around the small and suddenly very crowded table.

The mood was light and fun and I said a "Sure" to his request when he repeated it. We agreed to meet for dinner and a movie later that evening. His deep green/grey eyes had a very mischievous glint in them. He was so sweet and very gallant, if that was a term that could be used in this day and age. I felt an instant connection with him.

He was so handsome that I wondered just what might be his problem. After all a man this uniquely good was a find. His facial features were more boyish than chiseled. His dark hair was thick and playful, like he could never quite get it exactly the way he wanted it.

During that first night he often seemed to be deep in thought and I wondered what that was all about. Every time I would say, "Penny for you thoughts?" he would quickly reply something like, "Just thinking that I got really lucky today." And then he kissed me on my forehead, and even though we had just met, it felt natural. It was all quite comforting and sweet and innocent.

We began almost immediately to spend all of our evenings together. He was always interested in my work, and while I couldn't share everything, I would tell him some of the details of my day. He was always genuinely interested in everything I did. I loved it. This was the first man that didn't constantly talk about his day at work, leaving me out of the conversation altogether. It too was another one of those comforting things that I loved about him.

We dated regularly. Movies and book stores, dinner, quiet walks, and even ball games of every kind became the normal evening adventure for us. He seemed to have season tickets for every home basketball, football, baseball and even hockey team there was within a hundred miles. It was a fun adventure.

Every moment that we were together made me feel more beautiful and special than I had ever in my life. I slowly began to realize that I was in love with him.

One night we were discussing the hidden secrets of the history of the D.C. area from a movie that we had just seen. Our common interest in our nation's history was a great topic for us as we both worked within the government reaches in the area. So it came naturally that we would be talking about those types of things. I was in research with government funding and private funding on various topics. He was employed in some agency that kept him involved in undercover work, "for the protection of our nation." He had said.

I was on a roll now, telling my story as if there was no one listening, my eyes closed in the reverie. I continued.

Once he told me that he really was in the kind of work that "If I told you I'd have to kill you" was a real possibility. I ignored it. I had heard it before. The NSA was local, the Secret Service, the FBI, the CIA, and since 9-11 even more secret agencies seemed to have popped up.

He suddenly looked in my eyes and took my hands in his. I sensed it was coming. "I love you." He said it quickly. He dropped my hands and went back to the book we were looking over. I quietly said, "I love you too." Not looking at him. That was it. It was out in the open. We were in love.

We had been dating for over a year. Having fun and working and dating when he was available. Summer was fast approaching, and things were different this time. We were making plans together. I had grown up in the south and most of my family was there. My family had gone to Myrtle Beach, South Carolina, Carolina Beach and the Outer Banks of North Carolina most every summer. We planned to go visit some of my favorite vacation haunts together.

It was then that I would introduce him to my family. Killing two birds with one stone. We were so very much in love.

Our vacation started out beautifully. We stopped for a couple of days with my parents. They were all as impressed with Warren as I was. But, I was eager to leave. I didn't want any awkward parental questions to spoil the trip. Besides I had planned a full on assault of all of my favorite childhood vacation destinations. I loved it here along the eastern coastline. And there was no better place to be in love either.

As we were getting into the car to drive away, my father pulled me aside and said. "Don't make any rash decisions." I raised my eyebrows at him but he continued. "Do everything as you always have done. Study them out, research everything."

I thought it was a weird thing for my dad to say. Looking back now, it was foretelling. As we spent most of the week going to all the planned stops, Warren said. "Why don't we just slow down and enjoy where we are. It's so beautiful here. Let's stay and take a moonlight stroll on the beach."

I thought that a moonlight stroll was just the best of ideas. We packed a few things to snack on and some sodas and went down to the shore. We placed all of our things on a blanket and waited for the sun to completely set.

He held me in his arms as the moon rose over the ocean. It was at this precise moment that he brought his hands around in front of me and presented me with a ring. I looked at it. He was proposing! I squealed with delight as he took the ring from the box and placed it on my ring finger. I turned my head to my left to kiss him. And he said, "Let's get married. Let's do it tonight."

I was in shock. My mouth wouldn't form the words I wanted to say. He continued. "Why wait. After all, isn't this the Las Vegas of the south? I understand that you can get married here in about twenty minutes." I nodded. But I was answering his question, not really saying yes to getting married. I was already speechless and he took my not talking as an affirmative answer. He pulled me to my feet and gathered our things. We walked back to the car and he began to drive.

We were in Dillon, South Carolina in less than two hours. It was near midnight. But just like in Las Vegas the "wedding chapel" was of course open. The vows were short and sweet and we were done in less than the advertised twenty minutes. As we left through the door, I turned to him. "Promise me happily ever after?"

"Of course I do." He answered.

"Can we do it up right on our fifth anniversary?" He took me in his arms and said, "This is as right as it could possibly be." I kissed him passionately and we walked to the car.

The trip home made me realize that I was indeed a married woman. Now one knew. I could not wait to tell all of our family and friends. I felt so very completely loved.

Returning home meant going back to the everyday living of our lives. We needed to set about getting a home to live in and getting out of our respective leases. Neither one of us had anything big enough to accommodate all of both of our belongings.

The next few weeks were a whirlwind of activity. We found the perfect little townhouse to live in. It wasn't too expensive, which was our plan as we hoped to save enough go find our dream home to begin our family in. We built our lives around spending time together in the evenings when he was in town. Even if we just watched TV at night, we had fun. We were together and that was all that mattered.

My first experience with Warren's work interfering with our lives came sometime near the end of fall. It was before the schools went back in session.

The phone rang out and Warren answered it. He said that he had to go out of town. I was curious but also a little afraid for him. I didn't know what his work was about. He was always so secretive about it. How many times I had asked only to hear that same phrase. Sometimes I would laugh, other times I would wonder just how serious that statement was to be taken. This time, I left it alone. I asked him when he would be back, and he said that he didn't know. I knew that this would take some getting used to. All I had were phone numbers that would relay me to him if it was an emergency. That lifestyle had never really been as close to home as it was now.

I thought about it often, but I knew that in my own work, many of our co-workers had aliases. I had one sometimes myself when doing my research calls. No one wanted to have some angry participant in one of our studies or trials come to cause problems on site.

I helped him pack. After all, we were happily married and I trusted him completely. I had been single for long enough to manage on my own but we said our goodbyes and held each other just a little longer and tighter that night. The next morning he was gone.

He was gone for almost a month. I would receive an email about ever other day, telling me that he would be home soon but could not give an exact date. I was really not happy with not knowing but what could I do?

When he returned, we fell back into our normal routine. We still loved going out and did so regularly, but we had more fun just being in each other's arms in our own place at night. We spent the next year just getting our lives back into a regular happy couple life.

I was still participating in a cancer research study at work.
The regular physical requirements were wearing thin on me. I was
becoming increasingly tired and weak from all the new blood work and
tests. Now injections had been added to the list. The first round
anyway and I needed to stay focused. Although other employees had
been asked to participate, I was the only one in full participation.

None of the others were doing the whole process. And they
complained about the two to five year commitment that a study of this
magnitude meant.

One night, cuddled in front of the TV screen, I complained to
Warren saying that everything I was doing was taking a toll on my
body. I was weak all of the time and every injection made me
nauseous. I told him that I was going to request that I be dropped from
participation in the study.

He listened to me complain and then turned to me and said, "I
understand if you quit, but I've not known you to quit anything. I think
that you should see it through. You've always told me how important
your work is and even though it gets tedious, it is a worthwhile study.
Think of the future generations you will be helping."

I knew he was right but I didn't say anything. He added, "You
have said all along that these studies are important to more people
than just you. Look at the big picture and really think about it before
you quit. Haven't you often said that you were doing this for the
women of your life like your grandmother?"

I thought about it and I guessed that no matter what I could handle it if it meant that by the time we had children, cancer was only a memory. "Don't worry; the injections are for thirty months right? Two and a half years for a new lifetime for so many others. Besides, I'll help you get through it all. I like having a helpless female depend on me."

I said "I've been doing them for two months now and they don't give me any more information. They just have me turning in reports. It's so frustrating."

"I am sure it is. It's up to you, but we can work through it if it is really important to you. Lay out the pros and cons. Then tell yourself that it will end and when the end comes, it will all be worth it."

Once more, I knew he was right. His encouragement meant the world to me and I really did deep down want to do it. It did feel good to know that I was doing something important for the world. So my time would end just before Christmas two years from now. I could make it.

Chapter Six
And So It Goes On

Time seemed to pass by quickly and we were happily living our lives in society. I was shocked when Warren announced that he thought that we should start looking for a home of our own. We had just passed our one year anniversary!

Neither one of us had anticipated that we would be ready this soon. I was surprised. We had now known each other for two years and life could not have been greater. Only two years together. It seemed like he and I had never been single.

The shock of his announcement moved me to tears. I knew that this would mean that we were ready to start a family. I was so very happy.

I remember asking him if he was sure because I didn't think that we were financially ready for our dream home. He assured me that we could but it didn't matter, I trusted him. I would be happy to have the picket fence with a back yard for children to play in. We could still save up for the dream home as we had planned.

October was here and the fall colors were in full bloom all around us. Halloween decorations were going up everywhere and I found myself daydreaming about what our future Halloweens with children would be like. I would make all of their costumes and have the scariest house on the block. My thoughts were always on what was our next success story.

I loved the fall and knew that November would arrive soon enough so I went about purchasing Christmas decorations in anticipation of our new home. Warren had promised that we would find a place before Christmas.

I was already packing any unnecessary thing that I could. It was fun to plan for the holidays in a new home. I could not have been happier. Married life was wonderful!

Life was moving steadily along and both of our agencies began to hold various "holiday parties". It started with a big Thanksgiving celebration with all the trimmings. We had been told that it was to avoid the discrimination of other religious affiliations and that we had to attend them. Next would come the "Winter Festivals" that would cover those with Christmas on their minds. It was going to be a very busy eight weeks or so.

Three weeks before Thanksgiving, Warren told me that I needed to get dressed up for a surprise. I got dressed in my dressiest clothing, thinking it was another impromptu holiday gathering. We began to drive towards the Silver Springs, Maryland area. I knew that area well as each year I had made the drive up to see the beautiful decorations at the Mormon Temple that was there. I wondered if this was where we were going. They would be stringing the decorations now as they didn't actually get turned on until the first of December. I began to be a little excited but I wanted it to stay a surprise so I kept my mouth going about other things.

Finally, I could stand it no more and I began telling him that most of my life I had called the Mormon Temple "Cinderella's Castle."

Most of the people around here did. I loved going there. It was just peaceful and lovely and you always left feeling like you were a part of something much more than the beauty that was clearly evident.

The homes in that area were akin to the dream homes that we had discussed. Though they didn't have the extra acreage that we dreamed of, they were beautiful to look at. They were magnificent and well taken care of. That was the ideal of what we were looking for as a home by the time we had children old enough to actually celebrate Christmas with.

As we got closer to the highway exit to the Temple, I could hardly contain my excitement. It was a wonderful place to spend a cool late fall evening. I wondered if Warren knew that the Christmas Decorations didn't actually go up until December first. Should I tell him or just let it all unfold? I decided that I would once more wait it out.

We were driving slowly in the neighborhood that you drive through to get up to the Temple. Some of the houses were already decorated. They were lovely. I couldn't wait till we found our own home. We had taken to driving into the various cities in the area just to look at the homes so we could get ideas for our ideal home. I was glad that every time we went anywhere we found a neighborhood to dream about.

Without warning, Warren pulled into a driveway. Without a word, he opened the door to get out. I looked at him but he got out of the car and walked around to my door. "Is this where the party is?" I asked him.

"I just have to meet with someone for a few minutes. I thought that you might like to see the inside." I responded, rather unenthusiastically with, "Yea sure that's fine." I really didn't want to. I was sure that it would make me feel anxious about finding our home.

We walked casually up to the front door and rang the bell. A tall very distinguished man answered the door and escorted us in. We followed him to a very large "den" that was very ornately decorated. Christmas decorations came down the banister of the stairs that you could see led to a large upstairs.

The room opposite was decorated as well but the room that we were escorted to was the most beautiful. There were already stockings hanging from the mantle piece. A beautiful Christmas tree, elegantly trimmed was already standing in the big bay window. It was the picture perfect postcard of a Christmas home. I sighed.

The fireplace was roaring with a warm fire. The two men shook hands and the tall gentleman excused himself asking Warren to accompany him.

"There are holiday treats and cookies on that platter on the piano", he gestured towards the back of the room, "Please help yourself and make yourself at home." I hadn't even noticed the baby grand.

Hot coffee and hot chocolate were in two carafes on a silver tray with several different Christmas treats. I murmured a quick "Thank you" but he and Warren were already gone. I sat daydreaming by the fire. I wondered if Warren was killing two birds with one stone as they say so that he could accomplish his business

70

with the man and still get to the party or to the temple on time. I waited patiently in the lovely room wondering where we were going that was so special.

One day, I thought, one day in the not too distant future, we would own a home like this one. This was as close to perfect as it could get. Thirty minutes passed before the two of them returned to the room. I had not touched any of the offerings and I hoped he would not be disappointed or worse yet, offended that I hadn't.

His soft-spoken Middle Eastern accent was almost delicate as he asked if there was anything that he could get for me. "No thank you, I was just too busy admiring your lovely home." He nodded his head. "My wife decorated it for the holidays already. Decorating is her passion." I thought that it was obvious as I had seen some very feminine details. But the dark leather couches and furnishings were definitely masculine.

"Well" he said. "I must confess that I need to leave. I have another meeting in a very short time. I am always so busy at this time of year." I stood and began to walk towards the door. He reached out and shook my hand and then took Warren's hand in the same manner. He handed Warren a large envelope. Warren said, "Thank you for everything," as the man walked out of the room and out the front door. I stared at Warren. Why weren't we leaving? He pulled me close to him and said the most wonderfully magical words to me.
"Welcome home, Mrs. Stone."

I did not immediately understand. He walked me over to the deep brown leather couch and we sat down. He reached into the envelope and pulled something out of it. Then he spread my hand open and into cupping position. He dropped the keys to the house in my hands.

"You now have your dream home." He said with a huge grin on his face. "What do you mean? How can we afford something like this? Or even anything close to this?" I was stammering.

"Take a look in the envelope." He said. "I have friends in some very high places."

I pulled out the papers from the envelope, hands trembling; it was the paperwork and deed for the house. It was in my name. On the top was a hand written note:

"To my beautiful wife:
I hope this will qualify as your dream home. Our dream home. A place to raise a wonderful family in. It is my gift to you my darling, Bria. Everything is taken care of. It is yours forever. May your heart always beat strong in the love created in this home.
My love always,
Warren."

I looked up at him, my heart in my throat.
Warren smiled, "Some times the right opportunity opens up and you have to jump at it."

*Here it was between seven and eight weeks before Christmas and I, we, were in our own home. Not a townhome or a rental. **OUR** home. It felt wonderful.*

I stood up and slowly began to explore our new house. I walked through touching things to feel the warmth of them on my fingers.

Warren let me move through the house and then finally took my hand and led me upstairs to the doorway of a very spacious bedroom. It was luxuriously decorated with a large four-poster canopied bed and matching furniture. There was a huge master bath and two very large walk-in closets.

The bedroom was strewn with rose petals to add a delicious aroma and a romantic feel to it. Warren picked me up and carried me over the threshold of the bedroom and then to the bed itself.

It was the first night that we forgot all about birth control and began trying to have a baby. We stayed in bed for the rest of the night. It was glorious. It was passionate. I could not be happier. I was safe in the arms of the man that I loved and we would soon be raising a family here within the walls of our dream home.

The light streamed in through the windows and I got up to open up the window and feel the morning air. "Well, shall I get breakfast? We do still have to go to work, don't we?" He nodded his head. "I'm afraid so. Especially if we are going to have children around here we have to pay for them by going to work." It was almost a sad moment but it was tempered by the fact that we were in such a beautiful home and that we would be coming back to it.

"We need to pack the rest of our things and move them over."
I was very aware that I would have to put on the same dressy clothes
that I had worn over here the night before.

"Let's just go home and get dressed for work. We'll stop and
get a drive-thru breakfast on the way. I'll get someone to pack the
apartment up so we can move in soon."

I threw my arms around his neck and we danced around the
bedroom for a few more minutes. We were passionate enough for
another tryst in the canopied bed, but Warren just laughed, spanked me
lightly on my bottom and both of us quickly got dressed and made our
way downstairs.

We went about the day as we had been doing everyday. I went
to work. He went to work. It was a normal day. Except that I had the
most wonderful husband and now the most wonderful home to match.

The day floated by under my cloud nine.

Five o'clock came and we both raced to meet at the townhome.
I was completely surprised when I walked in to find that it was
completely empty. Nothing was there. "Does this meet your standard
of clean?" Warren asked as he stepped in the door just a few seconds
behind me. I put my arms around him again and let him know how
much I really appreciated not having to pack and move.

He laughed and twirled me around. "Well! I am batting a
thousand these days." He grabbed my hand and we walked over to the
rental office just minutes before they were to close at six. The secretary

was really happy for us, but she said that they didn't ordinarily let people out of their leases without prior written notice. That was one of those things that neither one of us had thought about in the past while looking for a home. Never mind that it was found and we had already spent our first night in it.

We both thanked her for allowing our little mistake. My heart was so full and I was so completely in love. From that point on things were continuously better and better. I truly couldn't count all of my blessings. I was; we were so very happy.

Thanksgiving arrived quickly. It was wonderful. We invited friends and family up to start up a new tradition for our family.

I wanted to host a Christmas party at our house and Warren was all for it, but we couldn't seem to find a free weekend to do so. All of our weekends were covered with parties that we were already invited to. He laughed when I finally gave up and said, "We'll just have to beat out all of the invitations next year."

A week after Thanksgiving, Warren came home and told me that we had to attend a "black tie affair" the next week. I was excited.

I thought it would be fun to get that dressed up. Warren was not excited at all. In fact he didn't want to go. He began sulking about it. I squelched my excitement and said "Well then we don't have to go."

He turned to me and snapped: "We do have to go. It is not an invitation. It is an order. This is not something that we can actually stay away from."

It was the first time that I had ever heard him that angry. He really didn't want to go but we had an obligation to go anyway? Why? Did he really have that heavy handed of a boss? I wanted to ask questions, but his demeanor had changed so drastically, that I left it alone.

The next week I set out buying the appropriate host gifts and formal wear. Warren's attitude and personality changed completely from the wonderful man that he had been just twenty-four hours previously. He also worked quite late almost every evening. I was getting worried.

When I chose to interrupt his thoughts or whatever he was working on, he would snap at me. I walked on eggshells around him. I found myself wondering if this was what I should have been expecting. I knew just how tough work was at times for both of us. Each of us had our secrets that we couldn't talk about for one reason or another.

I threw myself into work that week, trying to focus on things that I couldn't do during the holiday vacation days. I wanted to be finished so that I didn't have to worry about them. I found joy in my work as things progressed towards a greater good. I was even handling the first round of injections better.

My little commitment to the program was so important to me now. I had been able to handle the nausea as I got further into it. I had even talked with my mother about it at Thanksgiving. She was thrilled for what the possibilities were.

My mother, the cancer survivor, was the strongest person I knew. My grandmother had lost her fight with cancer, but I knew that wherever she was she was proud of me too.

Every night, I brought home my work with me as I entered personal information on my laptop. My observations were an important part of the research.

My genetic code meant that I could pass on the cancer gene to my children. Now that we were actively trying to conceive, I was happy to be involved in a possible cure for this most deadly disease. A vaccine just might be possible and best of all; I will have been a part of it!!

Chapter Seven
The End of …?

The night before the party, his demeanor changed again and he seemed happy and back to his normal self. We got dressed and when he saw me in my emerald green formal evening gown, he whistled. He pulled me into his arms and said, "I have an early Christmas present for you. I am sorry for my behavior this past week or so. I wish I could explain it all, but I can't."

He pulled a box out of his pocket and put it in my hands. "I do love you, you know." I carefully opened the beautiful wrapping and discarded it on the bed. I opened the box to find that there was a matching bracelet, necklace, earrings and ring.

"It is made with both diamonds and emeralds and it's the perfect complement to your new dress. I know you love emeralds. Wear this tonight and always remember that no matter how bad things get at work and no matter how often I bring it home, it is never directed at you. I just need to get a better handle on separating work life from home life."

He paused and took the ring and placed it on my right middle finger. "I will never love any one or any thing as much as I love you. Remember that." He helped me to put on the remaining jewelry and I spun around for him to view me.

"Prettiest girl at the prom." He quipped. I blushed. We were close to each other and he leaned in to kiss me. His soft lips caressed

my bare shoulders and I was suddenly aware that I no longer wanted to go to the party.

Warren sighed and pulled away from me. He held out his arm and said, "Let's get this over with Mrs. Stone. I can't wait to get you back home." I giggled and together we walked down the stairs and out to his Escalade. I loved him so much.

We arrived at a private exclusive home on a golf course. I wasn't sure whose home it was, but it was massive. When we walked, in people began to introduce themselves to me. Most of them were colleagues of Warren's. Others were people I had met at other holiday affairs and I found that I knew them by sight. I realized that we had indeed attended a lot of parties.

The evening slowly developed with people joining in on the festivities by drinking the alcoholic drinks that came with the season. I didn't drink at all but about every five or so minutes someone would make the offer to me. Warren didn't drink either but it was normal for the catering employees to offer drinks to everyone that didn't have a glass in their hands.

We somehow got separated when his boss took Warren aside. I watched from a distance as he offered Warren a drink. Warren shook his head and passed on the drink. His boss took the glass back and placed it into Warren's hand. He touched the drink glasses together and then they both drank a toast. I could see that Warren was not at all comfortable. Perhaps this was the reason that he didn't want to come.

The beverages were flowing freely and it was all too frequent that someone handed me a drink that I would then set down. Warren seemed to be behind me at every turn picking up my glasses and disposing of them in various ways. I watched as his boss would occasionally lift his glass from across the room and Warren would lift one that I had sat down and chug it down with his boss. It was very strange to see Warren drinking.

As I watched and he began to mingle, I noticed that he was becoming more and more flirtatious with the women and overly friendly with people in general. He was also a little sloppier in his speech. He began to wobble a little as he walked within the crowd. Finally I had seen enough. I wanted to go home and put my husband to bed. Hopefully he would be fine and tomorrow life would get back to our version of normal. The party would be over and all the worrying that Warren had done because of it would be past us. I left to go to the bathroom and steeled myself to find a way to get Warren safely to the car.

When I came out of the bathroom, another one of the servers was handing him a drink. I walked over to him and whispered in his ear. "I am ready to go home when you are."

His voice was suddenly very angry. "I am finally around people that I am actually happy to be with and you want to drag me away from it?"

He took the glass that I had been given by the server and drank it down. I was sure that it was the alcohol talking so I put my arm through his arm and said, "We really should leave now." He jerked his arm, almost sending me falling down, but I caught my balance and said as I linked my arm again in his, "Can I have the keys so that I can drive?"

Instantly, I knew that I had crossed some kind of invisible line and he was not the man that just a few short hours before had presented me with the jewelry and told me that he loved me. He reached for me and pulled me towards him.

Everything suddenly went into slow motion. His hands began to wrap around my neck. I began to sputter, trying to cry out for help. For that first second, I was taken by surprise and didn't get out a scream for help that someone could hear. The pressure was so great on my throat that I thought I would die. I twisted and his hands slipped a little and I screamed. People began to pay attention to what was going on.

Men and women both were now trying to pull him off of me. His hands seemed to tighten with every attempt that someone made to pull Warren away from me. Finally I heard some call out to others to call 911.

It seemed to take forever though it must have been only a few seconds. When his hands were pulled free, I fell to the floor and several men and women pulled me to the opposite side of the room. Two men took Warren and I watched him being dragged away. At first, some of the women were still laughing.

"That's the worst I've ever seen him." I heard one say. "I didn't know that Warren Stone even drank alcohol." Someone held my head while someone else took my hand. I couldn't see them, but I could

hear them. "Hang on Mrs. Stone. The ambulance is on the way."

That was the last I even bothered listening to until the paramedics arrived.

When the paramedics arrived, they gently aroused me by holding an oxygen mask in front of my face. Swelling and bruising all over my neck began to appear in the less than three quarters of an hour that it took them to get to me. The police came and took a report of what had happened from the people around me.

The policemen went to the room where Warren had been taken only to find it empty. "Warren is gone." I heard someone say. And I wondered what had happened to him. "He probably went somewhere to sleep it off." The first police officer said. "They say that he doesn't drink." The other police officer was worried and sent someone out to see if Warren's SUV was still here. He was worried about Warren behind the wheel so drunk. I was too. I couldn't believe that my wonderful husband was acting this way.

Excuses were on everyone's lips saying that he was out of control and no one else wanted to get hurt. They made sure that the police knew that this was out of character for Warren.

I signed the police paperwork and the officer gave me a directive to file domestic abuse charges against Warren. I shook my head. I felt so helpless.

I was eventually rushed to the Emergency Room of a nearby hospital. I promised myself that I would file charges the next morning, though I wasn't sure that I would be able to keep that promise. After all, he hadn't wanted to come to this stupid party anyway. He hadn't *wanted to drink and he was practically forced to. All of those things led him to act so badly. I couldn't believe that my Warren was capable of the things he did.*

The ride to the ER seemed unending, and I was so weary that I closed my eyes and waited for that inevitable stop and bump out of the ambulance. Time seemed to stand still. I didn't answer any questions and even though I could hear what the paramedics were saying, I seemed unable to speak.

The doctors brought the police that had followed behind the ambulance into my room and they continued to take down the doctors reports of my injuries to add to their paperwork. Again, I was in my own world. "She's in shock now." I heard the doctor say as he started an IV, in response to the police officer asking the questions.

A woman that the doctor introduced as a hospital social worker with the domestic violence center came in and walked over to the opposite side of the bed. "It will be okay, I promise." I was sure that she couldn't promise. My world had fallen apart.

She handed me some paperwork and I signed where she pointed. I didn't know what it was, but I couldn't think straight. I realized that I was losing focus and that I was slowly drifting in and out of the conversations around me. I looked up at the IV and the thought came to me that there must be something in it that was making me sleepy. My eyes closed and I could not open them again.

Several days passed with me drifting in and out of sleep. I was aroused by the social worker. She said that I would be taken to the courthouse for the domestic abuse and protection hearing.

"Has Warren been here?" I asked her. "No, Mrs. Stone, not today either." I guess I must have asked her before.

She led me to a van that was waiting in the front of the hospital. We drove to the local courthouse and I was escorted by her and a male nurse into the private chambers of a judge. It was all very strange. Why hadn't Warren come to get me when he had sobered up? I couldn't believe what I was about to do.

The judge was kind. He gave me thirty days of a protection order. "When you come back, you will need proper representation. Your husband will be served this paperwork and he will undoubtedly have his own representation. Don't come unprepared."

He then asked the police officer to read his report from the night's events. He also read into the records the doctor's reports. "Do you think that he might have gone back to your home?" "I really don't know. I have been stuck in the hospital since that night." He nodded his head, "Don't worry, we'll find him and get him served."

When it was all over, I silently followed my two companions back to the parking lot and into the van. The drive back to the hospital seemed to last forever. I needed to go home. I didn't want to be in the hospital any more. As soon as the nurse wheeled me back into my room, and he helped me to get into bed, I asked to speak with a doctor.

"He will be in this evening." The nurse answered me. He re-hung the IV and immediately injected the port with pain medicine that I wasn't sure I still needed.

I knew it was morning when the change of staff happened and I could see the light filtering through the drawn blinds putting stripes on the floor.

I realized that I would have to do things on my own. I needed to get back to my life and the way things should have been. I was never the weakling that I felt like I was here in this hospital. I reached down to my arm and swallowing hard, I lifted up the tape, so that when I was ready to yank the needle out it would be easier.

I decided that I needed to get dressed first and so I looked in the small closet and dressed leaving out my right arm. I bit my lip and then pulled the needle quickly out of my arm. I knew I was still bleeding as it began to spurt some on my arm. I ran to the bathroom and grabbed a hand towel from the neatly folded pile left by the nurse. I tied it as tightly as I could around my arm hoping to suppress the flow. I was getting dizzier by the minute.

I walked quickly towards the nearest elevator and rode to the first floor. I walked out and called a taxi immediately. Within half an hour I was on my way home.

The Christmas lights were still turned on the way we had left them several days ago. It was now only two and a half weeks before Christmas and I just knew that Warren would come home when he realized that I was there.

That night, I took the jewelry in my hands and remembered the words he had said. "I will never love any one or any thing as much as I love you. Remember that." I still believed him, in spite of the things that had happened. I waited and waited for Warren to show up but I kept falling asleep and waking up to some abstract noise that wasn't him.

Every day I seemed to be seeing Warren everywhere. He didn't speak to me, but he followed me all of the time. The protection hearing date came quickly and we both met in court. I was provided with a domestic violence lawyer to represent me. The judge extended my protection order for another thirty days but again admonished me that I should have "regular legal representation for any petition from this point further."

The judge then asked the police officer that had been there the night of the party, to make sure that I was safely off of premises before Warren would be released.

I cried as I walked out to my car. I had been living with Warren tailing me almost daily. I opened the door and sat in my car crying for no more that a few moments when the police officer tapped on the window. "I know it's hard, but you need to leave here before we will let him leave." I shook my head and started my car and drove away scared to death that I was still going to be followed by Warren on a regular basis.

When I had finished, Mr. Laughton looked as if he himself had been hurt. Kim was sitting beside me with tears in her eyes. I hadn't even noticed that she had joined us. She reached over and took my hand in hers and quietly said: "I'm so sorry." I shrugged my shoulders. I didn't know what else to do. The words had flowed from me and felt like they were from a book I had been reading. They were all true, but the whole truth was, it still seemed very unreal to me.

Chapter Eight
Making Plans

I looked down at my hands in embarrassment that I had been so emotional and so involved in the telling of my story.

Finally, after a couple of minutes of silence I looked up into Mr. Laughton's eyes. I did not know exactly what to expect from him. How could he believe that I had been unaware that Warren would become violent? I didn't want to know the answer and I hoped that he had more important cases to work on than mine. I was feeling overwhelmingly sure that I had already been enough of a burden to both him and his secretary.

I needed to be alone with my thoughts. Having to tell everything brought up questions that I needed to really examine myself. I was questioning what signs I myself had missed. I wanted to get up and leave but the silence held me in the room. I couldn't make myself move. Instead, I lowered my eyes again to my clasped hands in my lap. It was as if I could hear the wheels of our three brains turning, processing every word I had spoken. Somehow, it had all been much more real when I said the words out loud.

I really was becoming uneasy and was sure that it had taken forever to tell my story. I lifted my eyes again and watched them both for several minutes. Before I could let my eyes meet theirs again, I put my face in my hands. I was going to cry. I couldn't hold back the tears. While the three of us were busy sifting through the details, I let the tears flow freely down my cheeks. I was only vaguely aware that I was actually sobbing.

Mr. Laughton's voice became stern and calm when he interrupted the sound of my sobs. I could tell that he was frustrated with my situation. Like most men, he had trouble when women cried. Somehow he held his emotions in check.

He began, "We need to put together a real plan for your protection. It's obvious that Warren can be counted on for many interruptions to your life." It was then that our plan really took on the little details that we had put in motion today.

Our adventure in court would lead me to a new life. As the time grew shorter to actually go to court, Mr. Laughton said that we could ask for a continuance so that safety measures could be put in place. I knew that my life was changing. It was changing in a far different way than I had ever imagined. It would never be the same again.

Over the next few weeks, I managed to call Mr. Laughton several times while we waited on my new court date. April 6th. Wow, I thought, what a random date. In the middle of the week and in the middle of spring.

I would make frequent trips home, but I would also stay hidden in the hotel room that I was still living in. I worked as best as I could from the hotel room. I would go in to work every day for the continuing injections.

I was driving the Nissan Pathfinder that Mr. Laughton had given me to drive. I was grateful for the tinted windows. It gave me a security that I didn't have with the Mustang.

So here I sit, waiting on my lawyer to arrive. I knew it would not be long before permanent changes in my life would be made. I had arrived early, as Mr. Laughton had instructed. He didn't want the possibility of an attack in the parking lot. Since he had shown up at the parking lot at Mr. Laughton's office we were both reasonably sure that attacking me in this parking lot was not out of the realm of possibilities. I was in disguise with what I thought was no possible way that I could be recognized. We were taking every precaution to make sure that I would be safe.

I was also just as sure that until I was in my own clothes, that I was well hidden from Warren in plain site. It was easy sitting where I was lost in the crowd. Physically, anyway. Emotionally, I was in turmoil. My nervousness grew as more and more people filled up the waiting area. I began to worry that as the crowd increased I might be forced to be close to Warren. At least in a small crowd I could watch him and move out of his way. I pulled out a magazine and tried desperately to watch for Warren and pretend to read.

Various courtroom dramas would be taking place in this building today and I knew that I was one of them. I hated the turn my life had taken over the past two and a half years. I tried to keep myself 'reading' but I couldn't.

Tears began to trickle ever so slowly down my cheeks. That made it worse. I was really angry with myself for being weak and letting the sorrow overtake me.

I shook my head slowly trying, to no avail, to clear away the sorrow and the fears. I had to remind myself over and over again that I was doing the right thing. As I thought about all the damage that was done by one little broken heart, I realized that the tears had changed from tears of pain and anguish to tears of temporary strength and I had a powerful resolve to get on with my life and doing what was right for me.

Today I was here seeking a divorce and protection from a man I no longer knew. He was not trustworthy. He was cruel. He was a criminal. How many news stories I had heard that the "protection order" offered in domestic violence cases didn't stop someone intent on doing someone harm. Many women had been killed with a protection order in place. That little piece of paper didn't stop the violence.

Mr. Laughton had warned me of that fact time and time again. I knew that he was genuinely concerned for my safety. I was both curious and anxious to get the day over with. I couldn't wait to find out how everything would play out in the courtroom. The fact that I was in disguise was a very telling part of today's scenario. Mr. Laughton's words rang in my head over and over. It was a constant reminder that a "piece of paper can't stop a bullet."

God this was getting long! My mind kept reverting to all the things that had taken place since my first meeting with Mr. Laughton. Would he show up? Would Warren? Or had Warren done something to Mr. Laughton. Suddenly I realized that that was indeed possible. I looked around more fervently for the two of them.

I really did like Mr. Laughton. He was nothing like what I had expected. He kept me sane during the weeks and months leading up to today and I was appreciative of his efforts to calm my fears. Of course he would show up. I was just panicking a little.

I wondered why he would agree to take on a case like mine. Why was this taking so long? I looked at my watch and realized that I had only been sitting here for thirty minutes or so. I rolled my eyes. Time was going by so slowly or I was just running through so many different things that my brain was on fast forward.

This was why Mr. Laughton had told me to keep busy. "Don't let your emotions get the best of you." He had said. So the weeks and months before today had been filled with as much hustle and bustle as I could bear. I was needed to do the work that I had missed out on. I had to go in every day, but I only had to stay long enough to get injections and download my findings from my thumb drive. I had begun to be completely focused on everything else in order not to think about what was going to happen today.

Now that the day was finally here, I was sure that I was ready. Okay maybe 'sure' wasn't the right word. I was resolved to whatever fate there was for me.

I started looking at things logically. I was sure that I was safe in the courthouse; after all there were policemen everywhere. All those fears and all those concerns that had led me here could be put aside while I was in this building. Even so those fears kept filling every fiber of my being with worry and I would suppress them as quickly as I could. The waiting, watching, and worrying, didn't help. Finally I decided that even though I was scared, I was more than ready. Ready to move forward.

I went back to my pretending to read. A picture of a girl snow skiing as an advertisement for lip protection products somehow pushed my thoughts back to before I met Warren.

Wasn't I happy in my life? I had led my life to be exactly where I was before he came into my life.

Research had been my life's calling. I always wanted to know why to any question. The mystery of everything fascinated me and I hoped that I would again be able to find that fascination. I had loved life. I could go back to that, right?

It was then a thought crossed my mind. Every mystery? I was in the middle of the biggest one of my life.

What had made Warren become the man he was now? What makes any man turn against his wife in such a violent way? I really wanted to know. I really wished that I could be strong enough to help others who found themselves in my situation. I started looking around the lobby. What other women were here for the same reason that I was?

An argument between two men interrupted my thoughts. Bailiffs and sheriff deputies were immediately dispersing all the "extra" people. They were now going around the foyer asking each person what their business was at the courthouse today.

If a name wasn't on the list of business for the day, they were escorted out of the courtroom foyer and into the main foyer of the building.

Like a shot to the heart, I was aware of Warren. He was dressed nicely in a suit. His eyes were blazing their hazel green gray. He was acting completely at ease and there on his face was that smile that melted my heart. It was as if everything he had done disappeared and the love of my life was standing across the room. I was openly staring. This was not going to be easy at all.

He was looking over the room, probably scanning for me or Mr. Laughton. His eyes locked on mine for only an instant. I flinched, but he nodded and smiled at me. I did not smile back. He hadn't recognized me I was sure of that. I hadn't even recognized myself in the mirror that morning. He was just acknowledging that I was staring at him.

Then, a woman appeared by his side. She had apparently seen his eye contact with me because she acted like she was jealous and began playing with him. She reached her hand up and almost seductively she pulled his chin so that he looked at her. It was a playfully intimate gesture. My heart broke all over again. This, I hadn't expected.

I wondered who she was. We had only been away from each other for a few months! How could he be out of love with me and in love with someone else in such a short time? We had taken a year to even declare our love for each other! I looked her over from top to bottom.

Her clothing was quite business like but I could tell that she was not his lawyer. There was a closeness and familiarity between them that was far more than it would be for a lawyer. I had been worried about facing Warren in the courtroom and now, now it looked like I would be facing her as well. Her face, her eyes, her smile, and even her makeup were a vision of perfection.

My heart was racing. How was she involved? Was she just moral support? What role would she play? After all she hadn't been kicked out. Why had he brought a woman here if not but to hurt me even more than he already had?

I turned away from the scene. It was killing me. They were presenting to everyone that they were intimately connected, but I knew, I thought I knew, that it was for my benefit that this show was being put on. It didn't help that Warren was to me that dream that any woman would want to be in love with and have him love them back. My heart did a back flip as I recalled us making love and the feeling that I was his whole world and he mine.

Minutes later, thankfully, while I flushed in my remembrance, Mr. Laughton walked into the room. He walked over to where I sat, pretending not to notice me, he put his briefcase down and reached to pick up a newspaper that was on the bench across from me.

I looked back at Warren signaling to Mr. Laughton with a simple nod in that direction that Warren was already there. Warren's posture changed. I surmised that he had obviously recognized Mr. Laughton from his office that day. He began to stand a little taller and look a little crisper. It amazingly added to his air of confidence. He fairly glowed with strength and I knew that he would put forth a monumental effort to be liked in court and come out a winner. He pulled the woman close to him and looked away, whispering in the woman's ear.

Mr. Laughton took a couple of steps towards me, leaning over to put his brief case down, he nonchalantly said, "It's time."

Chapter Nine
Unmasking the Future?

Finally! It was the signal that I was waiting for. My time had come. I took the backpack that had been on my lap and swung it to my shoulder. I would have to pass by Warren to get to the bathroom and change.

I was frightened. After all, the disguise would be removed and I would be vulnerable to Warren's direct attention as I returned to my seat by Mr. Laughton. I was shaking slightly when I rose to my feet. I stayed close to the wall for stability and made my way over to the bathroom.

I chose the handicapped stall to dress in and sat down on the toilet to calm myself. I pressed my hands against the cold of the walls and then brought the cold to my cheeks hoping to remove the heat that brought color to my cheeks. This trick I had used in school when I was nervous about a test. How silly I was to worry over such things when this was more devastating. I was too flustered.

I carefully removed all the different aspects of my disguise. I removed the over exaggerated makeup and applied my real makeup and let my hair escape from the tight bun that it had been in. It fell down my back and I immediately clipped it back from my face. I had purchased a brand new outfit for today. I suddenly laughed. I was playing the same game that he was. Jealousy. I was going to look like a million bucks. I wanted to remind him just what he was missing. I put my disguise into the backpack and took a long satisfying look in the mirror before I began my walk back out into the foyer.

There were much fewer people in the foyer now. It was emptying fast as people were being called to go into each opening courtroom. Warren would easily be able to see me now. I didn't look in his direction and somehow I managed a weak smile as I approached Mr. Laughton.

He walked over to me, meeting me half way and held out his hand to shake mine. I put my hand in his and he said. "Keep your chin up. You look amazing." He took me in. "He is watching you. I'm sure that's what you were going for." He seemed a little upset with me about that. "We'll get through this as fast as we can."

I for some reason didn't want Mr. Laughton to be upset so I said, "I look this way for me. Not for Warren." I paused. "This is me, starting over and feeling good about it." He smiled down at me and I was happy to realize that my words were true. So dressing this well had accomplished two tasks and that was a good way to start this horrible process.

I did not want to look in Warren's direction and so we walked back over to where I had been seated and I sat down. Mr. Laughton stood beside me and I swung the backpack back into my lap.

Casually I looked up and glanced in Warren's direction. It was a mistake. His eyes locked on mine and his mouth dropped open as he realized that I had been the woman sitting there before. I lifted the little backpack and smiled broadly. I was trying to put on a very brave face.

In that split second of recognition, he took the opportunity to try and hurt me again. He took the arm of the woman that stood with him and pulled her in front of him. He kissed her in what was meant to look like a passionate manner but I could tell that it was not. I had felt his passion and I knew it well.

I turned away from him. It was embarrassing. I knew it was designed specifically for me.

He took a step in my direction and released her from his grasp. Mr. Laughton had taken in the whole scene and stepped in my line of vision with Warren. He totally blocked the two of them from my sight. I looked up at his tall and imposing frame and knew that he was doing his best to shield and protect me from any confrontation with Warren. Whether it be physical or mental.

The pain from seeing Warren's intimate interaction with the woman at his side must have been very visible on my face.

Mr. Laughton reached down and cupped my chin in his hand. He gently tilted my face up until our eyes were forced to meet. "Look at me. Don't let go of me. I want you to take my arm and let's go in."

I took his offered support and stood as he continued. "Don't break now that we've come this far." I knew that he was afraid I wouldn't be able to walk in without stumbling while looking back at Warren. I wanted to scream out at him.

The emotional pains I was feeling now were unbearable. I was dying inside. My heart hurt. Physically hurt. I suddenly felt sick. I crossed my hands over my chest, still holding onto Mr. Laughton's arm. I wasn't sure that I was going to make it through the day.

Mr. Laughton took his arm and placed it around my shoulders. "Stand tall. Remember that you are here to fight *against* him." He led me up to the list of cases that were posted on the cork board on the wall. "We're first on this docket in courtroom C." He gently but firmly guided me through the doors of the courtroom that we had been assigned to.

Filled with nervous energy, I stupidly giggled. "Stand tall" he had said. I was a mere 5'2" and he towered over me by a foot and a half. I found it funny for some reason. He looked at me, questioning my sanity, I suppose. I just shrugged my shoulders. "Good girl. I'm proud of you." For that moment, I had passed my first real test with Warren. What would happen once everything started; only time would tell.

Mr. Laughton led me to the front of the courtroom. He opened the short swinging gate almost with a flourish and holding it open for me, motioned that I should take a seat at the table to the right. Both tables were empty of everything except for a pitcher of water and several glasses set on a tray.

So much was strange in here to me. I looked around and realized that I was on the right side of the courtroom. I hoped that that was a sign. I smiled.

The door at the back was pushed open and laughter spilled into the courtroom. I turned to see both Warren and his friend walk in. They were cuddling with each other as a clear indicator to those present that they were "in love." My heart did a painful but powerful leap into my throat.

Mr. Laughton put his briefcase on the table and looked at me watching the pair as they walked down the center of the courtroom. He leaned down once more to draw my eyes to his. He put his hand on my shoulder. "This is an obvious attempt to distract you and make you emotional. Don't let him, or them, do that to you. You are stronger than that."

When I gazed about the room, others that also had business here were watching the outrageous public display of Warren and his friend. I hoped that the display would put others in the courtroom on my side. Or at least root for me. I didn't know any of them, though some looked familiar, but for some reason, it was important to me that they thought I was in the right.

The two took their time walking to the front of the courtroom. The bailiff watched and waited as he stood in between both tables. I continued to glance back at them. The bailiff cleared his throat. "Mr. Stone, your place is at this table." He nodded his head towards the one on the left and then he said: "Please." He looked at them as I did as they made their way through the swinging gate. A strong resentment was building in me. I hated we were here because of him.

"There will be no shouting or outlandish behavior in the courtroom." The bailiff spoke softly to us at both tables. "You will speak only when spoken to and you will answer questions directed to you and you only. Does anyone have questions before the judge comes in?"

I sat where I was only thinking about what was happening. Did I really want him to pay for all the pain he was inflicting or did I just want to get away from today as unscathed as possible? It was tearing me apart. I wanted him to hurt and yet I wanted him back. Why? I couldn't look at Warren and his, whomever she was, any longer.

I heard the water pour into the glasses. I heard the clink of the two glasses together and it seemed to me that they were actually toasting to a victory they were planning on having. I was so annoyed. How arrogant could you get?

My hands immediately went to my face. I wept silently into them trying desperately to keep my makeup in tact. Mr. Laughton pulled out a handkerchief and handed it to me. I tried to keep the mascara in place as I dabbed my eyes.

All too soon, and yet not soon enough, the formalities of the courtroom began when the bailiff called the court to order. The judge seemed to be reading over the paperwork that filled his desk in front of him. The room was completely silent. It was maddening. My thoughts betraying my broken heart, I kept finding ways to blame the woman beside Warren for everything. It wasn't reasonable, but it somehow was all I could think of. Surely he wasn't really trying to hurt me. Why had my marriage failed?

The doors closed at the back of the room and it hit me like a bolt of lightening. They were closing the doors on my marriage as well.

When I was able to sit down again, I kept going over everything. I was sure that this…this situation, was all my fault. My head was spinning. I tried to put my finger on just what I had done. What had happened to the wonderful man that I had married? What had I done to make him hurt me?

I was called back to what was happening in the room as I listened to Mr. Laughton read a statement with the charges of abuse against Warren. The judge looked down and asked if these were also the reasons for the divorce request, or if the charges were the result of a divorce request from me.

I didn't understand what the reasons were for this question. What did it matter? My marriage was ending with as little fanfare as it began.

Mr. Laughton cleared his throat. "We will establish that the first act of violence has led Mr. Stone to continually stalk and terrorize Mrs. Stone." Mr. Laughton said as he continued to address the judge. "It was that continued violence that has led to the divorce request."

He looked down at me. "The act itself was unexpected and his actions since have left Mrs. Stone in hiding and unable to continue her regular routine in life. Her day to day activities are no longer normal." He turned to look at Warren. "We will establish that he has the potential for even more violent acts given his training and his current employment. He is also a flight risk as his employment takes him frequently out of the country."

I wondered why that was important. Wouldn't I be safer with him out of the country? "We have sufficient testimony to prove that the defendant was drunk the night of the attack, and that divorce had never before been even discussed between the couple."

The judge's eyebrows lifted and he looked over the top of his glasses. Mr. Laughton continued, "Mrs. Stone was blindsided by his behavior and is now unable to return immediately to the life she had before her marriage. Her lifestyle has changed and she lives in daily fear of his next outrageous confrontation. We are asking that he be given a jail term that will keep him off the streets long enough to allow Mrs. Stone to return to her former life in safety or re-locate to a safer place."

I heard his words and though we had discussed them they were hard to hear spoken out loud like that in the courtroom. Mr. Laughton, looked down at me, and then back at the judge, "We are asking for the maximum of a year to be added to the current protection order and for a complete and final divorce with spousal support to cover the household expenses for their new home that Mr. Stone had paid before the incident. The home was purchased in November and given as a gift to Mrs. Stone, by Mr. Stone. It was deeded in her name." He walked forward and gave a copy of the paperwork that Warren had originally given to me on that wonderful evening several months ago.

The judge looked up and interrupted Mr. Laughton. "And if she decides to move to a safer location, then what is to become of the house?" Mr. Laughton looked back at me. "I suppose she would sell it." I nodded my head.

"Do you have any witnesses to present for your case?" the judge asked my attorney.

He quickly answered, "Yes." And for the first time, I turned around as Mr. Laughton motioned that our witnesses should stand.

There were about twenty people there on my behalf. I saw Kim sitting near the back. She must have come in after the doors had closed.

"Are they all your witnesses?"

"Yes. These are just a few of those in attendance at the party the night of the attack. We have taped their testimonies and have signed affidavits, but we would like to present some of their testimonies in court as well."

"That is not necessary, if you have their testimonies already submitted to me, but it is your right to do so. We could just have them read in court." He paused but when Mr. Laughton didn't answer, he said. "Call your first witness."

I found myself at this point listening to the various points of view from each person as they stood between the two tables. None of them had seen how it had started, but each one of them had their version of what had happened from the time he had pulled me to him shouting. There wasn't a single testimony that was favorable to Warren.

The testimonies went on for quite a while when the judge interrupted once again, "I am satisfied that the attack was unprovoked. Shall we hear from Mrs. Stone?"

Unlike in a regular trial, since I didn't have to go the stand to testify, I knew that I would be standing right beside Warren. Each person so far had just stood at the swinging gate between the two tables. The judge must have seen the look on my face because he motioned that I should stand where I was, and then asked Mr. Laughton to proceed.

"Judge? May I first call your attention to the photos from the hospital records? There are pictures of the injuries and descriptions by the attending physicians."

The judge picked up the medical records and thumbed through them, scanning them. He then picked up each photo and looked at them.

He shook his head and then gently asked: "Mrs. Stone, are you okay to proceed?"

My voice was soft and low, but I said: "Yes."

"These pictures are a graphic display of your injuries, and I have heard testimony after testimony that have told me of the intensity of the attack. However, it appears that you are the only one with the how and the why of what triggered the attack. In your own words, would you please tell the court what happened the night of the party?" I looked up and Mr. Laughton, who was still standing beside me and he nodded. I sighed and then began.

"We dressed for the party, which he really didn't want to go to, but he put on a happy face and seemed resigned to go and at least make an appearance. Before we walked out of the door, Warren gave me a present and told me that I was to always remember that he loved me, no matter what. It was a matching ring, necklace, bracelet and earrings set with emeralds and diamonds. He helped me put them on as he whispered those words to me. I went to the party quite happy and quite sure of our love." My voice was trembling and tears were streaming down my cheeks as the memory of that night swept over me.

Mr. Laughton reached over and touched my shoulder, patting it. He put the handkerchief I had left on the table in my hand and I took it gratefully.

"Do you need to take a break, Mrs. Stone?" the judge asked. I shook my head. I had to continue. I needed to get it over with so that I could sit down. At this point, Mr. Laughton sat down, and I was able to glance over at Warren who was representing himself, and I noticed his eyes looked as if he too were remembering the beginning of the night with fondness. When he realized that I was looking at him, he turned an icy glare towards me. Immediately, I turned back to the judge and continued with my story. The details were pretty much as I had told them to Mr. Laughton and by the time I had finished, I was near sobbing.

"Thank you, Mrs. Stone. You may be seated. Is there anything further, Mr. Laughton?" Mr. Laughton answered, "No. That is all I have."

Chapter Ten
Appearance of Evil

The judge spoke again after writing on a note pad, "That any man raises his hand to a woman is beyond my personal comprehension and yet day in and day out I have cases of that kind of abuse cross my desk."

For the first time that day, he showed his disgust with the situation. "You may present your side of the story now, Mr. Stone. State your defense of your actions for the night in question."

Warren stood immediately. He appeared to be very cocky. He opened his mouth and his words were as smooth as silk, and my heart melted again as I heard him speak. "I admit that I got drunk, your honor. I don't normally drink."

He looked over at me. "There was nothing I could do when my boss actually put one in my hand. I had already turned him down once, and I felt obligated. I thought it would be fine if I took one sip as he toasted our success on a project."

He looked down at the floor and then back at me. "I honestly think that it was a stronger drink than I thought I was given," he turned to look at me, "because I never would have intentionally hurt you. Bria can testify herself that I wasn't really myself. I quickly became someone I am not."

He looked at me again, his eyes boring through me. Our eyes locked and the moment lingered longer than it should have. The judge cleared his throat. "However, her actions since have been completely of her own making. I just wanted to talk to her but the restraining order was in place before I sobered up."

The woman with him coughed. Warren looked back at her and he continued. "It was Bria however that attacked me first." I gasped. "She didn't want to stay at the party with me completely intoxicated. When I wouldn't leave, she tried to physically pull me to the car. I didn't realize that I was even choking her until they pulled me away from her. I really thought that I was just pushing her away from me."

Once more he looked back at me, his voice becoming almost tender. "I would never have hurt you intentionally."

"That's enough Mr. Stone. Do you have anything other than your testimony of the fact that she 'attacked' you first?" "Yes, I do." He pointed to the woman beside him. "My witness was at the party and she was by my side when Bria attacked me."

I gasped again, knowing full well that I had never seen that woman before in my life. I knew that Warren was lying. Mr. Laughton reached over and patted my hand under the table.
I was stunned into silence as I listened to her words.

"Mr. Stone was indeed highly intoxicated when Mrs. Stone approached her husband. We had been talking but she interrupted us. She demanded that they go home. She reached out and took hold of his hand and Mr. Stone yelled that he didn't want to leave the party. Mrs. Stone at this point pulled her husband's arm as if she was going to drag him away. This was when I interrupted her and offered to bring Warren home at a later time. It was up to her, I said, but if she really didn't want to stay, that I would make sure that Warren got home in one piece." She glanced over at me while she paused.

"Mrs. Stone then slapped Warren. It was a hard slap that turned his head and this was when he reached out to her shoulders, but he was off balance and his hands went instead momentarily to her throat. He was so drunk and off balance that he didn't immediately realize where his hands were. They were not wrapped that tightly around her neck, but when Mrs. Stone looked around and noticed that others were now watching, she put on the performance of a lifetime and made it appear as if she could not breathe."

She stopped abruptly when the courtroom began buzzing with whispered conversations.

The judge banged his gavel on his desk and the room immediately got quiet. "You may continue, but I warn you that you can and will be held and charged with perjury if your version of events turns out to be false."

She continued, her voice now much louder and defensive. "I was there! I saw her attack Warren first. I saw what I saw. Warren simply reacted. As the crowd began to get close to the situation, I backed off, knowing that Warren would need to be taken home. He was pulled off of his wife, by several of the men, and a few whimpering women gathered around her."

She then looked at me again. "I saw her look up at her husband. He was shouting at her but she smiled just as she pretended to pass out. I know it was an act. She meant to embarrass him in front of his boss and co-workers."

She looked back to the judge. "I followed the men that were escorting Warren to another part of the house. When they left, I gathered Warren together and we left right out of the front door. No one even tried to stop us because they all knew the truth about what had happened. We even waited and then followed the ambulance to the hospital.

Warren was completely passed out by the time we reached the hospital parking lot. I walked in and tried to get back to see her, but it was her version of events that everyone had listened to. The police were there and I knew that Warren couldn't go home. He has been staying with me since that night."

She looked over at me one more time. "He has only tried to talk to her and every time, she gets hysterical and cries for help pretending to be helpless." She stopped and sat down abruptly.

Warren stood again. He said. "I have a right to demand justice and I am asking that all charges be dropped. The charges are ridiculous. It was self defense that I even reached towards her. The fact that I was too drunk to recognize what I was doing, is proof enough that it was not at all intentional."

"First of all, Mr. Stone, you cannot demand anything in any courtroom. The law demands justice, not you. If you have no more witnesses to your version of events?" he paused once more looking over his glasses at Warren. "Then you may calm yourself and take a seat."

The room was quiet.

"Are there any witnesses that can testify as to whether Ms. Coronado was at the party?" We all turned around to look at the people in the courtroom. No one raised their hand.

"Well then, Mrs. Stone, did you attack your husband at all at the party?" "No." I replied. "I have a very clear memory of what happened and I have never seen Ms. Coronado before today. And I wasn't the one drinking either. I don't drink. Warren was in conversation with several different women at the party and I can point most of them out, but I have never seen her before." My voice shook. It was not as strong as hers had been, but I did not whisper.

"I can see from all of the testimonies that you were intoxicated," the judge began. Warren interrupted him. "May I speak with my wife for a few minutes alone? In the foyer?"

The judge looked at me. I didn't know what he expected of me and so I simply stared back at him.

"Yes, you may have a conversation with your wife in the foyer, but the bailiff, Officer Marks, and Mr. Laughton will accompany Mrs. Stone to the foyer."

He turned and nodded to the bailiff. "Officer Marks, would you please escort Mrs. Stone and Mr. Laughton to the foyer? However you are to give Mr. and Mrs. Stone some privacy in their conversation, but do not let them leave your sight."

Mr. Laughton reached the doors first. He held it open for me and I walked through them with Officer Marks behind me. I was trembling, not sure what to expect from the man I knew I still loved.

His eyes bored into me as I waited with Mr. Laughton and Officer Marks.

Warren moved rapidly behind us and crossed to the opposite side of the foyer. I followed him slowly scared to death of what he might say to me.

When I was close enough to him, I looked back at the two men making sure that they would be able to come to my aid should I need them. Warren noticed them start to move towards us, getting closer when he stopped them. "This is a private conversation. The judge granted me that much."

"The judge also sent us out here to be with Bria so that you don't get that much privacy." James answered him. It was the first time that he was informal with me today.

He seemed very protective. Using my first name made Warren scowl at Mr. Laughton. "The judge said not to let us out of your sight. Not that you could listen in on our conversation." He grabbed my elbow and led me to the opposite corner of the foyer just about thirty feet away.

I kept looking back at the bailiff and my attorney. I wanted to have them safely near by. Warren then turned around, facing me with my back towards the two men. He was watching to make sure that they were not moving any closer. Warren's eyes stayed focused on the two of them while he spoke. He became a little animated talking more to himself than to me.

"I don't believe this. How did it get to this?" Things like that he kept repeating. It looked like we were in a legitimate conversation.

Suddenly, he reached up and put his arms around me as if we had agreed to hug each other. He whispered in my ear: "You think you had it bad before, you are in real danger now." He paused. "You don't know what you're dealing with Bria." He paused again, "Or what I'm dealing with" he added under his breath. I was shaking.

I wanted to call out for help but he whispered again, "**Bria, just listen to me.**" He sounded as if he were pleading with me. I glanced to the side and in the corner of my vision; I realized that both Officer Marks and Mr. Laughton were slowly making their way towards me. I knew that neither one of them trusted Warren.

He noticed their movement as well and between clenched teeth, he said. "I could easily snap your neck right now. One simple movement of my hand and it would be over with before anyone could save you. I have been trained to do whatever is necessary. You just don't know who you are messing with. I will do what I need to do."

And once more he added under his breath. "What I have to do." By this time I was shaking uncontrollably. "I meant what I said Bria." I turned my head away ever so slightly, not knowing what was coming.

"Step away from her." Officer Marks spoke sharply. The two men were only a couple of feet from us now. Warren instantly dropped his hands and put them into his pants pockets. He looked at me and I could see only the slightest resemblance of the past tenderness that we had shared.

Tears were streaming down my cheeks. The bailiff motioned to Warren to walk with him back to the courtroom.

Warren began talking with the bailiff as if they were old friends. I was sobbing. My body shaking and heaving in the silent sobs when Mr. Laughton directed me to a nearby bench, I collapsed onto it.

"We won't let him get away with that. Both of us heard and saw what he did." I didn't care. I needed to cry. This was so hard. I kept mixing up my feelings for him. I loved him so very much and yet he had once more threatened my life. I couldn't take this. It was too much for me.

Mr. Laughton sat down beside me and put his arm around me pulling me into his chest, comforting me like a father would. "I wish my parents could have been here."

Mr. Laughton whispered, "Do you want me to get them here for afterwards? I know that it's too late for today, but maybe you can use their support for a while."

I was already shaking my head. "No, this trip was everything they had planned and saved for all of their lives. Ninety days traveling to all their dreamed of places. How would they have known that I would need them?" I was trying to stop my sobs. I needed to be reasonable. Or at least try to be.

The doors to the courtroom opened. The bailiff stepped out and when the doors were closed, he said. "Take a few minutes for yourself." When he noticed that I was sobbing, he walked back through the doors for a split second and then came back out and stood in front of the closed doors.

Tears continued streaming freely down my cheeks.

Mr. Laughton said. "Look sweetheart, it's almost over. We need to get you cleaned up and back into the courtroom. It's okay. We'll make him pay for his threats." He was doing his best to be comforting. Even his endearing terms, though I knew that they were meant, I was sure, to soften the blow of going back in the courtroom, did nothing. It was simply too much to bear.

Chapter Eleven
Facing the Truth

At last, Mr. Laughton reached under my chin like he had done before, to tilt my head to look up at him and said. "It's okay. We will take care of this. Don't worry. Please dry your tears."

Again words that were meant to calm me down. Instead I turned even further into his chest, needing to feel protected, needing to hide. I could imagine my father caring for me in just this way and it felt safe. For a single moment at least, he took my father's place and I became again a little girl.

After several minutes, I stopped sobbing. I wiped my tears and pulled gently away from Mr. Laughton. "I'm so sorry. I didn't think I would be this out of control." He stood and pulled another handkerchief out of his pocket.

I stood and reached out to shake his hand, stepping back into a more formal mode with him. "Thank you. I have been so much trouble for you. I wish I could say how much I appreciate it but words don't seem to be enough."

I paused and looked towards the courtroom doors and Officer Marks that stood there. "After today, it'll be over and you can go back to your more important clients."

"That's not important, Bria. What is important is that you can get your life back. I have others who can handle any case if you still need my help."

I looked up at him. I knew that he was telling me the truth. He would indeed help me as long as I needed it.

I cleaned up my face as best as I could. He took the handkerchief and slowly wiped under my eyes where the mascara had smeared. I took a deep breath. "Okay." He held out his arm and I grabbed hold of it and we walked slowly back into the courtroom, followed by the bailiff. Officer Marks walked past the judge's bench and exited out a back door. I knew that he had gone to speak to the judge and let him know that we had all returned to the courtroom.

While he was gone, Mr. Laughton leaned across the aisle and said to Warren, "You will pay for that threat. I'm on my own mission now. I will prosecute you to the fullest extent of the law. With any luck you will be put away for a long time."

I knew that Warren had crossed a very important line with Mr. Laughton making his threat right in front of him. I could see the anger in him.

Warren's eyes shone almost with amusement as we stood for the judge to re-enter the room and take his seat behind the bench again. I took several deep breaths making sure that I was calm. I put my hands on the table in front of me. I meant to steady them and force them to stop shaking. It didn't work. I was still terrified. Every part of my body felt like Jell-o. I knew that Warren would carry out that threat if he could.

Sitting down again, I pulled my chair as close to the table as I could so that the desk would be my physical support. I didn't want to just sit there trembling.

Whispering to me, Mr. Laughton closed the gap between us. "Make sure that you maintain eye contact when the judge speaks to you." I wasn't sure I could look at anyone without bursting into tears, but I nodded.

My attorney stood and asked, "May I speak with you privately?"

"There is no need. I have already been informed of the events in the foyer. Is this what you were referring to?"

Mr. Laughton replied. "Yes that's it."

"The bailiff will recount what he witnessed in the foyer and to what he actually heard for the record."

As he stood by the judge's bench, he spoke quickly about what had occurred and what he overheard. Sounds of shock erupted throughout the courtroom.

As Officer Marks finished telling for the court recorder, what he witnessed, the judge looked at Warren and his witness. The whisperings in the room were growing louder. The gavel slammed on the desk or bench and silence fell over the room.

"You seem to think that you can play this court and me for a fool, Mr. Stone. I will not tolerate it. I don't tolerate it." Warren leaned forward in his chair.

The judge turned to look at me. "Your petition for a divorce is granted. An extension of one year on your protection order is also granted. You may come back in eleven months and extend it for another year if you need it. Everything you ask for is so ordered. Mr. Stone will pay all of your legal fees since it is a direct result of his actions that you have had to use an attorney. Mr. Laughton, please compile a ledger of all bills and submit them for my signature."

There was a sigh from Warren's table. Then the judge spoke again. "Mrs. Stone, you will be given as much protection as possible until this situation resolves itself. Mr. Laughton, you will make sure that this is carried out?" Mr. Laughton said that he would.

"Those of you associated with this case are excused with the exception of Mr. Stone. Officer Marks, please place Mr. Stone in temporary custody until Mrs. Stone is safely off of the premises." He nodded and the bailiff began to walk across the room to Warren's table.

Both Mr. Laughton and I scooted back in our chairs. I closed my eyes, tears easily gliding down the well known tracks to drip from my cheeks and chin. I was no longer Mrs. Warren Stone. Relief and sorrow flooded me. I lowered my head into my hands once again.

"And you," the judge looked at Ms. Coronado, "will be held in this courtroom." She gasped and slouched forward leaning on the table in front of her.

It was over. Now just who was I? I wasn't Mrs. Stone. I wasn't a wife. I had not yet become a mother. Could I go back to my former life? Those thoughts crowded out the fear that had been in my mind since he first attacked me.

All I had to do now was wait until Warren was escorted from the room. I intentionally kept my eyes closed. I did not want to see him taken away. I didn't think I could bear it. I silently wished that I could disappear. Behind my closed eyelids my blue eyes hid the pain so that Warren couldn't see how devastated he had left me.

Chapter Twelve
Unexpected

My head ached in my hands. My sobs were silent as I tried not to show such deep emotion to the rest of the room. I could feel my body lift and shudder as each sob coursed through my soul. My tears were flowing freely with the relief and the sadness that would hopefully heal my soul. I knew that I was at the point of starting over, but was all of this really now in my past? I felt so alone. I didn't want to hurt this badly.

The weight knocked me to the floor. I felt the chair slide out from under me. Warren's hands were around my neck. I opened my eyes and saw him on top of me, his hands closing off my air. Mr. Laughton was beside me trying to push Warren away and Officer Marks was behind him pulling at his arms. I could hear the cries of the people in the courtroom.

I heard the back door open and I knew that people were both running in and out of the courtroom. My head was swimming as oxygen became scarce in my lungs. I was going to pass out if I didn't die first. I thought, why doesn't he just snap my neck like he said he could?

I knew the answer. Mr. Laughton and Officer Marks were trying to remove his hands from my throat. Trying to pull him away and off of me. The weight of all three men was on top of me.

I tried to scream, but no one was getting enough leverage to actually dislodge his hands. The little air getting through seemed to only keep my lungs inflated. Finally, others came forward to help.

Everywhere I looked, there were people crowding around me, but my eyes kept coming back to Warren's. Why was this happening? "Why?" I mouthed. "I loved you." I finally whispered. Above the din of the room, I heard a laugh coming from the back of the room. I knew Warren's new love was getting away.

The ceiling began to spin. The voices began to mix together. The faces began to swim in front of me and then they began to fade.

My body went limp and my throat was free. I heard, through the tunnel that my brain was becoming, someone scream for the second time because of Warren, "Call 911!" My throat was free and I could breathe! The air seemed to whoosh in my throat as I gulped it in and swallowed hard.

My head hurt, my throat burned for the want of fresh air, but I could not lift my head. Even as Warren's hands had left my throat I knew that I was falling into darkness.

Somehow I was lifted slightly and Mr. Laughton held me in his arms. My head cradled in his lap on the floor. I did not remember actually hitting the floor. I could not focus on anything much except for the laughter that had come from the back of the room.

I tried to lift my head again and I still couldn't. I tried to lift my hands and I couldn't. My eyes were closed and I couldn't open them. "Please," I prayed, "let this not be real. Let this just be another nightmare."

The back of my head was pounding in pain. I was sure that pain meant that I was at least alive. That was something at least. The courtroom faded away. The darkness became complete. I slept. I was safe in this darkness. That's what I wanted most of all. To be where it was safe.

The scene of the courtroom drama kept playing over and over in my dreams. I would see Warren's face and his new love's face as I floated through the darkness.

Many other people, including Mr. Laughton, the judge, the bailiff and of course all those faceless people screaming and shouting flitting through. Weaving in and out was that bizarre laughter that left me feeling like the whole thing was nothing more than a nightmare scene from some carnival thriller movie.

Pain surged through my head. My throat was tight and dry. I looked around and could see the dimly lit hospital room. Taking in my surroundings, I saw that I was again connected to an IV. In fact, fluid was dripping ever so slowly from several bags. I watched as each one dripped and met in one line to make its way to my arm. Bruises covered my arms. How on earth did I get those? I didn't remember.

I tried in vain to lift my head. I tried to clear my throat and realized that something was in my throat. I knew it was a breathing tube when I brought my eyes in to focus on the tip of my nose. I could see the tube and though my hands couldn't reach up and touch it I could feel the tightness of the tape on my skin. It was uncomfortable and it did not allow me to speak. I wanted to call out to someone, anyone, to let them all know that I was awake and I wanted to get the tube out.

The voice startled me. "Good morning, Mrs. Stone." I heard the voice call softly to me from across the room. It startled me and sent chills running through me. The interruption breaking the human silence in the room, was making me panic.

Was I still dreaming? I was sure that the voice I had heard was Warren's, but that had to be impossible. I closed my eyes and tried to think clearly. Had everything been a dream? It was not rational. I was not rational. I started thinking of all the possibilities that might have brought me here. Could I have been in an accident? Could it really all be a dream? A car accident *would* explain the unknown bruises. I tried once again to clear my throat and swallow but it was too tight and too dry.

I caught his movement from the other side of the room in my peripheral vision. It wasn't clear, but he seemed to float to my bedside. I looked at him, my eyes questioning him silently. Our memories washed over me. This was all too real. He leaned over me and whispered. "Don't be afraid. It will all be over soon, I promise you."

Reality smacked me in the face. He had said similar words before. It flashed before my eyes as if it were happening right then. He reached towards me and then gently stroked my cheek. He leaned over me and kissed my forehead.

I began to try and move away from him. I wanted to push him away. My arms and hands were not moving how I wanted them to.

There was little or no movement at all. My body was not

responding to the threat that I knew was imminent but there was nothing I could do.

He leaned over me, embracing me and I felt his body press against my hand under the sheets. Something was in my hand and I felt it as the weight of his body pressed hard against me.

I recognized the feel of the call button and knew immediately that this was my one chance to survive. With all my strength, I pushed it. Over and over again I pressed it, hoping someone would answer it quickly.

The door burst open. Surprise crossed Warren's face as he watched people rushing in. His face became a mixture of pain and anger and excitement all at the same time.

He turned back to me and smiled. In an instant, I knew that he would always be able to find me. He turned back to his audience and slammed through the door and all the people that were suddenly rushing in to my room.

The nurse he had pushed aside scrambled to my side. Behind her came a doctor and Mr. Laughton. Warren ran right into the arms of either a police officer or a security guard, I could not tell. Three of them grabbed him just outside the now wide open door. Mr. Laughton saw my face and realized that I was watching the scene and swiftly kicked the door closed.

Fear was coursing through my whole body as the three people surrounded my bed. The doctor moved the sheet and began to pry the call button that I was still pushing from my fingers. I looked up into his eyes, begging for some kind of understanding. My other hand had somehow found the railing, and was now gripped to it, my knuckles white as I held on with every bit of strength I could muster.

Mr. Laughton reached for that hand and gently began to loosen my fingers. The doctor, Dr. Wilbrandt, if I was reading his name tag correctly, spoke for the first time, his voice worried but soft. "Let's remove that tube from your throat so that you can tell us what happened." I was trying to talk. "Obviously you can breathe on you own."

A second nurse came in and asked how she could help. Dr. Wilbrandt spoke to her quietly, and she moved around the room gathering things that they would need from the drawers and cabinet. The first nurse joined Mr. Laughton on the opposite side of the bed. She began to peel off the tape that held the tube firmly in place. As she loosened the tape, Dr. Wilbrandt gently pulled the tubing from my throat. I began to gag and felt sick.

The second nurse took a spit tray and a wet rag up to my lips and held it there just in case I did get sick. They were being so very careful. Dr. Wilbrandt took the rag and lightly cleaned up my face and mouth. It felt so good to be able to move my mouth and to breathe on my own.

The second nurse took all the tubing and tape and put it all in a trash bin and left the room. The first nurse, still standing by Mr. Laughton, held an oxygen mask just at my face. I could feel the cool oxygen hitting me and it felt wonderful. I turned my head more towards it enjoying the feel of it and breathing it in deeply.

I noticed her kind eyes and tenderness and she put her hand to my forehead, brushing away my hair and stroking my head. It was so comforting. I was grateful and I mouthed, "thank you".

"Here, sip some water," Dr. Wilbrandt said, and I turned once more to him on the left side of the bed to look at him. He held a cup of water with one of those bendable straws and put it to my lips. I sipped it slowly.

The water was cool and soothing to my throat. It was very sore but the cool water made it feel much better. I looked at the faces to find such tenderness and compassion in the eyes of all three of them. I had questions I wanted to ask, but I was afraid to try.

Finally, the doctor spoke. "Do you think you could talk to us? Maybe tell us what happened? I could still hear a little of the confusion in the hallway and I tried to feel for the call button again. Dr. Wilbrandt's hands took my hand in his and said that everything was fine. "They are just holding him until the police get here." I was tense and speechless nevertheless, still watching the door until Warren's voice faded. Then my whole body relaxed and I tried very carefully to speak.

"What happened to me?"

"Mrs. Stone," my eyes raised towards the doctor. "My name is Dr. Wilbrandt. This is my nurse Melissa Clover. We all call her Missy. And of course you know Mr. Laughton. James. Do you know what happened to you?"

I didn't really so I shook my head. "Not really. I think I remember some things." I whispered.

"Maybe Mr. Laughton can tell you in a few minutes. He has been almost always by your side since it happened. You have been with us for quite a while. What do you remember?"

I closed my eyes. I remembered the courtroom and the judge and the final result. I remembered Warren on top of me and the voices and that horrible laugh. Tears welled up in my eyes and slid down my cheeks detouring around the sticky residue of the medical tape.

"We have talked to you every day." Her comment stopped my remembering. Her voice was soft and almost musical.

"You were resting so peacefully. We just wanted you to recover and we left you to do so." Missy looked in my eyes and I knew that she was truly in the right job. A nurse really had to be a compassionate person.

Finally I turned to Mr. Laughton. "What did happen?" I paused. "There?" He knew I was speaking of what had happened at the courthouse. His hand held mine as it had since he removed it from the railing. He looked down at it, tiny in his and he stroked it comforting me.

"Warren dove over me and knocked me to the floor. He leapt on the table as the bailiff approached him. And before anyone knew what had happened, his hands were all too quickly around your throat."

He paused, "We were all trying to pull him off of you when you passed out. You went limp and Warren let go of your throat. I watched you fall the rest of the way to the floor and tried to catch you but your head banged against the separation wall. I tried to stop the bleeding with my hand until the paramedics finally arrived."

He paused again. "Warren escaped. He left during the commotion again. We think that he left through the bailiff's door to the judges chambers. The courtroom doors were guarded by too may people and still he managed to escape so that is the assumption.

I interrupted him. "Why? How does he keep getting away?" My voice cracked and even in the whisper that it was I could hear my throat straining to complete the sentence.

"Everyone was so worried about you and no one thought about that other door. He was already under guard and even handcuffed so we all thought he was secure. While we all watched you, he apparently just backed out through the judges chambers. It happened so quickly that he was long gone in a matter of seconds."

"It seems like so long ago." I tried to clear my throat. "Like another lifetime ago." Dr. Wilbrandt spoke again, holding the straw to my lips. "Sip slowly. Your mouth is just dry."

"How long have I been here?" I asked after taking several small sips of water.

"Almost a month now." Missy answered. My eyes grew wide and I shook my head. How could I possibly still have a life? I was missing out on so much of it.

What had happened to my life? My family? My work? My home? It had seemed that only a few hours had passed since my courtroom experience and yet forever ago at the same time.

A million questions were popping in my head. I wanted to have answers, but I doubted that anyone actually had them but Warren.

I could not remember how I had gotten to the hospital and yet here I was again.

"You were able to get the rest you need and that's what was important. So we left you to recover on your own, giving you what pain meds we thought you needed and keeping you breathing." Missy said. "You are a very lucky lady."

"The good news is that you are still alive and you are relatively well. You may be weaker for a while but you will eventually get stronger." Mr. Laughton stated it as if he was sure.

"But where can I go that Warren can't find me?" I whispered. It was a question that I knew by the silence; that they themselves had been thinking these same thoughts.

"Would he really kill me?"

"I don't know." Mr. Laughton answered quickly. "He has had several opportunities to and yet you are amazingly still alive. Either you get really lucky and somehow get saved just in time or he is enjoying playing with you like a cat with a mouse. He has the skills. He is highly trained and yet..." his voice trailed off.

We were all silent thinking about what he had just said.

The phone rang loudly, breaking that silence that had followed his words.

Dr. Wilbrandt answered the phone and then turned to his companions in the room. "We have to move." He controlled the volume of his words but there was a tense undertone that meant that something bad was happening.

I could not move easily. I realized that the others would be helping me. "Missy, take only the IV with us! We don't have time for the oxygen." Dr. Wilbrandt was giving hurried orders. "James get them going now."

Missy took the IV bag and taped it to my upper arm. Dr. Wilbrandt scooped me up into his arms and both Mr. Laughton and Missy went to the door. Cautiously looking out into the hallway, they watched as armed security guards ran in every direction.

"Hold on to me if you can. This might get a little rough." Dr. Wilbrandt said and I tried to tighten my grip around his neck. I couldn't. I didn't understand what was happening. I didn't want to understand. I knew it had to do with Warren and that was all I needed to know.

The four of us were moving very quickly towards the stairs only slightly pausing at the elevator. When it didn't open immediately, we continued to the stairs. A throbbing pain was getting sharper in my head. My arms were slowly slipping and they got weaker and weaker as I bounced unsteadily in the doctors arms.

We climbed the stairs to the next floor and Missy exited ten steps ahead of us to see if the elevator was available. She called to us and we stepped out into the hallway, she was pushing the elevator button over and over again. The door opened after just a couple of seconds and Mr. Laughton held it open as we all stepped into it.

Mr. Laughton's cell phone rang. He looked at the screen. "They're here." He said. We rode the elevator up to the top floor. "I think I can stand on my own." I said.

"I really don't think that you can." Dr. Wilbrandt said, but he put me down nevertheless. He and Mr. Laughton held me up. I was so dizzy. The vertigo that swept over me as the elevator climbed up to the top floor was unbelievable. When the doors opened, once more I was scooped up into the arms of the doctor.

We ran out into bright sunlight and I realized that we were on the roof of the building. The noise level was so loud but I didn't immediately know what it was. We rounded the enclosure where the elevator was and sitting in the middle of the roof was a helicopter, rotors going, pushing air out and over us as we approached. I started to scream. I did not want to get on that thing. I had never flown in one before and they scared me.

My screams were drowned out by the noise of the blades as they chopped speedily through the air. I squirmed and tried to get away from the doctor. I was thrashing about so much that the IV bag and tubing pulled from the taped down portion of the IV. Blood quickly began to spill out.

"We're trying to keep you safe!" Mr. Laughton grabbed my chin. "Be...still." He was yelling it into my face. He sounded angry.

He got into the helicopter. My head dropped back and I looked up at the spinning blades and I closed my eyes to block out the dizziness that swept over me. I was being pulled from Dr. Wilbrandt's arms and into Mr. Laughton's.

My body dropped quickly into the seat next to him, facing the rear of the helicopter and the front facing seats that were opposite us. My head dropped into his lap as someone reached out to close the door behind both doctor and nurse.

The sounds of the blades diminished as the door closed and all of us were encapsulated within the relative safety of the helicopter. Where were we going to go if even a hospital wasn't safe for me? I tried to sit up in my seat. I slumped back and my head rolled to the side. I could no longer hold it up.

I let my eyes drift down to my arms. They hung limply at my side, one dropping to the floor and the other dropping onto the seat beside me. My eyes were trained on my arm as I watched my blood slowly spill to the floor. The blood was pooling and then trailing away with the movement of the helicopter.

Mr. Laughton reached up and pulled my shoulders into his lap again. Missy turned my body, raising my legs and feet to the seat. I saw Dr. Wilbrandt place a cap of some sort on the dislodged IV and felt it sting as he threaded it back into my vein. I watched as he inserted a needle into the IV but I was out before it was removed.

Chapter Thirteen
Fight to Flight

The sound of the IV machine whirring was the first thing I heard. Then slowly as more of my senses awakened, I could hear birds chirping in the early morning. The light seemed especially bright as it streamed in through a large bay window in the room.

I pushed myself up and felt pain shoot through my arm and realized that I shouldn't be bending it. I sat up on the bed pulling my legs cross-legged in front of me. I straightened out the blankets and sheets over my legs and looked around the room.

Ten feet away was a sitting area with two recliners and a rocking chair. A small table with a lamp flooded light over the small area. A large TV set was on in the open armoire. It was sending a flickering glow just on the floor in front of it.

Sleeping in one of the recliners was Mr. Laughton, his hair mussed and his suit coat crumpled on the floor beside him. He was leaning on his hand which was propped up on the armrest of the chair. His mouth was slightly open and I watched as his chest rose slightly as he breathed in and out.

I did not speak because I didn't want to wake him. I had no real sense of what time it was. Surely I hadn't slept another month away.

The bed I was in was not a hospital bed. That was of slight relief for me. There were two bedside tables on either side of the bed and on one was a phone, a pad of paper, several pens and my cell phone. The room was obviously someone's bedroom. It was much more home like in it's appearance.

On the second table lay what looked like a medical chart and on top of that were two bags of IV fluids and smaller bags that I knew must be some kind of pain medicine or antibiotic meant for me.

Across the room was an open door that I could see led to a large bathroom. Beside that was a closed door that I assumed was a closet of some kind. The bedroom door was open slightly and I could see light filtering in from the hallway. No wonder I was awake, I thought, there was lots of light finding its way into the room while I slept.

I slowly straightened my legs out and turned to my left side away from the sleeping Mr. Laughton. My plan was to make my way to that large bathroom.

I slid slowly as close to the edge of the bed as I could. I tried to touch down softly to the floor with first one foot and then the other. I was using my arms to brace against the bed but realized that the IV hooked to my arm was hanging from a rolling IV pole on the opposite side of the bed. What had I been thinking?

I looked over my left shoulder and sighed. I would either have to slowly make it to that side of the bed and then wheel the thing with me or once again take the IV out of my arm. I was actually getting good at that. Though that second time was unintentional. I smiled. What a ridiculous thought that was.

I was still debating what to do from my perch on the left side of the bed, when I heard, "I wouldn't try that if I were you."

I jerked my head towards the chair where Mr. Laughton was rising from sending pain shooting through my head, and asked, "How would you suggest that I get to the bathroom?"

"That's what I'm here for." He answered, his voice tired and slow. He walked over and grabbed the IV pole. He herded it over to where I sat and then helped me to my very unstable feet. I shuffled over to the bathroom and went in with Mr. Laughton trailing right behind me.

"You're not coming in here with me, are you?"

He chuckled, "No, just going to set the pole here. Call out to me when you are finished."

"Thanks." I said to his back as he walked out of the door closing it behind him. I suddenly felt sorry for him. He sounded and looked so weary. I knew it was my fault. I took a deep breath. I would have to figure out how to heal quickly and get out of this man's hair.

I didn't know exactly what I was doing. I had already finished and had stood using both the counter and the IV pole as support. As I washed my hands, I looked at them and found that they were bruised in several more places. If I had been in the hospital for almost a month, why had they not healed?

I reached for the towel to dry my hands and looked up for the first time into the mirror. My hair was a long and tangled mess. I could tell that I had tossed and turned and I could feel it wasn't clean and I suddenly wanted nothing more than to shower.

I wasn't sure that I could do so but I carefully shuffled over to the side of the tub and sat down on the edge. It was one of those large Jacuzzi tubs and there were (amazingly) hand rails all around it. I reached around and untied the white and blue flowered hospital gown that I had been wearing when we were whisked away from the roof of the hospital. I turned on the water, touching it to make sure that the temperature was right. I kept my hand under the water turning it over and over feeling my spirits lift as the water played and danced over my hand.

Mr. Laughton knocked on the door. "Don't do that, wait for Missy to help you."

"Okay," I said, but I knew that when he went to get Missy, I would already be sliding into the tub. It was good that the IV was in my right hand because then the tubing wouldn't be going across the tub and I could keep that hand out of the water.

I carefully removed my panties and my bra. It was difficult to take it over the IV in my arm and past the tubes and the bag that held the fluids. I swiveled on the tub and scooted to the back. I grabbed one of the hand rails and slid my too weak body down into the rising water. I turned on the power to the Jacuzzi and relaxed, sinking down to my neck.

I realized that I had made a mistake only when I had to hold on to the hand rail so that I didn't slide all the way under the water and drown.

"Oh crap, I should have waited for Missy." I spoke the words out loud but they were just barely above a whisper, talking to myself.

As soon as the words left my lips, I knew I had made a mistake. The door blew open and Mr. Laughton walked in. "I'm sorry, I'm sorry," he stammered. "My eyes are closed I promise." Holding a towel over his face, he walked over and sat on the back edge of the tub. He quickly laid the towel over me. I was embarrassed that I had put myself in this situation. He reached up and turned off the water.

He didn't act angry or embarrassed at all now. He rolled up his sleeves and slid his hands under my arms lifting me slightly out the water. "We can't have you drowning in my house."

Without asking permission, he reached over and grabbed some shampoo and put it on the top of my head. Massaging in the shampoo with one hand, he sighed.

I could not speak.

I was too embarrassed and I couldn't really say anything about him coming in, since I knew that had he not come in, I probably would have drowned in the tub. I didn't know my own limits and I was stubbornly trying to do things on my own. I was kind of known for that.

His motions were automatic. Pulling up the long loose strands of my hair into the foaming bubbles, he continued to lather my hair and work his way around my scalp. I kept my right arm on the side of the tub and my left moved from supporting my body to holding the towel over my body.

"Missy will be here in a minute and she can help you finish bathing." I nodded my head, afraid to hear my own voice in this strange and unusual situation that I had put myself into. He reached over me and turned on the shower head that was hanging down into the water. He rinsed my hair, squeezing as much as he could with one hand. His movements were again automatic. I wondered briefly why that was.

Missy rushed in, looking flustered and stopped dead in her tracks, "What?" she paused. "What are you doing?"
I could feel him shrug, but I said quietly, "It's my fault. I tried to do it on my own and failed."

James interrupted me, "Well, let's just say she didn't listen to my advice. After I called you, I overheard her say that she should have waited for you, and I guessed," looking around at me from above and to the right, "correctly, I might add, that she was in trouble."

He paused and looked up at Missy. "I have been here before, remember?"

She walked over and kissed the top of his head lightly. "I'll take over now. Scoot downstairs and get Jonathan. Maybe between the two of you breakfast can be ready by the time we're through here.

She sat on the edge of the bath and took my shoulders from James. Mr. Laughton stood and traded places with Missy. He held my shoulders until Missy got into place behind me and then turned to walk out of the room.

"James?" she swallowed as he paused to look back at her, "I'm so sorry. I should've come up a little faster than that."

"No problem." He answered and turned again and walked out the door, closing it once more behind him.

Missy took over where Mr. Laughton had been sitting and grabbed a clean rag from the rack behind the toilet. She handed it to me and I held it in my open palm anticipating that she would squeeze a liquid soap onto it. "I know that must have been uncomfortable for you, Bria, but trust me James has done it many times before."

"Why?" I asked her.

"This was once his wife's room when she was extremely ill. He would come in and help bathe her from this same position or perhaps behind her in the tub itself."

"Where is she now?" I had a feeling that I knew but I had to have it confirmed.

"She died three years ago." I wanted to know more, but I didn't want to ask. She finished my hair and when I was finished, she helped me to stand, wrapping a dry towel around me.

As we opened the door we saw Mr. Laughton. He immediately got up to leave the room. She looked at him.

He smiled, heartwarmingly, "Just waiting to make sure that everything is fine." He left and we made our way over to the bed. Missy draped a second towel on the edge of the bed for me to sit on and walked over to the armoire. She pulled out packages of matching bras and underwear sets. Grabbing a brush and a few other necessities from the top of the dresser she came back to help me get dressed.

"Can I get rid of this thing?" I asked her as I held up my right arm with the IV attached to it.

"Of course you can. Besides it will be easier to get you dressed." She answered. She reached up and turned the IV to stop the fluids from flowing into my arm. She removed the connection that held the tubes to the needle in my arm and carefully taped down what she called the "cap" of the IV to my arm.

"This is the best I can do. We need to leave that on for easy access until you completely recover. Plus you have been getting your research injections through that IV port."

I nodded, I had forgotten about those but I was just happy to be un-tethered.

She then handed me the clean underclothes and told me that I could choose anything from the closet that I wanted to wear. With her help, I was able to get dressed in what I thought was a pretty casual dress and a sweater. Even if it was now May, I felt cold.

"You look like you feel a little better." Missy said. "Let's see if maybe we can get some real breakfast food up here for you. I'll be back in a few minutes. Do you think that you can manage on your own while I check on breakfast?"

"Sure, but I think I'll sit in that rocking chair if that's okay." She nodded and she watched as I made my way slowly over to it and sat down. She walked out of the room and I pulled my legs up underneath me.

What was I doing here? And just where was here? I had been given that this was Mr. Laughton's home since he didn't want me "drowning" in it. And that maybe this was his bedroom, but where were we? I wondered just what the next few days would hold as we waited out getting news about Warren.

Sitting alone for a few minutes I thought about what had been happening in my life and what it was coming to. I was missing my work, and yet, I suddenly had a new understanding of people, women, in my position. Abuse had become an epidemic in American culture. Most women didn't have the resources that I did. I had money in my account. I had a good job to pay my attorney. I did have places that I could go to, but they would require me to move back to the Carolinas. That? I really didn't want to do.

But just where would I find another career? I love my work. I leaned my head back, closed my eyes and made the chair rock. Rocking back and forth, all I could think about was what the next step in my life would be?

Missy, Dr. Wilbrandt and Mr. Laughton walked in the room with several trays of a great variety of breakfast foods. The trays were set on top of the dresser and the little table. Fruit, yogurt, scrambled eggs and toast with juice and milk filled the three trays. I suddenly realized just how famished I was and the smell of the food was so enticing. I waited only a moment before grabbing a fat red ripe strawberry and biting the point off the end of it.

"Mmm, that is so yummy." I smiled.

"Juice?" Mr. Laughton asked chuckling as he handed me a glass. I mumbled my thanks but continued to munch on the strawberry.

The three of them began to put things on the small plates and I reached over to do the same, enjoying the feeling of food reaching my empty stomach. It was very satisfying. It felt like forever since real food had passed through my lips.

"There's plenty more where that came from." Jonathan laughed at me as I reached for another lemon poppy seed muffin. "We aren't going to starve you, you know." I laughed myself and mumbled again through a mouthful of the creamy scrambled eggs.

"Sorry, nervous eating I guess." Mr. Laughton reached over and patted my hand. "Eat all you want. Don't worry about it." I pulled my hand away and put it to my mouth. Suddenly I was embarrassed about what he may or may not have seen in the bathroom.

"Do the clothes fit?" Mr. Laughton asked. I nodded my head. "Yes, and thank you so much for it. I guess I wasn't thinking ahead when I decided to shower this morning."

I paused and finally looked directly in his eyes, deciding that he probably hadn't thought about it as much as I had.

"Thank you for the help. I am sorry that I have become such a burden to you. That was another thing I didn't think through this morning. I really do appreciate you," and then I looked at Missy, "both of you for your help this morning."

"Well then, maybe you would like to go downstairs and get around a bit. A little exercise to get the blood moving might do you a world of good." Dr. Wilbrandt joined in the conversation. "And maybe we need to give you your regular injection?"

"What?" I asked.

"You know the trial medicines that you have been receiving? I am an authorized physician on the trial and for the study itself."

I had forgotten again about the study that I was participating in. Missy had said that I had been receiving the injections. I wondered, had my absence from work caused the study to be compromised? I would try to write up a good report.

"Sure," I answered. We all stood up and Mr. Laughton looked at the trays. "Nothing left but the dishes. Now that's a really good sign." He laughed and gathered the empty trays and dishes. Carefully stacked, he headed towards the door.

"Stay where you are, I'll get what you need and come to you." Dr. Wilbrandt said. Missy and I sat side by side and waited on him to return.

Chapter Fourteen
Day to Day

When he returned, I asked if maybe we could hold off on the injections for a little while. "I just think I want my breakfast to stay put." He laughed and nodded, "that may be a good idea after all."

Together the three of us went out of the room. We slowly began to make our way downstairs. I put my right hand on the banister as we walked down the stairs. The rich deep brown tones of the wood had a very luxurious feel to them. You could tell that they were crafted by an expert.

The banister curved down and around to the right coming to a point about twenty feet from a very large double front door. Ten feet across was another set of stairs identical to this one leading back up to the second floor.

The stairs were identical opposites of each other and they made for a very grand foyer to the home. The doors both had a wonderful stained glass picture inset into the wood and I was immediately drawn to look at them.

To the right, past the other side of the stairs was a dark room and that was the one we all headed into. Dr. Wilbrandt reached in and flipped a switch and several lamps around the room suddenly glowed with a soft ambient glow.

I looked around the room and could see that this was clearly a very large library. Two of the walls had floor to ceiling bookshelves completely filled with thousands of books. The room was beautiful.

I loved to read so I could easily see myself curled up in front of the fire reading several books at a time in this room.

Missy led me to a deep and plush sofa and we both sat down. Both men walked around the room opening up the ceiling to floor drapes that covered three sets of double French doors that opened up onto verandahs or porticos.

As the drapes were drawn, I could see meticulously landscaped property out in the distance. This was a very upscale home. Further up on the grand scale that my home was, and I had considered mine to be "grand".

The room became silent after the drapes opened up and let light in on the dark luscious room. The smell of paper and polish permeated the room. I sighed, completely at ease here. I leaned my head back against the sofa and relaxed.

Everyone sensed the need for silence it seemed. James and Jonathan were by the front French doors whispering and somewhere in the back of my mind; I had memories of quiet conversations just like this one that were held around me as I slept. I knew that I had questions, but I wasn't sure how to ask them.

And so I sat still, kept my mouth shut, and waited for the conversation now to bring us to a point that I could easily interject my questions.

The door bell rang and immediately Mr. Laughton walked out of the room and to the front door. A loud boisterous voice echoed through the foyer and filtered into the library.

"How are things this fine morning, James?"

"Fine, come on in, Mr. Hudgeson." We could all hear them as they made their way into the library.

Mr. Hudgeson was a large man with a body not unlike Santa Claus. He was dressed in a dark gray suit with a black overcoat which was draped over his forearm. He walked straight over to where I sat and took the chair to the left of me. His huge jeweled hand reached over and patted my knee.

"And how are we this morning?" he asked in a light French accent.

"Fine, thank you and yourself?" I returned the question.

"Well, very well. Did the clothing fit?" I nodded my head. So this was my benefactor.

"Bria, this is Mr. Hudgeson. He is one of the financial backers for the research you have been working on." Missy put her hand on my right shoulder. "He has been very generous and was worried when he heard of all the trouble you have been having."

"Thank you for everything." I reached out my hand as if to shake his, but he left my hand in mid air, seemingly distracted. He waved his hand instead in front as if he were swatting away flies. "It is nothing. Nothing at all. Just tell me you are doing better."

"Yes, much better, thanks to the generosity of so many others."

He stood quickly. "Well, I had better be going, just wanted to check in. Will you be returning to work or shall we have the work sent to you?"

I didn't have the answer and so I simply shrugged my shoulders. Dr. Wilbrandt stepped closer to Mr. Hudgeson. "Mr. H,

Bria can do her work here. She shouldn't be any where near where her ex-husband can find her, don't you agree?"

"Naturally, I suppose you are right. Let us know when she can continue."

With that he strolled out of the library and out of the front door, without so much as a proper good bye. It was strange, like a tornado sweeping in and moving on.

I was left a little breathless. "Just how many people know about my situation, Mr. Laughton?"

"First of all, let's quit with the formalities if that's okay. Call me James. This is my brother Jonathan and Missy is his wife."

"Oh" I said. Well that answered another one of my questions. "Now, to answer your question, well, plenty of people. Let's see," he started ticking them off on his fingers. "People at your work are aware of your situation, since you were unable to return immediately. All of those people in court who were witnesses and officials from the courtroom and also all of the people at the hospital, as well as most of the police department personnel."

"Does everyone know where I am?"

"No, no one but Mr. Hudgeson. He insisted that he needed to see you and know whether you were able to continue with your part of the program. We could not say no, since he has been so generous."

"I don't think many people ever say no to him." I said. Jonathan laughed. "You pegged him in the two minutes he was here." Missy slugged her husband in the shoulder as he had now taken a seat beside her on the couch.

Silence resumed.

Once more, the silence was broken. But this time it was by loud barking from outside. James and Jonathan went to the front set of french doors and looked out over the property. Opening the doors they both stepped out to search more closely what was happening.

"Does he have dogs, did they get loose?" I turned to ask Missy.

"No. That's why they're looking. It's probably nothing, but we're not taking any chances these days. The property is huge but oddly shaped and there is a point where the road winds into the property close enough to look out to the road. Usually that's where we see things happen. It is a blind curve with people speeding down the road and all kinds of joggers and people walking their dogs."

She was rambling, telling me more information than was necessary. I think that she knew that I would soon be asking other questions.

"Mr. Hudgeson has run into someone walking two very large dogs. The dogs don't seem to like him very much. The owner is struggling to keep them off of his suit." James chuckled as he said it.

"He probably doesn't want to have his thousand dollar suit soiled."

"Why would he have stopped to talk to him at all?" Jonathan asked. "The driveway, is a good half mile long, he couldn't have seen them."

"He's probably trying to buy them off of him. What a strange man he is." James shook his head but both men kept watching the scene.

The barking kept going and it seemed that they were watching for a very long time. I sat still. Not knowing what I was to do. I picked up a book that lay on the table beside me. "The Illustrated Life of George Washington" was the title. It looked like a very old book. It was leather bound with gold lettering on it but it looked well worn. It matched the room.

I opened the book and thumbed through the pages. I adored history. Maybe this could distract me from the thoughts that kept creeping in on me.

I had been reading for several minutes when the two men walked back into the room and closed the doors.

"Great book to read," James stated. "There are many more books here on the history of not only this area but the whole country. Take as many as you like to read."

"Again, thank you all for everything." I paused. No one spoke. "Now what?" I said. The silence was now tense with the unanswered questions hanging in the air.

Finally, I thought, someone is going to have to answer my questions. No one said anything. They all seemed to be waiting on each other to start.

"You really do look great in that dress." James said breaking the silence in an unexpected way. That was one of my wife's favorites."

I ignored his comment. I needed answers. "What happened to Warren after court that day?" I didn't want idle chatter. James looked at me, but shrugged his shoulders as he answered.

"They were supposed to hold him until we were clear of the building. But he escaped through the judge's chamber door. We can only assume that Ms. Coronaco was ready and waiting on him.

"And at the hospital? What exactly happened there? How did you know to have an escape plan? It all seems to be so..." I paused, searching for the right words, "so planned out? Did you know he would come after me?"

I sat back. I had asked my most important questions. I could see that they didn't want to get into it all but they knew that they had to. I waited and watched as they each looked from one to another. Finally I could take it no more. "Just tell me and don't spare me please. I can take the truth. I need the truth for a change."

"Well," Jonathan began, "It really has to do with the fact that he threatened you in the courtroom. We agreed to have you transported to our hospital under armed guards after his escape. We all suspected that he would eventually find you no matter how many precautions we took. We always had to have a contingency plan in place just in case."

"We?" I asked. "Who is this *we* that you are talking about?" No one answered immediately.

"We've only just found out most of this, but you deserve to know." Jonathan said. "Even if it is painful."

"Your participation in the study you have been involved with is what makes this hard." James took over the story. "You know of course that your family history made you a great candidate for it as well as your skills in research. You know the questions that are asked of each patient and you were more able to keep accurate records than almost any one else in the study." He looked over at Jonathan.

"However, no one was sure that you would recognize all of your side effects of the injections that you were given. You could report on what you saw and felt, but sometimes what seems rational and normal to you, might not be to someone watching you. So someone was needed to be that outside recorder to report everything you missed." He paused, letting it all sink in.

"You know that some of the participants are already in late stages of cancer. Their participation is their last or near last resort. Hoping for miracles." Another pause.

Most of these things I already knew. I knew that I was part of a study and that some things were indeed hidden from me. It was how these things were done. I had been involved in research long enough to know that. So what was the big secret?

"Are you all a part of the study also?" I was sure I already knew the answer.

"Missy had cancer. She is currently in remission. Jonathan is one of the consulting doctors. My wife died of cancer, and that is how we all came to be involved. I had to do something." He stopped, his voice cracking under the emotional strain that the memories flooded him with.

I tried to put it all together in my head. What exactly was so painful about this?

"So, if you are all a part of the study, then why and how did I get to you, as my attorney?" I looked directly at James.

"That's where Mr. Hutcheson comes in. James is not really a part of the study. He was hired on as an attorney for the investors of the pharmaceutical companies. They did not know at the time that we were brothers. They only knew that we were acquaintances. That part, we didn't feel was important to share with them. I on the other hand have monitored your health from the beginning. Both Missy and I. We, well, we're assigned to you."

Missy took over. "We only know this because of Mr. Hudgeson, and like we've already said, we've only just found out about the rest of these things when you were admitted to the hospital. Warren was brought in by Mr. Hudgeson. He was meant to be introduced to you casually and that you would become friends, maybe even more than friends."

She stopped, watching me for a minute before she went on reading my reaction. "You really do have to understand that we knew nothing of these plans or we would not have been involved in any of it. We don't know how or why he took your relationship any further than what he was hired to do."

Jonathan began again, "We suspect that it was not to the liking of the backers of the project. He was supposed to record your every mood, emotion, health and whatever else he could while you were away from your office. We simply don't know what is going on with him."

That was it. Warren was a spy of some kind for Mr. Hudgeson? His love for me was all an act? I couldn't believe it. What else did I not know? Oh my goodness, I thought. The question popped out.

"Do I have cancer?"

"No." Jonathan answered.

"Then what is making me so weak?" I didn't know why I was asking such ridiculous questions.

"There have been a few cancer cells injected as a result of the vaccine that they are testing, after all that's how vaccine's work. You are currently experiencing all the symptoms and eventually they will be destroyed. In the mean while, your own body is attacking the cancerous cells. That is causing you to be exceptionally weak and more vulnerable to other illnesses or injuries. Because your body is attacking those cancerous cells, your natural defenses are seriously depleted."

The injections you receive daily may help to maintain your strength to do daily activities, but their purpose is to enhance the 'vaccine's' abilities. By mid December, you will be finished with the injections, and the cancerous cells will be destroyed completely." He stopped again and looked at James. He looked at me for a moment before he took over speaking again.

"Only one of my clients is the pharmaceutical company. You happen to be another. I do have many others you know. I was hired to take care of any issues that occurred as a result of the study. It is yet to be determined whether your case is as a result of any of their actions. Mr. Hudgeson is behind sending you to my office."

"Was your wife a part of the study?"

"No. She passed away before it started."

There was too much going on here. I needed to sort it all out. I had so much that I had to do.

"I need to be alone. I need to go home." I was already crying again. The medical things alone were something to make me cry, but the fact that Warren was some sort of spy and not really in love with me was something that I needed to process and then deal with on my own.

"You can't go home." James' voice was stern but soft. "Warren is a free man. Who knows where he will turn up next. In order to make sure that you are safe, you have to stay here."

His voice was sad and ordinarily it would have tugged at me to be obedient to his request, but I was angry. Who *could* I trust?

"Thanks for taking such great care of me. All of you have been very kind. I just need to leave. That's all there is to it." My voice was raised. I was trying not to sob.

I stood up and started towards the stairs. I knew that when I reached the stairs, I would have difficulty climbing them but I didn't care. I couldn't let them see me struggle with it, but I didn't know what I could do to prevent it.

This was so much more than I bargained for. I reached for the banister as I lifted my foot to place it on the first step. I looked up, my vision blurring behind the veil of tears that were building in my eyes. James put his arm around my waist and helped me slowly climb the stairs to the room.

"You are not a prisoner here, but I can't let you leave."

Silence.

"I'm really sorry Bria, had I taken better care of you, all of this might not have been necessary."

"Just discount my bill." I snapped sarcastically.

He continued to walk me up the stairs but his voice was even sadder than it was before. "When all of this is over, I will personally deliver you to your home again."

I remained silent again.

"The work that you have been doing is so very important. I really believe that. No one should suffer through that horrible disease. It's not just the patient that suffers. It's also their family and friends." He stopped talking,

I could tell that it was a very painful memory for him. I too knew the devastation of cancer. How horrible I felt when my grandmother died and how much worse it had been when my mother told me she had cancer and had to have a mastectomy.

When he continued, I had softened. "As for all the underhandedness that is going on, we honestly didn't know anything about that." I kept quiet, still listening to him. "You know, there are many people that would pay big, big money to have the information about the study that you have. There are many other companies that are in the race for the cure to cancer.

You have an intimate knowledge and I am sure that that is what is behind all this. Why? I don't know. I can't fathom what they needed someone like Warren for. Your computer, your results are all a part of the study that people want to get their hands on. Your information is the only missing part of the study. When you are finished, all of the information that has been gathered will be what the big companies will fight for."

"And Warren? What role does he play?"

"No one really knows. He seems to be playing by his own rules now. Apparently his violence and his sudden change towards you was not in anyone's plan. We're only guessing. We just don't know.

Because we have only just found out, when I represented you in court, I didn't even know that he was a part of this. Not until after the escape at the hospital. It was then that Mr. Hudgeson stepped in and told us everything. We don't really know what to do next ourselves. We only know that no matter what, we want to keep you safe."

I thought, they really are trying to make sure I know that they didn't know. So if they didn't, then why did Mr. Hudgeson suddenly tell them? Because he had lost control over Warren? I didn't understand.

We had reached the door to the room I was using.

"Thank you." I said. "For telling me." I stepped through the doorway and closed the door behind me without looking back.

Chapter Fifteen
Run to Nowhere

I walked straight to the bed and crawled in. Instantly I was sobbing into my pillow, I was so confused. I curled up into a ball on the bed, finding comfort in the fetal position. I was sure it prevented my heart from breaking further. I thought. I pulled the covers over my head and took a deep breath of the heavy air.

It was nighttime when I finally awoke. I could tell by the darkness that enveloped me. There were so many things I needed to do. How could I get them accomplished? I sat alone in the dark room planning a way to escape from the house. I didn't know where to go to, but I knew where I needed to be away from. Here.

Before I could make a decision, I heard a voice in the hallway. It was a new voice. A voice I didn't recognize. Who else lived here and why were they awake? I picked up my cell from the bedside table. It was nearly four in the morning. I tiptoed to the door and pressed my ear against it. I turned the knob and slowly opened it. Ten feet down the dark hall I heard a male voice was in a whispered conversation on a phone.

"What do you mean he knows where she is?" The voice continued with irritation now. "He knows we are not in Maryland anymore? Or he knows exactly where we are?" The anxious voice was angry and had he not been whispering, he would have been screaming.

Who knows where I was? For I could only assume he meant me. Was it Warren? That was the only answer. Now I knew that I needed to make my escape from them. I needed to get out of here as soon as I could possibly figure it all out. I waited, listening until he finished his panicked conversation.

"Okay, I'll leave as soon as I can and try to pick up his trail." I heard the snap of a cell phone close with its familiar sound and waited.

When I heard a door close, I opened my door further. Peering into the darkness, I felt my way to the staircase. Putting both hands on the left side railing and hugging the wall, I crept down the stairs.

I was terrified when I finally found the bottom step and fell to the floor. I had not realized that the stairs had ended. I was sure that someone had heard me. I waited for a moment silently on the floor and then slowly I pulled myself up to stand at the bottom by the banister's end.

Nothing. No one came rushing down the stairs. No lights were instantly turned on. I fumbled my way to the front doors. They were locked. Of course they were! I could see small lights from a touch pad and knew that an alarm must have been activated. I didn't need to nor want to take a chance.

I walked slowly towards the library. One set of French doors were just to my left, facing the front of the house. How far of a drop could it be and would I survive it? I walked over to the doors and looked down at the handle. It was not locked. Did this one have an alarm?

I hoped that since it was left unlocked, an alarm might not be active on these doors. I cautiously turned the handle. The door opened easily and I stepped quietly out onto the verandah. I hugged the wall trying to find my way to the furthermost edge of the decking. My hand reached a hand railing and I was surprised to find stairs that led to the ground. I could not see clearly but my eyes were adjusting to the darkness that surrounded me.

Stepping onto the dark stairs was terrifying, but no more terrifying than staying here where Warren apparently knew I was.

Each consecutive step was bringing me closer and closer to my supposed freedom. I knew that the three people I knew of in the house would be worried about me. I felt that I could almost trust them but I wasn't really sure where their loyalties would lie. I had been so very wrong about Warren. Was I wrong about them as well?

I continued step after step until I found the bottom. I wanted immediately to turn towards the driveway, but I wasn't sure that someone else wouldn't see me. That someone else that had been on the phone in the hallway.

I followed the walkway that I had ended up on as it followed the length of the house and turned to the right. As I approached the corner, I could see light. I hurried to the corner and stopped, looking tentatively around it to see where the light was coming from.

A garage was barely one hundred feet away from me. In front of it stood several different cars. The two SUV's that both James and I had driven over the past few weeks and months and…my little black Mustang! I had no idea that this is where it had been brought to.

Great! I thought. I knew where I had kept the spare keys for emergencies and I knew that I could get them. I was getting weaker by the minute but I supposed that if I could get to my car, I would be okay to drive. I hugged the wall of the house until I came parallel with my car. I looked up and around for any sign of anyone watching and then walked as quickly as I could to the front of my car.

I dropped to my knees and reached my hand underneath the front grill of the car. My hand hit the dangling keys and they clanged against the metal. I crouched even lower.

I finally grabbed them and yanked hard. The cord that held them in place gave way and the keys were in the palm of my hand. I crawled around the front of my car to the side and opened the driver's side door as silently as I could.

As I climbed in, I felt the leather seats and reached instinctively for the stick shift for support. I cranked the car and prayed that no one had heard me. I backed out turning around and drove slowly over to the driveway.

I let neutral carry me down the long and winding driveway. It meandered back and forth and just as I was rounding one curve in total darkness, I glimpsed the glimmer of headlights come around the corner or two behind me casting shadows through the trees. Someone was after me!

I put the car into gear and I sped up. When the driveway ended, I turned to the right and pulled as far off the road as I could and cut the car off. I ducked down in my seat and waited. I heard the car finally hit the main road and held my breath.

Moments later, a dark limo turned onto the road. It sped past me, and I once more waited to see if someone else would follow him.

The wait was only a couple of minutes but I felt sure that I could finally leave. I cranked the car and sped away, not even sure where the heck I was. I followed the winding road until I came to a stop sign.

Across the street was a convenience store. I had traveled several miles already, but nothing was familiar. I decided to risk being seen. I parked in the direct path of the doors and quickly went inside.

Asking directions, I told the attendant that I had gotten lost coming home from a friend's new home. I needed to get back to 495. He didn't blink or stare at me but pointed out the door. He began giving directions to I95.

"You'll run into 495 somewhere along the way."

No joke! I thought but that was good enough. I95 would get me into familiar territory and then to 495 and then to my home. I would have to break in if the spare key was no longer in the globe of the back yard light. I didn't care.

Dawn was slowly breaking and I really wanted to try and make it to my home before people left for work. If I didn't, I would be breaking into my home in broad daylight. This was not a good thing in my neighborhood. Not at all.

The roads were empty by comparison by the time I reached Silver Springs. That was a bit unusual. How late was I? I had driven many miles and when finally I was able to make it to my neighborhood; I could see dogs being walked in the early spring morning. People were already on the exercise trail in the park as well. Oh well, if someone saw me, then I would just say that I had lost my keys on vacation.

I slowed down tremendously, purposefully cruising the roads of my neighborhood. I drove by once, twice and then a third time before I reached my driveway and pulled in. If I could make my way to the back yard, I might be able to enter my house without too much noise and disturbance.

I carefully and quietly got out of the car and shut the door as silently as I could. I walked towards the back gate and opened it. I walked over to the back deck and up the few steps and to the back door.

It was locked. There was no window so I couldn't break in there. I went to where we had hidden a spare key, in the globe of the deck light fixture and looked up. It was still there. I could see the outline of it at the bottom of the globe. I didn't have a screwdriver to loosen the screws, but we always said that if we needed it in an emergency, that we would just break the globe.

I thought about it. I didn't want the noise but I saw no other way to get in. I looked around for something that I could use to muffle the noise of breaking glass.

There was nothing I could think of and then my eyes settled on the cushions of the seat of our outdoor furniture. We had never used it. How funny that the first time it was used would be to break into the house. I grabbed the cushion and standing on the chair itself, I wrapped it around the globe and tried to crush it. That didn't work at all.

I stood on the chair trying to decide just how I was going to do this. I took off my shoe and whacked the outside of the pillow. I felt the globe break. It wasn't broken all the way, but it was enough and I dropped the cushion and reached my fingers in and withdrew the key. I breathed a sigh of relief, unlocked the door and walked in. I was home.

It wasn't what it was meant to be but it was still mine thanks to the judge. I started to walk away but turned instead and locked the door behind me, fearing someone coming in behind me like I had before. I shoved a chair underneath the door handle.

I walked around the dining room and looked around my home. It was sad to look at what had happened in it. Someone had been here.

There were papers strewn all over the table. There were broken glass snow globes all over the floor. My collectables. I searched the large living room and found that the rest of my collection was smashed to the floor. Some of them were still salvageable, others completely destroyed.

A lifetime of collections no longer sat on the pristine shelves where they had been so lovingly placed. I wanted to cry, but I had cried over so much more than this. It somehow didn't seem like the right time for something so trivial. I couldn't worry about that now.

There would be time later to worry about the little things.

I tried to clear a path so that I could walk without stepping on the broken remnants of my many memories. It was impossible. I stepped gingerly over it all and walked around to the stairs. I climbed them slowly and made my way up to our bedroom leaning against the wall. My fatigued and weak body made the climb up the stairs almost unbearable.

My dresser drawers were all emptied on the floor. Warren's had not been. Well that left no question as to just who had been here. My mind was racing with possible explanations to everything that seemed to have occurred here. They all defied reason.

So now I knew that James was right. I would not be safe here either. But, where would I be safe? Was I really safer in James' home?

I knew that I would be, but I didn't want to have all of my privacy taken away from me. I packed a few of my things and grabbed my important paperwork from our nightstand lockbox. Why hadn't Warren taken this? I wondered. What was he looking for?

I made my way back downstairs and went into the study. My laptop computer was still in the case where I had left it the morning I had gone to court. I remembered how I had hated being at the hotel only coming home for things I needed. I had checked out for good that morning and had brought my laptop home anticipating that I would be living here. What a joke that was.

I looked around the room. The monitor for the desktop computer was crashed on the floor. The pc unit itself was missing. I never used that computer so I didn't worry about it too much. Warren had all his private work on that one so if he took it, it was his to take.

All of my work had been saved on a memory stick that I kept in my purse. Even if I worked on it at home, when I was done, I would slide it back in before signing off of the computer. Thank goodness that those old habits were kept.

It had taken me leaving it at home several times and having to retrieve it before it became a habit for me, but it now came in handy. I knelt down under the desk to get all of the cords that I knew belonged to my laptop when my battery was low. I had color coded them with painters tape because I was forever unplugging the wrong computer.

As I unplugged the cords, I heard a key in the front door. Why hadn't I thought enough to park down the street? If it was Warren, I was as good as dead. I froze where I was.

Whoever was trying to open the door was having difficulty and I rose from my hiding place meaning to try and make it to the back door. Just as I stood and made it to the back of the couch, the door opened and I dropped to the floor behind the couch. I hoped that whoever it was wouldn't try to come around the couch to the desk.

I held my breath and waited.

Chapter Sixteen
A Place For Everything

I stayed as still as I could, barely breathing. I hoped that whoever was here would not find me but I couldn't be sure. I could see my bag of clothing and other things that I had sat down at the bottom of the stairs. I berated myself for leaving it there.

I listened intently as two different sets of footsteps looked casually around my house. One ran quickly up the stairs and I could hear him searching the five bedrooms up the stairs. The other person, lighter on his feet, made their way around the formal room and then into the dining room and the kitchen.

I continued to hold my breath as both sets of footsteps headed back to the foyer in front of the room I was hiding in. The combination library, office, study and family room was still decorated somewhat for Christmas. I had started to take things down on my various short trips before my court date.

"Her car is here. But I don't see her anywhere! Do you think she called a taxi, knowing Warren would look for her car?" Missy's voice was so worried that I could hear the tears in her tone.

"I don't know." Jonathan answered as he moved into the formal room, dining room and kitchen, checking behind Missy. "It's a mess in there," Missy called out. "I know and I'm betting that Bria didn't do this either. She wouldn't have had the strength to do any of this." He paused and continued to look around "I'm calling James."

Jonathan was sounding more than a little worried himself.

"Do you think Warren found her here?" Missy asked as they waited on James to answer. She sounded terrified at the thought.

They both walked back into the room where I was hiding and sat down on the couch. I wasn't ready to go back to James' house yet so I stayed hidden. Once more I was holding my breath in an attempt to keep them from noticing me.

"She's not here," Jonathan said into the cell phone. I could hear James on the phone, but I couldn't make out the words. "Yes, we think either she was here and Warren took her, or that she left in a taxi to throw Warren off her trail. The house is a mess. Broken glass all over the place."

Again he was listening to James for a couple of minutes. "It is impossible to tell. It looks more like an angry rage than a struggle." He listened once more before he hung up, snapping the phone closed. "He is really worried. I think he may be trying to save her."

"Save her?" Missy asked.

Jonathan replied slowly. "Because he couldn't save Joanne." Missy began to cry in earnest now and I could hear that Jonathan had taken her in his arms. He was soothing her, grief taking them both over. I suddenly felt that I was wrong to be hiding from them. I was causing someone else pain unintentionally. I shook my head. I had to trust somebody. I was choosing them. And James. But that was as far as I could go with it for now.

I tried to stand on my own, but I couldn't so I called out. "Can you help me up?"

Both of them jumped off of the couch. Jonathan looked over the couch and then came around to where I had hidden. Missy leaned over the couch taking the wires from my hands.

"What the hell do you think you are doing?" Jonathan yelled at me, anger and relief showing both in his voice and his face.

I stammered. I needed to choose my words wisely. I didn't want to offend them. "I just wanted to get out for a while. I thought that since I was out, I would get some of the things that I needed."

I paused and dropped to the sofa. "Every one was still asleep. I thought I'd be back before anyone got up, but I didn't know how far away I was from civilization." I smiled. I knew that what I had said was only part truth, but I hoped that it was good enough.

Missy was tender with me, Jonathan not so much. He was worried and like most men, that showed up in the form of anger. "What else did you need?" he asked a little louder than I had ever heard him.

I spoke softly, "I needed to be alone and have some time to think. Away from everyone and everything." I looked directly in his eyes. "I didn't know who I could trust anymore."

He softened. "I'm sorry. I know that you don't know us well yet, but we are still worried about you. James most of all."

I stood up and walked slowly over to the bag I had packed, hoping to feign strength, and started to pick it up. I got dizzy as I leaned down towards it and as I lifted it off the floor, I dropped down on the stairs.

Jonathan jumped up. "Okay, it's time to get you safely back." He picked up the bag and I said, "I need the laptop and its cords." And I pointed back towards Missy. She grabbed the cords she had dropped down on the couch and then grabbed the laptop.

I rose from the steps and started towards the back door.

"No, no, come out the front door." Missy said. "We're all going home together."

I could tell there was no use arguing with them. Jonathan spoke again as he took my arm. "We can't have you passing out while you are driving. You haven't had any injections in more than twenty-four hours."

I thought about that while I allowed him to walk me out the front door. He was probably right.

He took the laptop and cords and turned my support over to Missy. She put her arms around me and together we walked down the front step and towards the Nissan they had driven up.

When we reached it Jonathan helped me into the back seat with his wife beside me. I leaned against the door, realizing just how very tired I was.

Weak and tired. It was obvious that I had been carried along in my everyday life by the injections that I had been receiving. It explained a lot. Why my weekends before had been what I had called my winding down periods in the beginning before the injections changed to every day.

As we made our way back to James' home, I quietly wondered if they were intentionally not bringing my car back so that I didn't have any possible way of leaving on my own again. I wanted to think the best of them but every once in a while, I questioned my thinking.

All I really wanted was a place of my own that I could be safe in. I did not belong hiding out with people I barely knew. My mother had always taught me that there was a place for everything and everything had a place. I was suddenly overwhelmed with the feelings that I didn't have a place anywhere. I started to cry so I leaned my face closer to the window, letting my tears fall against the glass and the door.

I heard Jonathan call James and let him know that we were on our way. He had already called the police and needed to let them know that I had been found. I got the feeling that he was in the same position as Jonathan, a little angry and a lot worried.

Secretly, I was finding myself thinking more and more about James. He had lost his wife and yet he still lived and worked. He was the picture of strength, where I was the picture of weakness. How long had it taken him to become himself again?

He was a very handsome man, I could see that, but something about him was just so gentle and tender that I felt sure that he was genuinely concerned for my well-being. Even if his feelings were as a result of the loss of his wife, it felt good to have him really concerned about me as a person, and not as a client.

For the first time in a very long time, I fell asleep thinking about someone other than Warren.

When we arrived home, James met us out front of the house. His emotions were evident on his face. I felt like the worst person in the world. I wanted nothing more than to get in the house and upstairs and into the shower. It had dawned on me that I had been in the same clothes for over twenty-four hours also.

I started up the front steps, determined to make it on my own. The car door slammed behind me. I was sure that it was just frustrating to them that I was trying to prove once more that I wasn't that weakling.

I was able to make it up two stairs before I collapsed on them in tears. Jonathan rushed to me but James stepped down from the front of the house and took the steps two at a time down to me.

He lifted me in his arms, and I cried on his shoulder as he headed back up to the open door of the house. Jonathan and Missy trailed quickly behind us and we went up to 'my bedroom'. I whispered, "Can I please just take a bath and get cleaned up?" I said through the tears that just wouldn't stop. I figured that at least I could be alone. He didn't say anything.

When we walked finally through the doorway, James went straight into the bathroom. He sat me on the edge and began to run the water for me. I was still crying, tears flowing freely, exhaustion overcoming me.

"I can't do this anymore. It hurts so badly. Why?" I cried. "Why?" I slid to the floor and my face fell into my lap. I was sobbing now, my body shaking.

My heart was breaking with every thought of what Warren had meant to me. James knelt in front of me, his hands on my shaking shoulders. I looked up at James from my position "Why can't I just die? Maybe if my heart stops beating, it will stop hurting." I felt so broken. Like the glass of my snow globes, my heart had shattered into so many pieces I couldn't see how it could be mended.

James pulled me up lifting my shoulders and pulling me to his chest. I saw Jonathan and Missy at the doorway their own emotions easily visible as they watched my heartache unfolding in front of them.

James turned back to look at them both and motioned them to come in. The emotion was so much for all of us to bear. I knew that I didn't really want to die, but I was so very tired and so very weak and so very damaged by Warren's betrayal.

Missy and Jonathan came into the bathroom and Missy sat down behind me on the closed toilet seat. She spoke softly. "Bria, it's hard to know what such heartache feels like, but right here, there are three people that really do care for you. I might even go so far as to say that we love you."

She paused looking up at both Jonathan and James. "Bria, we have known you long before you knew us, because of the study, but trust us, please. We won't let you down."

James turned my body around, pulling my back into his chest as if I were sitting on his legs. He wrapped his arms around me from behind and whispered in my ear. "I know what heartache feels like. I know what loss feels like. I can't take it away, but I have been exactly where you are now. There is a saying that 'This too shall pass.' Bria, it does. It takes a while, but it does."

I lay back against his arms and continued to cry. They all sat there with me and waited for my tears to run out. It seemed like forever, as each little tick of someone's watch counted the slow seconds until my silence finally came.

"Let's get you in a warm bath and maybe that will help you relax a little. Then we'll get you some lunch and some medicine. Maybe you really need to rest." Jonathan said. I didn't answer, I was numb, not thinking, not reacting, just letting them move me.

Missy and James helped me to stand and then James put me back onto the side of the tub. "I'll be right out here if you need me." He said. I nodded my head as both he and Jonathan left the bathroom.

Missy turned on the Jacuzzi part of the tub and helped me to get undressed. I carefully got into the tub with her help and she sat on the edge of the tub where I had been sitting. "Don't get your arm wet; she looked at the IV that was still taped to my arm. I leaned my head on the side of the tub and she moved closer and lifted my head into her lap.

So much tenderness, tenderness I didn't really deserve since my actions had shown them that I hadn't trusted them. I wanted so much to believe in them.

She smoothed my hair and patted my shoulder. I wanted to feel some peace but I just couldn't find it.

Finally, I spoke. "I heard what the two of you said on the couch at my house." I wanted to ask Missy about it. "We worry about James." She stopped playing with my hair. "He was also very broken after Joanne died. In fact, he died a little as she slowly deteriorated. We didn't know if he would come back around."

She handed me the scrunchy and poured soap again on it. "We can see that he has become attached to you. He really cares for you.

Whether it is because of your circumstances or because he finds you as irresistible, it is hard to say. But Jonathan knows his brother more than anyone else in the world and he thinks that James will do anything to prevent you from being hurt any more."

I took in her words. "*Am* I just a substitute for Joanne?" I asked, knowing that it was a possibility.

"I don't know. Let's just leave it at this. He really cares about you and your safety. That I know for certain."

I lay back against the back of the tub, the bubbles surrounding me and closed my eyes. I was through talking. I just needed to not think about anything. I let my hand slide into the railing on the left side and my right hand hang over the right side of the tub. I knew that I was almost as weak as I could get but I suddenly didn't care.

"Missy, did my bag get brought in? I have some of my own underclothes in that bag. I want to wear them instead of all of the frilly expensive stuff Mr. Hudgeson purchased." She patted my arm and stood. "I'll go and get them. That I do understand. It's a comfort thing." I smiled up at her. "Exactly."

She walked out of the door and I pulled my arm out of the railing and sank further down into the water. I wet my hair and began to wring it out with my free hand.

I wanted to never cry again, but as I waited on Missy to come back, I couldn't help it. The tears were so easily spilling into the tub of water.

I lay my cheek against the opposite side of the tub and closed my eyes. I did feel like I could soak here forever. I drifted off into a semi-sleep, the warmth of the water on my body, the cool of the edge of the tub against my cheek leading me into a small bit of relaxing peace.

Chapter Seventeen
Two Broken

Missy walked in and I tried to pull my eyes open. I heard her call my name but I was so tired. I raised my hand an inch or so and lifted my head slightly. "Bria, let's get you out of that tub, okay?" Again I raised my hand a couple of inches but it fell back and splashed into the tub.

Missy stepped closer to me and touched my head. "Come on, Bria, you're going to have to help me get you out of there." I tried to turn and grab the bar but I didn't have the strength to lift myself out of the tub.

Missy pulled my body forward and patted my cheek. "Wake up a little bit please, Bria." I forced my eyes open and tilted my head up to look at her. My head fell backwards and my eyes closed again.

"Jonathan, will you come in here please?" Missy's voice was neither panicked nor worried. She held my shoulders in place as my head still hung backwards. I heard the door open and I had a stray thought that I was naked in the tub but I couldn't move again. My limbs were not cooperating.

"Just help me get her out." Missy asked him a little tentatively.

"I'll try to get her dressed on my own."

"No. Missy, you're not going to be able to do it alone and you know it. It's not like I've never seen a naked body before."

"Let me help." James said from the door. "I've done this before too."

"I know you have." Jonathan said. "But this is different."

"I really don't care; let's just get her out of there." Missy said. She took a dry towel and draped it over me the same way that James had before. "Okay, now get her out."

James stepped to the side of the tub and Jonathan took my shoulders and lifted them. James lifted me from the tub and Missy took another dry towel and placed it on top of the wet one and dropped that one back into the tub. I heard it splash beneath me.

"Bring her back into the room." Missy said.

James carried me to the bed and lay me down on it. Missy quickly covered me with the blankets trying to dry me as she did so. My brain knew what was going on, but my body did not respond and do what I wanted it to do.

"Get me a gown out of the armoire." Missy said and I heard one of the men cross the room and open it. James came and sat down on the bed, holding my shoulders and lifting my dripping hair. He took it and wrapped it with the towel that now lay on top of the blankets wringing out the water. Missy took the gown that Jonathan handed her and slipped it over my head, pulling my arms through. She let it fall as far down as it would go and James lifted me under my arms while she pulled it down to my knees.

Jonathan said; "I think this is going to be bad, her body and her mind is just completely exhausted and she hasn't had any injections in over a day, and no food since what, breakfast yesterday?"

James lay me back down on the pillow and asked, "What do we do now?"

"We wait." Jonathan said. "Let her body recover with rest before we give her any injections. I'm afraid that she is too weak to handle that." I tried to lift my hand and my head but I wasn't strong enough to hold it up. "Just relax. It's okay Bria." James reached for my head and cradled me against his chest and shoulder.

"Have other patients reacted this badly?" James asked.

"Worse," Jonathan answered, whispering "some have lapsed into comas and others have…" he stopped there shaking his head. I had known that some had already died, but, I felt positive that I would never be one of them. I didn't have cancer. I couldn't die, right?

Their quiet conversation continued but I was lost in my own thoughts and my pain. I didn't care. Why hadn't I died? I was so tired and so broken.

Daylight streamed in again through the large bay windows. My eyes opened briefly but I was still so weak and tired. James was no longer beside me. I was lying on my side and as I saw the open bathroom I knew that once again, my body had failed me and put me in a very uncomfortable position. I smiled. In the grand scheme of things, who cares? I was being ridiculous.

I moved to the center of the bed and sat up. I watched the door waiting on someone to notice that I was awake. Surely they were watching. For several minutes I sat there. Finally I decided that I had to go to the bathroom. I carefully slid to the side of the bed and put my feet on the floor. I was not taking any chances so I immediately moved to the wall for support. I walked this way to the bathroom and closed the door.

I looked in the mirror and decided that I needed to brush my hair and my teeth. I spent several minutes just doing ordinary everyday things.

When I finally, slowly went back into the room, I decided that I could get dressed. I was feeling okay so I walked over to the armoire and got out the things I needed and then went into the walk in closet and chose something to wear.

It seemed to take forever before I was dressed and ready for the day. Whatever it might hold. I walked, ever so slowly over to the rocker that was fast becoming my favorite chair and sat down picking up the remote for the TV. The instant noise was unsettling. I quickly turned the volume down and gradually returned it to a level that I could hear what was being said on the early local news.

I sat rocking in the chair and watching the news for quite a while. I was half-way falling asleep when Missy walked in the door. Not seeing me in bed, she inhaled sharply, but calmed herself when she realized I was in the room. She walked over and took a seat in the recliner opposite me.

"I'm sorry about everything." I said quietly.

"It's okay. Really it is. We can sympathize with what you are going through." She looked at the TV.

"We've seen heartache before. He went through so much with Joanne." She glanced around the room as if remembering Joanne here in this room.

"You just have the added disadvantage of being on a medication that makes you exceptionally weak. It's not unlike chemo. I remember being so weak that I couldn't even feed myself. Blood transfusions, chemo, rest. Life generally sucked." She paused remembering her battle with cancer.

She switched topics quickly not really wanting to recall her own pain. "James went through a very bad phase after Joanne died. When he finally was able to get back to living his life, he became so driven that work was almost all he did." She grinned and then added seriously, "We don't want him to ever get hurt again. His heart was broken by the loss. Our hearts were broken. Joanne was a wonderful person and a great part of our lives."

We both turned to the TV, not ready to go on, processing the conversation.

"He seems to have taken quite a liking to you. It's the first time he has even been interested in someone. Maybe he recognizes a kindred spirit and I know that he understands your broken heart. I don't know if his has yet to mend. Or…maybe it's just two broken hearts needing each other to mend."

"I didn't ask for this." I dropped one foot down and pushed the rocker into motion.

"I know." She said quietly. "None of us asked for any of this at all. I didn't ask for cancer. Joanne didn't ask to die. You didn't ask for Warren to be who he was or to get hurt by him and you certainly didn't ask to be this weak."

She stood. "Let's go get something to eat. Are you okay to make it down the stairs?" I swallowed. "I think so."

We slowly walked down the stairs. I was hugging the wall and the banister and Missy was holding my other arm. It was a tediously slow process but we made it. We wound our way around to the kitchen and found both James and Jonathan in a little eat-in breakfast nook.

We both took seats, Missy giving a quick peck on Jonathan's cheek.

James handed me a plate filled with food, "I'm sure you need this." He looked at my face, catching my eyes.

"James," a first for me, "I need to apologize. I just needed to feel like I had some control in my life. I know I *should* just trust you all completely, but…" I reached over and placed my hand on top of his, "I needed time away to think. Alone. To see things through my eyes and not through everyone else's. Please, understand."

He took my hand in his.

"Thank you all for everything." I looked at the others. "I'll try not to do that again."

His sigh said it all. It was one of resignation that any scolding was over and we were moving on.

"Now what?" I had been asking that question a lot lately.

"We wait, we live, we go about our lives and hopefully find things returning to normal." James said.

"What are we waiting for?" I wasn't sure what he meant.

"For Warren to be captured." He said quietly as he put a torn piece of toast in his mouth.

"Oh."

We ate pretty much in silence after that. All of us were in our own world of thought. What more could we say? We knew that I was in danger both from Warren and from my weak and fragile state. I silently promised that I would work very hard to regain my strength.

After breakfast Missy and Jonathan walked out on the verandah and James stood to take the dishes to the kitchen sink. I began to clear the rest of the table while he rinsed the dishes and placed them in the dishwasher.

"Where can I put leftovers?" I asked him, wishing I could talk normally with him. He reached into a lower cabinet and handed me several containers. Putting the containers into the refrigerator, I decided to make my way to the library rather than try for an awkward conversation.

"This is my favorite room in the house." James said, startling me twenty minutes later. I had been looking over the books on the shelves as he noiselessly walked up behind me.

"I always come here to wind down after a particularly hard day in court." I smiled. It was already my favorite room in this house. I understood completely. The room had an air of calm and quiet and a sort of reverence that made you want to stay here. There was a mustiness that came with the pages of old books and shelves. I looked at the height of them as they went all the way to the ceiling. I knew it would take a lifetime to read all of them. The silence was broken now, only by the hum of the large ceiling fans that hung from the high ceiling of the room.

"I could read for hours. Falling into a story or history and lose a whole day sitting in one spot."

I agreed with him. Many times I have done exactly that so I said, "Yeah, I know what you mean. It's like jumping into the pages of someone else's life without all the stress of actually living it."
He laughed. "Exactly, all the fun without all the work."

We browsed the books on the shelves and I took one and sat down in a big comfy chair. I leaned towards the table so that the light from the lamp glowed on the pages. It gave me a very secluded feeling and I was for the first time in a long time comfortable.

James strolled over to the chair on the opposite side of the same table and began reading a book himself.

I glanced up, and then back to my book. It was a fascinating book and I felt sure that I could finish it in one day or maybe two. This too was a genre that I loved. Mysteries. I loved them and now I was living my own, sort of.

I tried to keep my eyes on the pages but I found myself watching James in little glances. I was trying to feel out his emotions and whether he was too angry at me or was I really forgiven.

He also wasn't hard to look at. Totally handsome but darker than Warren. His hair was dark brown to black. His eyes, ooh his eyes were so deep and so blue that you could almost swim in them. They were penetrating in their gaze as well and you knew that you had to tell him the truth. He was well over six feet and his shoulders were broad but not over bulky. He was built well, but not so muscular that you were sick when you looked at him. I thought, he would make a good Prince Charming in a Cinderella movie. Just too tall unless they got a really tall female to play Cinderella. I giggled at the thought of dancing with him. He must have thought it was the book that I was giggling at because he said, "Isn't that a mystery?"

"Yes," I answered quickly and then added, "just thinking about my life and how it has become a mystery."

I was serious but I was also sure that I didn't want him to know that I was thinking about him.

The day dragged on and another meal was prepared and we ate together like a family. It was great to find some form of normal in this world of hiding out from Warren. It was like a family being born out of tragedy, we were thrown together and we had to depend on each other.

Several days passed on and we fell into a routine. Injections, breakfast, reading, lunch, board games or walks, lying out by the pool, reading, dinner. All the same even for James as he went to work and would come home shortly after lunch to share afternoons with the three of us.

Jonathan would occasionally go in to work when called, but he had plenty of "vacation" days. He was also getting paid by the pharmaceutical companies to be my personal physician. Missy too was getting paid to be my nurse and companion and even I was earning some money as a participant in the study and thanks to James, leave of absence pay. All of my work and my reports on how I was doing and feeling daily were being sent in thanks to my bringing my laptop back with us.

James hired someone to temporarily house-sit while cleaning up my home. They were to clean up any signs of the damage that was done while I was gone.

The days turned into several weeks and I began to be bored with not having my life back. I would go through various levels of weakness depending on how much physically I did during the day, but if I was careful, I suffered through it for only a little while.

The nights were still hard. Nightmares of Warren attacking me and dreams of our life together made nights difficult until I would finally fall into a deeper sleep that let me be rested enough for the morning.

Warren had not yet been caught, though recalling that late night conversation left me with no doubt that he knew where I was. The late night conversation was still a mystery, and though I wanted to find out, I was too afraid to tell anyone that I had heard it. I was still having some trust issues.

Chapter Eighteen
Monotony Over

I woke one morning, stretching only to find that I could barely move. I was weak. And for some reason I was terribly thirsty.

My throat felt dry and all I wanted was to get up and get some water. I slid to the edge of the bed and put my feet on the floor. My plan was to go to the bathroom and freshen up and get water there, but instead, I collapsed just beside my bed. I tried to get up but it exhausted me. My breathing was shallow. I sucked in air as hard as I could but every time I tried getting that deep breath, I ached.

My lungs ached, my back ached, and I hurt all over. Something wasn't right.

I couldn't reconcile the change in me. Yesterday was normal. Yesterday was good. Was there any difference yesterday? I wasn't able to receive my injections until last night because we had waited on Mr. Hudgeson. They had been being delivered by a service, but instead he delivered them himself late in the evening. That didn't make any sense because I had definitely been longer than that without injections.

So that wasn't it. Was it the swim yesterday? No, I had done that before too. It had been weeks since I felt this bad. I shook my head and again tried to rise.

I tried to pull myself up using the blankets but I was too weak and having trouble getting that deep breath. I heard slow footsteps in the hallway. I called out, "I need help," as loudly as I could, but even to my own ears; it was a feeble, near silent attempt. The knock on the door startled me when I realized that someone *had* heard me.

"Bria," James paused, "did you say something?"

Again I tried to call out, "James, please help me." My voice was barely a whisper.

James slowly pushed open the door, "I'm coming in," he said, still not sure if he had heard anything.

At once he saw me crumpled on the floor and ran to me. He bent over, lifting me from the floor. My head lolled back over his arm as he put me gently on the bed. "What happened?" I couldn't answer before he called out, "Jonathan, Missy, get in here, I need your help!" I could hear the panic in his voice.

Good grief, I thought. How could everything seem to be going well one minute and then the next it was crashing down around me again?

My breathing slowed. I gave up on trying to get a deep breath. I knew my sight was dimming, my eyes closing, I could feel myself slipping into unconsciousness just as Jonathan and Missy ran into the room.

"What happened?" Jonathan asked, as he began to take my pulse.

"I don't know." James' voice cracked with worry, "I thought I heard her voice, and opened the door to find her on the floor."

Missy took a quick look at me as she turned on the lamp. My pale face frightened her into action. She grabbed James, forcing him to look away from me.

"Go, James, get Jonathan's bag, NOW!"

Instantly he was gone running down the stairs. It seemed like only seconds before he was back with Jonathan's huge backpack. I knew what was in it as Jonathan carried it everywhere.

Jonathan reacted quickly and took the bag from James. He threw it open, quickly pulling out a portable oxygen tank and turned it on. He put the mask over my mouth and nose.

Within seconds, fresh oxygen was being forced into my lungs. I took a deep breath enjoying the cool oxygen as it filled my lungs to capacity. I felt better, but not by much.

Soon I could feel the color slowly returning to my cheeks. My eyes finally began to focus and I was shocked to see that Missy was in tears.

I turned to look at Jonathan and James and saw the concern in their eyes. I was frightened.

"What happened to me?" I managed to ask, my voice muffled as I spoke out through the oxygen mask.

Jonathan smiled, "We were hoping you could answer that question."

I thought for just a minute. "I just felt really weak when I woke up. My body aches and I'm very thirsty." I answered him.

"Thirsty?" Jonathan asked. I could tell he was running through various reasons for my conditions.

"It was like cotton clogging my throat." I answered him again. He looked at Missy and then at James, a shadow of concern now completely over his face. "I just don't know," he said as he continued to take my vital signs. He was writing them down when you could see that a new question had formed.

"Did the doors get locked after Daniel left last night?" James sat down on the end of the bed, looking at me, "Why? What would that have to do with this?" He looked at Jonathan questioningly. An unspoken conversation passed between them through their eyes. "I really don't remember doing it."

They were all quiet for a moment. The only sound was the hiss of the oxygen tank. I was breathing better but I still couldn't follow what they were talking about.

Moments later, Missy suddenly said, "Oh no!" Both men looked at her.

"Think about what Daniel said?" Missy stopped. "Do you think it's possible *he* was able to get into the house?"

I didn't need an interpreter to know that the *he* she was talking about was Warren.

I interrupted her before she could go any further with the conversation. Struggling to get a deep breath so I could talk, I spoke. "I didn't want to say anything," my voice was not even a whisper now, it was so parched dry, "but I heard someone the night that I left."

I paused licking my lips as my mouth got dryer with each word. "It was a man speaking and he said that 'he' knew that I was here."

"Do you know who you heard?" James asked.

"I didn't see his face." I was struggling even more now but I had to get it all out. "But he was standing right outside my room just a few feet down the hallway. I didn't recognize his voice and I didn't know who he was talking to."

"Daniel!" Both men said at once.

I briefly wondered who Daniel was, but I didn't think I could open my mouth again.

It took only a quick motion and James had his cell phone out and pressed to his ear. The rest of us waited, only hearing his side of the conversation.

"It was Daniel. He said that the night Bria left, he received a call from Edward." He turned to me explaining. "That's Mr. Hudgeson." Then he continued. "Edward told Daniel he was sure Warren knew that Bria was staying here. He says that Edward didn't disclose how he knew this information so he decided to just keep an eye on things and do some extra investigating on his own.

So far, he hasn't found anything suspicious. The only thing out of the ordinary was that last night while he was on guard, he saw a car stop underneath the lights by the road. He followed the car but it was nothing. A woman he supposed was looking at a map or making a call.

He turned around and that's why he came back here to tell us what Edward suspected. He didn't have any proof. But he felt he should tell us about it so we could be on guard as well. Only those few minutes that he spent here in the house, was the only time no one was on guard."

"I'm still really thirsty." I said trying to clear my throat. "I really need to get some water." My voice fading to just a whisper.

Jonathan looked back at me. Transforming back into doctor mode, he got some water and helped me to sip some through the straw he held to my lips. I was grateful and looked up to mouth "Thank you". I realized that this situation had gotten very bad very quick. I wondered what he was thinking.

I continued to sip the water. It felt cool as it flowed down my throat but it still didn't remove the cotton dry feeling that coated both my mouth and my throat.

In fact, it seemed almost to be making it worse. I tried to swallow. What was happening to me? I opened my mouth trying to push out the drenched cotton that wasn't really there. I tried to breathe in but that feeling was overwhelming me. Darkness was going to come; I knew that I was close to passing out.

My thoughts made me panic. I didn't want to be this weak again. I tried quickly to put together the conversation in my head. Had I been poisoned? Oh my God, had Warren been here in another attempt to kill me? I was pretty sure now, that I had put my friends in danger. Thanks to Warren, my soap opera life was taking on another dangerous twist.

Their voices eventually faded into the deepest recesses of my consciousness. Pictures of people I knew and people I didn't know began floating through my head.

First, Warren was lovingly holding my hand on the beaches down in the Carolinas proposing to me in the twilight. Next we were sipping hot cocoa in our favorite bookstore the night we acted like kids at a book signing. Next we were making love for the first time on the first night in our new house.

Then came the unhappier memories, turning my dreams into nightmares. Remembering his hands as they wrapped around my throat both at the party and then again in court.

There were the different people from both occasions intermingling. Mr. Hudgeson was laughing out loud, his belly shaking under his three piece suit like a fat mall Santa.

Missy and Jonathan were there, holding each other in tears while James stood at a coffin, stoic and strong. Faces I had never even seen shuffled through the projection screen in my mind. There was that woman laughing. A man was pointing a gun at me. A group of people for some reason standing around my office at work. Finally my vision focused on one single scene. I strained to understand what it was I saw. I watched as my own crumpled body lay on the beach amongst the hermit crabs and sand fleas.

I woke with a start, gasping for breath as the last scene in my nightmare played over and over. I realized that I was breathing and not dead on the beach. The oxygen mask was snug on my face. The elastic straps were giving me a headache.

I tried to sit up but was instantly so dizzy that I let my head fell forward to land in my lap. Immediately cool, almost clammy hands lifted my head and softly pushed me back to lie again on my pillow. I saw through the haze that was my vision that it was James standing beside me holding me on the bed to prevent me from falling out of it.

I screamed, some part of me recalling that last vision of my body on the beach. James held my shoulders, I screamed again, pushing the oxygen mask off, "I don't want to die, I don't want to die." I was hysterical.

Missy and Jonathan came in through the open door, once more rushing in response to my screams.

"James hold her down before she pulls out that IV."

I heard Jonathan tell him. "Watch the IV!" he said as he saw the tubing pull tight from where it hung. I was strong. My fear of dying and an irrational thought that they were the ones killing me overtook every cell of my body and I was actually winning. I was pushing them all away, my hands flailing, the tubing bending backwards at the needle that was trying to release itself from my arm.

The three of them were trying now, holding me, without much success. My thrashing took on an even more powerful adrenalin push and I tried to get away from them.

And then it happened. James movement was instant. He was on top of me, straddling me and holding my shoulders down with his hands and my body down with his. I didn't understand and the weight of his body was too much for me. Eventually my movements slowed.

My arm felt hot, burning me, and then slowly the warmth spread over my body, my mind slowly numbing. I looked up at James pressing down on me and wrapped my one free arm around his neck. I looked up at him in desperation, "Don't let me die, please." I was pleading with him with everything I had, "Don't let me die, don't…

let… me… d…" I could no longer speak. He pulled back a little when my voice stopped and looked directly into my eyes.

I saw his tears. Somewhere in the jumbled recesses of my brain, I knew he was remembering another occasion when someone else lay dying in his arms.

He gently stroked my forehead and rolled off of me to the side, not leaving the bed, staying very still beside me, lost in his thoughts.

He continued to watch me, his tears falling freely on my cheek. He kissed my forehead and whispered. "I won't let *you* die." He emphasized the word "you" and I realized that he was suffering.

He put his arms around me. "Stay with me." Another pause. "I *want* you to stay with me." He began to kiss me on my forehead as it rested in his arms. His small gentle kisses calmed me. I relaxed and put my hand in his open shirt collar. I rubbed his skin, familiar and yet foreign, finding comfort. I felt his arms wrap around me completely and I felt safe.

I smiled as I snuggled under his chin, "Love you," I whispered, and I felt his body tense against mine….and then moments later relax.

I don't know how long I was out but when the light filtered in through the window, I shifted. I tried to turn and realized that what I had thought was part of a dream, was in fact reality. One arm was resting over mine, the other under my neck enveloping me, keeping me safe.

I remembered what had happened and felt ashamed knowing my drug induced inhibitions had put me in this awkward position. I turned my head. I only knew he was awake when he lifted his head.

195

"I'm so sorry." I said softly, not knowing what else to say.

He shrugged. "I'm getting kind of used to taking care of you."

"Me too." I answered back.

I heard him sigh deeply, his hot breath filtered through my hair and onto my neck. I felt his chest heave against my back. I didn't want to move and I didn't really want him to move either. I closed my eyes again, waiting.

He kissed the back of my head and gently moved my hair from my neck, exposing it directly to his hot breath. He kissed me again, gently, on my neck and then again behind my ear. Shivers ran through me. What was I doing? Finally, I turned my head up and back towards him and he kissed my cheek lingering as he did so, *his* eyes closed.

As suddenly as it had begun, the tingle in my body, the freshness of his touch, the smell of him against me, it was over as he pulled away from me and stood up beside the bed.

Just a few seconds later, Missy and Jonathan walked through the open doorway. I hadn't heard them at all; I had been so wrapped up in James that the noise of their coming had escaped me.

"Feeling better?" Jonathan walked over to stand beside James. Missy walked to the other side and picked up my wrist. She smiled.

She could tell my heart was beating faster than normal.

She smiled at Jonathan and he looked at James. The smirk on his face was enough to let me know that he had read the situation a little too perfectly.

"I think she's doing much better." It almost sounded like he was laughing as he said the words. He proceeded to check me over, doing his doctor thing with a mischievous grin on his face.

"I am going to need to draw some blood, Bria, We really need to find out what happened." I nodded, afraid to speak for the moment.

It was over with quickly. I watched as he shook the vial. I hated that I was becoming squeamish. It seemed to me that all this familiarity with the medical stuff was having the opposite effect on me. It wasn't getting easier. In fact I was getting sick just thinking about the next time Jonathan might have to do it again.

Chapter Nineteen
Recovery and Discovery

I couldn't think straight with the three of them all staring at me. My feelings were so jumbled. James was worse. If he could have blushed, he would have.

"What's the diagnosis, Dr. Wilbrandt?" I asked addressing him formally in the vain hopes that he would stop his grinning and be serious again.

"I won't know until we can get this back from the lab." His tone switched to match mine. Then he added. "No sense getting snippy with me, little miss Bria." He was putting on a façade but I could see that he was doing his best to hold back the grin. "No need to call me Doctor Wilbrandt, either" he paused and under his breath, just loud enough for everyone to hear it, he continued, "we're family now."

He laughed out loud and Missy joined him, while James and I remained very tight lipped. This didn't help things at all and instead made both Jonathan and Missy laugh even harder. It was so infuriating.

After a couple of minutes, they settled down and Jonathan nodded to Missy as she began to check what I had affectionately called, 'my wiring'. I saw the needle she held and turned away. I hated this part of it.

I wasn't ready to watch it go into the IV as I had before. It was making me more and more squeamish each and every time.

Nausea swept over me as the meds entered my system. I thought I would be sick, but James pushed past Jonathan and took my hand in his. "Don't think about it. He said.

As if something new had dawned on him, he turned back to Jonathan, whispering, "Could it be the meds that are making her sick?" his tone was genuinely curious.

Jonathan shrugged his shoulders, "It shouldn't be, but with trial drugs, you can never tell." His voice was low, talking only to James. "That's why it's a trial, James. They all knew what they were getting into. Even Bria. Especially Bria." He put his hand on James' shoulder patting it in that brotherly way.

Looking back at them I watched their faces, trying to read between the lines of his words I realized just how close they were. They were as close as regular brothers instead of half brothers. They both had suffered because of what cancer and tragedy had done to their family.

James had lost his father when he was but an infant in a horrible accident. His mother married Jonathan's father and less than a year later Jonathan was born. The two were best friends as well as brothers.

Cancer had now taken their mother, but also James' wife. And now Missy was a survivor in remission. Did Jonathan fear losing Missy as James' had lost his wife? I knew the answer and suddenly, even though I was no one of real consequence in this family, I meant even more to them because loss of any kind was something they didn't like to deal with. They had suffered through so much of it already.

I sighed heavily fighting back the nausea. James' hands stroked mine, softly caressing the joints and fingers and palms. I felt serene and anxious, worried and calm. There was just too much going on.

I spent another few days in the bed before Jonathan would allow me up with assistance. I was never left alone. Someone was in the room with me at all times. James took up his place every night in one of the recliners. I knew he was uncomfortable. His restless sleep keeping me awake even when I was under the influence of drugs. Nightmares came more frequently for me now, every night seemed to hold the same horrors but I tried to keep them to myself.

"James?" I said as he entered the room one night with a throw pillow and a blanket. He stopped by the bed I was already in and looked down at me exhausted.

"Do you need something?" He was so tired and seemed so worried about me. I could see it in his face.

"Please, could you just lie down beside me?" He looked at my eyes, questioning me. "I'm fine; it's just that I can't seem to sleep." I pulled the blanket flat beside me and slid over. I patted the spot on top of the blankets. I hoped that this let him know that I wasn't asking for anything else, just the comfort of another human being to fight away the demons.

"Are you sure you're okay?" He asked. "Yes," I answered, "I just need to feel safe. The nightmares just keep coming and I can't shake the fear of them." He climbed up beside me, taking up the same position that he had before. This time, I turned towards him purposefully burying my head on his chest under his shoulder.

I sighed as deeply as I could without pain and closed my eyes. I would sleep tonight, hopefully, and maybe he would too.

I raised my hand to his face, tilting my head up, eyes still closed, "Thank you." He pushed my head back into its previous position and stroked my hair. He gently took my hand in his and held it as I drifted.

I don't remember falling asleep. I could remember his heart beating underneath his chest. I remembered my hand clutching at his shirt holding on to him as if my life depended on it. I remembered hearing my screams all through my dreams. I felt myself struggling to breathe, although it, too, was part of my dreams.

Half in and half out of my nightmare sleep, I could hear his words, feel his breath in my hair, and feel him comforting me. I would drift off again into peaceful slumber, if only for a few minutes at a time. Over and over during the long night, I would relive the same nightmares.

Each one would always end with me watching my body on the beach. It was so real. So vivid. So hard to watch.

Night after night, even after Jonathan let me get up and around on my own, James would still come to my room and crawl in bed with me. Always on top of the blankets beside me. Always comforting, always safe in his arms. I would drift through the nightmares. Every morning I would wake exhausted.

The nightmares that were becoming more and more vivid kept me from ever sleeping soundly. Every morning, James would be there, his arms around me, protecting me from the seen and the unseen dangers.

I couldn't understand our relationship. He was much more than a friend and yet we were not in any way comfortable with moving towards anything different. Both of our hearts still ached. Neither one of us seemed ready to cross the boundaries that we had set for ourselves. It was a very symbiotic relationship.

The phone rang sharply, interrupting any chance for staying in his protective arms. He reached back getting his cell phone off of the nightstand and drowsily placed it to his ear.

I could hear the excited voice so loud that it almost bounced as it echoed from the phone.

"What?" James' voice was alarmed by whatever he had heard. He practically leapt from the bed. "Stay put!" he was ordering me and he took off down the hallway.

What now? I thought. But I did not get up. I would not move. I had to wait. This knight in shining armor had kept me safe for quite a while now, and I had to trust him.

I waited.

Another set of loud voices came down the hall. Missy ran into my room grabbing clothes out of the closet. "We need to get out of here for a while." She was trying to be calm. "Come on, I'll help you." She was mothering me, trying to not cause panic.

"What is happening?" I was worried now. She didn't look at my face. "Bria, Daniel is coming with the car, we need to hurry." She was dressing me, not giving me a chance to dress myself.

"Please," she begged, "we have to go!" her voice was reaching hysteria and high pitched decibels that hurt my ears.

"James!" she yelled for him. "Jon!" She was calling them to help her. I was doing my best, but I was still weak and I found myself dizzy from standing up too quickly.

Both men reached the room and Missy handed me off to James like I was a toddler she had just gotten ready to go. I tried to walk to the door while Missy and Jonathan got his bag from the closet where he now kept it most of the time.

James lifted me off my feet, sweeping me up in his arms, and the four of us flew down the stairs. I said, smiling; "I think you like having me in your arms." I didn't want to think about what might be happening but as we reached the bottom of the stairs I asked, "What is going on?" I was afraid to scream it out and yet I wanted to know.

Daniel met us at the front door, limo doors open and waiting for us to get in. He didn't wait to shut our door but ran around to his own.

Jonathan pulled ours closed just as Daniel slammed his door and gunned the engine. We were moving quickly down the long driveway.

We slowed only when we had to drive around a car that I knew belonged to the additional guards that had been watching over the outer boundaries of the property. I leaned forward to look out the window that James was trying to block. I could see the guard, but he was slumped over his steering wheel and blood had sprayed all over the front and side windows.

I screamed. Loud and long and fierce, then clamped my hand over my mouth. I was in shock. I knew he was dead. I put my head between my legs and took deep quick breaths between screaming into my hands. I couldn't think.

James held my shoulders keeping my head down. I wondered why. What could possibly be worse than that? I didn't want to know. "I'm going to be sick." I said. I could feel it coming up from deep inside me, and I needed to stop.

Jonathan came to my rescue. Sitting across from me, he took my face in his hands cupping them he talked to me.

"Don't think about it Bria." He paused. "Bria, look at me, we can't stop. This is too important; you need to calm yourself down Bria.

Come on, look at me. We are going to get through this. Don't worry. You really can't afford to worry about this. Look at me."

His voice droned on and on, forcing me to watch his face, to breathe, to try and not think about what I had just seen. James continued to hold my shoulders but not down any longer. He was massaging them instead.

Missy, crying, leaned against Jonathan's shoulder, watching me, adding her soft, soothing voice, speaking through the tears and the near hysteria that she herself was fighting down.

A few minutes later James lifted my head slowly. "Lean back. Relax against the cool leather of the seat. It may help." I was trying to stay calm.

"The blood," I finally whispered swallowing hard and forcing myself not to throw up mid sentence. "There was so much of it." Jonathan began tapping my knee. He was holding the outer sides of my knees tapping on the kneecap itself. The movement was slow and steady. It was annoying, but it was monotonously soothing and it drew me away from what my mind was trying to process.

It helped a great deal. Missy, crying still, began to sob into her husbands shoulder as her own release came. We were both in shock now. The scene would play in our minds over and over as we escaped the area. The soft and soothing voice of Jonathan and the passing of the town we were in helped to reduce the urge to be sick. We entered the highway and the smooth fast driving let each of us relax, if only just a little.

I realized that Jonathan had stopped talking and I lifted my head. I looked at each and every face and I knew that *all four* of us were in a state of shock.

What had happened? I had to know. I had to know if it had anything to do with Warren. I simply could not believe that he could really be a killer. He couldn't be. He simply couldn't. But I still could not speak. I was afraid that if I opened my mouth, I would again be all too ready to throw up.

It was James that spoke first. His voice trembling with emotion, he spoke softly, almost pensively, "How could this have happened?"

He wasn't really asking anyone, more himself. Not having an answer, he looked devastated. I realized immediately that this had put us all in danger. Not only did it mean that someone very evil was lurking around our supposedly safe place, but an investigation would easily uncover that the dead man had been employed by James as protection for a client. It got even worse. Not only a client, but a client living with her attorney.

I knew this was bad...for everyone.

Chapter Twenty
A New Threat?

Missy was still crying, only more silently than before. I could tell that even though Jonathan and James had probably been in circumstances where they had seen violent death before, this was not ordinary and it was too close to home. Too close to them and the ones they love.

They, the three of them, were family. They had suffered much together.

It was at that moment that I made up my mind. No matter how much I now trusted them, I had to leave. I knew that this was my fault and as soon as possible, I would find another way and go somewhere else. Anywhere else but with them.

My mind was whirring with details that I would have to put into place. We were all going to have to deal with things that we hadn't dealt with before. I needed to take my part in it out of their equation. It would be safer for them.

As we drove along, Daniel rang back, asking James where to drive to. He hadn't thought that far in advance, so he looked at Jonathan.

"Home," was his one word answer. At first, James looked at him as if he were crazy. Then Jonathan said, "Our home."

James nodded and I heard him tell Daniel to "head south." Daniel must have gotten the message because James answered, "That's right. And as fast as you can please."

I was once more quite aware that I was the one outsider here. The three of them, no, make that the four of them, Daniel included, knew where we were headed. I was going to be in a place that might be very unfamiliar to me and I would have to make my getaway from there.

What did I have with me? Who could I call to help me, if I needed someone? I didn't know. I didn't have any idea.

I turned my face to the window I was seated next to and cried. I had been living in a place that was not my own. And living a life that was not my own.

My heart was aching. The hole in my heart where Warren had been firmly planted still gaped wide open. No matter how evil he might be my shredded heart was still pained because of him.

And even though there was an inkling of a thought that James might be able to repair some of that hole, all of this made me wish things were different. I knew that I had to give that thought up so that they could all be safe. I was the problem. *I* was who people were waiting for, or looking for, the study needed me.

What I had thought was wonderful was no more, and for some reason Warren had changed. He no longer needed me, but he now wanted me dead.

I tried to cry silently, letting the sobs get caught in my throat, but I knew that I was shaking. I needed fresh air, I needed to stop. I needed them to let me breathe, but I was afraid to have them stop. I wanted us to be very far away from the scene at the end of James' driveway. I scooted closer to the window and the door, plastering my body against it in my attempt to escape the scene in my mind.

Once again, I don't know when I fell asleep. I woke to find my head in James' lap and his hand holding mine.

Heartache again. I didn't want to feel the closeness. It would make it all that much harder to leave, but I couldn't let go too fast. It would make it easier, but it would be more suspicious, after our interactions at his home had been so close.

I turned my head, looking up at him. I smiled. Not that there was much to smile about. "Thanks." I said. He just looked at me and lifted me up to snuggle under his arm. It was safe and comfortable there. I questioned my senses. Why exactly did I want to leave this? I closed my eyes debating, and the picture of the man dead in the car, blood all over the windows, came rushing back to me.

In my head he (the dead man) suddenly changed to James and I knew that no matter what, I had to leave my companions, my friends. Friends that were almost like family.

If they were to be safe, I had to make them that way.

We had been driving for several hours. I knew by the look of us that we would have to stop soon. It was then that James called up to Daniel.

"We need some lunch. Drive to Mia's. Park in the back."

"Mia's? I knew of a Mia's restaurant. It was a great Italian place at VA Beach. I popped up and looked out the window.

I knew where we were. I smiled. I had spent many weekends here. Warren and I both had. We had practically made it our weekend haunt before we were married. After we were married, it was our once a month trip in the spring and summer.

I loved this place! Excitement filled my heart, I knew many people that could help me here. There were too many things that I knew about this place. I could literally hide in plain sight.

In twenty minutes, we were pulling up to the back of the same restaurant where I had eaten way too much lasagna. Their portions were so large that we always went home with extra for the next day. The family that owned the restaurant worked hard to make it like home.

You knew "Mama," and you knew "Papa". They were wonderful people and they would stop by your table to ask if you were satisfied. Suddenly, all the fond memories, were painful. I would be here with someone other than Warren. What would that be like? We walked quickly through the front door of the small restaurant and walked to a table for six. There was "Mama" asking what we wanted to drink as she placed soft warm breadsticks on the table in a little basket covered with a red and white checkered linen napkin. I reached for it, not to get a breadstick, but to feel the napkin itself. A tangible item of what had been.

Slowly, I uncovered the breadsticks, took one in the palm of my hand, still too hot for my fingertips, and lifted it to my face. I inhaled, smelling the bread, the yeasty warmth mixing with the butter and the garlic and Italian spices. Memories flooding back from every single time we visited here. I broke off a piece and placed it in my mouth. I seemed to be moving in slow motion and I couldn't get back to reality.

"Bria, what do you want to drink?" James nudged me. I swallowed quickly, "Lemon water." I replied lazily. They had intruded on my reverie. But, it was an intrusion that I needed. It was increasingly hard remembering the good things about us, about Warren and me.

After our drinks were brought back, James ordered the "family platter" which had several servings of different Italian dishes. Hushed conversation began the second "Mama" left.

"Bria, I know you haven't been formally introduced, but this is Daniel. Daniel, you know, but this is Bria."

I reached my hand across the table to shake his and he took it. "I'm sorry we are meeting like this." He said. I waved him off. "It's not your fault; it's all Warren's fault." I sighed.

I wanted to ask him questions, sure he knew more than most, but I didn't have them formulated in my mind yet. Daniel took control of the conversation.

"Okay, I've called the police but as far as they know, you were not yet at home." He said speaking to James. "The story will be that you had been staying here and that the reason he was on duty was that you, James, were to return home for work sometime later this afternoon."

I looked at James. He simply nodded in response to Daniel's words. I couldn't believe this. We were going to lie. I had to say something. "We're going to lie? We can't lie."

Jonathan looked at me. "Would you rather let them know that you were there? Someone killed that man. Someone killed a man! A member of a protective detail, specifically there for you." He emphasized each word.

"You two were in bed, we were in bed. Daniel was on guard in the house. We have plenty of proof that we could not have done it, but that's not the reason for the lie."

"Then what is?" I questioned.

Daniel answered. "To keep you safe." He said a little perturbed as he looked across the table at me. "It's so that Warren believes when the news is reported that he has been mistaken. Maybe he'll believe that he had it all wrong about where you were this whole time. Warren may take the bait and actually believe that you haven't been staying there. It may be the monkey wrench that we needed to throw him off of *your* scent."

I shook my head. "Haven't we learned anything? He would know. No matter what, he would know."

I shut up. I didn't know what else to say. I knew that none of us had anything to do with that man's death, but I also knew that I was responsible for it none the less.

"So what you're saying is that it's my fault that that man is dead. It's my fault that his family is going to suffer. It's my fault that you are all in danger!" I was shaking. I stood up. I needed to get fresh air. I didn't know what to do, but James was up instantly and Jonathan also came to my side.

"I don't want company." I said through closed lips. For a split instant I thought that they wouldn't let me go. I must have looked like

I was losing it, because they followed me as I started towards the door. "We'll be back." James said to Daniel and Missy.

I walked to the door with the two of them walking behind me. I turned right onto the sidewalk, though I didn't know where I would go. I tried to walk ahead of them but they were so tall and I was so short and their strides were two or three times the size of mine.

I finally slowed, no longer caring, just thinking, mulling things over. I turned down a side alley, thinking to just make a turn around the block and then back to the restaurant. When we turned, I continued to walk, and it was then that I realized that it was not an alley but a dead end.

I stopped, knowing that I had no choice but to turn around. Instead, I dropped to my knees. Sobbing, I wouldn't move. I needed to sit here and cry. I couldn't be consoled.

Both men, not knowing what else to do, dropped beside me, both holding my shoulders on each side not wanting me to fall and trying to comfort me.

"I put every one of you in danger." I sobbed the words. "I got that man k…k…illed." I pounded my fists into the concrete. "Ow!" I cried even harder.

It was too much for them. "Stop! Stop that! It is not our fault. No one could have known." James turned me towards him and was shaking me. My head snapped back and Jonathan pulled me away from James' hands.

"James, that's not helping things." He said as he folded me into his arms protectively. "It's too much for any of us to handle alone.

Not me, not you, not Missy and certainly not Bria, but you can't shake her like that!" His tone was scolding.

James rose and took several steps away. "Bria, I'm sorry." He looked down at his hands. He paused and I heard him walk back to me. "I can't lose anyone else I love, don't you understand? Suddenly his voice dropped to a whisper, angrier than ever.

"It's Warren." He said, "I'm sure of it."

I took in the words he was saying. "How do you know? It didn't have to be him." I stopped, biting my lip. Why in the hell was I defending Warren?

"Who else could it be?" James said. Jonathan pulled me to my feet as he rose. I turned from Jonathan, looking past James.

Suddenly, I just wanted to get back to the others. The sooner we were finished here, the sooner I could leave them.

I pulled away from Jonathan and started to walk back down the alleyway, wobbling on my unsteady legs. Both men took hold of my arms as we headed back towards the restaurant and I tried to calm my furiously racing mind. I lifted my eyes, looking around, remembering.

I suddenly had the feeling that I needed to hide.

"It's Warren." I said.

James looked down at me. "I'm glad you finally agree."

"No, NO!" I was whispering but I was looking across the street. Jonathan followed my gaze before James did. When no one said anything for a second, James followed both of our gazes. Walking on the sidewalk on the opposite side of the street was Warren. Beside him stood Mr. Hudgeson!

214

James and Jonathan picked up their pace, practically carrying me back to the restaurant. We entered the restaurant nearly breathless. Daniel and Missy both picking up on the terror etched on my face. And the rage that was on the faces of both her husband and her brother in law.

Our food was on the table, and everything was ready for us to eat. James quickly told them both what had happened. Daniel rose from the table, walked to the door and stood, watching them.

We could see them too through the windows if we stared closely enough. The two men seemed to be arguing with each other.

Several minutes passed and the argument looked to be over. Mr. Hudgeson put his arm across Warren's shoulders and they walked to the corner. Almost instantly, a large dark limo pulled up. Twice as long as the one we had arrived in, both men crawled into the back of it. The vehicle drove away heading towards the highway. I hoped that meant that they were gone.

Daniel returned to the table. We were all starving but, we were all anxious. "Why don't we eat quickly and get out of here?" It was Missy that spoke. I just wanted to 'get out of here' now. I couldn't eat. I picked up the single breadstick I had started to eat before and picked off little pieces and dropping them on my plate. The food smelled delicious, but I knew that one bite would mean a trip to the toilet instead of to safety.

The others ate quickly, automatically, just filling their stomachs and not really tasting the food.

Daniel left first. We paid for the bill and wrapped up leftovers, at the insistence of "Mama" and stood by the door. None of us wanted to have to wait on the sidewalk in full view of anyone.

When Daniel drove up in front of "Mia's", he hopped from the driver's side and rushed to open the doors before motioning for us to come out side. We exited quickly, James and Jonathan flanking both of us, Missy and me.

We drove off quickly, everyone keeping their eyes on the roads, watching for the large limo. The window separating the front from the back rolled down, "I don't think anyone saw us." Daniel said.

"Change of plans. Take us to the cove instead. I think that we should hang out around town just in case. But we should still go somewhere very peaceful and relaxing." James told him. "And Daniel?" he looked up at him in the rearview mirror, "Leave the window down."

Daniel nodded his head, making eye contact with James in the mirror as well. We all felt the need to have everyone in sight of each other. Somehow it felt safer, though I don't know why.

The tension was way too high amongst the five of us. You could almost feel it weighing down on the whole car.

Chapter Twenty-One
Hermit Crabs and Sand Fleas

Fifteen minutes later we pulled into the parking lot of the campground to the bay. Daniel got out and walked down to the beach.

"Looks innocent enough," he said as he opened the car door for us.

James took my hand and Jonathan took Missy's. Daniel stayed with the car. "Keep us posted. If you notice anything or have to leave, call one of us and let us know."

James was still very protective but not too panicked. Daniel reached up and grabbed James' shoulder. "Don't worry; I'm on top of this. We'll meet things as they come." He smiled and went back to get into the car as we walked away.

We crossed the parking lot and walked on the path through the small wooded area that was a barrier to the ocean. We could smell the campfires of the campground that was part of this seashore park.

When we reached the beach, I suddenly and inexplicably felt free. Looking out over the bay and seeing the Chesapeake Bay Bridge Tunnel, I was suddenly taken back to more peaceful and fun times on the beach.

I reached down and pulled off my shoes. Letting go of James' hand I almost ran to the waterline. I breathed in deep the ocean breezes. I walked out just a little, holding up my skirt, so that the waves wouldn't crash over it and get it wet. My feet sank in the sand, squishing through my toes as each new wave buried my feet deeper in the sand.

Again I breathed in the air, a deep wholesome breath. I could feel the spray from the beach on my face and I was completely relaxed. I spun around, only to see the three of them watching me. Half smiles plastered on their faces, trying to mask the horror of the morning. I began to walk, just edging the water as they followed me, thirty feet further up on the sand, keeping pace with me.

I knew they were talking about me. About Warren. About the dead man possibly. I hoped that this would present the perfect opportunity for me. The perfect place to leave them. I could easily get lost here. It was now late in the afternoon and in another hour or so, the sun would begin its trek down the horizon. If we could manage to stay here long enough, I could disappear.

The hours passed quickly on the beach. I could almost forget the horrors of the past seven and a half months. Almost.

"Come talk with me." James had somehow come towards me without me noticing. I needed to stop that. I seemed to be unaware of a lot of things these days. He grabbed my hand and pulled me closer to the tree and bush line at the top of the beach.

Campers slept in tents and trailers just within the confines of the trees. Densely populated, the trees formed a natural barrier from the ocean itself, but made for a great campground. I used to love camping here.

I let James lead me to a piece of driftwood to sit down. It was a little wet and so James took off his jacket and we sat on top of it. He pulled me to him and held me protectively close for a while. We sat that way for a long time.

"You wanted to talk?" I finally asked him.

"Yes." He paused. "I want you to know and understand that none of this is your fault. Seeing Warren here today, I have to admit that it might not have been him. There are only two things that that might mean. Either someone is following his orders or that there is another enemy that we don't know about."

He squeezed my shoulders.

"You're caught in the middle. I don't know how or why. Either way, you know that you don't influence who someone is or who they become. People make their own choices. No one else is to blame. It is a simple choice to do right or wrong." He stopped again. I didn't say anything. I couldn't say anything.

"Bria, do you understand me?"

I nodded my head. "But if it weren't for me, you all wouldn't be in this situation." He clutched my hand even tighter, talking through clenched teeth.

"No Bria, I was always going to be in this position. I made the decision to bring you to my home. I *wanted* to protect you."

He stiffened, pain crossing his face. "I have failed you on too many occasions. The incident at my office was bad enough but then right under my nose in court." He stopped talking, pulled his hands in front of him. He was shaking his head. His hands were shaking, his voice trembling with anger at himself.

"You know I've fallen for you." He said. "I hadn't planned on it, but from that first day I saw you when you couldn't open the door and walk into my office. I knew you were coming. I knew who you were. I could have sent you to someone else and never seen you again. I chose to help you because I felt a connection with you. Maybe it was just two broken hearts that would mend together. I don't know, but I chose this."

I couldn't talk now for a completely different reason. I found myself holding my breath. I was not ready for this. I wanted it and didn't want it at the same time.

"It has been a long time since I have felt anything. You were, uhm, quite unexpected."

I looked up at him. I wanted to be in his arms. I really did. But, the confession of his feelings made me even surer that I was going to leave. I had to leave.

I slid down off the driftwood and onto the warm sand. I pulled my knees up under my skirt, wrapping my hands around my knees and propped my chin up on my knees. "I love having you protect me. I feel safe. But now there is nothing that can actually protect us. If we go home now, someone will know we are there."

He stopped me, "So we'll stay here for a couple of days. Our old family home is here. We can't seem to sell it and each summer we rent it out to vacationing families. We can stay here for as long as we feel safe."

I breathed a sigh, knowing that no matter what he would argue for his point of view.

"Okay. I just need to think." I put my head between my knees and closed my eyes. I finally looked up at him.

"I think I sort of fell for you too, you know?"

His eyes lit up. "When?"

"When you stayed with me the first night after," I paused, "you know, and you stayed with me. When I said 'love you,' I suddenly realized that I meant it. And I do love you. I just don't know how. This isn't what I had planned." I smiled but I laid my head sideways on my knees and watched the ocean.

"You don't have to pretend you know." He said. "I know it must be hard for you. Your heart is so newly broken. I can wait this out. I promise you." He could see the conflict on my face. I hated that.

I pulled my knees up even closer and hid my face in them, my arms wrapped protectively around my head building my little cocoon.

There was really no need for words as we mulled over what we had already said. I felt tired all over again and for the first time, in a while, completely peaceful. I kept my little cocoon for a long while, listening to the small waves and the seagulls. I looked down and watched the hermit crabs and the small sand fleas on the beach and realized that this was almost identical to my nightmare. It was strange that it was so peaceful.

Soon enough Jonathan would remember that I hadn't had injections and I would be weaker again. Especially since I hadn't eaten anything.

221

Nothing made sense to me anymore. But, this place? This place comforted me. The water lapping up further and further onto the shore lulled me to sleep. I don't know how long after that that James left but I did remember him placing his jacket over me.

The sun had gone down when I lifted my head. The night was dark, too dark. I could see in the distance, lights from the bridge and I could smell campfires burning behind me in the woods. Where was James? Missy? Jonathan? I could not see them and when I tried to stand, someone reached from behind me and pulled me back down. I almost screamed.

"Stay low." It was James. "Listen, if you can." He said. I could hear voices and saw a circle of people maybe fifty to a hundred feet away. They were talking, rather low but animatedly. You could tell that they were excited about something.

I heard a female laugh. It was her. My stomach turned. Her laugh rang through me like a hot branding iron.

James whispered, "Listen closely to them, Warren's not there, but they are talking about the two of you." I leaned forward slumping down behind the driftwood we had sat on earlier. "Don't move! His voice whispered, worried that we would be spotted.

We both held still and listened.

"Warren said it was all on her computer." The woman was talking and I hated her voice.

"Then we have to get that computer." It was Mr. Hudgeson. I started thinking, what could be on my computer that was not available to him? All of my research was always downloaded to the ones at work. Only since I have been at James home have there not been daily reports. I didn't understand.

James tapped my shoulder. "Let's go. We need to get out of here." He whispered. I waved him away. I was intent on hearing her.

"He will try again. You know he will." She was getting upset. A second male voice spoke. "We could just try and get rid of Warren." Man number three cleared his throat. "He's right you know? And what if he succeeds this time? What if he succeeds? Would it be more difficult to just remove Warren from the picture all together?" The question posed caused mumbling amongst the group.

Mr. Hudgeson took charge. "No! He's important for now. He will continue to try, but we still have some pull with him. He will listen to reason, and if he doesn't, then, you can do what you want to him."

"What about that attorney and the doc?" She spat out the question. "They'll have to go only if Warren doesn't succeed. If he does succeed, then they will not be any wiser. We'll just take care of things with Warren then."

I gulped. I didn't know what was going on, but I knew that I had what they needed. If Warren got what he needed, which might mean me being dead, then he was dead? Am I missing something? This was all too complicated.

James was pulling me away from the scene. I knew I wanted to stay, but I had to go or risk being discovered. The moon was bright over the ocean and I felt sure that if they paid enough attention, we would be found quite easily.

We wound our way out to the parking lot and to the limo. Jonathan and Missy were not there, but James was sure they were close. I got into the car and waited, thinking. After a few more minutes of waiting, James opened the door, "Stay with Daniel at the car." He left me to go and find Missy and Jonathan.

I nodded my head. More time to think. I watched as James walked back toward the beach. Daniel leaned on the side of the car waiting. I wondered what he must be thinking about. Did he have friends die often? What a horrible thought.

Ten minutes passed slowly and Jonathan and Missy were seen walking towards the car. Daniel walked towards them. I was sure that he was telling them that James had gone back to look for them. He told them what was happening on the beach and once more, we were all waiting.

When James hadn't returned in another ten minutes, Missy climbed into the car with me and Jonathan walked back towards the beach.

Finally, I couldn't stand it any more. I opened the door and stepped out. I had to breathe. Missy followed me. We stood talking to Daniel and waited. This was not what I had expected to do.

I was hoping that everyone would make it back quickly so we could leave. I didn't know if or when Warren would show up. In fact I knew that I couldn't *take* it if he did.

I stood silently by the car.

Waiting.

Daniel kept pacing near the edge of the parking lot. Back and forth, back and forth. It added to the feeling that things were not right.

A scream suddenly penetrated the darkness. Loud shouts and running all startled us. I wanted to think it was the campers and children pulling pranks but I knew different. I wanted to run and yet inexplicably, I was drawn to the woods and through to the beach.

Daniel called after me, too far away to stop me before I entered the woods. I had my own fears.

I walked carefully through the dark underbrush and was immediately aware of people talking all around me. Campers were coming out of their respective tents and trailers with lanterns and flashlights.

When I reached the beach, the sand felt much wetter than it had been less than an hour ago. That it would be much harder to run in if I had to. I hadn't thought about that. I wouldn't get far anyway because I was even weaker now than I had been when I sat with James on the beach.

I bent over and took off my shoes again and as I came back up, my head began to swim. I knew then that I was in trouble.

It had been a long day and I hadn't eaten but the little bit of a breadstick. Bending over always made me light-headed these days. I tried to catch my breath, and steady myself when I saw them. The crowd of people that I had been listening to were only feet from me. It wasn't that I could see them clearly, it was more their shapes that I was familiar with. They were all speedily walking away from the beach.

As they began to separate, I tried to keep track of the number of people and compare them with my memory of earlier. I waited and listened and watched them as they disappeared into the trees. Where was the woman? Ms. Coronado. I dropped to the ground, hoping she wasn't near me and wishing I had the cover of the driftwood that I had had during the day.

The crowd had begun to disperse through the woods. I walked quiet and low over to where they had been. I couldn't see who might have screamed. I suddenly really wanted to know what had happened to Ms. Coronado. Had I seen her when I walked up? I couldn't remember, but I didn't want to be caught by her either.

I thought about it for a minute. It really could have been campers or their kids that screamed. After all, camping had that effect on people. You often did things out of the ordinary. Teens in particular, got away with almost anything on vacation.

Exasperated, I shook my head. This was really stupid of me. No one was on the beach. I was alive and not lying on the beach. I was sure now that the scream had been someone scared by a sibling or a playful husband.

I began backing up to the shore line, scanning for anyone on the beach. Looking left and right, I still saw nothing. I had just decided to go back to the car when I fell over backwards.

The driftwood was probably pulled into the woods to form a place to sit for young lovers to make out on. I laughed. It was just one more obstacle for me. Driftwood was wonderful when you needed it and a hazard when you didn't. I stood up again and begin my new route through the trees.

I looked back at the beach one more time and made my decision to go as quickly as I could to the parking lot. I needed to get back to where there was relative safety. Fear overruled curiosity.

I must be crazy to have run off into the woods towards the scream. What was wrong with me? Didn't I have enough drama in my life? A change of heart occurred in me just then. I suddenly felt that I needed to stay with James and his family for just a little while longer. I realized that I really did care for them. And besides, I could gather more information. I walked slowly, looking all around me, hoping against hope that I had not strayed to far south of the parking lot. I didn't want to run into any one of those people on my own.

I tripped again falling backwards. I cried out and then screamed. I covered my mouth shutting off the scream almost as soon as it left my mouth. I couldn't stand up. I looked at what my legs were draped over. I was screaming again. I closed my eyes and pulled myself away from her. I put my hands over my ears shaking violently.

"Bria! Bria!" Someone, I didn't know who, was pulling me to my feet.

"Bria, stop screaming! Stop!" I couldn't hear them for my screams. He put his hand over my mouth and stepped back as if to drag me away. We bumped into Jonathan.

"It's okay. You're all right." He pushed my hair back out of my face. I was trembling uncontrollably. I looked down at my feet and began screaming again, trying to get away from the scene that played out on the ground before me.

There she was, the woman Warren had been with. Blood was all over her head and her neck and her clothing and around the ground where she lay. Jonathan stepped up beside James.

"Bria, stop." James elbowed Jonathan and looked down. They began to move, walking as fast as they could, with me in between them towards the parking lot. In a matter of minutes we reached Daniel, who had been circling with Missy.

When we stepped through the woods, he sped to where we would step out onto the blacktop. When we were in the door of the limo, Jonathan turned around and spoke quietly to Daniel. Suddenly we were moving fast, making our way to the exit.

We entered the four lane street a little too quickly. I wasn't ready, my body and mind numb, so when Daniel turned to the left, cutting across the lanes, I slammed into the door. The side of my head hit squarely in the metal window frame. I looked up at it and noticed that it hadn't cracked but my head really hurt. I felt the oozing blood pulse down my cheek but I thought for sure that it was minor, given all the blood I had already seen today.

I struggled to keep calm. Hadn't I been through enough? I reached up and touched my head. No one had yet noticed it because of the dark interior of the limo. I slowly pulled my fingers away, knowing what I would see. "Too much blood," I said to myself.

"Jonathan?" I held out my hand for him to see. He looked at me, not grasping yet that I had been injured. He pulled out a handkerchief and wiped my hand.

It took only a second to understand that he thought I had touched the woman on the beach. I put my hand to my head again and brought back down a fresh coating of my blood.

"Jonathan?"

"Bria, we're okay, and we're going to call someone to go there." He said taking my hand again. Fresh blood back on the hand he had just cleaned. He wasn't thinking clearly at all.

"Jonathan…" I pleaded. He looked at me. I pulled my hand away and reached up to my temple. He followed it with his.

"Oh, Bria. No." He sounded exasperated. I didn't know what to do, but I knew it was too much. He leaned me over and into James' lap, blood streaming from the laceration, he took the handkerchief and pressed it against the side of my head.

"How did that happen?" Missy asked as she reached up into the front seat through the still opened window. She unzipped the backpack, pulling out gauze and medical tape.

"What do you want me to do?" Daniel asked from the front seat. "Just keep driving. Take us home." James was wasted. His hand began rubbing my arm shoulder to fingertips, "What am I going to do with you?" I didn't speak. All I could do was glare at the sticky dark liquid on my fingers.

Minutes passed. My head was throbbing in pain. Wasn't it enough that I had seen other's blood spilt? I was ready to give up. Maybe that was the answer, I could call up Mr. Hudgeson and offer myself up for whatever his purposes were if he would get Warren and everyone else to just leave us alone. The terror had to stop.

Chapter Twenty-Two
Only For a Little While

The car turned left, right, slowed down and sped up. I could tell that I was getting completely lost. It didn't help that my head was spinning and throbbing like every beat of my heart was sending crashing courses of blood ready to spill out of my barely bandaged head.

Missy was huddled in Jonathan's arms and I lay still in James' lap. I could hear the three of them whispering but I didn't want to open my eyes. I let them believe that I was sleeping. I didn't move.

"What happed back there?" Missy whispered.

"You don't want to know." James sounded so tired. As did Jonathan. Jonathan said. "She stumbled across another body." Missy gulped in air. "Oh no." I could feel her trembling in the seat across from me.

"It was Warren's girl from the courtroom. I could tell by her face she was the same woman. She had that smug look just as she did then." He stopped. "I don't think that even she deserved this." "Who do you think did it? How do *you* think she died?" Jonathan sounded like he already knew.

"I don't know, I didn't even kneel down to check if she was still alive." I knew he was looking at Jonathan, unsure of everything. "She was dead. Her throat was slit." Jonathan said. "The amount of blood on her neck and her shirt," I heard him sigh, "It must have been a very vicious attack."

231

Silence.

Nothing but the thump, thump, thump, of the tires broke the silence as we drove over some poorly maintained road. It was occasionally joined by the sound of cars that rarely passed us by. I noticed the difference when we pulled onto a much smoother road. There were now no other cars. We were slowing down. No. I thought. I don't want to get out. I am just going to stay here and sleep. Forever. If I didn't go out, no one could see me and I couldn't put anyone else in danger.

"Don't wake her." Jonathan said. "She is going to be in even worse shape than before." I was grateful. I heard the door open and felt them leaving the car. That's right, I thought, just leave me here. No such luck though.

Of course!

Jonathan came around to the opposite side and told James to get out. He slid out from underneath me, Jonathan crouching over me from my knees, lifted my head and shoulders, slowly passing me into James arms.

I could feel his chest rise and fall in that now all too familiar way as he carried me up front steps. I heard keys jingle and then fit into the lock on the door. I felt the light as it was turned on through my closed lids. Daniel closed and locked the door behind us and everyone walked into another room.

James lay me gently down onto the couch. Moving my head hurt. "Oh," I murmured not meaning to and tried to open my eyes again for the first time since I had been bandaged. Instantly, James was on his knees in front of me.

"Bria just lie still, you'll be fixed up in no time." He meant the words to be encouraging, supportive, but what I heard was the sound of a man that was completely coming apart and didn't need me adding to his troubles.

I sat up, pushing his hands away. I needed to stand and I needed to pace. I needed to be doing something. I needed to get away from them. My 'change of heart' plan to stay with them was now thrown out the window. I would get away as soon as possible.

Missy stepped in front of me, preventing me from moving. Her eyes met mine, her tears fresh on her face.

"I know." She said as she looked at me. She reached her hands out, taking my shoulders in hers and pulled me to her in an embrace.

She whispered in my ear. "I know." She said again. "I want to run away and hide, too." I nodded into her shoulder.

Why did I have to feel this so deeply? My tears came so easily now that it seemed as if I cried every day. My tears now were staining her pink shirt brown as it ran through the path of the blood that clung to my face.

"I know you think that it is your fault. It's not. Bria, it's not. Who knows why, but you are the one in danger. We are trying to make it right. I know what you've been thinking. I see it in your eyes."

I pulled away from her shoulder looking intently at her face. "I'm so afraid."

"So am I." She whispered. I closed my eyes to her tears. They would not prevent me from leaving them…at least until it was all over. "Don't hate me if I do, please." I whispered.

I sat back down; eyes still closed, and dropped my head onto the back seat cushion of the sofa.

Jonathan touched my arm. "Bria, I need to clean that wound better and maybe give you some stitches." I groaned. "Just let me die." I whispered.

I was too exhausted to give a damn any more. My patience had worn thin.

He dropped to his knees on the couch beside me. Removing the bandages from my head; he began the slow process of cleaning my face and assessing the damage.

"Bria?" It was Missy. "Mmmm," I answered. "We don't have any thing to numb you with, but you do need stitches. Do you want to go to the hospital?"

"No! Just do what you have to do." This time my tears were silent. I didn't want to sob. I didn't want any extra or stray needle holes because I couldn't control myself.

"Will you let Daniel hold your head still?"

"Whatever needs to happen."

"Daniel, come and hold her head still. James you hold her as best as you can. I don't want her moving." He drew in a deep breath. "Ready?" I didn't move. He took that as my sign to begin. And in truth, I guess it was.

Ten minutes later, he added a new gauze bandage to my head. Daniel released his hold on me. James pulled me closer to him, drawing me under his protective arm like he had so many times before.

The house slowly became silent. I realized no one was talking or moving when the clock above the mantle tick, tick, ticked loud and clear, moving second to second around its face.

No one had been ready for all of this. Even Daniel, whom I had assumed had been on much more important guard details than this one, seemed to be at a loss for words. We stayed where we dropped, all of us listening to the slow tick…tick…tick…tick.

Falling asleep wasn't so easy this time. It was uncomfortable and it was nerve wracking. First one, then another and then another, each person falling asleep. We all slept where we sat, uncomfortable or not. Daniel had pulled a chair up and placed it under the door knob.

It had been discussed that there was no protective detail here, but no one wanted to actually call and give away our location. We were frightened, but between the five of us, no one had any idea how we would keep from being found. We couldn't trust Mr. Hudgeson since we had seen him with Warren and on the beach in the circle of people. Someone in that group had killed Ms. Coronado. It was maddening. How many people were out there trying to kill me?

When I could find a way out, I would disappear from here. Maybe that was a good thing. I didn't know where here was and so how could I possibly endanger anyone else. There had to be somewhere that I could hide out at for a while.

It came to me in my drifting sleep. I would find a domestic violence shelter. I knew that they would help me without many questions. Now I had a plan as to where to go. I would leave soon. I had to leave them, no matter how perceptive Missy was, this was the best option.

The morning dawned but the sun was blocked from shining through the windows. The house was surrounded by trees. The thick shelter the trees provided could be seen through the curtains, but you could barely tell it was morning.

Daniel was the first to actually get up. He stretched and I watched him look around the small room we were all huddled in. He went to the fridge, looking in, shaking his head. It was empty. He opened cabinet doors and he closed them quietly as well. They too were empty.

Jonathan woke up next, his voice tired. "We'll need to make a run to the store." He walked over and clapped Daniel on the back. He looked back at me, and he put his finger to his lips, asking me to be quiet. "We'll be back in a few." He whispered.

The two of them opened the door and left through it, locking it as they shut the door behind them. I lay there, cuddled in the arms of a man terribly spent. Drained as he was, he was still trying to protect me.

I slipped out from where I had tried to sleep, and stretched slowly. I didn't want to get dizzy and end up on the floor. I'd probably just get another injury that would put me in the "oh Bria," category.

I was done. I didn't care if I went off and died somewhere. I couldn't take another minute of this cloak and dagger and hide and seek that we were playing.

I tiptoed around the house, checking out every room. I went to the bathroom, washed up and ran fingers through my hair. There was nothing I could do just now to fix it. I looked like I had been in a horrible accident.

The back of the house had three bedrooms and a mud room that opened into a massive back yard. There was a garage of some sort there and a storage building. I turned the doorknob and slowly opened it.

I walked out onto an attached wrap around porch. A porch swing grabbed my attention. It looked like it should be a part of some early 1900's novel. A young girl being courted by her true love as they sat on opposite ends of the swing, hands together in the middle.

What a foolish woman I was. I could see those things with my minds eye because that is what I had hoped for in my life.

A life I now doubted that I would get to live for much longer. I wasn't suicidal. I was just overwhelmed with it all.

I sighed as I stepped off the porch and walked towards the garage. Nothing was in there. I slowly strolled over to the storage building and looked inside.

Old couches, chairs and mattresses stood against one wall. On the other wall there stood several bits and pieces of someone's life. Toy chests, clothing, mirrors, a rocking horse. I was sure that these were memories stored here from Jonathan and James' childhood.

I opened the door, dust flying; I walked over to the couch and removed the sheet that draped over it. Again dust flew. I sat down on the exposed upholstery and pulled my legs up underneath me.

This was the remains of their youth. How I longed to be back in my youth, away from the horrors that were plaguing me and my friends. My eyes stung with the tears that streamed down my face. No sobs. No hysterics. Just tired tears. I lay down, folding my arms around my chest, again trying to keep in what was left of the broken pieces of my heart.

I only slightly remembered reaching down and pulling the sheet over me. I woke to find that I was completely covered. It was dark outside. I had slept the whole day away. Why hadn't they come and gotten me?

I sat up. Sweeping over me was a sense of relief. Had I escaped without even trying? It seemed as if no one had realized that I was still here on the property. I moved towards the door and stood.

Could I chance leaving and peering in to find out what was going on? I knew I had to risk it. If I was caught, it was simply an accident that I fell asleep. That at least was, after all, the truth.

I walked carefully to the back part of the porch. I looked in through the window and could not see anyone. I walked around to the left side where the kitchen was. I didn't know if there was another door or not, I had not been paying that much attention. I hoped that there were windows for me to peek into.

One step at a time, I moved along my path. I didn't hear anything or anyone. Were they even still here? I saw the light streaming from a window and crept low towards it. I rose up on tiptoes to peer in through the bottom of the window.

Missy sat at the table, her head in her hands. Crying. I knew what she must be feeling, but I would not go back to them until everything was over.

James walked in from another room. His head was down, his eyes sullen. He plopped into the chair at the table beside Missy. He covered his face with one of his hands, slumping down so low in the chair; he looked as if he would collapse out of it.

My heart was aching. Yearning to be in his arms and protected. But I knew what I had to do. I was sure that they would forgive me if I lived through it.

I still had to get past them without being seen. Just where were Daniel and Jonathan? I followed the porch towards the corner of the house. The car wasn't there. Maybe they had gone looking for me. I walked down the stairs and staying in the shadows, followed the driveway from the trees.

I knew that I was taking my life into my own hands. I knew I was weak. I knew I needed the injections at regular intervals, but I had to take this chance. I would rather die than to have one more death on my hands.

It took me twenty minutes or more to reach the main road. I looked out from behind the trees for any sign of Daniel and Jonathan. I didn't know how far I would get, but I had to try if I was to spare them of the killer or killers that were tracking me.

I kept off the road, watching for signs of traffic of any kind. Several hours later, with way too much stopping and starting, I found my way to a convenience store.

It had probably been less than five miles but I walked in and went straight to their bathroom. I took my time, breathing in and out, relaxing. I kept pushing the dryer button to have some kind of noise around me.

When I finally exited the bathroom, the woman behind the counter stared at me. I walked up to the counter. I cleared my throat.

"I'm sure that you don't get many questions like this, but do you know if there is a domestic abuse shelter near by?" She looked at my haggard appearance and the bandage on my head and she nodded.

"Finally had enough?" she asked. I answered. "Yes. I just need to rest and put together a plan." She reached up and switched off the open sign. "We close in an hour anyway." She winked at me.

She took the money out of the drawer and dropped it uncounted into a floor safe. She walked around the counter and took me by the hand. "Come with me." I was too worried about the danger I had put James, Missy, Jonathan and Daniel in to not follow her.

"Elaine," she said. I looked at her. "What?"

"My name. It's Elaine."

"Thanks. Umm, I'm Nikki," I told her taking the name of my cousin's daughter. I often used her name as an alias when we had to work on certain research phone calls that required us to not use our real names. It was all that came to me at the time. I couldn't and wouldn't give her my real name. It would lead too many people out searching for me.

She unlocked the doors and motioned for me to get in. I did so without hesitation. Death now would still be better than subjecting the others to whatever cruelty Warren or whoever, was planning.
She drove for over an hour. Maybe, I didn't really know. She never said a word. Never asked a single question. Finally, we entered a highway and I decided to question her.

"Where are we going?"

"To a home for battered women." She looked as if I should have known. "But where is it?" She looked over at me again. "Honey, don't you know where you are?" I shook my head. "No, I've been walking and running for a day." I lied.

"Poor thing." She picked up her cell phone and called someone. "I'm bringing you someone," she said into the small phone. I could hear only mumbling coming from the phone.

"I don't think she has anything. She has been walking and running all day trying to get away. We'll be there in another hour." Again she listened. When she hung up the phone she said. "You're all set."

"Thank you so much." It was all I could say.

An hour or so later, we were pulling into the driveway of a large Victorian home. I had seen the north signs on the highway, so I knew that we were probably just before the border to Maryland. If I still had any sense of direction left at all.

There were windows everywhere and there was a plaque on the door. "Never believe no one will believe you." I thought about that. I understood it. I stumbled my way in behind Elaine. She talked to a tall and very statuesque woman that looked as if she could take care of herself and probably many others.

"Keep in touch, Elaine. Don't be a stranger." Elaine then turned and walked out the door. The tall woman introduced herself.

"Just call me Dee." She said and she walked over and locked several locks on the door.

"Nikki? Elaine said your name was? There is a room here for you until you are able to go to the next step. We will help you as much as we can, but you are not to tell anyone where you are. It will put others in jeopardy. Do you think you can honor that?" I nodded. We headed towards the stairs when she stopped, "Do you need medical care?"

"What?" I asked her. But then I saw her eyes linger on the bandage on my head. "Not any more." I answered her.

She walked me slowly up the first flight of stairs and handed me a key. I turned the lock and though the room was plain and simple, I was happy to see that there was a bathroom and a bed.

"Thank you so much. Really."

She smiled. "Just get some rest. You look as if you need it. We'll plan tomorrow." She pulled the door closed and I heard her descend the stairs. I locked the door, walked over to the bed and toppled into it. I was beyond tired. I hoped that I would be able to make it until the morning.   At least here, there was a sense of peace.

Chapter Twenty-Three
A Little Band of Women

Peace.

Well sort of. At least no one here knew what I was going through. No one knew who I was. No one would come for me here. I closed my eyes and I knew that the nightmares would come and there would be no James to sooth them away and lull me back to sleep.

I kept seeing new scenes in my dreams. Blood splattered across a windshield mingled with the blood soaked shirt of the woman on the beach. What was her name again? My brain was so tired I couldn't remember. She had a name. I began to cry. She was somebody's daughter, somebody's sister maybe, and someone's girlfriend. I knew who that someone was.

His face came glaring back into my nightmare. I saw us standing by the Christmas tree in our new home and I followed the scene up to our first night in the new home. I watched it with tenderness as we finally collapsed into each other's arms spent and happy. His arms were around me and he promised to love me forever.

Where did that moment go? Even though that was now a distant memory, I did not want him to hurt as he had hurt me. I wondered, somewhere in my sleeping, if Warren even knew that his new love was dead.

I was suddenly very awake as her bleeding body entered my nightmare. Did *anybody* know that she was dead? My dreams had pointed out the fact that none of us had reported what we had seen.

How could we not report it? What was wrong with us? We were so wrapped up in our own misery. We forgot or at least, I forgot. Maybe Daniel had called. I didn't know but I couldn't help but think what if no one knew?

I shook my head, pain shooting through it. Oh my….What if I died and no one knew? I didn't want to think about that. I couldn't think about that.

My brain was frazzled. I pulled my knees up into me and hugged them.

I found my heart breaking for her family. Suddenly, I realized that I didn't even know if the murder of the guard had been reported. Not for sure anyway. I was sure that someone had. Yes, I was sure. Wasn't I? I remembered Daniel saying it had been reported. But why would we report one and not the other? I shook my head. I couldn't be sure of much these days.

No! I could trust them. They were doing the right thing. I chose to think that way.

I don't know how long I sat up in bed. I vaguely remember sliding back under the blanket and back onto the pillow. Everything was in slow motion. Sheer exhaustion kept the nightmares away from then on.

I heard the door open, but I couldn't open my eyes. I heard someone walking in my room, but I hadn't even the strength to acknowledge it. I lay there motionless. My mind, trying to focus, simply would not allow it.

Hours later, I finally came out of my stupor. I rolled over to find that a breakfast tray had been placed on the top of a dresser I hadn't even noticed the night before. A note lay on top of it.

"Nikki, Get some rest. You arrived late and it looks like you still need it. When you are ready, come to the office on the first floor. First door on your left. We'll discuss what your options are. Dee"

I was grateful for the non-suspicious nature of the woman. She had probably heard and seen much. "Nikki," oh yeah. I had forgotten. I would probably have to come up with a last name. I decided that I would use Nikki's whole name. After all, she was only two. She would have no traceable record of any kind.

I had to think. As a researcher, I was well aware of how people were found. LexisNexis, Elocate, Edetective, USAtrace, all of these could be used to find a person. Sometimes, even if they were working very hard not to be found.

I would have to be careful how much information I gave out. I looked abused enough. It was true enough. I was physically, mentally, and emotionally damaged enough. I wondered just how long I could stay here and use this place to hide out.

I took the toast from the tray and took a bite. Dry. Very dry. I quickly picked up the glass of juice. I didn't like that feeling of dryness in my mouth. It was too much a reminder of how really sick I still was.

I didn't know what I would do about the missing injections, but I felt that I would survive. I had to survive. I giggled. "Or die trying."

Wasn't that every hero's last words? What the heck was wrong with me?

I finished what I could of the now cold breakfast and almost crawled to the bathroom. I needed to at least freshen up. Maybe that would give me a boost of energy. It had before.

I was surprised to find that on the toilet seat was a bundle of clothes and towels with trial packets of all the toiletries that I might need. A printed note this time stated.

"These are for you. They aren't much and they may not fit correctly. All we ask is that you send us a replacement outfit when you are back on your feet."

I smiled. If I survived, I would make sure that there were fresh new clothes for everyone at the shelter. They seemed to have thought of everything.

I knew that I was so weak that I wouldn't be able to do much, but I ran the bath water and washed up from the side of the tub. I put on the clothing that had been left for me and pulled the covers up on the bed.

I knew that I had to make my way down the stairs somehow. I put the room key into my pocket and grabbed the tray. I carefully pulled my door closed and leaned against the door. Sliding down the wall, my one hand holding on for dear life to the banister I made my way to the bottom step. I stood leaning against the doorway at the bottom of the stairs.

To the right was a TV and a kitchen just beyond it. I murmured hello and lowered my eyes. I walked through, hoping I didn't really look like death warmed over, to place my things where it looked like everyone else had on a counter by the sink. For some reason I wanted to fill up the sink and wash the dishes but I was so weak, I knew it was next to impossible.

I smiled, feeling good about the fact that some things still were instinctual. I walked slowly back through the TV room and across the hall to the first door to the left of the stairs. I knocked and leaned against the door frame.

"Come in." A pleasant voice called out. It was not the voice of Dee, but I couldn't think about that. I shyly opened the door and walked through to a lovely little office with a small elderly woman sitting behind a desk.

"Nikki?" she asked. "Yes, that's me." She motioned for me to sit down in the chair in front of her desk. I practically fell into it. She stared at me. "Child, do you need to go to the hospital?

"No!" I said a little too quickly. "He'll find me there." I said hoping she understood.

"Dee said that you looked bad. She'll be back for her shift later. I'm Ruth. I own this house." She looked at me. "Nikki, I need to ask you some very hard questions. Do you think you can answer them for me?"

I nodded. What choice did I have? If I wanted their help, I had to be ready.

I was in her office for less than an hour. The questions hard to think about, but not hard to answer. I simply told her the truth. My abuse was at the hands of Warren. There were already police looking

248

for him. There were no children involved. The end result is that I can stay here for thirty days before they will place me somewhere else.

I was happy that it was that easy. I would have to work around the house, taking my turn with chores. "I won't require them until you at least look like you can do the work." She had said. I felt guilty. I knew it would only get worse from here.

I was expected not to ask personal questions. I could make no calls without one of the workers beside me, and I could not give out my location to anyone. I would be given a weeks worth of clothing and I was responsible for them being kept clean as well as my room.

Now all I needed to do was stay well. I would listen to the news and see what was happening. I would call the authorities to see if he had been captured. That would be easy to do in front of the "phone police", since I really needed to know.

The first two days was easy. I was not required to do much but try and recover from my injuries. The next two were very difficult. I could barely get out of bed. I was weaker and weaker and finally I knew that I could not go much further with my charade. It was easy around here after all there wasn't much to do. I stayed in my room or watched TV but even that was too much for me without the injections. The next two days I didn't leave my room.

I spent too much time listening. I had listened to other women and their abuse stories. How many of them really were just like me. I discovered that no one ever really marries an abuser. We are all in love with those men before they ever lay a hand on us. We blindly believe their words *and* their apologies.

I was lying on the bed when Dee knocked on my door. "You have a visitor." She said. I looked terrified I'm sure because she quickly added. "It's Elaine. The woman who brought you to us?" I breathed a sigh of relief.

"Are you okay to take visitors? You look like road kill and getting worse by the day." I nodded. I did not get up.

"I'll send her up." She walked back out the door and down the stairs.

A couple of minutes later, Elaine knocked on the door. "Come on in, Elaine." I tried once more to sit up. I couldn't. Elaine walked over and sat on the end of my bed.

She didn't beat around the bush. "I know who you are." She said it way too fast.

I dropped my head back on my pillow. Tears that I hadn't really shed in a week flowed immediately down onto the pillow. I swallowed hard, choking off the tears. "How, what, do you know?"

"Private detective came by asking questions about whether or not anyone had seen you. He had your picture and everything. Said you were really very sick and would need medical care if any of us ever saw you."

She stopped. "I told them I would call them if I found a sick woman anywhere."

I tried again to sit up on the bed. She reached out and helped me. "You look like they were telling the truth."

I sighed. "They were. I am very sick. I was just tired of my ex trying to kill me. I didn't want them to get hurt in the process."

"That's what friends are for." She looked down at her hands. "I know. I've been there. I abandoned mine years ago, and I know how much it still hurts to be without them."

"Can you help me? I need to get away from here. I appreciate their help, but I will not put anyone here in another bad situation." She stayed quiet for a few minutes. I could see the wheels turning in her brain. "I'll help, but you have to let me call them and get you medical help at least."

"No!" I begged her.

"Look you're no good to anyone if you're dead. There has to be a way to do this. I don't know why you're sick. But even around here they have noticed that you always wear you shirt sleeves pulled down. Are you recovering?"

"Recovering?" Slowly it dawned on me. "Drugs?" I shook my head. "No. I have been taking trial drugs designed to help create a vaccine or a cure for cancer."

"Do you have cancer?"

"No. Not really. Not yet."

She took it in. "We have to get you out of here. You'll die if you don't get what you need, right?" I nodded my head.

She wrapped her arm around my waist and stood me up. Together, we walked down the stairs. She nodded towards Dee as we met her at the bottom of the stairs. Dee helped me the rest of the way to Elaine's car. The rest of the abused women of the home stood on the front porch, watching. Apparently, every one knew I was in bad shape.

Dee, put her arms around me and said. "You need your friends. They really can help you where we can't. But when this is all over, come back for a visit. We could use another voice against domestic violence." She backed away, shutting my door. I knew that I would come back if I survived. I would be that voice. I would be heard.

Chapter Twenty-Four
A Really Bad Idea

My head dropped back against the seat. "Thanks Elaine. I didn't know what to do any more but do we have to call them first?"

"No. In fact, I have another plan. I'm gonna take you to another place. It's one of the hotels that I stayed in. They never think to look in fancy hotels."

"What exactly are we doing?" I was too weak to be afraid.

"We're going to put you up in a hotel, and then I will go somewhere else and call your detective friend."

I wanted to protest, but she kept going. "I'll tell him that you want to be alone but that you really do need some medicine. I'll make sure he understands that you're really sick but that you're not willing to compromise."

I hoped that would work. But I wasn't sure. No matter what, I would have to depend on someone else for a little help.

We drove on. When she pulled into a Marriot parking lot, I asked her if she was sure about this. She nodded and then went in and got a room for me. I stayed just where I was. By the time she came back to the car, I was sure I wasn't going to make it. The medicine would be too late.

"You really need to pull it together so that we can get you into the room." She helped me out of the car and helped me to stand. I didn't think I could make it.

"Nikki, you have to stand up. We'll walk arm in arm and hurry to the elevator. Then you can rest while we ride to the floor and we'll take it slow to the room."

She seemed to be good at thinking on the fly. I guess that comes with the territory of abuse. I had begun to do so as well.

Although my decisions weren't always the wisest of choices.

We linked our arms together and walked as quickly as I dared to the elevator. We stood for only a few moments when one of them opened. Stepping in, I only barely waited for the door to close before collapsing against the corner railings.

We reached the room quick enough after that. Elaine left me then and went to make her phone call, not wanting to have her call traced to a specific area or to the hotel.

Things were happening too fast. I lay on my bed, wishing I were dead. My whole body was betraying me. I wanted everything to be better but I couldn't see how it would be. I knew that I didn't have the strength to help myself. Would Elaine be able to give me the medicine I so desperately needed? I didn't know.

She was gone for more than two hours. Elaine came back with news. "Daniel Massey? Heard of him?" She asked as she locked the door behind her. I nodded. I hadn't known his last name but it couldn't be anyone else.

She walked over and sat on the second bed. "He met me at the store. He said that he would get what he could from your doctor, and meet me back at the store."

I stared at her. "Daniel is a professional detective. He'll follow you." I was resigned to my fate, too weak to care just now.

She looked at me. "I didn't think of that." She began to fidget. I could tell that she was upset with herself. "It's okay. I don't care anymore." I looked over at her. I am just thankful for your help." She lay down on the bed. She was lost in thought about what had happened. I could tell that she really was upset.

"Maybe, I'll make it a couple of more days and Warren really will be caught. Just don't go back to meet him. I'll be fine. I have been so far."

She nodded.

"I'll keep checking on you though. Okay?" I smiled. I really did appreciate everything she did for me. "I'm ordering room service." She picked up the phone and placed a sandwich order. I wasn't sure how, but I was going to repay her kindness.

We both were lying down, the TV on, waiting for the order to come up. We were lost in our own thoughts about what we were doing. What we were going to do.

"When do you have to go?" She looked at her watch. "I'll call them soon and change where I want to meet them. Then I'll see if I can't be a little sneakier when I come back."

She was finally looking a little pleased with herself. "Just don't get into trouble. No speeding ticket or car crash or anything." I tried to laugh, but it hurt.

We both got involved with a movie that was on the TV and were a little shocked when the knock came at the door. She was up like a flash. "Who is it?" she asked through the door. We were both relieved when room service answered.

I tried to eat. She did eat. When we were finished, she walked over to the window and pulled open the curtains. "I hate to go and leave you like this, but I do have to meet them somewhere. I also have to go to work so I'll just get what he gives me and come back in the morning."

I thought, I might not be here. If I could save my strength, I was going to call myself a cab and get Elaine out of this mess as well. Everyone that was willing to help me would be in danger, and she only had a minimum investment in me. No sense in burdening her any more. I could see the conflict in her.

"That's perfect. I'll be able to rest up and you'll be safe at work. It works out great."

She looked skeptically at me. "I'll be fine." I reassured her. She looked at her watch. "Okay. I'm out of here." She hugged me gently and walked to the door. "I'm locking this, but you will have to flip the door lock." I nodded.

I didn't. The night was so long. I tossed and turned and when I couldn't sleep, I sat up against the pillows. I had to get to my work. If I could get there, I would be able to get the vials of medicine myself.

I knew the cleaning crew was at the office between four and seven in the morning. I needed to do several things in the meanwhile. I called to the front desk. "I need to switch rooms. Can you do that for me?"

"Is there anything wrong with your room?" I hadn't thought of that.

"I am highly sensitive to cigarette smoke. The room smells of it."

"That is a non-smoking room, ma'am."

I interrupted him, "Nevertheless I can smell it. Please switch rooms for me."

"Someone will be up to help you and bring up your new room key."

It was about thirty minutes before someone came to help me move. I walked so slowly down the hall to the elevator that the young man kept waiting on me. Finally I asked. "Are we going up or down?" "Up. The only room available is on the top floor. So you're getting a free upgrade for the inconvenience."

"The top floor? What type of rooms are on the top floor?" "The very best ma'am. Our luxury suites." I assumed he thought I was being even more picky, but I didn't care, I needed to lie back down before I fell down.

"Of course. I wasn't implying otherwise. I'm just very sensitive to smoke and I couldn't sleep because of it. I'm really exhausted." I hope that would stave off any curiosity.

He didn't answer. I was frustrated. I would probably need some help to get to the room if this took much longer. The elevator stopped at last and the doors opened. He stepped out but as I started to walk, I tried to move but I couldn't and ended up falling into him, my body just too tired to lift my feet. "Sorry," I said.

"Are you okay, ma'am? He seemed genuinely concerned now.

"No, I'm not." Tears of pain and exhaustion began, "I don't think I can make it to my room. Can you help me to it?" He put his arm around my waist and helped me limp to the room.

When he opened up the door I asked him, "Could you help me to the chair?"

Again, "Yes ma'am." I think he thought I was crazy.

"Listen," I said as he carefully put me in the chair.

"I need someone that I can count on and trust. Can that be you?" He didn't really look to be that old, but I didn't have anyone else that could help me do what I needed them to do.

"Sure ma'am."

"Okay, sit down for a minute." He sat down at the table across from me. I put my head in my hands and waited for a moment, trying to decide how much I needed to tell him.

I took as deep a breath as I could muster and then told him everything that I thought was important for him to know in order to illicit his help.

I told him nothing about the murders or my friends, just of me being sick and about Warren and his attempts to hurt me. Again I said nothing about Warren trying to kill me. His mouth hung open most of the time as if he couldn't believe everything I was telling him.

"I'll help." He finally said. "What do you want me to do?"

"I need it to look like I checked out of here. I don't want anyone to know that I am here." I watched his face. He looked like he was following my story. "Look, I don't want to get you in trouble, but I don't know who else to turn to. I don't want my family to get hurt. As long as he doesn't know where I am, they are safe."

"Ma'am?"

"Yes."

"My mom and I had to leave because my dad beat both of us. I got you covered." He smiled a big bright toothy smile.

I laughed, sort of. "Okay. Do you have a car?" His eyes went to the floor.

"I do have a car, but it's a piece of junk. That's why I am working here. To save up for one."

"I'll make you a deal." I was getting exhausted. Talking was hard. "I have a car that I'll give you for your services."

He was all smiles again. "Really? You're not screwing with me are you?"

I smiled. "No. What's your name?"

"It's on the tag." He smiled, "Sorry, it's Nick.

I had to laugh. "I'm Nikki." He laughed too. It just seemed funny.

"Can you come back tomorrow morning?"

"Sure, what time?"

"I don't really know where we are, but I have to be in DC by six. So what time shall we leave to get there on time?"

"Five."

"Is that too early for you?"

"Not if there's a car involved." He was excited.

"Thanks, Nick."

He walked out the door, locking it behind him. I felt better already. Mentally anyway. Physically, I didn't know just how long I would last.

Chapter Twenty-Five
An Unlikely Hero

The wee hours of the morning crept on with sleep having been little or non existent. I was up, ready and waiting when Nick showed up.

"At your service, Nikki." He smiled and together we walked to the elevator. "You don't look so good."

"Yeah, one of the places we have to go is to get some of the medicine I left behind. I have extras at work. If we get there before the cleaning crew leaves, I can get some to last until Warren is caught."

"Okay which way do we go?" he asked as we climbed into his little Honda Accord. It wasn't comfortable and it was very old, but it was his to drive. I remembered that. My first car was an old piece of junk but it got me around. I was glad I had decided to give him my Mustang.

"We need to head to I-95."

"On our way." He was too excited about this.

We got onto I-95 and headed towards DC. It was still very dark and I wasn't sure he was familiar with the area at all.

"Which exit?" he asked as he drove with that cocky ease of a teenager.

I told him which exit and we made our way to where I had worked for the past several years. I asked him to wait for me, but when I tried to get out, I could barely walk.

"You aren't doing this alone." He got out and came to help me.

I knocked on the door and waved to the cleaning crew chief. Yolanda recognized me and let me in. "You look like you still need to be in the sick bed." She looked me up and down, her grandmotherly eyes watching me closely.

"I know, but I have to get some things from the office and get back in time for my morning therapy."

"Oh, this is my nephew, Nick. I'm not supposed to drive so he's playing chauffeur today." She seemed appeased.

"Come on Nick, I'll show you my office. We'll be gone before you know it." I told her as we walked away.

We made it back to my office and I told Nick that we needed to get into the physicians area where all of my medicine was stored. We watched for the cleaning staff to move to the front offices to clean.

"Could you help me get in there and then watch the door for me?"

"Of course." He was loving this. I must remember that when this is all over so that I can straighten him out about everything. I made my way across the room and into the cabinets. I knew just how the vials were marked; I had gotten enough of my earlier injections in this very room. I grabbed several bottles and several syringes. I chose the smallest needles, because I knew that I would have to do it myself. The only thing I didn't know was how much to use. I thought about it quickly. I would have to try and steal the information.

"Nick, I'm ready to go but we need to stop at my desk for a minute." He walked over and took hold of my waist. "You really don't look like you're gonna make it." We walked to my desk and I turned on the computer. I tried to wait for it to boot up, but the cleaning crew was packing up and I didn't have time. The rest would have to wait.

"Nikki?" I heard his voice. "Nikki? We better go." He was getting a little worried.

"Okay, let's get out of here." I would figure it out. I couldn't take chances. Not here where people might suspect what was going on. We walked out of the office just before the cleaning crew unplugged the rest of their vacuums. Nick backed out and pulled out just as the Security guards were arriving. I had forgotten about them. What was I thinking?

"Nick, you need to head to the Connecticut Avenue exit off 495 west, do you think you can find it?"

He laughed, "Of course I can. I've been there many times. That's down by Cinderella's Castle." I smiled. "Mormon Temple." I whispered.

"Yeah, that's it. I hear it on the traffic reports every morning when I work the morning shift." He patted my shoulder. "Take it easy and rest a little till we get there."

It was more than thirty minutes that passed by before he reached over to my knee, shaking it gently and said.

"I'm getting ready to exit. Which way do I go?" I opened my eyes. "Keep going towards the temple. Take the first light to the right. You'll be cutting through the park."

He slowed and exited. He took the first right. "You need to be careful from here on. Warren may be watching the house." I directed him to my street and said:

"Do you see that black Mustang? That's your car." He looked at me, his cheeks fat from his smile. "You gotta be kidding me?"

"Nope. It doesn't mean anything to me just now. I can't drive myself around."

"I can't let you do that. Besides, my mom would kill me. She'd think I stole it."

"I'll make out a gift ownership title for you." He was shaking his head already.

"Look, I saved for years for a Mustang before I got married. It was my dream car. My original one my ex sort of crashed. This is just the replacement, though it is much nicer. But, now it is just a reminder of things that hurt me. It's yours. Trust me. I don't want it."

"No." he said again. "But I'll make you a deal. I'll help you out and I'll drive your car to do it. We'll even switch the tags over so your ex won't figure it out. Does your garage work?"

He was becoming quite the schemer. "Yes." I answered him. Again, another person with an abusive background adapting quickly and planning ahead.

"Okay, here's the plan. I'm gonna park my car in your garage. We're gonna switch plates and take off in your car. I'll drive it until you need it and we'll switch back. Deal?"

"Deal." I said. I would give it to him later. When my life was back on track. Right now, I just wanted to get out of here. It was early morning. I wanted to be gone before we got stuck in traffic.

"Just make it quick, please."

"Where are the keys?"

"Oh," I thought for a minute. "Oh yeah, they're on the dining room table." Thank goodness they were. I was suddenly grateful that I had been caught by Jonathan and Missy.

Oh no, I remembered that James had hired house-sitters. "Nick, they may be hanging up. Look for the green Irish medallion on it. Oh and there should be a check book on the mail station by the kitchen phone. If you see it, bring it for me please. Oh yea, and I forgot that we hired house-sitters. I don't know if they are still sitting. Don't run into anyone."

He looked at me. "Don't worry, I don't see any cars here but yours right now."

"You'll have to break in the back door. I don't have any keys. Just do it quietly."

He shook his head laughing. "Got ya covered." He hopped out going to the back yard.

I waited patiently. I couldn't do anything else. I took one of the vials out and looked at it. Could I possibly give myself an injection? Nick was back before I could answer the question.

"The garage door opener?" he asked. "In the car, Nick." He smacked the side of his head. "Duh!" He went to the car and opened the garage. He came back and pulled his little Honda into my garage.

He was on my side almost instantly and helping me to my car, license plate in hand.

"You do know how to drive stick? Right?" He was looking at me like I was crazy.

"Every man knows how to drive stick." He shut my door and ran around to the driver's side door. The whole thing couldn't have taken more than five minutes. It was either youthful exuberance or he was scared to death of getting caught.

We took off going back towards the highway. I could see that he was enjoying himself. The feel of a new car under his capable young hands. I smiled. I knew that I could never take it away from him. I would just keep him doing me favors. Hmmm, I thought, another symbiotic relationship.

By the time we reached the hotel, he was on a natural high that I didn't think he could come down from.

"Nick, I don't think I'm gonna be able to make it on my own." He got out and quickly opened my door. "Don't worry, I'll get you up the back way."

He pressed the button locking the doors on the car. He smiled again as he heard the quick 'beep beep' of its alarm. His arm around my waist once again, we made our way to a side entrance. He pulled his badge out of his wallet and swiped it. The door beeped and we walked in and to the elevator. He patiently held me secure. When the doors opened, we walked several steps until he could hear the second elevator coming.

"Sorry," he said, "We gotta be faster than this." He picked me up, and ran carrying me to the room. "Key?" I pulled it out of my pocket and swiped it, still in his arms. I pushed the handle down and he shoved the door open with his foot.

"I don't want anyone to see me. I called in sick today."

I was surprised but it was very funny. He was being so helpful. He locked the door behind us and sat me on the bed. "You need your medicine don't you?" He looked a little scared as I pulled out the vials and the syringes.

"I don't know if I can do it myself."

He gulped. Okay so maybe he couldn't do it either. I rolled up my shirt sleeve. The IV cap lock still in place where it had been for weeks now. My arm was bruised horribly. I had been using it too much.

His eyes got big. "You need a doctor."

"No. I can do this. Don't worry."

"I don't think so. There's blood in the bottom." He was really afraid now.

"I will do it. We simply push the medicine through and it will clear it."

I put the needle in the vial, and pulled out some of the liquid. I wasn't sure how much to give myself, so I only filled it up half way. I tried to put the needle in the rubber IV cap. I simply didn't have enough strength to push the syringe.

Nick reached over and took it from me. I knew how I was going to feel. I would be passing out soon.

He took a deep breath and gently, slowly, pushed the fluid in. I could feel it affecting me. At least if it wasn't the right dose, I was quite sure that it couldn't be an overdose. Nick put the needle syringe back in its wrapping.

I closed my eyes. Nausea swept over me but there was no food to throw up. Darkness followed all too quickly this time, my body over exhausted and ready to accept it. I don't know what happened with Nick.

My sleep was back to my normal. Nightmares floated through my mind. I would scream and I would cry. Sometime in the afternoon,

I opened my eyes to find the clock saying it was after five o'clock. I had been sleeping most of the day. My forehead was covered with a cool wash cloth. Nick must have hung around for a few minutes anyway. I fell quickly back to sleep, needing it desperately.

The worst part was the scene on the beach. My body crumpled on the sand. My hair was tangled and bloody. That was a new twist. I screamed, waking myself up. I wanted to sit up, but I couldn't.

"Don't move. I think I overdosed you." There was so much panic in his voice.

"No." I answered him weakly. "It wasn't an overdose. It always makes me this way. I just usually have someone holding me. It calms the nightmares."

"I'm sorry. I shouldn't have left you."

"You left me?"

"Yes, after you fell asleep. But I came back. Told my mom I was helping out a friend by taking his shifts. She was stoked. More money for college."

"What about the car? Did she say anything about the car?"

"I told her it was his. I lied to her, telling her that it was his way of making sure I came back to take his shift." She bought it. Hook, line, and sinker." He was so proud of himself.

I closed my eyes again. This was getting to be too much for me. I needed someone to take over, but I just couldn't.

"Nikki? Are you gonna be ok?"

My nod was almost imperceptible. "I'll be back in an hour." He said.

"Wait. Nick you need some cash." He started shaking his head. "No Nick, you have to do this for me. I'll write you out a check. You have to cash it. I need to eat something. We need gas in the car. Lots of things. Just cash it for me. Please?"

I took his waiting as a yes.

He cleared his throat. "Some one asked for you this morning."

I pulled up on the bedside table. He moved to sit beside me on the bed and helped me to sit upright.

"Do you know who it was?"

"We think it was the lady that you checked in with."

I caught the word 'we'. "Oh no, Nick, who is the 'we' that you're talking about?"

"Oh, it's the friend who is pretending to give me his shifts. I'm paying him fifty bucks to keep an eye on things at the front desk for me and to confirm my story to my mom."

"Can you really trust him?" I was worried again.

"Yeah, he's a great guy. Besides, he'll help you when I'm not here." My mouth dropped open. "Nick." I was exasperated.

"Don't worry; really, he's a great guy. I help him out of scrapes all of the time." He paused, thinking. "Look, I know what you are going through. Not like a lady does, but we had to hide out too, my mom and I. You don't think you can trust anybody. But me and Casey, that's his name, by the way; us you can trust. I may be only nineteen, but I've been through hell with my mom. Case, well he's twenty-two, but we've both been through all kinds of crap. Neither one of us like men who beat up on women, we've both come from that background. If your ex ever shows his face around here, he'll get what's coming to him."

He was showing that youthful exuberance again.

I smiled. "And I thought you were maybe seventeen." He looked wounded. Boys! Men! They worried about being older while all we women want is to be seen as younger than we are. "It's a compliment. Nick. Even though I thought you were only seventeen, I still thought you were mature enough to trust and to help me."

He smiled and I noticed that his brilliant white smile and his bright blue eyes were gleaming. What a handsome young man. No wonder his mother trusted him so much. I knew he must be her pride and joy. He had probably been the high school hero as well. I hadn't noticed all that before.

"What about girlfriends? I don't want to keep you from your girlfriends."

He was blushing. "I don't have any. They don't really go for boys with ratty little cars."

"Hey maybe that'll change with me driving around in your car!" He was getting even more excited. "Casey thought it was cool, too. He drives a Jeep. But girls love jeeps. But he doesn't have any trouble with girls. They fall all over him."

I was writing the check out for him to cash. "Nick, before you go, I need another injection." I had looked at the clock. It was after eleven in the morning now. I had slept through another too many hours.

"Nikki, I can't stay with you."
"Its okay, Nick, I'll be fine until you get back. I promise. I reached into the drawer and once again filled the syringe to halfway. He took it from me and told me to look away.

"Wait, here's the check." He took it and looked at it. "Twenty-five hundred?" He looked at me. I nodded. He looked back at the check.

"Hey, this isn't you." He was confused.

"It is me. Nikki is my cousin's two year old daughter. I use her alias in my work. I am Bria. Bria Marie Stone. Don't you see it on the top of the check? The domestic violence people, well they want you to use an alias. Since I used her at work, I used her there at the domestic violence home."

"That I do remember." He said as the painful past came out in his tone. "We had to change out names too, in the beginning. It's like changing who you are somehow." There was such sadness in his voice.

"Please keep calling me Nikki. Warren doesn't know that name; I never thought to tell him I used aliases. But if someone asks for either Nikki or Bria, you don't know me, right?"

He smiled again. I smiled back. He held up the syringe like he was toasting me. "Ready?"

I nodded. My eyes closed and I pulled my feet up onto the bed, Nick pulled the blanket up over me. He touched my hand. "Nikki? I'll hurry." I thought to myself, he really is just a scared little boy inside. I smiled and drifted into my sleep. The unwelcome nausea came and the nightmares would follow but, hopefully so would some measure of recuperative sleep.

Chapter Twenty-Six
A Pair of Young Heroes

The nightmares came. It seemed a vengeance was being waged against me for the few days of relative peace. Once more a wealth of scenes played on my own personal big screen.

Blood splattered on the windshield as I watched; his face hidden, but falling forward to slam against the steering wheel. The closeness on the beach was gone. Now the beach held the wild look on Warren's face as he closed his hands too slowly around my neck.

The hermit crabs were there with the sand fleas on the beach, but they were stained with blood. I tried to get my body to turn over so that I could see my face. The water cruelly came up to my body and I knew that it would float away into the ocean. I screamed. My heart was beating out of my chest, I was sure I wasn't yet dead. I wanted to make sure. I wanted to see my face.

"Nikki!" I heard the name echo through the screams. "Nikki! The voice was unfamiliar.

"Nikki!" Again, the voice was terrified, I had to help. I climbed out of my nightmare searching. Trying to help whomever was frantically looking for Nikki.

I left my nightmare realizing that someone was living a worse one and I had to help them. I couldn't hear them clearly now. I reached out and someone took my hand. His voice was suddenly stronger and very close.

"Nikki?" I sat up, wide awake. The room was dimly lit by the lamp on the desk. A tall young man sat on my bed shaking me, trying to wake me fully, my hand in his. I started to back away, "It's Casey, miss. Nick said you would need help." His eyes were pleading, trying to get me to comprehend. He looked so unsure.

"What?" I said trying to understand.

"I'm Casey. Nick asked me to check in on you and said that you might need my help."

I stared blankly at him.

He cursed. "Damn you Nick." He was furiously trying to figure out what to do next.

"You are Nikki, right?"

Finally realization dawned on me.

"Casey." My voice low because of my screams. "Casey, Nick's friend." It was a statement and not really a question.

"Yes, that's me." He still seemed shaky.

"Thanks." I stared at him.

"I'm sorry. I didn't know what else to do. You were screaming. Are you okay now?"

"No. I'm not okay, the nightmares are worse when I'm alone." I took a deep breath. "Nick told me. It's okay. If you need to rest; I won't leave you alone again. I guess Nick was right, you shouldn't be alone."

I turned on the bed, putting my feet on the floor. I felt slowly for it, inching further and further, testing my ability to remain stable as

I stood. He backed away. "Do you need help? I can get whatever you need."

Nick was right. They were just two young men that were terribly alike and in this day and age, terribly gentlemanly.

"I'll manage." I answered him, not really sure that I could. I stood still. Waiting until I could take the first step. He stood himself and backed away from the bed. I walked gingerly towards the bathroom, taking several small steps. I desperately wanted to splash water on my face and try to bring some life back into me.

I reached for the wall to steady myself and it wasn't there. I could see myself falling but in an instant he was there catching me before I hit the floor.

"No, you're not really managing." He said as he carried me back to the bed.

"Look, I get the impression that you are all about trying to do things by yourself. But, babe, you can't. You got to let me help you. Nick says you've been running from everyone that wants to help you. Do you have a death wish?"

I couldn't speak, letting his words sink in. Again, this weakness was more than I could bear. I wanted to be stronger. I used to be stronger. I cried. Angry sobs pouring from me.

I was shaking. "I'm just so scared. I would rather die alone, than have my friends and family hurt." I was crying hard, my hands covering my face. "I'm so sorry. Just go. I can't get someone else involved. Go. Please just go."

I heard the door open but did not dare to look. I was sure it was Nick. Just another person that I had dragged into my path of destruction.

"I'm not going anywhere. And neither is Nick. We're seeing this thing through to the end." He put his arm around my shoulders and pulled me into his chest. I couldn't resist his pull. I was too weak, and I sobbed, tears wetting his shirt.

Nick sat on the other side of me, draped his arm over my back as Casey held me. "He's right, Nikki. We're not going to let you alone now, you're stuck with us."

I could feel them looking at each other over my head. "We don't abandon damsels in distress." He added as the two of them carried on a silent eye contact only conversation.

Finally the sobbing stopped. I pulled away from Casey. I sat up as best as I could on my own. They both stayed by my side.

"Now what do you want to do about it?" Casey asked. I shrugged. I don't know what I can do about it I thought, but I didn't even know what to say. I turned my head so that I could lie against the pillow, but Casey realized what I was trying to do and picked me up.

They both stood and Nick pulled back the blankets we had been seated on top of. The two of them were actually tucking me in bed.

This was so not right, I was arguing with myself again. They were so not supposed to be doing this. They sat down on the edge of the bed I was in, blocking me in.

"Since Nikki's taken off from everyone that's tried to help her so far." He paused. "One of us has to be with her at all times." He was planning.

"She's a little bit of a feisty thing, isn't she?" Casey put in his two cents worth. "I think we need to erase her from the records all together. I can take care of that. Does she know how many people have been here looking for her?" Again their conversation didn't include me.

I stirred, trying to re-focus my thoughts. Their low whispering voices droning me back off to my nightmares. I was fighting it. I didn't want to see the pictures again. I didn't want to hear my screams.

"No." I whispered, but I couldn't say anything else.

"Man this is real bad." Nick said. "She's cool, though. She just got hooked up with the wrong guy." I was listening, trying to stay tuned in to their conversation. Anything to avoid going back to sleep.

"You were right about her nightmares. She was screaming bloody murder. I kept trying to wake her, calling her name and shaking her."

Nick laughed. "You called her Nikki?"

"Yeah. What else would I call her?" Casey asked.

"Bria," both Nick and I answered at the same time, my voice barely audible. He reached up and rubbed my arm. "It's okay to sleep. We'll be here."

In my peripheral vision I saw him nod to Casey who was sitting closer to the head of the bed. He leaned over and whispered. "Sleep heals. I promise. We'll fight the monsters off for you."

I smiled. They think they're my babysitters. He began to comb his fingers through my hair, but turned his head away once more talking to Nick. I continued to listen, trying to fight sleep still.

"Bria." He said. "That explains why she didn't come out of it." Nick said. "I think she's in real trouble. She's really sick. We had to steal vials of medicine from her work but it makes her sick too."

"Where did you steal it from?" Casey perked up.

"This place just outside of DC." Nick answered. "Why?"

"Well, if she's really that sick, we may need to steal some more if they don't catch the jerk. I wish I could get my hands on the guy. How do you beat up on a woman like this?" Casey began to show anger at the situation.

"Hey, I didn't think my dad would do it to us." Nick said. "But somehow, he just snapped one time and it was normal for a while after that."

"Okay, change of subject, been there done that, remember?" Casey began, "This girl needs food, and some clean clothes, and a little big of shopping for," he paused. "Personal items, you know, make up, girl stuff. "If we're gonna get her out of here and somewhere that we can take care of her, she needs to look like she's not on deaths door."

"Not a problem," Nick said. "She wrote me a check this morning for twenty-five hundred." He pulled it out of his wallet.

"What ever she needs, we can get for her. We gotta nurse her back to health. Now it's on us. If she doesn't make it now, it's the two of us that fail."

Casey was already on his feet, pacing the room. "Let's not move her from here," he stopped when Nick started to interrupt. "Let's move her here." I could hear the understanding register with Nick so Casey continued. "We can move her around from room to room here. We can fix it so that no one knows she's still here and yet still look like life is normal."

I couldn't help but think that if it were me at their ages, that it might have been more like a game. These guys were serious. They were thinking things through. I might actually make it through this.

I couldn't sleep. Their quiet but lively conversation back and forth, making plans kept me involved in what was happening rather than drifting solidly into sleep. No matter how much these two thought they could protect me, they didn't know about the two murders yet. If I was going to use them, they were entitled to the truth.

I stirred, "Guys, I need to tell you the rest." I sighed.

"There's more?" Nick asked.

Casey punched him. "Of course there's more goofball. There always is."

"Do we have to know?" Nick asked. "I don't want to not like you."

Casey came to my rescue again. "How capable was she of actually telling you everything? She's not been able to even think straight as far as I can tell."

"Thanks Case," I said leaving off the y unintentionally. Nick laughed. "I call him that too. He thinks Casey is a girl's name. I only use that when I want to piss him off."

"Okay, Case it is." I took a deep painful breath. "Help me sit up. I need to tell you everything." Both of them moved to help me sit up against the pillows.

Nick crossed the large room and grabbed me a bottled water out of the kitchen. When I had taken a few sips, I started my story starting with the Christmas Party. I told them about everything.

It was a slow and a very long story with their eyes getting bigger and bigger as it went along. I was exhausting myself. My words were barely above a whisper and I was sipping water every few words. I wanted them to understand just what they were in for. Every once in a while, one or the other would ask questions or curse at something that had happened.

Not once did I look at their faces after I spoke about the murders. The wide eyes in the beginning told me they hadn't been ready for it all, but I couldn't not tell them the truth.

When I was finished, stopping with Elaine helping me by bringing me here, I looked down at the water bottle in my hands, peeling the plastic shrink-wrap from it and waiting on their final opinions of me.

Case was the first to speak. "Wow! You really are a damsel in distress."

"I guess you weren't kidding when you said that the car didn't mean anything to you. You had more important things to worry about." Nick said.

I looked at him and smiled. "Yep, not really that important in the grand scheme of things is it?"

Case picked up the remote for the TV. He turned it to the local news channel. "I think we need to be listening to this." He said. "Why dude?" Nick looked at Case like he was crazy and tried to take the remote from him. "She's already got enough to worry about."

Case held it back from him. "Exactly. But we need to hear if they catch her ex. Or," he paused, looking at Nick pointedly, " if anyone else turns up dead that she knows."

Case turned to me. "Bria, I like that better, we have to decide what to do about the people asking questions about you. It's only been three or four, but there's something suspicious about that.

Elaine, the lady that brought you here was probably the first one. Nick says he moved you that time because you asked for it. The other people have been one woman and two different men. Do you have any idea who they might be?" I think I might be able to guess.

"Huh? Oh yeah, probably Missy was the second woman and Daniel and Jonathan were probably the men. I don't think that James would jeopardize my safety if he really thought I was here."

Neither one of them understood. "Warren knows James. You know, courtroom, hospital etc…" the light of comprehension dawning on both of them.

"Jonathan? What does he look like? He's the doctor, right?" Case asked.

"Well, a lot like James. Tall, but blonde, and really built." He clicked his tongue. "I don't want to date him. I mean the physical details so we can recognize him."

I smiled. Boys. I thought exasperated, no matter how old they get, that attitude that is given with the y chromosome comes shining through.

"Okay, he's about 6'5" tall, blonde hair, blue eyes, maybe two hundred plus pounds. Not an ounce of fat on him. When he has carried me or lifted me it almost hurts as my ribs bounced against him." They both rolled their eyes.

"Anything else, like his bulging biceps or his rippling thigh muscles you want us to look for?" Nick was laughing.

"No." I replied as sharply as I could.

"Oh, he sometimes wears glasses." I sheepishly added. Case stared at me. "Okay so the next Adonis we run into we'll frisk him to see if he's the doc." By this time they were thoroughly enjoying themselves, laughing at my way of describing people.

"That's okay. I can run away from them on my own. I've done well so far." I was pouting a little and, while I was appreciative, I couldn't see what they were so amused about. I gave them 'details'. I dropped back down on the pillows and turned my face towards the wall.

"Oh come on, don't get upset. We're just trying to lighten things up." Nick was once more consoling.

"Yeah." Case said, "It's not everyday that you meet a beautiful girl and she tells you that someone's trying to kill her and, oh by the way, one person that was protecting her has already been killed. Yeah, that's an every day occurrence."

"I guess you're right." But I was too tired now to think about it. I had fought off the sleep long enough.

"Time for some food." Case stopped the turn the conversation had taken. "When was the last time she ate?" He was asking Nick.

"I don't know. Not since I've been with her."

"Damn, we're gonna be the ones to kill her. Take some of that money and go get food. Make it look like you're doing some grocery shopping for your mom. Pretend you've got a list." He was back to scheming now. "And now that I think about it, I'm gonna move her. That way we're ahead of the game a little in case someone followed you already."

It was Nick's turn to show his bravado. "Hey, I was careful. I watched. No one followed me to the room. Don't you think that they might have broken in on us by now if they thought that I was coming to see her?"

"I suppose. Just don't take any chances. We can't afford that. How many of the suites are empty? Never mind, I'll find out. Just call me when you're coming back."

"K." Nick said as he picked up his things to leave, "Oh yeah." He turned and pulled his wallet back out again. "You better keep this, in case I can't make it back. I'm taking two." Indicating he was taking two hundred. He handed the remaining money to Case and walked out the door.

"Case? What aren't you telling me? Why did he say in case he didn't make it back?" I was worried, but suddenly excruciatingly tired.

"Nothing. He just knows that if someone starts following him, he won't lead them back here. He'll call though and we'll leave."

He left it at that and finally, fifteen minutes later, the silence of the room, the drone of the air conditioning, began to lull me back to sleep. I reached back my hand and put it on his arm. "Thanks. I don't know if…" The words trailed off and I was finally resting.

Chapter Twenty-Seven
From The Frying Pan into the Fire

Nick burst through the door excited and scared.

"Case, we gotta move it. I don't know if someone followed me or if its coincidence, but they're downstairs right now showing a picture of her right now. Someone must have followed me, 'cause they are downstairs. I saw them when I came in."

"Time to beat it. You ready?" Case looked at me like he knew I wasn't.

"Put the bags down, you idiot," he yelled at Nick, "we'll get them later." He pulled me up off of the bed and planted my feet on the floor.

"She can't do this." He said to Nick as I dropped back quickly to the bed. At least I was sitting. He pulled a key card out of his pocket and tossed it to Nick.

Nick looked at it and started back out the door.

"Hold the door. I'm right behind you." Case grabbed me again and held me by his side my feet not even touching the ground.

"It'll look like you're walking, I hope." I nodded my head.

Nick was holding the door and he took the other side of me. We could all hear the whirring of the elevator.

"Run!"

They were carrying me, down the hall as fast as they could, hands cupped under my elbows. We rounded the corner just feet from the elevator as the ding sounded letting us know the elevator had reached the floor.

I wanted to cry. All the jostling around between them was hurting me. I felt a sharp pain in my arm. The port was bending and slowly pulled out. Blood began dripping down to the floor as my arms were supported in their hands.

"Open it, I got her!" Case whispered, and Nick sprinted further down the hall. I heard the door open and prayed that whoever had gotten off the elevator didn't. Case almost dragged me in the room. The door did not close. Nick stayed at the door with it slightly open, to look out into the hallway.

"Lock it up, Nick." Case whispered as he sat me on the edge of the bed. The two of them looked at each other, breathless. They were both frightened but I could tell that neither one of them would admit to it.

"That was a little too close." Nick said breathlessly. He stood at the door peeping through the peephole in the door.

"I'm going back to the room." Case said suddenly.

"Why? You can't!" Nick argued.

"Because it will look really strange if they do get into the room and see all those groceries just sitting there with no one around. Besides, they haven't seen me yet. They don't know who I am." Case stopped him.

"But maybe it wasn't even them. And no one really knows what floor even if they do suspect something." Nick was really scared.

Case continued. "And my uniform vest is in the room so maybe they'll think I was just staying for free."

"My checkbook." They both looked at me. "Remember Nick? It's on the night stand. And the medicine and syringes are in the drawer." They both cursed.

"I'm leaving." Case said firmly. "Back in a few." And with that he was gone out the door.

"I'm sorry Nick." He was still looking through the peephole. He waved his hand back at me. "Nothing to worry 'bout." He kept up his vigil, anxiously waiting on the return of his friend.

I only hoped that it was Jonathan, James or even Daniel and not Warren. I couldn't even think of what I would do if Case or Nick were killed because of me.

My head was spinning through my thoughts as the pictures of them flashed in my head.

I had my hand over the now furiously bleeding broken IV site. I tried to stop the blood from being seen by both of them. Oh, I thought as I looked down at it. This would mean that my meds were now out of the question. I couldn't let them know that the jostling run had done the damage.

Nick didn't move. When Case wasn't back in ten minutes, he opened the door. "Nikki, I mean Bria? I'm gonna go look for him. You okay for a couple of minutes?" There was that little boy in his voice that asked the question. He really was a kid and only playing the part of a man.

"I'll be fine. I'm safe now." I said.

"Yeah, for now." He said disappointed as he disappeared out the door.

Alone in the new room, I pulled my hand away from the IV site. Blood poured down my arm and dripped all over the bed. It was an open vein and it wasn't clotting. I was wrong to look at it but I thought if I saw how bad it was I would know what to do. My head began to swim. What I wouldn't give for that drug induced sleep right now.

I wanted to try and make it to the bathroom so I pushed up off the bed with my one good arm. I fell back down to the bed again, feeling sick. I had to use both arms and as much strength as I could muster to stand. If I could just make it up, I might be able to make it to the bathroom.

I pushed off again with both hands, barely standing; I stumbled my way across the room, finding support in the dresser that was against the far wall. The bathroom was only a few more feet away and around the corner. I was sure I could make it.

Not now! I thought as nausea swept over me because of the blood I shouldn't have looked at. I was going to be really sick if I didn't make it to the bathroom and the cool water quickly.
I began talking to myself. "The bathroom is just around the corner, the entrance just past the wall where the dresser was. I could make it. I know I could make it."

I reached for the door facing of the bathroom and pulled myself towards it and around the corner. I could see the sink. I pressed myself between the door facing. I tried to push myself towards the sink.

My hand was too slick with blood to hold on. Just a little too late to make an adjustment, I scrambled as I tried to hold on, but I half slid half fell down the door frame to the cool tile of the bathroom floor.

My head landed with a soft thud on the open door as I went down.

I was dazed and already dizzy but my eyes were still open and staring at the sliding bloody handprint on the door facing. I wanted to shut my eyes against it, but I just kept staring at it. I was afraid that if I closed them this time, I might not be able to ever open them again.

Blood pooled around me and began to spread out over the tile. I watched it as it filled in the crevices where the grout was and fall even deeper in places where the grout had disappeared.

The door banged open. I couldn't move. I prayed silently. Please let it be Nick and Case.

"Damn it!" I heard Jonathan's voice. I didn't see him, but I heard him. "Where is she?" He shouted. He was angry.

"We left her right here, honest." The little boy again showing up in Nick's voice.

"Get over here." He said and I heard him shove both Nick and Case to the bed. I heard the springs as they both bounced onto it.

"Oh gross, what is this?" Nick pulled his hand away, blood staining it as he lifted it off the bed he had been shoved onto. Surely he could see my feet as they hung out of the bathroom.

"Oh my God!" he said it as he inhaled in a loud whisper and crossed to where I lay on the floor. I could imagine the terrified look in his eyes. I knew Case had realized what was going on because I heard him get up off of the bed.

"They got to her." Case slammed his fist into the wall as he slid under me on the floor. He couldn't believe what he was seeing.

"Get away from her!" He yelled as Jonathan tried to take me from him, "She ran away from you, remember?"

Jonathan stepped over to him, kneeling beside him.

"Look they didn't get to her, look, pay attention. It's just the IV. See?" and he picked up the ripped apart apparatus. He put his hand over it quickly to stop the still pooling and dripping hole in my arm.

"You," he said to Nick who was white as a ghost standing just outside the bathroom door looking at the bloody door facing.

"Nick." Case shouted. "You gotta help."

He stepped towards us. "Get me some towels would you?" Jonathan put his free hand up on Nick's arm. "It's okay; she's going to be fine. Get me the towels." He recognized shock when he saw it. Jonathan took control. "What's your name?" he said to Case.

"Casey. Case."

"Well, Case, lay her down on the bed. I need to help her and I need your help." He put both hands above the bleeding, forming a tourniquet with his hands.

"I have a cell phone in my pocket. Can you manage to get it out?"

Case reached in the pocket that Jonathan had nodded to. "Press and hold the number three. When it rings, put it on speaker." Case followed orders. Nick walked slowly back over to the bed where I was lying. I thought he was going to pass out.

This was too much for me. I thought I really was dying this time. My body would not move.

My brain focused on the tally of lives I was ruining because of Warren. Two more innocents had now joined the list. How many people was I needlessly involving in my situation? How many people can one person hurt at a time?

"Jonathan?" I heard James' voice on the speaker.

"Yeah it's me. Look I've got her but it's bad. Really bad."

"Where?" James' voice cracked.

Case's fingers covered the speaker. "No!" He whispered.

"Someone else was here just before you, showing a picture of her to the staff. They'll know she's here for sure if they see him. She told us that!" They looked at each other.

"Case, we can't move her. She'll be dead if we do."

"I'll lead him in. We'll get him to the service entrance."

"James, there will be two young men to meet you, fourth exit after Seashore."

He looked at Case, "You know where that is right?"
Case nodded. "If you're not here when I get back, I'll come after you."

"James, they'll be driving?" he looked at Case,

"Her Mustang." He said and Jonathan raised his eyebrows.

"They'll be driving Bria's Mustang."

"I've changed the license plate though." Nick said.

"Okay, James, they'll be driving Bria's Mustang. Follow them. Bring Missy and tell her that we need the surgical bag too. James? You had better break the speed limits getting here. And James, someone else came looking for her just before I got here so follow them around to the back."

"Damn it Jonathan, don't you let her die!" The phone was dead.

"Okay, grab that towel; roll it like you're going to have a towel fight with it. Lengthwise. Wrap it around where she is bleeding so that I can let go. The blood will speed up a little when I let go. It's not the best, but it's all I've got for now."

"Will this do?" Nick pulled off his belt and pulled it tight around the towel that was wrapped around my arm.
Jonathan nodded. "Good."

I kept secretly hoping that I was dreaming it all, that this was just another nightmare. I was still not strong enough to speak or move any part of my body. Jonathan turned to the two young men standing beside him looking like they had seen a ghost.

"You guys have done a great job. Sorry that it's like this."
He put his arm across both of the boys and turned them away from me.

"You need to hurry or everything all of us have done will be for nothing. I know you're both scared and I am too. This is probably the biggest thing you'll ever do in your lives, but if you're not back in under an hour, she might not make it. And I'll be forced to take her to a hospital where Warren will surely find her."

"Yes sir," Nick said.

"I'm not trying to scare you more than necessary. I just want you both to know that you had better hurry. He'll be in a black limo. He knows Bria's car, so don't waste time on conversation, just turn around and fly back. We've covered every place between here and DC and then some trying to find her. Just make it back. Got it?"

Case looked over his shoulder at me. "We'll be back as fast as we can."

With that, both boys were out the door. Jonathan walked over to the door and locked it.

When he came back over to where I lay on the bed, he began talking at me. Not to me.

"Bria? What am I going to do with you? James is in love with you. He needs you and you're killing him running away like this. I don't know if I can tell him if you're dead when he gets here. I should be taking you to the hospital but even they wouldn't be able to help you as fast as I can if James can get here soon enough."

He sat down on the bed, took my hand, putting his finger on my pulse holding it praying it wouldn't stop.

I wished I could respond. He removed the belt that Nick had left behind and pulled back the blood soaked towel. He pulled the buckle around my wrist and tied the other end of it to the headboard.

"Let's see if gravity will help slow this down to a trickle." He was talking to himself. "What else have we got to work with?" He walked over to the closet and opened it up. There was a bundle with a change of sheets in it for each bed.

"Good. This will do." He tore apart the bundle and then spread out the sheet; he pulled a pocketknife out of his pants pocket and cut through the seam. Over and over he ripped strips of the sheet.

"Guess we'll owe them." He took one strip and folded it over and over again zigzagging, making a four inch loop. He took the knife again and slit the edges of each fold. He was creating a layered bandage. He pressed first one and then another and another on the bleeding gaping hole in my vein that it had become. He reached up and released the tie on the belt from the headboard.

"I knew that would happen." He said as the blood began to pool again and spill over onto the bed. He grabbed the stack he had made and placed all of them over the pulsing blood. He took another strip and tied it around the stack wrapping my arm several times around with the long strip and then tying it off when the strip ran out. He lifted my hand again in the belt and tied it back to the headboard one more time.

His actions were calm. Methodical. I could see that he was worried. He could do nothing else until everyone returned and he had his bag of medical supplies.

"Bria, this isn't your fault. I know that you don't understand, but, we are all hurting now. You just don't know. I thought you trusted us. We have all grown to love you. Missy has cried every day since you left. It's not good for her."

He stood and walked to the door. He checked the door, peeped out the peephole as Nick had done, and walked back to sit across from me. He brought his hands together, fingers interlaced with his pointer fingers pressed together.

I recognized it as the same "thinking pose" that my father used. I watched him. Finally he leaned forward and he sighed and he began to shake. I could tell he was crying. Not out loud. He was silently sobbing into his hands.

I had so much pain for everything that was happening, that I couldn't think about what I would do next.

I needed him to hear me. I tried to speak, but the words would not come. I moaned, forcing the air to escape from my lips.

"Bria?" I blinked, so very weak. He jumped to his feet. "Bria. You're going to be fine. Hang in there with me. I looked up at my dangling fingers and wiggled them slightly with as much effort as I could, which wasn't much. They were white. He looked at me.

"Shit! I've gotta bring your arm down just a little. I'll prop it up but not so high."

I blinked again and tried to smile. I tried to swallow. He reached up and unstrapped the leather belt. He held it up as he scooted me over. He slid his arm under my head and lifted me a little. He propped my right arm up on top of a pillow he had grabbed off the second bed. He put his hand on my forehead. "A fever too? Well I guess this will have to do for now." My other arm he let fall in front of me on my stomach. He looked down at me. "You sure know how to get a world of people caring about you little Bria."

I closed my eyes. Okay, I thought, I have to live till James makes it here. My head slumped over and fell backwards. Jonathan let

295

go and came around to the left side of the bed. He slid beside me sitting with his back against the headboard. He leaned my head against him. "I always wanted a little sister. I thought she would be a pain in the ass so I guess that means you qualify."

He was talking to himself again. "I'll not let you die in my arms, Bria. It would kill James and Missy, not to mention two young men playing the role of hero."

He kept talking but I was no longer listening. Unconscious, I drifted into some dark sleep that held me hovering over a precipice. I could choose my fate. I could jump or I could choose to back away from the edge of the cliff. I really wanted to jump, but I couldn't make my feet step off into oblivion.

Chapter Twenty-Eight
Rescue

The banging on the door drew me back from the precipice that I was trying hard to step off of. I looked at the door. I couldn't move. Not one part of me worked. But, I was alive and it was James. I wanted to be alive when he got here.

"Break it down James!"

"No!" I heard both Case and Nick yell. "We got this."

"The boys have gone for tools. Is she alive? Please tell me she's alive." His voice weakened as he finished the sentence.

"Yes, James but you really have to hurry."

Case took a set of bolt cutters and snipped through the flip door lock. It was all that was needed since the card opened everything else.

The door burst open the second the lock fell to the floor. The four of them hurrying over to where Jonathan held me protectively, he yelled. "One of you, lock that damn door. Block it. Do something. We don't want any surprises." He breathed a sigh of relief as Nick got a chair and shoved it under the door handle.

"What do you need?" Missy asked.

"First we need to pull this bed out. Push the rest of the furniture as close to the other walls as possible. You have to move it with us on it."

Immediately everyone was moving. Chairs and furniture were stuffed on top of each other. Missy backed into the bathroom to get out of the way of the working men.

It was then that she noticed the blood. "Jon?" Her voice quivered and she knew by the volume that she saw that I wasn't doing well at all.

Every one of the men in the room turned to look at her, the near tears in her voice making them turn.

James looked at all the blood and then back at Jonathan.

"That's why we need to act fast. Any donors?"

It took a moment before they realized what he was asking.

James rolled up his sleeves, looking at the veins in his arm. Case and Nick, not wanting to be squeamish, did the same. Jonathan spoke quietly again. "I hope this works. Do you boys know your blood type?"

"Bria is A+ so if your are O or A either positive or negative, we're good. Do either of you fall out of those types?"

No one said anything.

"O+" said Case as he pulled a work ID out of his wallet. He elbowed Nick. "Ummm," he paused as he pulled out his ID. "O-". "James I know you're O+. I don't know how much this will take."

Missy pulled the smaller bag from the dresser and set up the night stand on my right as her station. She began pulling out tubes, and needles and medical scissors, clamps, and other medical supplies.

Jonathan looked at Missy. He mouthed. "I love you." And then louder so that everyone could hear: "Are we ready?" She nodded.

"James, I need you to support her for now. Take my place but on her right. But don't let her arm go any lower. I can't guarantee that it won't pour.

298

James, Nick and Case all seemed to turn white at once. I don't want to put it higher, because her fingers went white when I did that."

Jonathan lifted the pillow just inches. He stood up and James slid in to take his place on the opposite side. Letting the pillow with my arm rest on his legs, he pulled my head to his chest. Jonathan shook his hands, getting the blood circulating in his own limbs.

"Okay boys, we've got work to do."

He moved a dining chair to my left side. Missy stood on my right. He pointed to the chair. "Who's first?" Nick didn't move. Case walked around and took a seat. Jonathan sat on the bed and took my left arm. He tied the tourniquet around my upper arm and Missy handed him the needle. He threaded it easily in the best vein he could find. He taped it down and held out his hand for Case's arm. His muscled arm was full of veins showing visibly through the skin.

"Please tell me you don't use drugs."

Case shook his head. "We'd be fired."

"That's not what I asked. Do you or not? Even steroids?"

"No. Never."

Jonathan took the new needle from Missy and placed it into his arm, taping it down. He connected tubing to it and in no time, blood was flowing from his arm to mine. I am watching all of it, without moving. I know I am going to die. I feel so weak. I wanted to shout out, don't do it. I'm sorry. But I couldn't.

"Nick, do you think you could get something for everyone to eat. And some orange juice. Everyone will need to drink some juice so you're not lightheaded." Jonathan said.

"I just brought groceries up. They're in the other room." And with that Nick walked out the door.

In just a couple of minutes he was back and putting things away in the kitchen. He put out a plate of cookies and poured OJ into six glasses.

He walked back to sit on the opposite bed and remembered the blood on it. He began to strip the sheets and blankets that were bloodstained and to remake the bed with the extra blankets and sheets in the closet. Then he walked to the bathroom and began to clean up all of the blood. I heard him get sick and puke in the toilet. I felt sorry for him.

Missy walked to the closed bathroom door. "Nick? Are you okay?" "Yeah. I'll be out in a minute." He answered weakly from behind the closed door.

When he walked back out into the room, he dropped all of the bloody things into a trash bag that he took from out from under the sink. He sat down on the freshly made bed looking pale. Missy brought him one of the glasses of OJ and told him to drink it. "You're next, do you think you can do it?"

"You bet. It's just the cleaning up of it that gets to me." He slowly drank the orange juice.

"Okay Nick." Missy looked at him as a mother would to a child. "It's your turn."

He walked, robot like, over to where she was waiting. He pressed his body up against the wall. I thought he was going to faint.

Case stood up, wobbling himself, and as Nick stepped towards him to take his seat, he put his hand on Nick's shoulder.

"It's gonna be okay." He said as he walked over to the right side of the bed and slammed into the wall.

"Case, go lay down, Now!" He looked to where he stood leaning against the wall. "I have as many patients as I can handle. If you fall on your face, you'll just have to stay there for a while."

Case obeyed Jonathan's voice as if he had no choice.

Missy grabbed several cookies and a glass and took it to the bedside table beside him. "Eat these and drink the juice as soon as you can." She rubbed his sweating forehead. Then walked back to where she had everything set up to take her place as nurse.

After a second thirty to forty minutes Nick was through with his donation to my fading life. He stood and walked without missing a step to sit beside Case, still lying on the bed. They were both watching everything taking place in a very somber silence.

"Okay. James we've got to do this right." Jonathan spoke out loud but seemed to be pondering just how to do it.

"Why isn't the blood stopping already?" Nick asked. Jonathan sighed, talking as if he was teaching a child.

"The injections had some of the same properties as blood thinners in it. The IV was in her arm for so long that it's become like a water hose with a spray nozzle on it that has been turned on. It has been open and on for so long that the pressure has built up and was ready to be released. When the needle was pulled out, the blood just flows. Because it's thinner than normal now, nothing is helping to clot properly. It will soon, I hope with all of the thick blood going into her. If not, we will be flying to a hospital for surgery."

"We stole some vials from where she works." Nick said. "Does that make a difference?"

Jonathan looked at Nick. "Where is it?"

"Oh, in my pocket, except for the bottle that's in her pocket. That's the one we used." He pulled out everything that he had gotten from the other bedroom when he left.

"Come and get it out of her pocket so I can see if she has the right thing in her system. We're kind of busy here."

Nick reached into the pocket of my skirt and pulled out the half empty bottle.

"Well, that explains it. She should have died." He paused and looked at Nick. "Do you know how much she got into her?"

"Yep, we've done it twice, but only half of a syringe full. She was afraid of overdosing."

Jonathan looked at me. He reached up and pushed my bangs away from my face. "Smart little girl, you are, Bria."

I tried to smile. My lips twitched. I swallowed trying to open my mouth to speak but I still couldn't.

"Stop trying to talk." Jonathan said. "Nick you seem to be doing alright, take James place, carefully. James, hold the pillow steady till he gets in place." Nick took hold of my head and slipped in where James had been and then James laid the pillow with my arm resting on it on top of Nick's legs. I could barely tell the difference in the men. They were all about the same size except in height. Every one of them was over six feet. No wonder I felt small and insignificant when I was with them.

James walked over to the vacated chair and took a seat. James looked at Nick. He was overwhelmed by the two young men, barely out of boyhood, "Thank you both." Tears building in his eyes. Nick put his finger and thumb into an ok sign and lay his head over on top of mine.

After another thirty or so minutes James was finished with his donation.

"My turn," Missy said.

"No Missy, not unless we have to," Jonathan looked at her. She nodded her head, knowing that it would probably make her too weak to be of any assistance.

Jonathan took the chair and put the tourniquet on his upper arm pulling it taut with his teeth.

"Missy, would you do the honors?" She drew in a deep breath and inserted the needle into her husband's arm. She dropped the tourniquet off, untying it with one hand. She taped the needle down and waited for it to be done. Jonathan put his arm around her waist and pulled her to him. She held him tight until his thirty minutes or so were done.

"Now we wait." Jonathan put his head in his hands and Missy cleaned up the used tubing and tossed them into the trash can. She sat on the edge of the bed beside and in front of the chair Jonathan was sitting on. They leaned into each other silently consoling each other.

"So how did you two get involved with Bria?" James asked. Both boys said at the same time. "Nikki."

"What?" James looked at them.

"She called herself Nikki." Nick said.

"Okay, out with it all. I want to know everything you can tell me."

"She was with a lady named Elaine that checked in. When Elaine left, she called down to the front desk complaining that she didn't like the room she was in cause it smelled like cigarette smoke and that could we send someone up to help her change rooms."

Case interrupted, "Nick was the lucky one on duty. He came running up to help what he thought was an old lady that might give him a big tip and it turned out to be her."

Nick rolled his eyes. "I showed her to her new room, up on this floor and as we were leaving the elevator she sort of fell into me. I thought she was going to fall on the floor so I caught her. That's when she asked me to help her get to the new room. I sat with her because she looked like she wasn't doing well. That's when she bribed me with a car." James looked over to where I was still half in and half out of my stupor shaking his head.

"What about the drugs?" Jonathan asked joining in on the conversation.

Nick continued to tell our story with Case adding his part in it at just the right times. They told everyone what their plans had been and finally Nick said: "The rest you know already. From the time Jonathan got here, you pretty much know what went on."

James sat beside Case who had finally sat up in bed and put his arm around him. James clapped him on the back. "You did good son. Check that. You did great. Both of you did all the right things. I am in your debt. I don't know if we could have done any better had we been in your shoes. I'll never be able to repay you."

I could not hold back my thoughts. I wanted to let them know I was alive.

I whispered, "Nick Mustang, Case Pathfinder." That was all I could manage. I heard everyone's sharp intake of breath. Nick swept his other arm carefully up and took my fingers in his hands. "We did it." he whispered in my ear, barely able to find his own voice now.

Jonathan got up and walked around to the right side and took a look at my arm. The fact that I was conscious at all, the sign he was looking for that let him know that the four pints of blood were doing their job. He carefully loosened the sheet made bandaging and pulled it off. A faint trickle of blood, bright against the drying blood made him smile. It was still leaking but only a little. This was good news. Nick didn't want to pull his arm from under me and I could feel his chest rise, puffing up like he had rescued me all on his own.

Everyone chuckled or smiled, tension finally easing just a little in the room. I watched James for a moment. I said "thank you' through my barely open mouth and closed my eyes amazingly thankful for just being here and being alive.

Chapter Twenty-Nine
That's what Friends Are For

The room was quiet. The lights were all dim and all over the room my friends lay or sat. Sleeping through the night was out of the question for me. I was recuperating. My energy level was better than it had been in days, though that wasn't saying much.

I couldn't just stay put. I tried to get up, but Nick was asleep beside me with his arm underneath me and his other arm draped over his side and hip.

James was seated beside me in the chair that had been used to donate their blood to me. His fingers were intertwined with mine. His head laying in my lap.

Case had moved to the couch and Missy and Jonathan were cuddled up together on the opposite bed.

There we were this band of six different people with lives interrupted. Everyone had put their lives on hold for me.

I moved, hoping that my movements, something, anything would wake the others up.

I needed to get out of here and I needed to be somewhere peaceful. I gently squeezed James' hand. He lifted his head from my lap.

I smiled. I was surrounded by people who loved me and I knew that I loved them all. My two young 'heroes' that had gone out of their way to save me, had a piece of my heart. I was aching for them and the possible danger I may have put them in. James leaned in and gently kissed my cheek.

He whispered. "Welcome back, sleeping beauty." I shook my head lightly. "You are such a strange girl. I knew that from the moment I met you." I shrugged my shoulders lightly. "I don't mean to be. I've just been really confused and really scared. I didn't know what was going to happen next but I knew I didn't want anyone else to die because of me."

"No one ever knows. That's what makes life so grand. Every day is different. We strike out sometimes, miss a few curve balls, but every once in a while we hit it out of the park. That's the way the game is played."

I grinned, remembering, "My dad always said you have to learn how to hit the curve balls."

He smiled, raised his eyebrows and said. "Maybe so but you my dear, ran out on the game."

"I'm ready to get out of here. How about you?" Jonathan said from behind James.

Caught off guard, James looked up and over at him. "Should we? He stopped for a moment, "I kind of like the plan these boys came up with."

"I'm not abandoning these boys," Nick moved in his sleep and I stopped talking. I waited a few moments. "They were risking everything to help me out without knowing one thing about me. They're coming with us." They both knew that I meant it.

"Besides, they're kind of fun to have around."

James drew my hand to his lips. "I'll hire them right now if that's what you want. We'll call them "Bria-sitters." He laughed softly. I tried to pull my hand away from his but he wouldn't let it go.

"Seriously," Jonathan said, "They did put a lot of thought into their plan where as we were basically just running. I think that maybe we can make a few changes and then it will be more than just a good plan but a great one."

He looked thoughtful. "We'd have to put a little more than planning into it, you're right, but we could pull it off."

Missy was looking up into her husband's eyes from where she lay beside him.

Case sat up, "Okay, we're probably out of a job anyway. Do I get the Bria-sitting job and the Pathfinder?" he yawned as he said it and we all laughed.

Nick was jolted awake by the laughter and he pulled away slightly. "What?" he said when we all laughed again.

So here we sat the six of us. "Where's Daniel?" I suddenly thought of him.

"We sent him off on a mission." James said. "He'll be back by check out time.

"We're not technically checked in." Nick said. "What's the plan for today?"

"Yeah, what is the plan?" Case was wide awake and interested now.

"Food," I said sheepishly as my stomach grumbled loud enough for everyone to hear.

"Well, that's a good sign." Jonathan was up and on the phone immediately. He was telling Daniel that he could come at any time. He walked into the kitchen and pulling out a pad and pen began to write what Daniel was telling him.

James said, "Would you like some help up?"

It was only then that Nick realized that he was even still in bed beside me.

He looked at his watch. "Damn, I was supposed to work last night." He lifted his arm under my head. "Uh, can I get my arm back?"

I sat up slowly with James and Nick helping me. He rubbed his arm, waking it up and turned to stand. He was a little taller than Case, but he stood well over six feet and it seemed like his arms went on forever. He stretched up and touched the ceiling. I rolled my eyes. He was flexing for the older men I was sure, letting them know that he was more than a boy. It was a funny display given all we had been through.

"Okay, I'm done." He said as he dropped back down to the bed. Everyone started getting up and Case started moving furniture back to where it was supposed to be.

"I think that we need to move to another room if we are gonna stay here. That was our plan, but I'm willing to listen to yours." He was making sure that both he and Nick weren't left out.

"Well, here's my plan." I said. And everyone turned to look at me. "What? I know Warren better than anyone here. Even if there are things I didn't know. I know him intimately."

There was an odd silence in the room. "I do. I was with him for several years. Give me that at least."

"But so far your plans have almost killed you." James said. For the first time that morning he took his hand away.

"I owe you all my life. But that's a debt that I intend to spend the rest of my life repaying. Right now, it's time that I go back to being the independent woman I was before Warren walked into the picture and turned me into this, this, weak person."

Jonathan asked, "What about your health? That's the most important thing right now. You almost died. I won't sign off on letting you go without treatment again. We have to finish this if you're ever going to get completely well." He was adamant about it.

Standing he took Missy's hand and pulled her to her feet. "He's right you know." She said. "We've had our share of worrying over you, too; I don't think any of us could take it if something else happened."

"Don't you think that being pro-active is always better than inactive?" I countered.

"Okay, I can see that anything we say right now might just be superfluous, so you might as well tell us." Jonathan's eyes were flashing. He wasn't going to give up on my health after all the work he had put into it. I wasn't sure if it was all about me. After all, a successful trial would also mean a greater hope for the future with

Missy, but I wasn't sure that it was even all that important to me any more.

"I'm doing this with you, not against you." I wanted him to know that I cared for Missy too and that I wouldn't run away again.

"Okay, it's time for me to go home. It's time for me to take control of the house."

A chorus of vehement "no's" echoed off the walls.

"I need to sell it. It's my dream home, but I've discovered that it doesn't mean that much to me any more."

James rolled his eyes. "We're trying to save your life and you are worried about selling your house?"

Nick was looking at me. "I get it. It's like dropping off the face of the planet. No house, no starting point for Warren to look for you."

I smiled. I had heard the boys planning things in my in and out dreams.

"We need to do it quickly so that it looks like I am just packing up and moving away. I have a leave of absence, right?"

"Yep. Until further notice. They don't want to lose their data either, so you are getting," he paused, "the word they used was 'compensated'."

"Okay then." I took as deep a breath as I dared to.

I turned to look across the room. "Nick? Case?"

I paused, waiting on them to really look at me.

"Do you want new jobs? Both of you?"

"Sure." Nick said, "Since I basically blew off this one." His smile was broad, his white teeth gleaming.

"I already have a new job. Remember?" Case asked.

"I'll pay you better." I told him.

He looked at James. "Were you serious about us working for you or not?" Nick looked at him. "Us?"

"Yep. We're gonna be 'Bria-sitters', right James?" James laughed, "Something like that."

I rolled my eyes and sighed. "Whatever, I don't care if he pays you or I do, but I want you guys around." I dropped my voice and I could feel the tears coming. "I owe you both my life." I whispered, "I wouldn't be here but for the two of you."

Nick put his arm back around me hugging me. James picked my hand back up. "You weren't my first damsel in distress, remember?" I knew he was referring to his mother. I had a feeling that he was this way with her as well. Suddenly, I thought of her for the first time. "Oh no," I pulled my hands to my face and covered my eyes.

"What?" Nick asked.

"Your mom?" I answered him quickly.

"She knows I'm helping a *friend*." He punctuated the word.

"Besides, she's hangin' with her soon to be new husband. They're making plans and crap that I don't really care about. As long as I'm still employed, she's happy."

"Well, employed you are." James said.

"Okay, enough of this, we need food." Missy said.

She looked at Case, "Do we need to move to another room or not?"

He looked at his watch. He shook his head. "Not till eight. They start with the rooms then and I want to leave this one open so that they'll clean it before anyone realizes what kinds of things have been going on in here."

"How long before Daniel gets here?" Missy turned to Jonathan. He shrugged his shoulders, "I don't know." He didn't move and we all stared at him. Even the younger guys understood. "Well?" Missy asked.

"What?" Jonathan asked her back.

"Call him" she laughed, "and find out."

I pulled back the blankets and turned so that I could stand up, but James stopped me. "What do you need? Where do you want to go?"

I ignored him. "Missy, can you help me to freshen up." I needed to go to the bathroom. I wasn't sure that I would make it by myself.

She stepped over her husband's legs and came over to where James held me up and I took her arm. We walked slowly to the bathroom.

Once the door was closed, I put my arms around her neck. "I'm sorry that I caused so much trouble."

"You are what, twenty-five?" she asked. "I think you can manage your life on your own. I just think that you should know that we all really love you. And those boys, well, they acted more like men than most men twice their age. You got really lucky, Bria."

"I know. And I asked you not to be mad at me. Thank you for not being mad at me anyway."

I sat down on the toilet and waited, knowing that she was about to chastise me. When I had finished, she helped me to the tub, "Let's wash the blood from your hair and face." She turned on the shower and gently pulled the showerhead to me. She put a towel around my shoulders and rinsed the blood out of my hair. She took the shampoo and gently lathered it up. As she was washing my hair, she said. "I knew how you were feeling. When I was first diagnosed with cancer, I wanted to run. I wanted to die in peace. I wanted to never see Jonathan in pain. I understood you."

She rinsed my hair then wet one of the washcloths and washed the blood from my face. She took off the bandage from my head and washed carefully around the stitches that Jonathan had put in my head.

"Please, don't stay mad at me at least. I just didn't want to see your faces in place of those I've already seen. They haunt me. I am why those two people were killed. I know it. If that happened to any of you, I couldn't live with myself. I silently wished that Warren would just kill me and get it over with." I was sobbing. She sat down on the now closed toilet seat. "I didn't think your feelings for us had come that far, I guess. James maybe, but not the rest of us."

"I just look at you all, and, well, you're closer to me than family right now. Really. I'm not sure where my feelings are on plenty of things, but I know I'm not family to you guys. I was sure I'm just a client to James and nothing more than research to you and Jonathan. I know I'm just someone you all felt obligated to protect. For your own reasons."

She looked as if I had slapped her.

"You are wrong, Bria. Like I said, we really do love you."

"Missy, I thought Warren loved me. Please, understand. I seem to do nothing but doubt people these days. Even myself. I think I'm falling in love with James, but is it because of my own vulnerability? Is it because of the loss of his wife and his vulnerability? How do I know?" I put my hands to my face again, crying into them.

"How do I know how to trust my feelings again? Ever? It's not fair to my heart. I feel it beating but I don't know how when there is such a big hole in it." I was close to completely losing it. "I really loved him with every bit of my whole heart and he tried to kill me, Missy. He's still trying to kill me."

"It's okay. We're all going through so much, it seems like we're climbing Mount Everest without supplies." She chuckled.

"Aren't you glad we have so many men around us to do all the hard work?" She pulled my hands from my eyes.

"I'm not strong. I was called a goody-two-shoes all of my life. People think I'm too old fashioned. I have many faults, but Bria, we are strong together. Even I can knock down one fencepost. But together, we can break down walls. You don't have to be strong by yourself. We'll all be strong together."

I felt helpless. I hated being weak. "How long before I can stop being so helpless?"

She smiled. "December. When the study is over and you have regained your strength. Even then it might be a while to get back to normal, but till December you need our whole team."

She stood. "Ready?" I nodded. She held out her hand to help me up and I stood beside her. "Together?"

"Yep, together, all seven of us."

"Seven?"

"The four men in the room, Daniel, and you and me."

"The Magnificent Seven." She laughed.

We walked out of the room, ready to conquer... well... whatever came next.

Chapter Thirty
Highway of Fear

James knew when we came out of the bathroom that we must have had a discussion that included something about him. He looked over my head to Missy. I didn't see her, but I felt sure that she nodded her head.

I sighed. I knew that I had hurt him. Never mind what the reasons were behind how he felt about me, pain is pain no matter how it happens. He took my hand holding it tightly. I knew that he wasn't going to let me go anytime soon.

"Daniel is no more than five minutes away." Jonathan said. "We need to get down back soon." He looked at the two new cohorts. "Lead the way."

The room was already back to the way it was before we took it over. I noticed that every trace of blood and bloody towels and sheets and blankets were all gone. No one would even know that a life or death situation had happened here.

"We're going to make this as inconspicuous as possible." Case said. "Wait here." He slunk out of the room. A minute later he was back. "Put this on." He said as he handed me a baseball cap and a baseball jersey.

I looked at him, questioningly, "I coach these little kids sometimes." He reached behind me and pulled my hair back through the hole and tightened it so that it looked like it fit me. Nick shrugged.

"I guess that's the best you can do." He inhaled deeply and then blew it out.

"Let's go." He took my hand from James and Case put his arm around my waist.

We opened the door and the both of them started telling jokes and talking loud to each other like normal boys their age.

We made it to the service elevator without anyone noticing. We rode it to the basement and strolled out the back like everything was absolutely normal.

Daniel was waiting there with the limo. The door was yanked open and I was carried in.

Both boys laughed with relief. The window rolled down from the front and Daniel said, "I'm Daniel. Nice to meet the two heroes, in person. Who's Nick, who's Case?"

"Nick." Said Nick. "Case," and he bobbed his head at Daniel in a typical male greeting.

"Well, I guess you did get some planning done. These guys actually know what they're doing." Daniel said. "Even the FBI would be impressed." Both of them immediately puffed out their chests. I laughed. It really did feel good to laugh.

"Okay, Jonathan and Missy will join our little caravan in about eight minutes at KFC. James will be driving the Mustang and meet us three minutes later at the Sonic a mile further away." He looked at them. "Right?"

"Yep." Nick answered. "But if you don't haul it out of here, you won't be there before it looks like they're pulling in with us."

Daniel nodded and pulled the gear shift into drive. We drove for the few minutes that it took us to get to KFC "Nick? What are you going to say to your mom?"

"Well, first I will tell her that Mr. Laughton has hired me to work as his right hand man." He smiled.

"You mean gopher." Case teased.

"Whatever!" and he reached across and punched Case in the shoulder. "At least it's not 'babysitter'." He turned to me, "Sorry."

"No offense taken."

"Hey! I prefer escort."

I laughed. "You guys! Why don't we just call you both 'personal assistants'? That way you can both just help me out as much as possible."

"They may have a career ahead of them as CIA operatives, or Secret Service, or…" he stopped as Case reached through to the front and punched him on the arm. The grin on Daniel's face was priceless. Both Nick and Case were so easy to get along with and so much fun. Even if they were older than I had originally assumed, they hadn't turned into stuffy old men yet. I guess that might happen with marriage.

"Seriously, what are you, either of you, going to say to your parents?"

"Well, I already live on my own." Case said. My parents are in Florida." He lowered his eyes. "I, uhm," he stuttered, "moved here for a girl."

"Yeah and she left him after about a week." Nick said laughing. "She wasn't exactly a girl. I think she was what, about forty?" He almost doubled over laughing.

I reached across and patted his hand. "It's okay. The world is full of people who lie to us. You have to roll with the punches." I was mostly talking to myself. "Or hit the curve balls." I whispered.

"And age is just a number." Case defended himself. "I really liked her. She just didn't really want a thing with a real man." Again the bravado of youth was showing.

Nick rolled his eye. "Whatever. My mom is getting married. I was supposed to move in with Case here after the wedding. I can just move in now. My "step" dad, to be, practically lives there anyway." He was so quickly adapting and changing his life it made me wish that I could do things that easily. Youthful exuberance I thought. Don't I wish that I could bottle that as a cure-all?

When we were waiting in the parking lot, Nick got out and went into the store. I wondered what he was doing. We apparently were on a very strict schedule. I could see him talking to someone at the counter and I wondered if he really was that hungry.

Jonathan and Missy pulled into the parking lot and Nick flew to the car. His hands were empty. I said, "We could have waited for your food."

He shook his head, laughing. "That's not why we're here. My mom is the manager. I told her I would be gone for a few days on a job with Casey."

"Stop calling me that with your mom, I hate it." He turned to him. "What did she say?"

"She told me not to forget to call her and keep her posted."

He paused. "You know my mom. She's too busy wrangling that wedding stuff right now."

We were driving fast trying to reach the next destination in the three minutes that the boys had allotted for it.

Pulling up to the Sonic entrance Daniel saw that James was already there and that he didn't want us to turn into the parking lot. Instead, he pulled out immediately in front of Daniel. If we had not already been slowing down, we would have hit him.

It took only one look over our shoulders to see that Warren had followed the Mustang in his Escalade. So that's who was there looking this morning. How cocky was he these days? Daniel put on this act of blowing his horn at James in the Mustang. My Mustang, or as the guys would say, check that, Nick's Mustang.

He must have been waiting. Saw James hopping into what looked like my car and simply followed him. One more time, Warren seems to be either one step ahead or just on our heels. This was not going to turn out exactly how we planned it. It is exactly what everyone feared.

The chase was on, but it was only shortly afterwards that Warren caught up with and passed our limo. Daniel immediately called James and asked him, "What do you want us to do? Take him out? Or just follow behind?" He must have said to fall behind because the urgency with which Daniel was trying to catch Warren's vehicle slowed.

Both boys were now on the edge of their seats. Eyes forward, they were following the action of the two cars in front of us, weaving in and out of traffic. Warren was trying to get clear enough to pass James but he wasn't having much success.

Behind us, we could see that Jonathan was following as close as he could behind the limo. It was obvious that we were going to somehow have to intervene and put it to an end, but what would that be, how would it happen?

We were coming up on an exit when suddenly James scooted across the two right hand lanes and up the exit ramp. We watched as Warren slammed on brakes and pulled to the left hand side, traffic too close for him to accomplish the same thing. As we drove past, he was backing up in the hazard lane in an effort to wait out traffic and cut through those same lanes to take the exit. Immediately, the phone rang in the car and Daniel picked it up.

"Where are you?" he asked James as he listened to our ever changing plan.

"Okay, pick you up in a few."

All three of us in the back stared at Daniel as a grin crossed his face.

"What about the car?" Nick asked concerned that his new car was now lost.

"Don't worry, I don't mean literally 'pick you up'. We're going to catch up with him soon. With Warren now trying to get on the exit, James went straight across but took the state road beside the highway. He will be way ahead of us by the time we catch up with him. With any luck, Warren will be searching along the roads and restaurants at this exit for a while."

He was shaking his head. "I guess he's learned a few things over the years. That was brilliant,"

"Where are we going now?" I was in the dark.

"North, Bria, we're going north, we can't go back to the hotel now that we know that Warren knows about it." Daniel said a little tense.

"We've got a long drive ahead of us but first we're going to get food and supplies."

I wanted to ask questions, but I could see that everything was in motion. What I wanted to know, really, was that same old question... why? I kept going over every thing that I knew.

Warren was a plant to keep an eye on me as I participated in the trial. He was to monitor my moods and my mood swings, and my diet and apparently everything about me. Why? Was I not doing everything that I was supposed to do? I sat back trying to remember anything of a personal level that I might have missed. I crossed my legs underneath me and closed my eyes, pulling up memories of little every day things that should have been a sign. Maybe by the time we get to where we are going, I will have some answers. After all it was going to be a 'long drive'.

Nick and Case were all consumed like little boys in the 'chase' that we were in. Even if Warren was now not on James trail, they were

323

anxiously waiting for anything that might happen, peering over the front seat and talking with Daniel. I listened to them jabber.

I laughed silently to myself and thought about that saying, "Boys will be boys". It occurred to me that all boys no matter how old they are want to be the hero. I was way too easily playing the part of the damsel in distress, as they had called me.

Why was that? If I put, as they say, two and two together, would I get my answers. Why was I so weak when others were not?

Had Warren been poisoning me all along? Was there something else going on that I didn't know about? I had done enough of the interviews with the trial participants that I knew that none of them had the same reaction that I was having. Of course I had been out of the loop for quite a while now and only been able to know my own, but I had been through other physical and emotional injuries as well. Maybe that was the difference.

"There he is!" Nick almost bounced off of the seat as he saw the little black Mustang come into view. It had been several minutes before we caught up with James. Nick was extremely happy to see the little black Mustang and suddenly I realized how unimportant the material things in life really were to me now. I had wanted a Mustang so badly and now, it just wasn't a part of me any more. It was the same with the house. My dream house. It wasn't the house that made the dream. It was the love that should have been in it.

I had felt so loved and protected by complete strangers in the past few months that I realized, with a sudden intensity like no other, that what I had with Warren only felt like love on the surface. It couldn't have been real. Everything deep was somehow not any more.

I kept thinking, it's like when you're three years old and the three foot pool is too deep for you. When you're fifteen, the three foot pool is the baby pool. You learn that things could go much deeper. What a strange analogy. It was as if everything that I knew was tossed out the door and I was on a new path of discovery. I wondered where it might lead.

We were miles from the city when we decided to meet up and stop. It was an amazing adventure for the two young men with me. They both knew that they were in for a big change in their lives and they were almost electric with excitement.

James was there waiting on us when we pulled in. Jonathan pulled up last, only a minute behind us, and we all made our way into the local "Cracker Barrel". It was just the kind of place that no one would really expect this motley crew of ours to be going. James quickly came over to my door and opened it.

He pulled me out of the car and hugged me close. I was taken aback by his open intense public display of emotion. The only bits and pieces of this kind of display had been when I was either too sick or too susceptible to danger.

We joined in the queue to be seated in the very crowded restaurant. Ever watchful, Daniel seated himself outside in the rocking chairs until we actually found a table. He joined us only after our orders had been placed and his food was at the table. None of us spoke for fear of speaking too loud and for fear of appearing as if something were going on with us.

Food felt good. It had been too long for me. Maybe just a little too long, because the nausea swept over me with every bite I forced down. I was starving. I wanted to eat. But…I couldn't.

"Bria, maybe you should have something a little lighter. Do you want some soup?" I shook my head. "I'm way too hungry for just soup." I couldn't remember ever being this hungry and yet not able to eat. I stood shakily. "I'll be back." And I moved swiftly towards the restroom, I knew that Missy would probably follow me so I waved her off, "Just eat, I'll be right back. And if I'm not, come and clean me up off the floor." I smiled. I really was tired of everyone taking care of me.

I made my way to the restroom and I entered the stall. It felt cool in there and so I sat down on the toilet instead of in front of it. I didn't really *want* to throw up. I pressed my hands against the tiled walls of the stall, the cold feeling good on my hands. I leaned my head against it. If I could just breathe slow and work it through, I would feel that the retching that threatened to come up from the pit of my stomach settle down a bit. Just the thought of it was making it worse.

"Bria? Are you alright?" It was Missy checking on me anyway. Of course she would.

"Missy, I'm fine, honestly. I just think it has been a little too much for me."

"Well, you did just receive four pints of blood in the past twenty-four hours. Maybe we left too quickly."

326

"I'm okay, really. Go back and eat some lunch for me as well." I laughed lightly. "Really, I'm gonna just sit here for a few minutes and wait it out."

"Bria, it's okay, you don't have to pretend everything is fine. It won't be for a while. But hopefully, in the end, it will be good for lots of people."

"I know." I didn't know what else to say. I knew that she was one of those 'lots of people' she referred to.

"I'll be out in a few minutes, I promise."

"I'll be back if you aren't," she said and I heard her exit the restroom.

I sighed. I was helping out others and no matter how bad it got, it would never be as bad as it was already for them. I swallowed hard, hoping that the too little contents of my stomach would not come up.

It was from that one point of view that I knew would make me stronger. And that was what I had to focus on, and to pull from, to get through things like this.

I finally stood and opened the door to the stall. I walked over to the sink and washed my face and hands splashing my face and hair with cold water. I quickly dried my face and hands with a paper towel and headed towards the door. I had made it through without throwing up.

I knew I couldn't make it through the meal though and so I wandered through the little gift shop looking at the various oddities and old fashioned toys and candies.

In a few minutes I saw Missy and Jonathan both come my way. I stopped them before they could go into the restroom.

"I just don't think I can look at the food right now." I said. Jonathan took my wrist. Without being too conspicuous he slowly took my pulse. He watched my breathing like I was still as ill as I had been the day before.

"Do you realize that we haven't given you an injection yet? We need to get you taken care of." He pulled me outside with Missy trailing behind as we went to his car. He pulled out his life saving bag, "We can't do another IV port right here, I guess we need to give this to you somewhere else."

"I'll go get everyone else." Missy was gone immediately.

"Sorry." I whispered.

"No Bria, we're sorry. We've been so caught up in everything else that I should have weighed out all the options. We just thought that it was worth the risk to move you. My mistake again."
I patted his shoulder. "You have done more than you ever bargained for."

He smiled. "And yet it's still not enough."

"We'll get through this too." I said. I didn't want him feeling inadequate because of my mistakes.

Chapter Thirty-One
Making Life Hell

The rest of our group flowed out of the restaurant rather quickly after that. None of us really knowing what to do next, the conversation staged itself around the open door of the car I was seated in.

Nick and Case were just as involved as if they had been in on all of this since the beginning.

"Why don't we make a run for the house before we get too far away?" Jonathan asked.

"We have tons of supplies there and we can pick up clothes." James looked at him, "And just what will we do with Bria while we're getting supplies?

Case interrupted. "We can go back to the hotel maybe and sneak back in. Maybe now that they've seen us leave,"
Nick stopped him. "They didn't see us leave. They saw James leave. For all they know, we could still be there."

Daniel said, "It's true. That's why we came up with this new plan to begin with. We're working our way north remember?"

"Look, Missy needs more care than I have with me, and Bria's needs are even more extensive." He put his arm around his wife. "We don't need to take chances but somehow we have to get things from home."

Over the course of the next ten minutes or so, several options were talked over and discussed and when it was all said and done, we were at least on a course that might accomplish all of our tasks.

Nick, Case, Daniel, and I were going to be heading north to the Poconos while Jonathan, Missy, and James went back to the house.

Everything would be packed into both of SUV's that James owned. Groceries, meds, computers, clothing, all of it would be packed and brought with us.

Except for the two newcomers to our little troupe, we would have all we would need to stay 'hidden in plain sight' at James and Jonathan's vacation home.

We agreed that we could pick up some things for Nick and Case later. If they were going to be a part of this, the least we could do is outfit them and get them all the things they would need.

Pulling out of the parking lot, I was sure that I saw Warren's Escalade but when I looked back, I didn't see it again. I was getting paranoid. After all we would have seen him with all of us standing in the parking lot in a group like that.

The ride was going to be over four hours long and so I settled in the back of the limo with much to think about. We were going to be gone for as long as it took and both James and Jonathan had to make work arrangements. Their jobs were too important and I had taken them away from lots of it lately. Missy was now on disability leave so she didn't have too much to worry about.

Nick and Case would have new lives and careers. I didn't think that they were as disappointed to leave their jobs behind when we left. They were off on an adventure of a lifetime.

I watched the two of them talking back and forth. Nick had climbed into the front with Daniel while Case sat in the back with me but leaning through the drop down window. They were asking questions and listening to Daniel explain his exciting life.

I closed my eyes and tried to focus on what I would be doing for the rest of my life. I hadn't thought that I would ever want anything other than it was except to add in children when the time was right. I guess that's further away now than I ever imagined.

I couldn't hold back the tears but I didn't want the three men with me to know. I lay down in the seat and pulled someone's jacket over my head and shoulders.

I quietly sobbed into my arm hoping against hope that they wouldn't notice.

Falling into the dream was easy to do. I was back on the beach, looking down at my body curled into almost a fetal position, my hand stretched out with my wedding rings in my palm. I had taken them off and placed them in the magnetic ring holder by the sink when I had gotten home that first time after the attack. I couldn't imagine how they could have possibly come to be in my hand.

The scene changed to something new and I watched intently for clues to where I was. I was no longer crumpled on the beach but instead I was in a large open field of snow all around me. My body was in the same position, the rings glistening in my palm against its new white backdrop. I couldn't understand it at all. I looked around and no one was there. A shadow lurked at the edge of my vision, and I was sure that whoever hid there made me afraid. It was probably my killer.

I screamed. I was getting good at it but no one came. The ghost of myself that was watching my body couldn't wake me up. I couldn't get my body to rise from where it lay on the snow. It was the worst dream yet not to mention the most disturbing.

I tossed and turned in my sleep. Unknown assailants kept chasing me from place to place and Warren's hands coming for my throat every few minutes scared me to death. He would smile and be almost tender, reaching for me as if to embrace me and then his demeanor would change and I would suddenly feel his hands choking the life out of me. I never died at his hands that way. The scene revolved like a funhouse with different scenes within the mirrors.

I screamed again, my body shaking with fear and I felt someone lift me up off of the snow covered ground. I couldn't break the fear. The shaking continued, my teeth were chattering and the wet snow still clung to me.

I thought.

It was Case who held me, soothing my shoulders and pushing my hair back from my face. Nick was in front of me, his face filled with shock.

I heard Daniel, "It looks like she's having a seizure of some kind. It's been too long since she last had any of the injections."

My mind was racing, I could hear him, but where was he? I looked around and realized that I was in the back of the limo and not on the cold frozen ground. It was still summer but I was shaking uncontrollably and I was freezing.

"What do we do?" Nick's voice was trembling. Or was it me and it only seemed that his voice quivered?

Focus. I needed to focus. I was fighting my way again up a long tunnel. This. Was. Not. Right.

Daniel pulled off into some place out of the way and came back to where I lay shaking violently. "Bria?" he took my hands in his. "Look honey, we've still got a couple of hours to go. I need you to hold on. Can you do that for me?" I couldn't nod. I couldn't answer. He reached over to the little fridge and pulled out a bottle of icy cold water. "Sip this," he said but I couldn't grasp the bottle.

"I haven't seen this before or heard of this happening. Did it happen when she was with you?" Case and Nick both shook their heads.

"But her nightmares are almost as bad. I've seen her go through them, but she's never had this shaking while she is awake." Nick described what he had seen then and Case agreed that it was the same with him.

He cursed. "I need to call Jonathan."

"You know, it's almost like she's going through withdrawals from something." Nick interjected. "I saw it with my dad when we didn't have money for booze."

"I think you may be right. She hasn't had any of the normal injections that she has been on for over a year and a half now if not longer. Maybe that's exactly what is happening."

He reached in his pocket to call Jonathan but he quickly put it back in his pocket. "No signal." He explained. Both Nick and Case pulled out theirs and sure enough, the commercials had lied. You really can't get a signal everywhere.

I couldn't stop the shaking and I felt my teeth chattering even though I really was working hard to stop it. I wanted to talk but I couldn't. It just wouldn't come out. I felt my eyes roll back in my head. It hurt. Just the movement of my eyes made the front of my head scream in pain.

And then it was over. My body continued to shake because I could feel it. There was something calmer going on in my body. Somehow, my body was going limp replacing the stiff shaking little by little and my head dropped back over Case's arm.

"Okay, we've got to move." Daniel said as he hopped out of the back of the limo and got back into the front. I could hear it all, but I was completely a rag doll moving in motion with the car as he pulled quickly away from where we had stopped.

"Let me know the minute either one of you get a signal!" He was worried and I could tell that he didn't really want to take me to a hospital but would if he thought I was in trouble.

"Watch for changes in her breathing." He was giving orders now.

"We do know how to take care of her." Nick spoke softly. "We've been doing it for a few days now."

"I know you have. But I haven't. I've only been trying to make sure that no one could find her. And I haven't been as successful at that as I should have been.

His phone rang, interrupting his self loathing. "Yeah" He answered irritated. "Oh, sorry, we're in a bit of a bind here. She was seizing. Now she's just completely unconscious." He listened to someone for a while. "No, well, maybe another two hours before we're there. How far behind us are you?" Again he listened. "That's not quick enough, I can almost bet on it."

"Drive Dan, pick up the pace and let me talk to him. I can tell him what she's doing instead of you trying to do both." Nick was once again thinking on his feet, reverting back into his roll as hero. No longer the little boy enjoying a new adventure, he put the phone to his ear.

'This is Nick." He spoke with authority. "No. She was sleeping, screaming out in her sleep. I've seen her through the nightmares. Then she just started shaking uncontrollably, unable to speak. It reminds me of the withdrawals that my dad went through when he didn't have any alcohol in his system." He listened to Jonathan.

"Yeah, now she's completely limp." He listened again. "We need to get her some orange juice." He leaned up to tell Daniel through the open window. "We need to try and wake her and get her to sip it really slow." He said a quick good bye and slapped the phone closed.

"Hurry, Daniel. Jonathan sounded worried. He said that there are several reasons that she might have a seizure. We're gonna try one thing at a time. And we need a blanket. This jacket ain't gonna cut it." "Wal-Mart?" Case asked. "See the signs off that next exit?"

Before another word could be said, Daniel had switched lanes and was exiting the freeway. I felt like I would be sick. I had tried to get better, but apparently I really needed to eat something and the little bit that I had had at the Cracker Barrel wasn't enough to sustain me. Daniel was out of the limo like a shot and Nick had to run to catch up with him.

"It's gonna be okay Bria. Really you should give up on trying to do things too fast. I hope you can hear me. You are gonna kill us. I really like you and your friends but I don't think that it'll work out if you're not with us. You think you could try and let the rest of us take care of you until you get better?" He was droning on talking to me more out of his own fears than actually expecting me to hear and respond.

He was quiet for a couple of minutes.

"Where did they go to, China?" he asked the dead air in the limo. "You would have thought that they would have been rushing." I took a deep breath. I could feel the overwhelming urge to puke. I had to sit up.

He finally felt me pulling up. "Here wait a sec." He lifted my head. My eyes were still closed but I couldn't open them. His hands were holding me into position. My head rolled back. I was trying. I couldn't do it on my own. I finally forced my eyes to open and I raised my hand to my mouth. He got the sign. Quicker than I though possible, the door was open and he was holding me at the door.

I threw up, and gagged trying to throw up more and more until finally it was nothing but dry heaves. I could tell that he was getting sick. I heard him gag. I felt immensely better. I couldn't have done it without him, but he pulled me back into him and he held me up under my shoulders. I was again that rag doll hanging limply from his hands.

"What happened?" Daniel asked as they reached our side of the car. He stopped short. "Oh." He opened the front door and reached in for wipes. A second later he was cleaning my mouth, talking the whole time.

"You're both going to do this. We're going to break some speed limit laws." He opened up the juice. Cupping my chin in his hand he tilted the bottle up so that a little of it flowed slowly into my mouth. He dabbed my lips and my face again.

"Get in. Lay her head in your lap." Case hurried to do as Daniel told him.

"Nick you too. Just give her little sips of this." He handed him the orange juice bottle and then waited as Nick climbed in back with us. He unfolded a fleece throw and put it over me. I looked at him finally able to hold my gaze since Case was holding my head.

I breathed. "I'm going to die, Daniel." The words faint, snapped at him like a whip. "No! You're not. We've got no room for talk like that." And with that he slammed the door and ran to climb behind the wheel. In minutes we were back on the freeway.

I repeated myself. "I'm going to die." And then all was lost again. I was falling through that long tunnel of darkness. Voices pushing at my consciousness from some far away place.

I knew that it was too hard to try and find them. I was so very tired. My body and my mind were tired. I made up my mind. I wouldn't try this time and then as soon as I made up my mind, the world went black into nothingness.

Chapter Thirty-Two
Dying and Living

The voices were silent. I couldn't hear them any more. I was sure that I had died. But if I had died, surely there was something more. I believed in heaven.

So, I hadn't died?

Where was I? The dark nothingness of where I was frightened me. There was something. Pin points of light. I could see stars. That's what they were. I was sure of it. I just hadn't realized it before. I was getting closer to them. Or were they getting closer to me?

I started to walk to the stars but they moved with me. I looked behind me and there was nothing to see. I looked ahead of me. Again nothing.

The voice startled me. "She's just really sick. Others have had similar reactions, but they were within hours of having an injection." Jonathan was explaining things to someone. "It's like the body shuts down, trying to recognize the toxin and then expel it. I haven't seen her react like this yet, but others have."

"Has anybody died?" Nick whispered.

"Yes." I could hear him pat Nick on the shoulder. "But they actually were already dying."

"What do you mean?" Case asked.

"Well all of the other participants already had cancer. Bria was actually the only one that did not. This part was supposed to be a way to test it for genetically pre-disposed people that did not have cancer."

"Why would she do this?" It was all upsetting Nick.

"Because it is for her future and for her past. If it was successful in her, then there may be a way for them to zap that genetic link and remove cancer from ever rearing its ugly head in her life. Her grandmother died of cancer and her mother is a breast cancer survivor. She wanted to be a part of it."

"Sick." Nick said.

"Exactly," Jonathan said. "She is very sick. But we'll keep doing our best. I've never met anyone as strong as she is. She has been through more than any of the other participants, and I never would have guessed that she would have survived."

"She fights in her dreams or nightmares a lot." Case said. "She is fighting off demons or whatever and then she begins to feel pain or something because the whole look of her changes when she stops the fighting."

Jonathan said. "Yes, we've all noticed it. The emotional turmoil that Warren has caused that girl is beyond what any normal person would handle."

Silence.

I can see shadows. Shadows of people. I wonder who they are and so I call out. "Who are you?"

I heard gasps. "Bria?"

I answered, "Yes, it's me."

I can't see anyone clearly, just shadows hovering over me.

"Bria?" Missy's voice echoed through my senses.

"Bria? I'm here." Missy said again.

"Let me try something." I heard Nick. "Nikki?"

I knew then that I was still alive. I could recognize the voices as they became clearer and clearer.

"I'm here Nick." I was trying to see, wasn't I? "It's okay, don't be afraid."

"I'm not." He said and the room sighed.

"Bria, open your eyes honey. Open your eyes." Case was there too.

"They are open."

"No honey, they're not."

"I'm trying."

"Bria, what do you see?" Jonathan asked.

"Shadows and, and stars."

"Bria, try really hard. Try as hard as you can." James whispered in my ear. I could feel his breath against my skin.

"We're safe and no one is going to hurt you." James was whispering again.

"Why can't I open my eyes?" I wondered aloud.

"Honey, you're having a bad reaction or something. All of your muscles shut down on you. You have to try." It was Case again. That was why he was calling me 'Honey'; he was scared too but trying to be brave.

"Just let me rest."

"You have been resting, darling. You have been," His voice held me steady. He had my hand in his. I could feel him rubbing his thumb in circles on the top of my hand. He leaned over and kissed me on my eyes. I felt his tears drop as he hovered over my eyes and my face.

"Do you feel that?" James asked softly as he blew on my eyelids.

"Yes."

"Then open your eyes."

I tried and I tried and as if there was nothing else left to do, they slowly opened. Squinting through the shadowy veil that still seemed to want to close, I saw him.

"Hi." I said. He laughed and kissed me on my lips. Soft and supple and appetizingly sweet.

"Do you feel that?"

"Yes,"

"Then try and talk clearly."

Wasn't I doing that?

"Open your mouth a little more. We can barely understand you."

Jonathan laughed. "It's not like she's saying a whole lot, James. Give her a break."

"What happened?" I formed the words slowly and stretched my mouth to show that I was trying to speak normally.

It was Jonathan again. "Bria we don't know. It's a trial drug and you are an anomaly. No one in the study has had any of the same reactions in the same way you have."

"An anomaly?" I stuttered over the word as I blurred one syllable with another.

"It's okay Bria." Missy was there again. "I'm a bit of an anomaly too."

Now that I could see, I tried to turn my head and look for all the voices I heard. The only one missing was poor Daniel.

"Where are we?"

"Much better. We're in the Poconos. We have a little home here on a lake. No one knows you're here so you're safe." He was still whispering in my ear, his hands still massaging my hands in his. I heard snickering by the two new cohorts.

"We're not in a place in the Poconos?" I tried to look in their direction.

They burst out laughing. "There's nothing little about this 'home on a lake'." And they kept laughing.

"It's all about prospective." I whispered it as loudly as I could. The whole room erupted. Things would be fine. But the trial was literally killing me. I needed to figure that all out. Why was I an anomaly? I was so very tired. Okay, I had made my presence known.

I needed to rest and recuperate.

I closed my eyes again, and James put his arms around me.

"That is about as big a hint as you're going to get guys." Missy said. "Let's leave them alone." I heard the shuffling of the group as they left the room. I sighed. I tried to turn into him and snuggle, but I still couldn't move the bigger parts of me yet.

His smell was becoming so very familiar to me. When he was near me, I loved it. But it was also very distracting. I wasn't really ready for 'love.'

I knew that I could trust every person that I was with, but I wasn't ready to have my heart healed with the first person that came around. Hadn't I seen my share of heartache? I needed to take things back down a notch or two without making trouble. Besides, there were so many other things to think about. Like work. I was still participating in that.

I decided that I really needed to focus when I got better. I had to discover what was making me so much sicker than the others. Pretty soon, that was all I could think of. After all, Missy really needed to have this trial be a success. Not to mention, families all over the world. Including mine.

The days went by quickly with me recovering a little bit at a time. My body just couldn't get a handle on all it had been put through.

I wanted to get back to all the things that I had loved, skiing, both water and snow, tubing, again both water and snow. I wanted to be back to the way I was before the trial. I worked towards it every day. Nights were another story.

Nights were the worst. Nightmares were stalking me like predators that I could never run away from. Coming into the darkness of my mind as I would drift into sleep and rudely waking every fear that gripped me. It did not aid in my recovery at all.

One day as I sat by the window, reading another one of the books that were found wherever James seemed to dwell, I over heard Nick and Case talking about how much their lives had changed. I was really happy and they were happy with their choice.

Nick and Case had become part of the new house. We made plans to stay for the summer with commutes back only when absolutely necessary.

I had my laptop and of course Jonathan and Missy to help me record all of the data that was needed for the trial I was participating in. James was gone the most. He had to commute often and so he became a virtual stranger around the house. Instead, James hired Nick and Case to be around me constantly. They were to run errands and to 'guard' the house. They loved their new found 'family'.

Everything seemed so normal.

It wasn't. Around the everyday things going on was an undercurrent of anticipation and speculation of when the next time would be that we would find ourselves facing Warren.

.

Several weeks passed before we knew it. We didn't know what was going on and no one could say when it might be time to leave again and so we were determined to have the house be calm.

As the summer wore on, we decided that it was finally okay to let me out of doors. I loved to walk outside and would frequently be found sitting in the front porch swing. It was like the best log home you could dream of. I loved it here.

I had asked James to make arrangements for me to sell the "dream home" I had shared with Warren. I had wondered if it really and truly was completely mine or was Warren making payments on it somehow. I wasn't sure and I just didn't want anything to come back to haunt me.

James finally brought home the news that I could indeed sell my house. There were lots to do to get it ready but I was willing to make the trip and do the work. I decided that I would like to have it continue to stay decorated with the Christmas décor and that that would be our target period for sale. I hoped that we would have it ready for the holiday season and have open houses starting from November 1st. Until then, I wanted to do anything so that I could begin to be active again and feel like a productive member of society.

Missy understood me the most, while the men we were with just didn't get it. She had not been in remission for so long that she could remember being as helpless as I had been. We talked about it a lot. I began to love her as if she were on my own sister. We would even do short shopping sprees when we could get the men to leave us alone.

Because I was steadily improving, I felt my energy level growing and I was able to do more and more. The nightmares did not lessen, but each morning seemed to be better than the last.

I woke one morning with an incredible burst of new energy. I was feeling so much better than even the day before. The end of summer was finally here and the fall colors that were just barely beginning were calling to me much as they had every year of my life. I needed to be out doors today. Here in Pennsylvania, there was a plethora of pre-fall fauna that I could walk around and see.

It was early. No one was up and I decided to take advantage of the alone time and the very slight chill on the morning. I quickly got dressed and pulled on a sweater and went out the back door and down to the dock on the lake. There were fishing supplies there in a big truck storage box that anyone could use, and though it wasn't my favorite pass time, I could still do it. Today felt like that kind of day. The energy level I was feeling had me missing the things of my youth.

I picked out a fishing pole and some hooks and weights and bobbers along with a few of the rubber worms. I just wanted to sit and enjoy the beauty of it all and the feel of just passing time leisurely like when I was a young girl with my dad by my side.

It was a strange feeling. I hadn't felt this not stressed in ages. Something wonderful was happening. I felt it like a warm glove wrapping me in fond memories.

347

Warren and I had never done this. I wondered what else I had changed without realizing it while we were married. I used to go to the slopes. I used to go to the lakes. I loved going to the beaches with him, but we never had any adventures. I laughed out loud. I think we've more than made up for that afterwards.

I put my rubber worm on the hook and threaded the bobber on the line. I stood and cast it out as far as I could. It was nice to sit here waiting on a strike that I knew would never come. I thought it was the same with Warren and me now. It had been so long since my last Warren encounter. I wondered, just where was Warren? What had happened that the past three months had not been interrupted by him? I had even talked to my parents and my friends and no one had heard anything.

My dad had even warned me. "Don't get complacent little girl, because that will be when he decides to rear his ugly head again." I had laughed. "Don't worry Daddy," I had said, "I think my protective detail would love for him to do just that."

I smiled remembering. The sun had taken the chill off the morning as I sat there and now it was almost hot. I took off my sweater and tossed it to the side. I removed my shoes and dropped my feet into the warming water. It was the perfect late August day.

I heard the footsteps before my name was called. "Bria, what are you doing?" James asked.

Everyone must have been looking for me. Behind him trailed Nick and Case while up on the porch, Missy stood, her arms folded with Jonathan wrapping his arms around her in their typical loving embrace. They made such a great couple. I looked back at the people I now called family, and I was happy.

The three men got closer, "Bria, did you hear me? What are you doing?"

I laughed out loud. "Uh, panning for gold?" I said. "Isn't that what this thing is for?" Nick and Case laughed out loud, too, and just as they touched the dock, Nick shoved Case into the water. I reeled the line in quickly and tossed the fishing pole down on the dock beside me.

I stood up and turned around completely. Nick dove in, fully clothed and splashed water every where. Water dropping on both James and I felt just a little cooler than it had with my feet actually in the water.

"I'm just feeling exceptionally good today, so I thought I would relive a memory." James stopped just beside me. I looked up at him and he smiled down at me. "I'm glad you're feeling so much better. We've been waiting on that complete recovery level of energy for a long time."

"I know." I paused, a mischievous thought creeping in my head. I waved my hand out in front of me. "Just look at how beautiful this time of year is. The colors are beginning to creep in at the stem of each leaf. Soon it will be time for fall festivals and Halloween."

He looked across the lake at the trees in the mountains. I slowly stepped back a bit, and then with all my might, I shoved. James looked shocked as he reached for me and missed, splashing mightily into the lake. I laughed, almost in tears instantly.

I watched as he sputtered, in shock that I was able to do it. He swam back to the dock and tried to jump up and grab me to pull me in, but I dodged his touch. "Oh no, you deserve that, interrupting my quiet morning." He was laughing. Nick and Case both swam over to the dock and began their attempt to keep James from grabbing on to me.

I was laughing so hard. It was fun to feel this way again. My smile broadened and as James began to pull himself back onto the dock, I took a running leap and dove over the side into the water. I heard him yell "Bria" as my head went underneath the water.

I didn't care. Life was fun again!

Chapter Thirty-Three
Living

I was, for the first time, feeling completely free from everything. It felt good to let go. I swam underneath the dock without coming up in plain sight of everyone. Hiding like I had when I was a child, scaring my parents. James dove back in to the water and began looking for me.

The three in the water began calling my name. All too easily, it turned to panic. Oh good grief, I thought, and when James was close enough, I ducked back under the wood framing of the dock and popped up just in front of him, giving him a peck on the lips.

"Gotch ya!" I said. Laughing felt so good and I pushed off of him with my feet, but he grabbed me and pushed me under the water. Jonathan and Missy reached the dock in time to see me come up spitting water in James' face. Nick and Case were loving it. This was the first time they had seen me let go. After all, I was sick of being sick. This was my time for fun. I was going to get out of it all that I could even if I had to pay for it later. Now, was good.

Missy was laughing and Jonathan was calling out to James, "Be careful James, water is the great equalizer." I knew what he meant, even if James didn't seem to get it. How many times I had been able to come out the winner with my brothers in the water. It didn't matter how big or small you were in the water, it made every one weightless while you were in it. I ducked down again and swam away while James wiped the water from his eyes. I came up from behind him and putting my hands on top of his head, lifted my body out of the water, pushed him down. I dove backwards off of him as he sank. When I came up out of the water, everyone was laughing. It was so great!

James came up sputtering, I had surprised him again. He turned to me, wiggling his finger for me to come to him.

"Catch me if you can." I said. He laughed. He suddenly put his hand in front of him and stroked clean strokes to where I was. He pulled my shoulders to him and I kicked out, putting my feet on his thighs, standing on them. I pulled myself into him and kissed him full on the lips. Instantly, he had his arms around me and we were kissing passionately.

The world disappeared. I didn't hear the comments or the laughter from the others as I closed my eyes and wrapped my hands around his head, pulling myself in closer to him.

It was so good to feel that. That indescribable connection when passion ignites flames in two people at exactly the same time.

"Get a room!" Nick called out.

Suddenly, I was aware of just how passionate I was getting. I pulled away from him, turning around and pulling his arms around me. I wanted to let him know that what had happened was okay. I kicked my feet up and splashed Nick and Case.

The games were then on as they realized that I was in a very playful mood and would have fun with them as well.

The next couple of hours were filled with play in the water, getting in and out, clothes dripping as we climbed onto the dock. Diving back in and splashing each other like a group of kids.

Finally, so tired that my arms were almost too weak to lift my body out of the water, I pulled myself up halfway, and Nick, who was the closest, lifted me up the rest of the way onto the dock. I plopped down next to where Missy sat beside Jonathan. I was breathing hard.

"That's more like it. I've wanted to feel this good for a very long time." She patted my wet pants leg. "Do you think you could have done this with a bathing suit on?" She laughed. I shoved her and she almost fell into the water, she was so unprepared.

"Hmmm, stronger than you look when you're feeling good aren't you?"

I smiled. "Yep, I'm not always that 'damsel in distress' every one thinks I am. It takes major bodily harm to put me in that place." The shadow of my recent past flitted before my eyes and she heard it in my voice.

Missy heard it too and all too quickly she said, "That was quite a passionate display out in the water." I blushed. "I don't know what came over me. I don't want to start that kind of relationship with any one right now." Her eyebrows raised. "I want to be well away from the whole Warren situation before I open up my heart completely again."

I lowered my head. "I don't want to feel the way I do about James. Not yet." She put her arm around me. "It's okay. I understand. But don't lead him on. He's already trying to figure out his own feelings."

I nodded. "Okay, now, I'm exhausted." I yawned and lay back on the dock, my feet just barely hanging over the edge. The boys were still playing around and I noticed James get out of the lake. He began ringing out his clothes. He took off his shirt and I watched as he towered over us on the dock. His chest nearly bare of hair, his muscles taught and larger than you could ever have guessed underneath his shirts. I smiled up at him.

"You okay?" he asked.

"Yeah I'm just really tired now. Too much all at once I guess."

"Need help?"

"Maybe, but I'm going to let the sun dry me a little." I spread my hair out behind me on the dock. I closed my eyes and for the first time in a while I didn't feel like there was a need to fight away the scenes that would play in my mind. I was too happy to let them bother me.

He sat down behind me, his hands playing in my hair. I could feel the heat of the sun as it began the slow process of drying my clothes and my hair and warming my body. I was lost in thought and not really ready to give up the fun that I was having this morning and so I lay there, quietly and enjoyed the near silent rustle of the wind as it flowed around us.

Finally, grumbling stomachs talked sense into all of us and we slowly began to realize that our morning's fun was over. I sat up and gathered my hair to wring it out of any excess water. There wasn't much left, but that stiff feeling, like I needed to wash it that made me cringe. I hated that my hair was that stiff in my fingers. I shivered and rubbed my arms.

As I started to stand, James reached under my arms and lifted me off of my feet. He turned me around to him without my feet touching the ground and I knew it was coming before his lips touched mine.

The soft supple kiss, less passionate than it had been in the water, melted me. The others were already fifteen to twenty yards ahead of us; I would be in trouble if we didn't start walking. I completely relaxed as the kiss filled me, I held my breath. I could taste the pleasure of the moment and I wanted it to be more but not yet. I pulled away and he let me slide my body down to the ground. I took his hand and held it as I draped it over my shoulders. We walked slowly back up to the house wrapped up in our own thoughts and raging passion, keeping everything in check.

We walked together up the stairs and I went into my bedroom, closed the door behind me and dropped to the floor by the bed. I was so confused. I sat for a few minutes tracing shapes on the floor with the water that fell from my clothes

Finally, I stood and walked to the bathroom that connected to another bedroom that was currently being shared by Nick and Case. It was an odd situation. I knocked on the door. No one was in the shower. I walked in and locked their door and then back to lock mine. I turned on the water and quickly undressed.

My mind was turning over all the mental and physical feelings that were enveloping me. I could not believe that I was falling for James this hard. Dammit, I wanted to have myself free and clear of Warren before letting myself get into any relationship again. I was so mad at myself.

I climbed into the shower, and bathed. Washing my hair, I felt the dirt of the lake falling out of my hair and off of my body. I wished that I could wash away my former life with Warren the same way. But it still had too many questions about it all.

When I got out of the shower, my mind was racing with how I would put everything back and on the right track. I quickly got dressed, leaving my hair wet and dripping down my back. I ran a brush through it and tried to towel dry the ends so that I didn't trail water everywhere I walked.

I hopped up on the bed, continuing to towel dry my hair. It had grown so much and I hadn't cut it in years so I knew it would take a while.

I wrapped the towel around my head and lay down to relax for a little while. My body was overly tired but it felt good. There is a vast difference between being weak and sick and physically exhausted because of play or good honest work.

I wanted to revel in the moment. I curled up under the blanket and closed my eyes. I smiled. I was happy. Wasn't I?

I knew that something still bothered me about all that had happened but I couldn't quite put my finger on what it was. I fell softly into sleep for the first time in ages. My mind only on the passionate kisses that had been exchanged between James and I.

I could easily imagine much, much more. Somehow, I managed to wrap my arms across my chest. I smiled again in my sleep. Today, it seemed to be bursting from me. It felt amazing.

Chapter Thirty-Four
And Dying

The knock on the door interrupted my dreams as good as they were. I knew that I needed to get up and go get something to eat. My stomach was really growling and in spite of that I couldn't erase the smile from my face. I could still taste his mouth on mine.

I shook my head. What the heck is wrong with me? This is not good for either of us. I was an old hat at not being sure about the feelings of my heart.

"Yes, come in." I called out; I just needed to put up my hair. James walked in the room and over to the bed. I began to blush deeply and he reached up and felt the heat of my cheeks. I grabbed his hand and held it there. I wasn't sure what I wanted to do next, but I was sure that if I didn't get out of my room, we might do things we shouldn't be doing.

I wasn't ready emotionally for anything further. Besides I was an old fashioned girl. I really did believe in purity before marriage. Even if I have been married before, I like the thought of having a pure relationship with whomever I marry next, whenever that might be.

James pulled me to my feet. "I love this you, too. Maybe we can play that again later." He laughed as he pulled me out of the bedroom and down the stairs.

Okay this I could deal with. It was fun being this way. Of course it would go away again temporarily when I got my injection again, but I was okay with it. As I got better each day, the time that I was sick seemed to get shorter and shorter.

Lunch was superb. Simple. Wonderful. Maybe it was because we were so famished from the mornings play. It had been a long time since we just sat and had soup and sandwiches. I was so happy.

We finished but not one of us felt like there was an immediate need to get up and do anything else. I finally picked up the plates and walked over to the sink. I started washing the dishes. It was as if my moving was a cue to have everyone get up and do something. In short order, the rooms were cleaned again and we were ready to relax.

Jonathan hesitantly spoiled the moment with his words.

"Bria?" he looked at me and I knew it was time. I had been able to put it off so far this morning because we were all outside having a great day. "Are you ready? It's already been more than twenty-four hours. Daniel just brought in a new batch for us to start on."

I knew this and I was well aware of the consequences of me not having the injections. I nodded my head and got up to walk to my room. I had taken to going to my room to have my little bout of nausea, drowsiness and nightmares. I was fine in a couple of hours now as opposed to all day events from before.

As I passed by James, Jonathan already following me, he took my hand and stood, accompanying me up the stairs and to my room.

Jonathan looked at James, "Are you sure that you want to see this again?" James nodded his head. I knew that he hated watching me in pain and my nightmares were worse than ever. Mainly because it had been so long since we had had any interaction with Warren.

I climbed into the bed and held out my arm. I was no longer attached to an IV. Each day I would get stuck again. It was easier for me. He was just giving me a slow injection now. James pulled up a chair beside my bed and held my hand. I felt the burn and then the slow warmth and the nausea.

Without warning, I was sicker than I had been in several weeks. Jonathan must have known. It had been an active morning, I had eaten well, and of course, today would be the day that I would have much more than usual to throw up. That was why we had taken to always doing it before breakfast.

Jonathan laughed. "I thought it would be bad today, after all the exercise this morning and her energy level being so high. It was bound to happen." He pulled James out of the room and he sat with me puking into the trash can.

When that embarrassment was over, he helped to clean me up and I was suddenly very ready for the sleep portion of my daily routine. Being exhausted before taking the meds, made it worse. I should have known that.

"I'll stay with you for a while, or would you rather have someone else?" I shook my head. I didn't really want anyone there. My nightmares were bad enough for me to face much less have someone else witness them as they all had before. "Just until I get to sleep," I said.

He closed the shades, creating the darkest room possible at two in the afternoon. I closed my eyes and willed the sleep and nightmares to do their worst.

Sleep came and my body, weakened by the morning's activities as well as the puke session of moments before, led my nightmares to become more intense than they had been in quite a while.

I walked along a small path in the mountains in the snow. I was looking for something but I didn't know what. My heart was breaking and I was sobbing. Warren stepped from behind the trees.

His hands reached for my throat but instead he pulled me to him, whispering something unknown in my ear. He took my hand and kissed it and then suddenly there was blood all over the snow. I screamed and I looked at my body in the snow my hand out in front of me with my wedding rings in the palm of my hand. I screamed and screamed. I couldn't find my way back to the safety of my room.

"Bria, honey, you need to wake up." I knew instantly that it was Case. His voice was strong, battling to pull me back.

"Bria Stone today is your day to die." The voice dragged me back into the nightmare.

"No!" I screamed. "Stop!" I was being dragged through the snow by someone or something. I couldn't see anything but the trail of blood off my fingertips as I was being dragged in the fresh white snow. I kept screaming and couldn't stop. My breathing was becoming shallow.

I heard the panic in Case's voice.

"Jonathan! She's not breathing!"

I was breathing, I wanted to tell him, I was screaming, couldn't they hear me. The two worlds were colliding, half in my nightmare, and half in the light of day.

"Breathe Bria, take a breath." He was puffing air into my lungs. His head right over my face, his mouth on my mouth and my nose pinched. I knew he was breathing for me. I could see it as if I were standing there watching it.

In fact, I was standing there watching it.

I saw Jonathan come in with Missy right behind. Case was busy blowing into my mouth, Missy grabbing Jonathan's medical bag from where it had been stored and not used for weeks.

"She's not breathing!" Case was panicked and the tears were streaming down his face and onto mine. Jonathan pulled the bed from the wall, calling for Nick and James. I saw them come into the room and as the seriousness of the situation immediately showed on their faces, I watched as they ran to help pull the bed further from the wall.

Jonathan tilted back my head and I watched as he put a tube down my throat and I felt air fill my lungs, Missy pumping an oxygen bag steadily and I realized that I my chest was beginning to rise and fall.

Everything went black, and I knew nothing more.

"Bria, I'm sorry, please don't give up." Case's words were a whisper, almost a prayer. He sat in a chair pulled up by my bed. His head was bent over his hands as he laid his head against my bed. I knew that something bad had happened. I had seen me die. Of that I was sure of. Or was it a new twist to my nightmares? I had to think.

I *had* watched Case try to revive me and I saw his face as I died. I remembered James, his face white and poor Nick backing against the wall as if he couldn't get far enough away from the scene playing out in front of him. Missy and Jonathan, working furiously to revive me, no tears, just doing what they would normally do at the hospital. I had seen it all.

I raised my hand and placed it on the top of Case's head. Comforting him like a mother. He slowly raised his head and looked up at my open eyes. "Bria," he breathed my name. He jumped to his feet and yelled. He kissed my cheek and held my hand. Too tightly.

"You're alive. I tried to save you. I really tried. I'm sorry I wasn't…"

I stopped him, pulling my hand from his and turning it so that I held his and I brought it to my cheek. I could not speak, the breathing tube blocking words.

The room crowded quickly. I looked in the eyes of the people that I loved. So much more than friends, and so much more than family. I blinked back the tears. I knew that they had suffered again because of me.

Jonathan spoke. "I'm sorry Bria. I don't know what happened." I began to shake my head.

"Stop. Don't try and talk or move. You are going to have to be patient. I'm not taking out that tube until we figure out what caused that. That's two different times that you have had this type of reaction and I'm not willing to take chances again."

James stood on the opposite side of the bed. He didn't say a word. I was afraid to look at him. I had seen his eyes, his face when I died. Or whatever it was that had allowed me to move out of my body and watch it all. He had relived not only everything that he had gone through already with me, but he relived the heartache that he must have had with Joanne as well. I was overwhelmed at the pain I had caused.

Missy took my hand and said: "Bria, Casey saved your life. He kept you breathing 'til Jon got here. He's been by your side constantly, as have we all."

I turned back to Casey. I couldn't express my thanks just now, but I would. I squeezed his hand and he held on as if he would never let go. He was too choked up to talk, but Nick walked over and massaged his shoulders from behind. "Like I said, damsels in distress always need heroes." I nodded.

"Okay, everyone out. Let her rest. We've got plenty to keep us busy." Jonathan said. "Casey, it's time that you got some real sleep. Outta here, now."

With that the room cleared with the exception of Jonathan and James. "I've got lots to do Bria, but we have to take more blood samples and figure this one out. We think we understand, but we're not sure. Meanwhile, you've just got to try and get better. If you're breathing well and your oxygen level improves, I'll take out that tube tomorrow."

I looked at him. I blinked. He understood that I understood. He leaned down and kissed me on my forehead. "Look little helpless Bria, we like the fun girl you were the other day. It was great to see that side of you. We're going to bring her back. So work with me. Okay?" I blinked again and he looked over at James and walked out of the room.

I looked up at him. He reached underneath me and slid me over and crawled into the bed with me without a single word.

Carefully, he slid his arm under my neck and cradled me under his arm.

His voice cracked when he was at last able to speak. "I can't lose you. I didn't want to fall in love again. Ever. I was resigned to love only Joanne." He paused and I knew he was having a hard time with continuing.

"I'll ask you only once. Will you give up this trial? It's killing you faster than if you did get cancer." He paused again. "I only had a small glimpse of what life would be like with you, and I want it. I want it more than I can tell you."

He kissed my forehead and held me tight. "I love you. But, I'll not have another woman die in my arms. If you continue with this trial, I don't think I can handle it."

I turned my head away from him. My tears were silently flowing. How could I give it up when we are so near its conclusion? December. If I could make it to December, then it will be over. And what they learn because of me, could, I hope save millions. It was bigger than me. It was bigger than James.

I knew my answer. And I knew that no matter what he said, his heart would be there for me when I was able to give him mine. We would last.

Chapter Thirty-Five
A New Trouble

The morning broke with a thunderous clap. It was hurricane season down south still and a storm had been spun off and into the mountains. It would probably mean an early snow in some of the higher elevations, but here it was simply a downpour.

James lay beside me with a very somber look on his face and he looked like he hadn't really slept at all. On the contrast, I did sleep. I knew I was sleeping because the nightmares kept changing and changing, each one including my death at Warren's hands.

I had had enough of it all and I wanted to run again, but I couldn't. I wouldn't. The next time something like this happened would be my last. I was sure of it.

Lightning flashed. Thunder clapped. The electricity flipped off. The oxygen machine shut off. James jumped out of the bed and disappeared out of the room.

Jonathan and Missy came running in and immediately, she began the process of bagging the tubes manually pushing air through my throat and into my lungs. I tried to push her away to let her know that I was breathing on my own. I purposely sucked air in through my nose and blew it out. Jonathan stopped her and began to remove the tape from my face. The tube exited this time much faster and smoother than it had the first time. However, I did manage to slobber all over everything before the two of them could clean me up.

The electricity turned back on and the machines started up once again. James came back into the room with both Nick and Case trailing him. "I started the generators." He stood at the foot of my bed, "How is she?"

"She's fine, James." Missy said. "She's gonna be great."
I tried to clear my throat, but of course it was so very sore. Jonathan went into the bathroom and came back with a cup filled with water. He held it up to my lips. "Do you want me to explain what happened?" He looked at me and then away to the others.

"No, I saw it all." The reaction was expected.

"What do you mean you saw it all?" Nick asked.

"I saw my body. I saw Case breathing into my mouth. I saw you all working to save me and moving the bed and I saw everything that happened until just after the tube went into my throat." My voice was raspy. It hurt to talk. But I had learned that it only got better if I used it.

Missy covered her face, her hands trembling. She knew I had died and was brought back. She had seen many near death experiences in her work and so had Jonathan.

James went white. Case dropped to the chair he had been sitting in over the past few days before I woke up. Nick just stared.

"It's okay. I know that you were all fighting to save me." I looked around the room. "How long before we know what the heck is going on?" I looked directly at Jonathan.

"We are thinking that you just occasionally have an adverse reaction." I looked at him, confusion on my face.

"This is what you call an adverse reaction."

"It's like the people who have taken penicillin all of their lives and then one day they are allergic to it or have an adverse reaction to it."

"Oh."

"Well then what can we do about it?"

"Nothing for now. We just have to do things more carefully." He paused looking at James, "You can't stop the injections because it will also be damaging to you. Your problems would be just as bad or worse. We're stuck doing this to the end. We'll taper the dosages off as we will do with all remaining participants in the trial."

"'Til almost Christmas then?"

"But there is always something good that comes of everything. It will now be one of those side effects that well help us change things for future use."

I took in the conversation. One thing struck me. I was one of the remaining participants. Just how many had died? I was too afraid to ask. I was sure that the number was large.

"Okay, can I get dressed and cleaned up or is that an impossibility?" Missy laughed. "No, we can do it right now if you want to. Shall we have everyone help?"

I smiled. "If that's what it takes." She hadn't expected that response and everyone laughed. Jonathan reached up and tussled my hair like I was a two year old. It felt funny. But I knew that it meant that he loved me.

He reached towards Nick and Case and pulled them out of the room, leaving James standing at the end of the bed. Missy looked at James. He wasn't moving. "Uh, James?" She wasn't going to start helping me with him in the room.

He slowly moved his eyes to hers and then back to mine. "I've seen her naked. I don't think there is anything left to hide.

Missy sounded frustrated. "James, that's not the same and you know it." He shook his head. "I'm not leaving her."

She started protesting him, "James, you're being a little silly. You can't be with her every second. You simply can't." He was shaking his head again.

"James," I looked up at him. "I'm not leaving you." He continued to stare at me. "I can't leave you. I'm not going to leave you."

"Please let me keep some of my moral standards." I smiled back at him.

"I love you, Bria. I want you to know it. It's out in the open. I want to marry you. I want you to bear my children. I want it all, and I can't do that if you keep dying on me."

Missy's hand went to her mouth. "James now is not the time." She spoke loudly and clearly to him. "She is not Joanne. She is not in any way ready for this type of conversation."

James stared at her. It was as if he had been slapped.

"James," I cleared my throat. I wanted to be especially precise with my words. "James. I love you. I have begun to fall in love with you. But," I paused, "I have things to finish before I begin to think about marriage and family. I will not quit this trial. I will not give up on everything I've worked for and suffered for. We will work towards the rest when I have closure on everything else. That includes Warren. And," I paused again, "It includes Joanne. You need closure where she is concerned. I am not Joanne. I am Bria Marie Sutton Stone. That is who I am. When you are ready to love me and not a shadow of your former wife, then we'll be on the same page."

I watched his face and saw the signs of pain as he realized that I had spoken truer words than he wanted to admit to. He turned and walked out of the room without another word and without looking back.

Missy said nothing else. She helped me out of bed and together we walked to the bath and we went through all the motions of bathing and getting me dressed without a single word being spoken. When we were successfully back in the bedroom and I was once more propped up in bed, I asked. "Was I too harsh?"

"I don't know. I just don't know. It had to be said, but I don't know if that was the right time to do so. I don't know if it was right for me to say what I said. I guess we're all so edgy and you, well, you're so much a part of our lives now, that..." She shrugged her shoulders and left the statement hanging in the air. She walked out of the room closing the door leaving me alone with my thoughts.

I cried in my pillow for a long time. I did not eat when they brought food up to my room. I did not speak for a long time to any of them.

That night, Jonathan came in to give me my dosage of the meds. Sometime in the day he told me that he was going to be experimenting with when the dosage was administered.

So since we were now going to try different times of the day to see if it made a difference in how I felt, he decided that tonight would be our first of three days of night injections. We would record the differences in how I felt and how I handled it.

I turned away while he did it. I gagged furiously but I didn't throw up. There was nothing in my stomach anyway. He watched me as I began to drift off back to sleep.

"That was unfair Bria. It hurt James more than you could have possibly imagined." I didn't respond. He touched my shoulder and whispered, "We all love you." I kept silent. He left the room.

I watched the shadows of the night fall through the window. I couldn't think about that now. I had to protect my heart and his and neither one of us needed to be thinking about a serious relationship when we were both so obviously still tied to our previous loves.

The nightmares came raging on and I heard my screams penetrate the night. No one came to comfort me. No James was there to brush away the immediate threat and I died many times during the night in my nightmare. When the nightmares ended and I had slept some, I awoke to find Case sitting in the chair beside my bed and Nick standing behind him.

"Thanks." I looked at the two of them and then my decision was made. I had promised to never run away again and so I wouldn't. I would just leave. I was as free to do as I pleased as an adult.

371

"It's time I left." I said the words calmly.

Nick smiled. "We figured you'd be running soon."

Case added. "Ready when you are. But Bria, they will have to know where we are. I can't go through you dying in front of me again." He was shaking his head. Nick piped in. "James isn't the only one with his heart breaking. Both of us love you. You're like my big sister. Case, well, that's between the two of you."

"Casey." He cringed when I called him that. "Casey, I do love you. But, like I said to James. Not now. I can't do this now, with anyone. Besides you're like my brother. I would never tie you down to me. I have too much fun with the both of you. Don't put me in this predicament. I'll leave without you both if you can't deal with it."

"No!" both of them said it at once.

"No." Case said again. "I don't know what I feel. It's like I would die for you. Die trying to save you. I love you. But I don't know how I love you. Make sense?"

"Not really, but we're family, so we don't always have to make sense."

"That's how I feel. Like we're family. Like you're my little sister, but you're my older sister. And yet...I just don't understand." No one spoke for a few minutes.

"They're family too, Bria. Jonathan, Missy and James. We've all been through hell and back with you and for you. We gotta be honest with them."

"Okay. I'm going home. I have a house to get ready to sell. I have work to do. I have things I have to set in place before I can move on with the rest of whatever my life holds."

"We're coming. We'll help. But we're telling them the what, where, when, why and how of everything, right?" Nick was adamant. I nodded. "I don't need to get packed. I have things at my home I can use. I just need to leave a note or two."

Case walked over to the desk. "Do you want me to write it?" I chuckled a little. "No, Casey, sweetheart, this is for me to do. I do need to arrange for a car. I'll not be taking one of theirs."

"Actually, I have one here that James gave me to use. We'll use that one." Case said.

"The Pathfinder?" I knew it would have been.

"Yup."

"Okay. I'll be ready to leave in an hour. Can you guys be ready to leave then?"

"Of course."

I got out of bed slowly, carefully and shuffled over to the desk with their help. "I'll knock on your door when I'm ready." I wanted to have privacy when I wrote the letters.

I waited, pen in hand over the pad of paper that Case had pulled out of the drawer. When they left the room, I started my first letter.

My dearest James,

In my dreams you are my hero. You are the man that I spend the rest of my life with. You are the father of my household full of children and you are the love of my life. Know that I really do dream those things when I dream. They weave in and out of the nightmares that also haunt me. Warren is still a little bit of a mystery in my life. Until that part is solved and filled up with answers to all of my questions, I cannot give my heart to you as fully as I want to.

I didn't mean to hurt you. I can't wait to have you take me in your arms and share a passion that endures what ever the future holds for us, but there is no future when we are both trapped by our pasts.

Love me, James. Love me for me and not as a substitute for Joanne. There will always be a piece of Joanne in your heart, but I need a place there of my own. Maybe, when all of this is over, we'll find room for me and the hole that Warren left in mine will be very easily filled by you.

I love you,

Bria

I reached for another sheet and started on the next one.

Dear Missy and Jonathan,

No greater family could there be than the two of you. I have loved you as much as my own real family. More than friends. I just need some time to solve my issues. Yes, I will try to remember what my needs are. I have decided to quit my job. I no longer want to work in the research industry. I will continue with this trial, but after that, I am through. I will try and find another way to help other victims of abuse like me. I suddenly realized that all of my problems stem from abuse and not from some trial medicine that I happen to be participating in.

I've asked the boys to accompany me to my home in Silver Springs. That's where we'll be. Getting the house ready to sell, and getting my things packed. You're welcome to join us there.

I do love James. I'm sorry he is hurt. I just need to heal the hole in my heart with answers. That is, I'm afraid to say; the only way our future will be one.

I love you both so much.

Bria.

I turned over James letter again and re-read it, tears streaming down and dropping onto the page. I decided on a p.s. on his letter so I wrote.

p.s.

James, I'll be at my house. Please come by when you can. I love you the mostest.—lol.

I smiled through my tears using the term that my parents had used on us kids when we were little.

I left both letters face up on the desk and gingerly walked to the boy's room through the bathroom. I knocked on the door and both of them came through the door at once as if they were waiting right by it. Case said, "Bria, you're going to need meds, aren't you?" I shook my head. "I think that maybe Jonathan and Missy will come down and bring them to me. If not, we have that supply at my work. I am going to go in and clear out my desk and quit my job. We'll liberate some of the vials while we're there."

"But you're so weak now." Nick said.

"I know but I have my two heroes." I smiled and he hugged me tightly.

375

He held out his arms. "Need a lift, m'lady?" I nodded and smiled, happy to have help. Nick swooped me up in his arms and we walked downstairs and out the front door. I looked back over his shoulder at the lovely house that had become another on the list of homes that I loved. I finally realized that it wasn't the size or the build of the house that makes it a dream home. It was the hearts that lived in it. I was sure that one day soon, I would be back here. I didn't know how and I didn't know when, but I knew I would once more sit on that porch and look out at the beauty around me.

Chapter Thirty-Six
Much Work to Do

Nick, Case and I got into the Pathfinder that now belonged to Case and we made our way off of the property and out onto the highway before the sun even came up that morning. I sat in the front with Case driving. Nick was in the back but most of the time was leaning up in between the seats watching. I knew that the four to five hour drive would wear me out but I was determined to just keep going with my plan.

I had told them where I would be and who I was with. The decision was now up to them. If we never saw any of them again, it would break my heart, but I would at least know that they had been given a choice to make and it was up to them to make it.

Case rambled on and on about how much fun it had been on this adventure that we had been on. Nick said, "Yeah, Nikki." Emphasizing the use of the name I had first told him, "you've given us one great adventure." I laughed. "Not your everyday theme park kind, huh?" We all laughed. It was as if we were off again on our own new adventure and we could feel the excitement in the air.

When seven in the morning rolled around, I realized that the rest of the house would be waking up about now and someone would inevitably bring me breakfast. It wouldn't be long now before one of our cell phones rang. I was sure of it.

They didn't. By eleven we were at my home. The back window had been replaced and so I had Nick smash the window in again. When they helped me into the house, I could see some of the changes that had been made. The broken pieces of my figurines and snow globes were in a waste basket. The carpets had been shampooed and things generally straightened up. I had just a few weeks before I wanted it to be ready for open houses and for sale.

"Wow," Case said when he walked through to the living room. "This place is massive."

"And you're selling it why?"

"Because it was a gift from Warren. I always wanted to raise a family here, but now, it is just a painful reminder of what was and is no more." I put my hand on the banister. I felt the cool wood underneath my fingertips. I took a step towards the stairs, and I sat down on them. I knew that I couldn't go up to the bedroom. It held very painful memories there.

"Well, I guess we have some work to do but not too much for us to handle." Nick said

"I want it to be decorated again for Christmas. It looks like those things have now been put away." I looked around. Sure that if I decorated it as I had seen it, I would be able to sell it fast.

"There are lots of things to do but for now, let's order Chinese food." I looked around, "My checkbooks are in the office in the bottom drawer." I reached for the phone on the foyer table and dialed the restaurant number. It was written on the pad where we had last ordered from them. The memory flooded back to me when they answered and asked for my phone number. "Do you want the same thing as the last time you ordered?" I remembered it well. I couldn't talk.

"Nick, order for us, will you?" I handed him the phone and put my head down between my knees. I didn't want to cry any more. I just couldn't. I needed to maintain the façade in front of them, even if I cried through every night's sleep.

We sat in the living room waiting on the order to be delivered. I sat at my desk, and wrote out a list of the things I wanted to accomplish.

1. yard work
2. painting
3. repairs to the back door
4. new locks on all doors
5. put up decorations for Halloween
6. call real estate agent
7. close out all joint accounts
8. pack up Warren's things
9. pack up my things
10. change my name back!
11. enjoy Thanksgiving here with family and friends.
12. put up Christmas decorations and sell house
13. whatever else we discover needs to be done☺

The doorbell rang and Nick got up to answer the door. The food was really more for the boys, but I picked at it in an effort to build up my strength. I couldn't afford to throw up and I couldn't afford to have it weaken me further. I was days away from having died and I wasn't ready to go through that or anything close to it again.

"Why don't you take it easy up stairs and we'll begin the cleaning down here?" Case said as he finished eating. "After all, if people are going to want to buy this place, we better have it look like a million bucks."

"I'll help you get upstairs, Bria." Nick offered. I nodded. I guess I could rest for a while. "Don't let me sleep the afternoon away, please." Immediately Nick was on his feet, and I stood. I wanted to make it up the stairs on my own power. He held out his hand and I took it gratefully as we walked to the staircase. I put my hand against the wall and leaned into it as I put one foot on the steps.

I made my way up the stairs with Nick's help and finally found my way into the bed I had last shared with Warren. I could still smell his cologne from that night. The Christmas candles still sat on the dresser. I lay back on the pillow and on my side and leaned over the bed rubbing my hand over the sheets where he had last lain beside me. Maybe this wasn't such a good idea.

I was lying down on the bed for hours without moving and without sleeping. I heard the boys working around the house. The quiet movement of furniture along with quiet conversation carried through the first floor and up to the second in a mumbled jumble of words.

The doorbell rings and I am not sure I want to know who it is, but I know I should be downstairs, but I can't be. I want to stay here in my bed. In the bed I shared with my beloved Warren.

Where we fell passionately the first night we were here. I could remember it as if it were happening. My eyes closed and I watched the scene as before me on the bed lay Warren. His body close to mine and the smell of him as he pulled me on top of him and we collapsed in on each other. We were trying to bring children into our home. How could he have? What if I had become pregnant? Would that have changed things? I shuddered at the thought.

"Knock, knock." I looked up to see both Jonathan and Missy standing at the door to my bedroom. My hand still in place as if Warren were beside me. I pulled my hand away from the empty space.

I looked at them and I started to cry. The heartbreak so intense that I couldn't fathom that our love had ended. I hated these feelings. I didn't want them, but they wouldn't go away unless I grew out of them.

Missy and Jonathan crossed the room and both sat on the bed. Missy sat beside me and Jonathan at my feet. I cried and cried. "I don't understand. How can I possibly still love him after all he's done to me? My heart feels as if it will never truly be healed. I ache. All over. And not because of my health either. This is because I can't figure it all out. It doesn't make sense. It just doesn't make sense."

Missy slid over and put my head in her lap. Neither said a word. They just let me cry. I cried until I got sick. Missy still soothed me. My broken heart could not be healed until I had answers. Without them I would never be able to find peace.

Finally Jonathan said. "Maybe we need to get your injection over with so that you can rest. Relatively speaking. If you like, I'll give you something to help you sleep."

I looked up at him without raising my head. "Please." I said. Missy interjected, "I'll stay with you while Jon and the boys try to carry out the things on your list. I am no good at the lifting and moving part anyway."

I stayed where I was and nodded my head. I couldn't move. "I hate all of this. I'm really sorry. I do love James you know?" She continued to play with my hair. "Love is a very strange thing. I shouldn't have said the things I did, and maybe it wouldn't have triggered that reaction in you. I don't know either."

"James has grieved for so long. Too long. It was nice to have him back in love again." Jonathan said as he began to rise to go back down to his car to get the things he needed. "But just because he still grieves for Joanne, doesn't diminish his new love for you. He has had longer to heal than you have. It'll be alright."

He left us alone in the room, my tears silently falling now as I thought about the two types of love that I was feeling. I had been so in love with Warren. Warren had loved me and had made me believe that miracles were commonplace. It was exciting. It was fun, it was unreal.

James on the other hand, had suffered and his love was much more intense than anything that Warren had shown me, except in intimate moments. Why was that?

In several minutes, Jonathan was back and my ordeal of the medicine begun again. I was so nauseous that I was afraid that I would get sick all over the bed and I didn't want to lose Warren's scent just yet. I wasn't ready to let go. I held my stomach.

When the nausea had passed, Jonathan said. "This will make you sleep. I hope it staves off the nightmares. It should, but the mind is a strange thing to control. You might have them, you might not, but eventually, you will be able to sleep."

He leaned over me when he had given me the second injection and kissed my cheek. He pressed even further and leaned into his wife. He kissed her and whispered. "I love you my angel." I smiled. It was nice to see their devotion and love to each other. "I'll be back to check on you both in an hour."

I did not close my eyes. I wanted to smell the room, relive the moments of that first night when life was the happiest I had ever been. I wanted to carry that into my dreams. I wanted that love; that intense feeling as the two of us became one to push away the nightmare that I knew would follow. I paid no attention to Missy. I couldn't if I wanted to remember.

I fell into the dream much easier than I had on other occasions. I was beside him, happy in the thought that this home, our dream home was actually ours. I kissed his neck. I kissed his chest, and slowly took off his tie. I unbuttoned his shirt. I snuggled up against him and felt his arms wrap around me and pull me on top of him.

We were kissing passionately, his hands exploring my features, my body, my scent, my love. "I love you so much." He had said. "I would die for you. You know that don't you?" I nodded my head, too busy kissing his chest and playing with the little hair that was there.

He lifted my face so that I could see his, "Never ever forget that. No matter how bad things get between us. I will always love you and I will do what ever I have to do to protect you and our family." I was so in love with him. "Bria, promise me. I mean it, promise me you won't forget." I had looked up at him and stared into his eyes. I could swim in them. "I promise. I promise I won't ever forget how much you love me. I love you just the same. I love you more."

He had smiled and we were swept into the passion of young love. It was wonderful. I knew that we were molded for each other.

Almost as soon as my memory of that night faded into the moment I was reliving, another took its place and Warren's hands were closing around my throat. His eyes dark with fury and there was something else. Sorrow. He knew what he was doing. I screamed and I felt his hands tighten around my throat choking off the scream.

Missy was there stroking my head and soothing me. I finally drifted off into the no dream sleep induced by the extra drugs that Jonathan had given me. Gratefully, I slept through the rest of the night in relative peace.

Chapter Thirty-Seven
Days Go By

I woke groggy but rested. Missy was gone. The bed was empty and I was still able to feel the warmth in my cheeks from the glow that the first dream had left with me. The scent of Warren permeated the room. I drew in a deep breath and knew that this was something that I had done right. I suddenly had a new idea in my head.

This is where Warren had been coming when I wasn't here. That's why his smell was still so strong. That's why. Because he still slept here at night. It had to be that way. I was almost excited about. He too, had come home.

Then it hit me. Not any more. It was going to be sold. I was staying here. With company, as my mom would say. Friends that would never leave me to face this alone. I smiled. This was the right thing to do to get over him. He was here. And now he's not. And he won't be back.

I stretched and yawned. I looked up at the door to find that Case was watching me. "I guess you rested last night." His eyes curious at the expression on my face. "Yes, I did. Better than I have in a long time. Jonathan gave me the best of drugs to help me." I smiled.

"Remind me to thank him will you?"

"Uh huh. And were your dreams good ones?" I looked at him. My eyes suddenly burning into him. "Why?"

"Some of us couldn't sleep. You were very, umm, what's the right word to use, amorous in your sleep. Warren this and Warren that." I blushed, totally embarrassed.

"It has happened before, but the memories of my marriage fade away to him trying to kill me." I looked down at my hands. "There were good times for a couple of years. Those memories are still there. Even if they turned out to be a lie, they still happened."

Tears came easily. How I wished the waterworks would stop coming so quickly. I could feel the tension between us. Was that why I was left alone?

"I'm so sorry. I didn't mean to keep anyone awake again. I can't control my dreams. They are what they are. Just like the nightmares." He crossed to the bed. "I know." He said. "I just hate it because it makes him almost human to the rest of us instead of the monster we know he became." He sat down.

"It made me remember bad times with my mom. She would be beaten so badly that we were at the emergency room for hours on end. And who would she be asking for? She would ask for my dad; the one son of a bitch that beat her nearly to death every other week. And yet, she still crawled back into bed with him every night."

He was shaking. "I wished he would die for most of my life. And when he did, I cried. I loved him too. I just didn't like him. He was a monster. Just like Warren." He closed his eyes remembering and clenched his fists.

"He'll never change. He'll never come back. He'll never love you like you deserve to be loved. He'll always have that monster inside of him waiting to rear his ugly head and hurt you again. Just like my dad did, day after day."

"I'm sorry Casey." I reached toward him. I touched his cheek and he shied away from my touch. "I am sorry, too." He said. "Sorry that s.o.b.'s like that exist. But I wish that the good memories would disappear. It's easier to want to take care of you and stay around when you aren't pining for him."

"I'm not pining for him." I protested. "I was just reliving the memory of our first night in this house. It was supposed to be our dream home and the home we would raise children in. Now, I am just happy we didn't have any children. I would not want them to be without a father. And just so you know. I don't want to feel for him. I want to only hate him. I want it badly. That's why I came back here. To work my way through it all. To find a way to get past it. Once this place is sold and we can all leave it, then Warren will truly be out of my system."

"Can you understand that?"

"Yeah. I actually can. I loved my father when he was the dad at the little league or when we were fishing. I hated him when he beat us. I totally get it. I just don't like it." He smiled. "You are forgiven." "Thanks." I grabbed the pillow and threw it at his head. He tossed it back and I fell backwards on the bed. He took my feet and tickled them, and I laughed. He pulled me towards him, and tickled my thighs and I laughed as he wrestled me.

"Thanks. I needed to laugh today." And everything else, that was fun. I pulled his face towards mine and kissed him lightly on the lips. I held his cheeks in my hands. "Casey. I love you. You are my family. You are my little," he balked at that, "okay, my big savior.

You saved me and brought me back from the dead. I saw you breathing life into me. I don't want to ever hurt you. So when I sleep at night, don't hold those unwanted and unmasked dreams and nightmares against me. It's life. Things like this," I tickled him, "they erase the memories of my past."

"I'll be sleeping with you from now on." He said.

"What?" I asked shocked at his words.

"No, no, no. I mean that I will be on guard when you go to sleep. I will be the one holding your head while you sleep instead of Missy. I'll help you get through the nightmares and the memories. I promise. Deal?"

"Oh good grief." I said. He stared at me. "It's hard for me to sleep knowing that I almost slept through you dying. Just let me be there for you."

"Okay. Deal."

I started to stand and I immediately got dizzy and fell down into his arms. He immediately changed from someone having fun, to someone scared again. "Are you okay?" I turned around in his arms and smiled. "Yes, silly Casey, I'm fine. Getting dizzy doesn't mean that I'm dying. Don't get overly jumpy." I kissed him lightly, and pretending to swoon, I leaned over his arms. "My hero." He laughed and lifted me to my feet.

"Okay, let's go down for breakfast." He picked me up off the floor and slung me over his shoulder like a sack of potatoes and trooped down the stairs. When we made our way to the kitchen, and he walked in with me still on his shoulders, everyone looked at him. "She was being a little dizzy blonde." I kicked at him and pounded on his back like some cartoon character and laughed. He sat me down at the table and pulled up a chair beside me.

No one really knew what to say, so I piped up. "Look guys, I'm sorry about my outbursts last night in my sleep. They were unintentional I swear. I don't know why the new dreams were there, but I'll try not to broadcast them to the house."

Missy was the first to speak. "It was bound to happen. Too many things with memories attached to them here. Everyone does it." Jonathan pecked me on the top of the head. "We'll get it out of your system as we pack things away."

Nick just sat there. "Are you okay?" I asked him.

"I didn't hear a thing. I guess I missed out."

The rest of us laughed out loud.

"That might have been a blessing, you're so young, and you don't need to expose your virgin ears to such ranting." Case said. Nick punched him in the shoulder and Case pretended that it hurt.

Breakfast was filling even it if was a little much for me. We cleaned up and began the slow process of crossing things off my list. The lawn, the plantings, the repairs. We all were doing something, each person accomplishing tasks as quickly as we could. I was focusing with Missy on separating things into different categories.

Mine, his, later and throwaways. It was harder than I thought.
I wanted it to be over with but I knew that the whole process would
take us through Halloween.

The day was a long one. We eventually got around to going
grocery shopping and stocking up the foods in the kitchen pantry. It
was beginning to feel warm and wonderful again.

That night, Case slept beside me as the injections were both
given. I didn't want to dream the dreams. I didn't want to have the
nightmares. I just wanted sleep. The day had been long and hard.
I realized that I was dreaming again when I felt his gentle shakes
waking me. I could smell Warren's cologne.

"Bria. Come out of it." I mumbled incoherently, not
understanding . "Bria, it's me, Case."

"Ooh yeah. Thanks Case." He pulled me up into his arms and
I fell back to sleep.

I went right back into that phase of my dreams about the house
when the nightmare started again.

"Bria, wake up. You're screaming." On and on through the
night, Case would wake me and bring me to the brink of being
completely awake and I would fall back into one dream or the other.

Finally, they eluded me and I fell into the blessed black hole of
the deep dreamless sleep.

For several nights, Case would pull me out of the nightmares
and the dreams. He never said a thing again and I was grateful that
they were finally dissipating. I was able to fall asleep more readily and

more easily and we would simply cuddle together. He really was great.

We had an understanding.

A month later, was the first time that James came to visit. Our meeting was an awkward one. He wasn't exactly standoffish, but he wasn't overly touchy feely either. I tried not to be hurt by his cool attitude. I had wanted it to be this way. Just until I could get things figured out in my head.

He joined in on the packing and the redecorating. The house really was beginning to change back into a showplace home. I was increasingly proud of all of our hard work.

By nightfall we were all very friendly again, the ice had melted a little. We were all really ready for dinner. I was happy to be able to spend a few minutes just admiring the work around the house. We still had a little more to do, but it would be someone's pride and joy someday.

After dinner was over with and we were settling in for the night, Case went out for a walk with James and Nick while Jonathan, Missy and I played a game of Scrabble. The day was beginning to take on the feeling that was so wonderful in both of James' homes.

When the three men came back to the house, James walked in first and he was smiling. It was nice to see his smile and suddenly I wasn't able to concentrate at all on the game.

Case came to sit beside me. "Hey little sis." I looked up at his face. "What?"

"Well, I'm going to be gone for a couple of days. Nick and I both have a job to do. Do you mind?"

"No," I paused, not sure if I could do nights alone again. "What's going on?"

"Well, James brought news from Nick's mom. You know she got married, right? Well, she's pregnant and has decided that Nick needs to get his stuff out of the house."

"She's pregnant?" I couldn't put the two things together. "But, but, you're almost twenty?" I looked at Nick. He shrugged his shoulders, "My mom had me when she was fifteen and she's still young enough to have kids. I just didn't expect it." He blushed at the thought. "Congratulations then. Are you happy?

"I guess... I don't... I," he was stuttering. "I'm happy if she's happy. She deserves to be happy. We've both waited for it a long time." He seemed so stunned at the news. I was sure that he didn't know how to deal with it.

"I have offered them both full time jobs at a salary that will keep them from ever having to work at a motel again." James said.

"They will have housing wherever we have housing. I've decided to take on more domestic violence cases and see if we can't help out victims who are even less fortunate than you are Bria. I can't look in your eyes or theirs without feeling like I could do more." He clapped them both on the back. "And they've proven themselves often enough." It was the most he had spoken since he arrived.

"When do you leave?" That horrible thought again. Could I really sleep alone again?

"Tomorrow morning, early. We want to be back before the first open house the weekend after Halloween. In fact, we're kicking you off of decorations for Halloween. We're gonna turn this house into a haunted house from hell." Case said.

I laughed. Well, I had that to look forward to.

"Okay, but when Christmas decorations are ready to be put up, I expect it to go overboard. I want it to be the best in the city. Especially if we're competing with the temple up the road."

"Not a problem, Santa's workshop won't hold a candle to this house."

Nick was joining in on the fun.

I yawned. "Sorry." I guess I didn't realize how tired I was. I stood from where I sat and started towards the stairs. "Give me about ten minutes would you?" I said over my shoulder to Jonathan.

James caught me by the arm. "Do you mind if I come up with you?" I looked around at the others. I stopped on Case's face. His smile was bright. Then he winked at me and blew me a kiss. I laughed. I looked back at James and nodded my head and held out my hand for him to take. I walked up to the wall and put my hand on the banister and started on my way to my room with James beside me.

I reached the room and walked to the bed. He walked over to the bed and sat on the edge of it. I unabashedly took off my shirt. I had had enough of being embarrassed in front of him. I was still somewhat modest as I had a cami underneath. I walked to the back of the bed and grabbed my nightshirt. I pulled it on and dropped my jeans to the floor. I picked them up and folded them over the edge of the chest seat at the end of the bed. I crawled up in the bed without saying a word. I pulled the blanket up over me and patted the space beside me. Of course the blankets were pulled taut over the space. That's the way Case and I slept and it would not change.

I held his eyes as he stood and walked around to that side of the bed and sat down pushing his back against the headboard. I waited until he got settled and then snuggled up next to him, pulling his arm around my neck and buried my head on his chest. I put my hand in between the buttons on his shirt and slowly unbuttoned them. I wanted to feel his presence intently. I wanted his smells to take the place of the ones that had haunted my dreams and nightmares since the day I came back to this house. This house that wasn't a home any longer. I needed him to chase away the dreams and nightmares as he had so many times before.

"Thanks for coming. Now, maybe, I'll sleep."

He finally let go. "Oh Bria. I couldn't stay any longer. I do love you. I'll always love Joanne. But all I think about is you." He bent down, tilting my head in that familiar way, to meet his face, and kissed me passionately. Our mouths were easily moving in sync with each other. I was where I belonged. I knew it and he knew it. All that was left was to rid myself of this house and all its memories. I was ready to move on.

Jonathan walked in catching us in the act of kissing. He cleared his throat. Without looking away from James I said. "I'm ready, Doctor." I held out my arm and waited. I knew what was coming, but I didn't care. I was okay with being in James' arms the whole night long.

The warmth spread through me and the nausea swept over me. I swallowed hard and kept my stomach from heaving. I was getting better at it. I had to move and get a trash can, but I succeeded in keeping my dinner down. It was more than thirty minutes before the feelings were calmed down.

"Are you ready?" Jonathan asked when he saw that I had stopped retching and I nodded.

"James, you might want to leave for a while. I'll get Case to come up." Jonathan was protecting his brother.

"It's okay. Case told me what she says and does when she's drugged into sleep. I'm okay with it."

I smiled.

The needle burned and it was a sign that sleep would come and so would the dreams and the nightmares. James would hear me making love to Warren as Case had heard it each night. It would not be good. But we would work through it.

James held me tight and whispered how much he loved me as the sleep aid spread over me. I drifted into the dream and the scene transformed into that first night again. I could smell Warren and we were making love. I was feeling every bit of it. My heart was pounding as he whispered those words to me.

Somewhere, I could hear it from outside of my dream as well. I was reacting to the moment of my dreams. And...so was James.

Chapter Thirty-Eight
Love Comes To Those Who Ache

"Bria. Stop it." He was breathing hard. "Bria. If you don't wake up, we're both going to be sorry." James was shaking me, I could hear his voice and I could see him sweating even though the night was cool. We were well into the fall and I knew that it wasn't because of the heat of the house. "I'm so very sorry." I tried to turn away from him. Embarrassed.

"No. Don't turn away from me. I want to make love to you. I want to hold on to you forever. I want to remove his name and replace it with mine. I just have to be strong enough not to want you too much tonight."

I tried to pull away, but I was so drunk with the heat of the moment combined with the sleep aids, I wasn't anywhere near strong enough to resist him.

"Come to me." He said. And he pulled me into him and halfway on top of him. I could feel his breath on my face. "Just stay here with me and I'll control myself." He laughed.

I snuggled into his chest. I had no choice but to live through the night and what my sleep would bring me.

I tried not to close my eyes, but it was soon a lost cause as the medicine pulled me back in. I closed my eyes. I found it easy to sleep in his arms. Within minutes, the night was back, just as it had always been with Case.

My dream first, with Warren telling me of his love and that I was never to forget it. When the scene finally changed and his hands were around me, my screams were so violent that James was shaking me awake again. I started crying. "I can't get rid of them. They are going to haunt me forever." But almost as soon as I was awake, I was drifting back into the drug induced sleep. The nightmares instantly back.

James wrapped his arms tightly around me. He pulled my head right next to his lips and whispered till the nightmare ended. Exhausted, the deep sleep crept over me in the wee hours of the morning. James pulled the blankets on top of both of us and I felt the warmth of his now shirtless body against me.

When the morning finally dawned, James kissed me and propped me up on his chest. My eyes were still drooping, but he whispered, "I love you so much. I will never stop loving you. I will not take advantage of the nights. But I can't wait till you are calling my name in the heat of passion instead of his."

I laughed. "When it *is* right, we'll be in that happily ever after life. We just have to work through all the things I have left with Warren and with the memories that haunt me. I really do want to live and love again. That last day. On the lake. That was living."

He laughed, too. "Yes, that was," he paused, "amazingly, really living." His voice suddenly changed. "That's the day I knew I couldn't live with out you."

I lay back down on top of him. I closed my eyes and his hands rubbed up and down my back.

He sighed. "I guess we had better get up. I hear the boys up and getting ready to leave. We should probably get down to see them off." James was all practical.

He wrapped his arms around me and lifted himself up into a sitting position. I wrapped my legs around his waist as he stood and he carried me over to my closet. I clung to him, dangling several feet from the floor.

He reached in and grabbed a random dress and with one hand, removed my night shirt. His hands brushing away my hair as it dropped over his face. He kissed me under the cascade of my hair and he handed me the dress to slip on over my head. He watched and as his hands held my bare back, I raised my hands and let the dress fall down over me. He slid me to the floor, and straightened my dress before picking me up again. We walked down the stairs with my arms securely around his neck and his arms firmly around me, holding me safely against him.

At the bottom step, he set me down and together we walked into the kitchen where both boys were eating a quick breakfast.

"We'll be back in three days tops." Nick said. "Just long enough to put everything in storage."

"You mean my place." Case interrupted.

"That's okay. I'll pay the rent for the next two months then we'll get you out of your lease and move your butts in with us."

His arm was fully around me. I looked up at him. Case caught on quickly. "Does that mean its official?"

"What's official?" Nick seemed lost.

"Nothing is official." James said. "Except that I love her. I am in love with her and somewhere, sometime, we'll get married and have a family. But for now, she will still be living with us under our protection. Just like before. Until Warren gets caught."

"Good enough." Case said. "I told you the nights were very interesting." He laughed.

James immediately threw him a glaring look and shook his head. He took in a deep breath and exhaled it in a "whew". Case laughed again.

James reached into his pocket. He pulled out that same credit card that he had used with me. "This is the key to you both getting back here successfully and as quick as possible. Gas, food, lodging. And get a few gifts for your new baby brother or sister. Pay the rent through the end of the year and get back here as soon as possible. I get the feeling that we're going to speed things up as soon as Halloween comes and goes."

"Is there a cap on this spending?" Case asked good naturedly. "Cause rent is eight-fifty."

"Just don't go over ten grand." Nick dropped his fork.

Both boys looked up to see if he was kidding. "You gotta be kidding?" Nick said.

"Nope. Not kidding. But you also have to buy all the Halloween decorations to make your haunted house a reality. We're going to leave the neighborhood with a bang. Halloween, Thanksgiving and Christmas. We're going to do them all up right."

Both Nick and Case were almost bouncing off the walls. They immediately began talking over the decorations that they would buy. As they got ready to walk out the door, I grabbed both of them one at a time. "I love you Nick." I said as I put my arms around him. I kissed his cheek and whispered in his ear. "Come back soon young hero." It was corny, but it was real.

Then came Case. "I love you, too, Case." I put my arms around him and pulled his around me and I kissed him on the lips. Not passionately, but affectionately. "Thanks for saving me."

We both knew that I wasn't just talking about breathing life back into me physically. It was also because he let life come back to me here, changing my days as he spent each night with me and swept away whatever the nights brought. He squeezed me tight. "I'll be back soon." He winked at James. "We'll always be here to take care of you when you need us." He let me go and then, in a very little brother way smacked my bottom.

"Don't do anything I wouldn't do." He laughed and the two young men walked out the door.

I would miss them both terribly. They were really a big part of my life. I turned to James. "Can we adopt them?" He laughed and pulled me into him, we spent the next couple of minutes kissing and cuddling in the foyer right in front of the stairs. I was happy all over.

The next two days went by slowly but when Nick and Case showed up with the car loaded down with decorations for turning my house into a haunted mansion, life was suddenly back in fast forward.

It was unbelievable. We had such fun putting it all together and the weather turned cool which meant that it was time to light the fireplace and get the warm scents of fall going through the house. I even baked some pumpkin cookies and painted ghosts, witches, pumpkins and other holiday sugar cookies to put out for parents that were accompanying their children.

We put up a big sign out front that said that anyone was welcome to attend the Halloween haunted house.

The mood in the house was one of nothing but fun. Some of the fears and worries were vanquished in the hustle and bustle of the decorating.

James was joining in again on the daily fun when he could. He was going back and forth to work and trying to set up his new foundation with Jonathan to help out victims of abuse. I had not yet quit work, because James said to wait until I put the house actually on the market. I was on a "paid leave of absence" anyway.

Missy and I decided that all of us should be in costume and so we went out shopping. We came home with costumes for each one of us. We thought it was funny that we purchased the two of us "sexy" costumes and the guys; well we went more towards the goofy costumes for them.

We laughed as they looked at the scary clown, the Tweedledum and Tweedledee and the tall cartoon Frankenstein for James. It took less than two minutes for all the men to decide that those costumes were going back.

"I don't want to scare the children." I protested. Case quickly pointed out, "Then why are we doing this haunted house?" He took my hand and dragged me to the back yard and waved his hand towards it.

It *was* amazing. The children and their parents would come in through the front door. A series of child gates would lead them through to the back and they would go through a miniature 'trail of terror'. The trail wound around the back yard and would end with a large blow up slide that acted as the final scare after coming out of a fake haunted house. The slide was set up to come through the opened backyard (make that dismantled) gate. It would deposit sliders on the side of the house between the garage and the property line. It was well thought out and Case and Nick were proud of their design.

Missy and I conceded and the four men agreed that they would go and find their own costumes. We still laughed the night away as we put together little treat bags for each person. We were going to have hot cocoa and cookies for everyone as well.

I was having so much fun that those last few nights had fast become only annoying little blips on my daily schedule. They were still vicious but had become easier and easier to handle as James held me through each night.

The next day, after lunch, all four of the men headed down to the costume store. I knew that they would have slim pickings as they say, because Halloween was now only a day away.

Missy and I set about turning the front yard into a comic relief of Halloween. We had agreed that the front yard would be funny and the back yard scary. We set up wooden cutouts of tombstones with funny captions on them, comical jack o lanterns, and cheesy spiders and witches. It was as we called it, "cute." We plopped down on the front doorsteps with satisfaction as we waited on the men to return.

A huge dark green Hummer drove by, slowing to look at our decorations and we laughed and waved. It had been fun to watch the stuffy older neighbors shake their heads at us.

I had gone to great lengths to invite them all over on Halloween for the donuts and hot cocoa and to watch the children and parents come through our little haunted house. I wasn't sure how many would actually take us up on the offer.

Missy said, "I bet they're getting ideas for their own Halloween decorations." It wasn't the first car to slow down and look, but it registered with us because it was one of the more unusual expensive vehicles to roam the neighborhood. Most of the people in my neighborhood had Lincolns and Cadillacs and well, what I called "money cars".

It was past dinner time when the four men pulled up with pizza for dinner and costumes hidden beneath triple bagged packages. We laughed at them as they worked hard not to let us see what they would be wearing the next night.

Missy and I looked at each other. We had our own secrets as well. We sat around the pizza boxes and the fireplace discussing everything that would happen tomorrow from who would direct the children and their parents through the house and who would hand out the treat bags. That would be my job as I still had daily bouts of weakness. I was happy that the trial was drawing to its conclusion at the same time that I would be selling my house and moving further away from any Warren associated stress.

We were all keyed up and excited about the next day and night. When the night drew to an end at about eleven, I was still not ready to have the injections that would send me into my own haunted world.

"We've put it off long enough today. We can't have you sick tomorrow." Jonathan said. I noticed the look that he gave his brother over my head and James quickly took hold of my hand and dragged me up the stairs. I tried to be happy about the day being over. That meant that tomorrow would bring about the culmination of the hard work we had put into the past few days. I was really very happy.

Life seemed to have been changing in leaps and bounds. Warren was only a part of my nighttime. He had finally stopped haunting my days. I could finally see the light at the end of the tunnel.

Chapter Thirty-Nine
The Friendly Haunted Mansion

The night was long, the nightmares all the more fierce by the hopes that things might finally be winding down. We had not let anyone associated with the trial and study know of our whereabouts. After seeing Mr. Hudgeson with Warren that day in Virginia Beach, we hadn't thought it was prudent to let anyone know.

It was that scene that I fell asleep thinking of. I was really happy that the trial was soon to be over and that would mean that we all severed our ties with the scheming that had gone on behind the scenes.

My nightmares seemed to be even more extremely violent than ever before. Warren's face was contorted in pain as he tried to kill me. I was fighting harder and harder to stop him from choking me. I screamed and screamed. His words from that day in court came back hauntingly to my mind, "I could easily snap your neck right now. One movement of my hand and it would be over with before they could save you. I have been trained to do whatever is necessary. You just don't know who you are messing with. I will do what I need to do." He had said.

I woke screaming and bolted upright. Something wasn't right. He could easily snap my neck. Every time. "What's wrong? Bria? James pulled me back down to lie on his chest.

"Nothing. Just the nightmare." I didn't know why I didn't want to tell him what was coming to me. I lay back down and began to try and remember every word that Warren said on each of his attempts to kill me.

In the hospital he had said. "Don't be afraid. It will all be over soon, I promise you that." He could have killed me then. But instead he had been tender and even though he had been in the room for a while, he waited on me to wake up. He said that it would all be over soon. I thought he meant he was going to kill me. But was he? No. I was exhausted. Wishing that things were different wasn't making it so. I closed my eyes and drifted wearily into the sleep I needed.

The morning finally dawned. The mixed message of my dreams settled over me like the beginning of a cold. Wearily I kept the thoughts momentarily to myself. I was combining that first part of my sleep, the dreams of our first night in this home, with the nightmares. They were finally merging. Maybe this *was* the beginning of the end. Maybe the nightmares were getting shorter.

"Are you okay, darling Bria?" James held me to him. "You seem to have had a hard night. Harder than normal anyway."

"I don't know. My dream was confusing. Something Warren said haunts me." He rolled his eyes as I propped my chin up on his chest and looked at his face. "I'm serious. Even you said something about it."

"What?"

"Warren could have killed me many times over. And he didn't. Why is that?"

"I don't know, my darling. I honestly don't know."

I sighed. Maybe some of it was real. Maybe he wanted to kill me but his subconscious wouldn't let him. Maybe. I didn't know. "Maybe it's just a dream. Maybe I am just anxious to get things done with."

He stroked my hair, laying my head back down on his chest. "Let's just forget about it for now. It is just a dream. You were saved each time by someone else. Us in the hospital because you were pushing that buzzer, the people at the party were pulling him off of you. And in the courthouse, well, he just wouldn't have done it there. He would have been shot and killed."

He reached down and pulled me further up on his chest bringing my face to his. He looked in my eyes. "I love you, Bria. It is all going to be over soon. I'll make sure of it." He kissed me solidly, strong and then settled into the soft reassuring kiss that relaxed me in his arms.

"I love you too, James. I truly do." I kissed him back and made a trail of kisses from his lips to his chest where I again nestled in for a few more minutes of just relaxing in his arms.

Suddenly noise and excitement rose from the bottom floor. Nick and Case had risen early and were wrestling with each other. Excitement clearly was the mood of the day. I looked up at James and he shrugged his shoulders. "We'll be in for this all day; you know that, don't you?"

I nodded. "Yeah I do know that. It's nice to see them acting like kids. I get the feeling that they've missed most of their childhood."

I was happy to have a part in their revelry. It was fun to see it. It was fun to be a part of it.

"Everything's ready!" Nick called out as the five 'o clock hour approached. Most of the younger kids and their parents were going to be coming around soon. It was already beginning to get dark and the chill in the air was perfect for the hot chocolate that we would be serving. Take home cups sat with their lids ready for the parents and kids as they exited the 'haunted house.' The festivities out front were meant to take away the fright that our little activities had given them. They could stand around the front yard laughing at what had scared each of them. When they were done they would then be handed their treat bags and be on their way. The whole thing would take maybe ten to fifteen minutes. It was now time to quickly get dressed.

Missy and I walked up the stairs together and we hurriedly put on our skimpy "sexy costumes" as they were called. I was a vampiress with a black wig complete with dripping blood on my neck. Missy was a sexy sorceress. Both costumes were short, with fishnet stockings and over done jewelry. Our makeup was dark and red. We were surprised with how different we looked.

We walked down the stairs to find that our men and chosen to be various monsters of legend. The two werewolves of course were Nick and Case, meanwhile James, unbeknownst to me, was Count Dracula. Jonathan had chosen to be Jack the Ripper. Of course! What a perfect costume for him. Dapper murderer doctor he was known to be. This was going to be fun.

We were all in our places when the first children began to arrive. We had put out the word everywhere that we would be doing this and so parents with children were coming out of the woodwork. Pretty soon, the screams and sounds of the scary CD echoed from the back yard joining with screams and cries of the kids and their parents. I sat at the front with the treat bags, cookies and cocoa.

Missy sat next to the end of the slide as to direct them back to the front yard after their scare. Jonathan and James both took turns leading small groups into the back yard where Nick and Case took over and took them through the trail of terror and the haunted house that would lead finally to the slide. Parents could walk around if they wanted to but most were choosing to slide after their children.

Everyone was happy. Even parents were joining us in costume. It was the best! After about two hours, the smells of different perfumes and candies and hot cocoa, cookies and donuts began to make me nauseous. It was very overwhelmingly sweet.

I decided to take a break and get away from the smells. I called over to where Missy sat and asked her to come over and take my place. She wasn't immediately worried and neither was I.

"I just need a few minutes and some cold water."

She patted my hand, "It's okay; go on in for a while."

"No, it's just very sweet around here."

She sniffed the air. "Oh yeah, I see what you mean."

A couple of parents with children came up just then to be taken back to the trail. Both adults were dressed in costume. One was the same clown that Missy and I had brought back for our men. We looked at each other and smiled. Missy looked at the man, his clown mask scary and funny at the same time,

"My husband wouldn't wear that one." She told him.

"I don't think I really had a choice, there was nothing left by the time we decided to dress up."

We all laughed and waited while Jonathan who was next to come back to take the group.

"Go on up, or do you need help?"

"Maybe just a helping hand to get over the gate but I'll manage." I answered her.

"What's the problem?" Jonathan asked as he arrived.

"Honey, Bria's feeling a little sick, all these sweet smells are getting to her. Do you want to help her up the stairs?"

The clown spoke up, listening to the conversation. "I can help her up stairs if you want. As long as you'll go ahead and take the kids around." He looked down at his costume. "Maybe I'll skip the 'trail of terror' anyway. I'm not really interested in having to climb up a slide in these baggy clown pants."

Jonathan laughed, and pecked Missy on the cheek. "I told you it was a bad idea." He reached out to shake the clown's hand. "Thanks for the help. Your kids will be back shortly. The sorceress will show you where they'll land."

"Okay." Missy said. "You two go ahead, I'll be waiting over by the slide until another group forms here. I'll keep watch." The clown reached towards my hand. "Lead the way to my death, vampiress." He laughed and the rest of us did as well. I was happy even if I was sick as the proverbial dog.

Up the front steps we went. "Thanks for your help. I think that maybe the excitement and everything were a bit too much for me."

He nodded his head. "Sorry, you're not feeling well. This is such a good idea. It brings together the neighbors in a really cool way."

His voice sounded almost melodic in its cadence. I wondered briefly where he was from. When we reached the stairs, to go up to the top floor, he said. "Oh that gate. I wondered what you were talking about. Looks like you're well stocked for children." He looked over the gate that had been wedged in place. We had blocked it in so that wayward children wouldn't find their way up the stairs. It was very difficult to move.

"Why don't I climb over first and then help you over and up the stairs?"

"Sure. However it's easiest." I was feeling weaker by the minute.

He climbed over the gate and reached back to lift me off of my feet and onto the stairs. "Up the stairs then." He said as he sat me down and I almost fell back over the gate.

"Okay, you need a little more help than just dropping you on the steps." He gathered me to his side and held me up as we slowly climbed up the stairs.

Missy popped in at the bottom of the stairs. "You doing okay?" I looked back at her. "Yep, just weaker than I thought I would be. I'll send him back down once I make it to the top. I think I'll have him open the windows for me. That way I can still listen in on the fun."

"I'll let the guys know." She said.

"Thanks Missy. Maybe I'll just take a quick nap."

We continued up the stairs and the clown said, "Where's your bedroom?" I pointed the way, and he helped me into my bedroom.

"Thanks, I really appreciate it. Sorry you've missed out on the fun. Your kids are probably waiting on you." I pulled my body up on the bed and lay flat, not even bothering to get all the way up to the pillow. I took off the wig and dropped it to the floor, closing my eyes.

The clown turned and walked to the windows. "You want both of these windows open?"

"Please. And thank you." I untied the neck of the costume and began to fan myself. I was getting hotter in the nylon costume.

"I'm sorry." The voice was closer now. Clearer.

"What?"

"I said I'm sorry." His voice was right above my face.

He lifted off the clown mask. "Warren." I whispered.

I opened my mouth to scream but his hand was quickly over my mouth. I struggled against his weight on my body. I was already weak, but I was suddenly terrified. His hands moved over me, feeling my body as if he were remembering the first night in this room as well.

He began kissing my neck and my shoulders as he pushed the costume down uncovering my breasts.

413

He whispered. "I love you. I told you never to forget that. It looks like you have forgotten. I'll show you just how much I love you." His free hand lifted up the short skirt of the dress and began to pull off my panties. I knew what he had planned and I could not let it happen, I tried kicking but I was so weak.

He took off the bowtie that he had around his neck and lifting my head, gagged me with it tying it in the back. I struggled, trying to push out the tie with my tongue. He pulled my hair out from under me.

I tried to scream. "Even if you managed to scream, the screams will only mix with the ones from the back yard." He removed my panties completely. "My back yard. Our back yard." He crawled back on top of me and holding my arms down, began to rape me. Over and over he repeated. "I love you. I have loved you, always. You are always going to be mine."

My body responded to his touch unwillingly and he laughed. "I knew you would." The tears ran down my face, smearing the makeup. "It's okay," he whispered. "I have heard you call out my name in your nights and practically make love to strangers but I forgive you. I know it was me you were thinking of. I know you love me as much as I still love you."

His lips were kissing my body, his hands touching me in places that only he had ever touched before. "You're not going to die tonight. I'm here. You aren't going to die." I struggled again and again trying to raise his arms as they pinned mine down. "Forgive me Bria. I love you."

"Get away from her!" James voice boomed from the doorway. Warren looked back over his shoulder. He threw back his head in a laugh and said. "Take another step and she'll die right now."

James froze mid stride. He knew. We both knew. Warren could do it. Warren rose from the bed, opposite of James. He pulled me with him, my half naked body dropping to the floor as he stood.

Pulling me up in front of him, he backed to the open window. He pulled me to him as James began to step towards us.

"No you don't." He put his arm around my neck and his hand on top of my head. He would snap my neck and I was sure of it.

He kissed me with a ferocity that said to both James and I that he was the one in charge. We backed as close to the window as we could get and as he began to climb out of it, he shoved me forward toward the floor as James stepped in to catch me. He immediately took off the tie and I collapsed into his arms screaming.

"Jon!" James was yelling at the top of his lungs. He picked me up and carried me down the stairs. "Missy, get Jon, get everyone. Close this down now!"

Missy looked up, "What for, the kids are having a great time?" Her mouth dropped open as she saw me almost completely undressed in James' arms.

"Warren!" James spat the name out.

I raised my hand. "Please no." I tried to pull my dress down far enough to hide the fact that I was naked underneath and covered my breasts with my hand. Missy ran to grab one of the throw blankets off the couch.

415

She began to cry as she placed the blanket over my body. I took her hand in mine and said. "Don't scare the children." I smiled. "I mean don't unintentionally scare the children, or their parents. Just tell them that I'm sick and we need to close things up a little early. Don't let them panic. Let everyone that is already here go through but put up a closed sign or something."

She shook her head and she took off to tell Jonathan, Nick and Case. I was calm outside but totally shaking inside, my heart pumping fiercely. My muscles had fought off Warren. I was confused and angry. I had responded to his touch sexually as I never thought I would. Especially because it was rape. He may as well have killed me because my heart now was completely shredded.

Chapter Forty
It Gets Worse From Here

James would not put me down. His arms were holding me tight as he stood holding me, leaning against the wall as if he couldn't stand without the support of it.

"I'm sorry. I'm so sorry. I didn't mean for this to happen." He looked at me.

"Oh Bria, of course you didn't." He was crying. Full sobs being forced back as he held me close.

I leaned my head against his shoulder. "He raped me, James. He raped me. Why would he do that? Why?" I was sobbing into his shirt. "He raped me." I was whispering it in between sobs.

Missy, Jonathan, Nick and Case came running in. Stopping short, Jonathan walked to where James stood, holding me. "He raped her." He cleared his throat. "He was going to snap her neck in front of me. Out the window. He was the clown."

"Call the police." It was Nick. "Why haven't we called the police?"

"No!" I screamed. "I'm not going through that. He's already a wanted man. Can't we just tell the judge?" I was bordering on hysteria.

"Put me down. I need to shower. Put me down!" I struggled. Jonathan shook his head. "No. James, don't put her down. Take her back up stairs." He turned to everyone else.

"Lock down the house, every window, every door. Then come upstairs. Missy, you come with us now."

We made our way up the stairs slowly. I sobbed. My heart was aching. I felt so violated and yet it was my husband all over again.

How could these mixed feelings possibly be rational?

James carried me to my bed. He lay me down with the blanket covering me. My panties lay at the end of the bed where Warren had thrown them. Jonathan handed them to Missy and she took them to the laundry basket in my bathroom. She gathered a new set of underwear and a gown from my drawers and draped them over her arm.

Jonathan cleared his throat. "Bria, I can't get you anything to fix this," I didn't know what he was saying. "Just let me sleep, please, just let me sleep." I was crying.

James looked at Jonathan. Jonathan shook his head. "I doubt that it would make any difference." I was still lost.

"Do you want that shower?" Missy asked the question as if I were a child. I nodded. James picked me up again and carried me to the bathroom. I was so sick of being helpless, but I couldn't do anything but cry. He turned on the water checking it every few seconds for temp, while I sat on the toilet seat. Missy leaned my head against her waist and waited. When the shower was ready, he rose and left the bathroom.

"Missy?" I looked up at her. "He raped me." I was still crying and holding onto the blanket. I couldn't believe it at all. My mind couldn't wrap itself around this new terrifying event.

"I know Bria. Let's get you showered. It will help you feel better."

She pulled off the dress and turned me around and unsnapped my bra that had been pushed down below my breasts. I dropped the blanket to get into the shower. She gasped and I looked down, my breasts were already beginning to bruise from his rough hands. I stood in the shower and let the warm water run over me for only a minute.

I reached for the scrunchy as I called it and filled it with soap. I scrubbed my body, trying desperately to wash away his touch from my skin. Washing away every trace of him that I could, my body didn't feel clean enough.

"I'll be back in a minute, Bria."

I didn't answer. I was too busy scrubbing my skin.

A knock at the door interrupted me. I wondered who would be knocking. I put down the soap and the scrunchy and grabbed a towel.

"Bria?" Jonathan's voice was tender. "May I come in?"

I rolled my eyes, causing me to get dizzy. I shook my head and wrapped the towel around me. "Come on in." I whispered. I pulled another towel and spread it over the toilet seat. Jonathan walked in and knelt in front of me.

"Look, Missy is in tears. You've got bruises?" I looked at his face. I nodded.

"Bria, I love you and we're as close as family now, but I'm also a doctor. I need to see them, but I'll understand if you don't want to show me. If not, I'll call a colleague." I looked at him. His face, too, was stained with tears. I took a deep breath and simply put my arms around his neck. "I don't care any more." I cried softly into his neck.   He turned and called to the door, "James."

Immediately, James stepped through the door. He took the gown and my clean panties and handed them to me. I took my gown and slipped it over my head and let it drop.

The towel fell to the floor and I noticed for the first time blood dripping as I stood on the little carpet. I knew this was not the normal my time of the month bleeding. It wasn't a lot but it was more than just drops on the carpet. I looked up and my eyes caught Jonathan's, he had noticed it too.

He pursed his lips. James backed away and Jonathan carried me sobbing to the bed my panties still in my hand.

"Bria," he whispered, "he was so rough that he probably ripped you slightly, don't worry." And then louder, "Missy says that you have bruises all over your breasts. I can see them on your neck and shoulder beginning to turn. I need to examine you or" he paused, "you have to go in to the hospital. What do you want to do?" His voice was tender, explaining things as gently as he could.

Everyone was standing in my room. Case and Nick against the wall and Missy by the dresser. James sat down on the end of the bed. I turned to the side, taking the blanket and covering my body with it.

"Just leave me alone please." I sobbed into the pillow. "Please leave me alone. This is all my fault. All of it." I couldn't stop. "Just go away. Just go away."

"NO!" It was Nick. "I'm sick of this. You being brave just sucks! We're here because we all love you!"

I pulled myself up a little to look at him.

"Either you go to the ER or you let us take care of you. One or the other. No one is leaving!" He was shouting.

Case stepped closer to him, putting his hand on his arm.

"Whatever, I don't care any more." I couldn't stand it. Every way I turned I was hurting someone.

"Stop it, Bria." Missy came forward. "Every one out." They all looked at her. "Every one but Jonathan. Boys go get his bags." She pointed to the door, for them to leave. "You too, James." He balked. "I mean it." She walked to where he sat on the bed and pulled his hand. She lowered her voice, "She's been raped, James. She will not want you to see all of this, or the pain she's in."

James towered over her but she was suddenly the only one really in control. She walked him to the door as Case and Nick returned with Jonathan's bags. She took the bags and put them down before she closed and locked the door.

Jonathan sighed becoming suddenly Dr. Wilbrandt in spite of being my friend. "I'll give you something to help you sleep. But," he paused. "You can't have the trials on this strong of a dose." Missy sat down next to me. "I will take care of what I can." She whispered. She reached down and pulled back the blanket raised my gown and I watched as the needle jabbed into my bruised and broken body. I did not watch any more, I turned away not wanting to see their eyes. I was pushed by the medicine into a semi conscious state. Aware of what was going on and yet completely unable to do anything.

Between the two of them they undressed me as quickly and as gently as possible to assess the damage. I saw him thread a needle and I knew that I had indeed been ripped. Somewhere in my head I murmured a drowsy "ouch". My body was softly explored as bruises were checked over. Missy and Jonathan quickly became a skilled team addressing my injuries one by one.

I began to drift into that sleep that comes as the drug finally kicked into high gear. I was redressed and back under the covers on my bed. Jonathan sat by my hip and Missy sat with my head in her arms. I don't remember anything else. I was blessedly asleep.

Darkness still enveloped me when I groggily moved. Missy and Jonathan were still where they had been hours ago. Jonathan was asleep as he sat leaning forward on his hands. Missy too was asleep leaning against the headboard. James had come in and he, too, was sleeping there beside me.

Even Nick and Case were seated against the wall by the door snoring away. Apparently, one more time I had caused them to come to wait out whether I survived or not.

I moved slightly again. The movement caused pain to shoot through my body. "Oh" I gasped as the pain took the breath out of me. Immediately everyone else in the room was awake. "Bria?" Missy put her hand on my cheek, "Its okay. Get some rest."

"I hurt." I said. "I'm sorry. All of you go to bed."

"Not a chance." Jonathan said. "We're a little too invested."

"Then make the pain go away, Jonathan. Make it all go away." I pleaded with him. "I really do hurt like crazy."

"It's because you fought him so hard, sweetie. You fought him, and now you need to stop fighting. You have to rest." Missy was talking low, almost whispering in my ear.

"Jon can you give her anything else?"

He looked at his wife. Something passed between them and he got up and went for his bag. I watched him choose and fill a syringe. He walked back to the bed and Missy once more exposed my hip to him. I cringed as the needle jabbed sharply into my hip. I closed my eyes, feeling the sting as the pain killer spread through my blood stream. Warmth spread over me. Sleep came seconds later. I think I smiled.

The sun was up, and people were talking around me. I tried to pull myself out of the debths of my sleep. I would partially open my eyes and they would close again quite on their own. Every couple of minutes, I would try to open them again. The conversations around me were becoming clearer.

"We just need to watch her carefully. I don't think she could but it's possible. More than one woman has." It was Jonathan. James sighed. "It would completely devastate her."

Missy spoke thoughtfully, "Maybe not. Maybe nothing will happen. Don't talk about it; she's beginning to come around."

"Because," he paused, "there is more than just Bria at stake. If she pulls out at this point, things everywhere will be jeopardized. We are six weeks away. That's all. We can handle this for six more weeks."

Jonathan was trying to make James understand. "In two more weeks, the tapering off will begin. It takes a month. Just before Christmas she will be completely free of the drugs and she'll be able to return to her normal health slowly after that. Trust me James, cold turkey is not the way to do this. Do you remember what happened the last time she missed too many in a row?"

James nodded. "All right but she is never to be out of anyone's sight. We can't have him getting to her again. His eyes were wild last night. He would have snapped her neck, if I hadn't started towards him at that window. I had hoped he would fall out of it, but…"

He didn't finish. I could tell that he was torn between what he wished had happened and what he wished hadn't.

They all stopped talking at once, realizing my eyes were open.

"It's time for Thanksgiving and Christmas decorations to come down from the attic." I startled them with my words. All three of them looked at me like I was crazy.

"What?" I asked. I wasn't going to let Warren ruin my plans for the next few weeks. This was my favorite time of year. Halloween would always be a reminder of what had happened, I was not about to let him taint my future holidays.

"I'm gong to go shopping for some extra stockings." I looked at Missy, "Care to join me?"

She looked at Jonathan helplessly.

Jonathan took a step from the end of the bed to stand beside me. He spoke quietly and calmly. "Not today, you're not, and maybe not for a couple of days or even a week."

"And why not?" I protested.

Missy reached for the silver mirror on my vanity and then slowly walked over to stand beside Jonathan. She put it in my hands and I slowly pulled it in front of my face. My neck and my shoulders were black and blue. Bruises were everywhere, even light ones where the gag was pulled tight across my face. I pulled back the covers and slowly raised my night gown to my hips. Bruises covered my thighs.

"Oh."

I handed the mirror back to her.

I was silent for a while. I didn't want to cry. I wouldn't cry. He was my husband. I had loved him. He raped me. That was that. I took a deep breath and finally I was okay to talk.

"I'm not going to sit here and do nothing. I have to do something. I can't just sit and think about it. Please just let me do the things I can do."

I tried to get up. My muscles were so tight and hurt so badly that I would need their help to do anything. James laughed.

"What are you laughing at?" I shot at him.

"You are such a fire cracker. Do you always have to get us all worked up and worried about you?"

I smiled. "If that's what it takes to get you all to let me do what I want, then yeah. Besides, I'm getting used to having you all around."

Chapter Forty-One
Happy Holidays

James crawled in bed next to me and gingerly held me in his arms. "Have I told you today that I love you?" I shook my head slyly. "Well, I love you, my little minx, you. Or should I say wolverine? The way you were fighting, even I was afraid of you." He lifted my chin to look up at him.

"Well then you had better watch out." I laughed. "I just might get feisty and attack you." He pulled me into his arms wrapping them around me. "Ouch," I said and he loosened his grip on me. I laughed again and snuggled up as close as I could to him.

"Okay, it looks like we've got work to do. Let's get back to the list, shall we?" James handed me clothes from the closet. I pulled on a wrap around dress and a sweater sitting on the bed. It was colder today than yesterday. "I may not be able to do things exactly like I wanted to, but we were still going to make this house a home for someone."

James came to me and gently lifted me in his arms, kissing me softly before we walked to the doorway to go down stairs. Today was the day that we would begin putting all of my things in storage. We called one of those pack your own storage container places and made arrangements for them to drop it off in two days. Boxes were first on the list of things to purchase. I wanted everything to be put away that had any personal touch to it. I sat on the couch to go through things as they were brought to me. I was going to make this a showcase. The new owners could move in immediately and set up their own house at their leisure.

The day passed and I put many of my plans in action. Plus, by doing things this way, the house could be sold for more. That made me happy. I would have money, lots of it, of my own, so that I didn't have to depend on James or anyone else.

The night went by slowly. I couldn't wait to get up again. My nights were different now as Jonathan gave me some help with sleeping. If I dreamed, if I had nightmares, I didn't remember them and James refused to tell me. I was sure he was hearing painful things, but he kept them to himself.

I slowly began to go through everything that was brought to me. I tried to stay very busy because if I had time to sit and think, I would break down. I was sure I would.

Case and Nick would look at me with so much tenderness as they sat down each load of my personal belongings that finally I could take it no more. I reached up to them both and asked them to sit beside me.

"I want you both to know how sorry I am for dragging you into my messed up life. I am so sorry that I am such a wuss and that so many bad things keep happening to me."

Casey started to say something, but I stopped him.

"I can't stand the way the two of you look at me. I'm really sorry that you aren't really happy anymore."

Nick covered my mouth.

"Can you stop talking? You are making no sense at all. Do you think that's why we are looking at you in any way? What's really happening is that both of us, all of us, are just pissed the eff off that we weren't there to beat the shit out of him."

He moved his hand. "Sorry about my language, but Bria, we love you. It's not like we're both boys with some silly teenage crush, but you're part of who we are. Who I am. I wasn't but a lousy hotel employee with no immediate plans for the future. I was part of a broken family, and now it feels whole. Don't you get that? And Case, well he was in the same boat. We were both living paycheck to paycheck, trying to find someone to love us or someone to hang out with."

Case started in on me then, "Neither one of us led lives we were extremely happy to share with others, and yet you walked in and suddenly we have plenty of things to do. Plenty." He laughed. "With your luck, maybe, we'll have plenty to keep us busy for a while." He laughed again.

"But I don't want you to look at me like I'm that damsel in distress all of the time. That I constantly have to be protected and rescued."

Nick patted me on the head. "Stop being silly Bria."

"You can't change the way we feel about you." Case added.

"It's just who we are for now."

I started picking through the things that they had just brought to me, the things from the dining room that I wanted to store and not leave here. My fingers traced over each one as a fresh memory of how and why it came to be in our home. Nick and Case both got up at that point and left me to my thoughts.

Pictures that hung now changed to generic scenic pictures. I had to take all of my Kincaid's and I had to take the ones that Warren had painted. He really was very good, even if he was officially off my list of even someone I hated.

Within a week, we had filled up the moving container and all that was left was food and clothing. The furniture was all cleaned and ready for a new family to move in and take over.

We were ready when the real estate agent came with the inspector. Everything passed and he was quite impressed with the house. I, we were all so proud.

I stood waiting for the inspector to leave and when the real estate agent came back in she was ready to list my house.

"You know we could list it for one point five million."

I dropped to the couch in shock. I had no idea! I looked up at James and he winked. The rest of my little family were as excited as I was.

When the real estate agent finally left with a promise to come back in a week with a contract, we erupted in excitement. "One and a half million!" I squealed. "Well, thank you Warren."

My bruised and broken body healed as they tend to do in about a week or so. We began putting up decorations for the holidays with a vengeance. I strung garland, hung stockings, hung mistletoe, hung lights, you name it, it was a pretty decked out house.

Thanksgiving seemed to come up so quickly after that. We invited family and friends. Everyone was excited to come to the house and see all the work that we had done. Even Daniel was here, making our "magnificent seven" complete.

Family and friends were completely unaware of the twists and turns that our lives had taken. They could however see that we had morphed into a family. The protective nature of each of us towards each other, but particular towards me, was quite evident. My parents adored my new friends and could easily see how much I loved them all. It was obvious to them that we were a tight knit group.

Missy and I made homemade pies, and as many homemade foods as we could. We cooked two turkeys, and as guests began to arrive, I was really happy that family had been able to make it.

Dad and the guys all watched football and mom and the other women gathered around the dining room table to play Scrabble and talk. We chatted easily and my mom was happily talking with Nick's mom about her pregnancy. She was absolutely glowing.

I couldn't wait for that part of my life. Looking at her, how could you believe that she was anything but happy? I smiled. Mom noticed and reached over and patted the top of my hand.

"Someday."

I leaned in and hugged her.

"I know."

The day slowly progressed. When family began leaving late into the night, I was tremendously sad. I wanted to have them all stay but there simply wasn't room. They were all going to get early starts back down to their homes the next day and needed a good nights sleep.

We had booked them all in the nearest hotel.

I was exhausted by the time we locked down the house for the night. I crawled into bed without changing. By the time James had come to take his normal position next to me, I was already asleep.

Jonathan warned me that the nausea might be worse tonight, given all that I had eaten, but I held it down too tired to even throw up.

The next morning dawned bright. Almost too bright. I was nauseous. I raced to the bathroom and hung over the toilet, ridding myself of the food that I had consumed the day before. I had known that it was too much, but it was Thanksgiving. I could endure the ill effects afterwards. I was sick for quite a while, and kept wondering how all of that fit in my little stomach.

James knocked on the door. "You alright in there?"

"Yes, I just ate too much yesterday. I'm paying for it now, but yesterday it was so great." He laughed. I was brushing my teeth now. "Just because I'm not the bottomless pits you men are." He laughed again and I threw a towel at the door.

When I came out, I looked over at the window, I said. "Why is it so bright?" I walked slowly over to it and gasped. "Snow." I squealed. "I love snow."

I opened the window, and scraped some of the fresh white powder into my hands. I formed a ball and threw it at the shirtless James. He shivered as the snow melted on his warm body. He was at the window in no time, and threatening to throw me into the snow below. Instead he reached out and grabbed his own handful and rubbed it all over my face. It felt wonderful.

In no time we were both dressed and on our way down the stairs. We knocked on the other's doors as we went by. "Rise and shine, sleepyheads." I called out. "Time to go Christmas shopping." I heard the groans of my sleepy little family and started to prepare breakfast. I would do omelets. I knew the smell of bacon and other breakfast goodies would manage to pull them out of their beds.

I started out with the bacon and before the first omelet was made, sure enough everyone was sleepily standing in the kitchen. "It's about time." I began putting things together on plates and handing them out. They could find their own silverware and juice. I had done the rest.

"You are so funny, Bria. Near death one minute and the next ready to hike the Appalachian Trail." Case said it sarcastically. "Not so ready as you might think, I ate too much yesterday and it tastes horrible the second time around."

"Eww. Thanks for sharing." Nick said as he walked over to the table.

Suddenly the thought of it made me sick again. I ran to the downstairs bathroom and knelt down by the toilet. "Okay so maybe only a neighborhood hike is in store." I swished my mouth and cleaned up. I had to go brush my teeth again. Ugh, the thought of the toothpaste was making me ill.

"I need to keep it to just a few calories today." I started up the stairs. "Turkey is out for me." I went straight up to the bathroom and brushed my teeth again. I gargled with mouthwash and then went to the bed. I laid down on it, catching my breath for a minute.

Jonathan was at the door. "Bria, we need to talk." I wasn't really feeling like much just then but I motioned him over to sit on the bed. "Bria. You are tapering off the trial drugs now. You shouldn't be getting as sick. I'm worried about you. Do you think this is the same feeling you have had before or do you think it really was that you ate too much yesterday?" I looked at him.

"Jonathan," I whined. "I ate too much. I don't normally eat all those pies and cakes and my system wasn't used to it. I think I've probably thrown up every Thanksgiving. I expected it. Besides, I was already weak, and maybe just a little more susceptible to it now that my stomach has gotten used to it." He just looked at me. "Jonathan, I'll be fine. Now go get ready to shop."

I got up and walked to the closet as he walked out of my room and shut the door behind him. I couldn't believe that he was worried now. I was within a few weeks of being rid of work and this trial forever. No one would need anything from me after that.

I changed into a nice pair of ski pants with my parka and my boots and tromped down the stairs. "I'm ready."

When no one answered I said. "I'm leaving. Ready or not." I opened the front door, and the blast of chill air took me by surprise. Black Friday it was called but I'll bet that not one person stayed home because of the snow. It was just all part of Christmas. I stood in the door, waiting on everyone else.

Daniel had joined us for Thanksgiving but as he said, "I don't do shopping unless it's on the internet." He was the only one not going. "I hate the mall at Christmas." I had laughed. "It's not all about the mall." I said but we left him home to do turkey sandwiches and football by himself. All the rest of the men were quite jealous. I stepped out into the snow. I felt alive and happy. Right behind me everyone else slowly came.

"You wouldn't really leave us, would you?" It was Nick. I rolled my eyes. "I'll never leave any of you behind." He smiled. We all hopped into James' SUV. It seated eight, so that left us plenty of room for presents.

We reached the mall and traipsed all over the place, making purchases. I kept wishing that I felt this good every day. By lunch time, we decided that we would eat something light at the food court. I settled on a gyro. I did good to get most of it down.

Nausea was still part of my day, but I refused to let it get to me. I excused myself and went to the bathroom again. I didn't lose my lunch but I came awfully close.

When I came out of the bathroom, I must have looked horrible because James decided that it was time to go home. I protested, but he said, "You look very pale Bria."

Jonathan piped up. "You're not taking to this tapering off very well." Missy linked arms with me and we walked several feet away. She whispered, "Ignore them. I do."

I looked at her she was being a little strange.

"I felt that way this morning as well. But they see you sick and they think the worst. Me, I'm just pregnant."

"Missy, really?" I felt better already.

"No one knows yet," she put her finger to her lips,

"Not even Jon. I'm saving it 'til Christmas."

I hugged her tight.

"Want to help me plan an interesting Christmas present to tell him with?"

"Sure." I couldn't contain the excitement in my voice. "I am so happy for you." She nodded and put her finger up to her lips again,

"Not a word. Look at him; don't you think he'll make a great father?" I looked at Jonathan and then I looked at James. "Yes, I do. I can't wait to see his face Christmas day."

Chapter Forty-Two
Happy For Missy

Missy and I skipped around the mall like teenage girls with the four men trailing behind us like our own personal slaves. There was no way that I was going to go home now. We had to look for things that she could use to surprise him with. And we had to do it surreptitiously. They couldn't know what we were looking for.

After another hour, I had to make another run to the restroom and this time I gagged and threw up my lunch. When I came out of the stall, Missy was waiting for me.

She quickly took my arm. "Okay, enough for today. You're not going to have another bad episode on my account. We'll come back out next week. We still have almost a month." She went right to Jonathan when we went over to where they were waiting. "We need to get her home."

Jonathan looked at me. "She's as white as a ghost."

That was all it took for the rest of the men. We headed out to the exit so fast; you would have thought that we were in some kind of race. When we got to the SUV, I stopped in front of it and threw up again. I grabbed a bottle of water out of the little cooler in between our seats and swished, spitting it out. I poured the rest of it out to 'clean up' my mess, thoroughly disgusted with myself.

I started to climb up into the front seat, when I got so dizzy that I fell back into James' arms. "Yep, you're done for the day." He laughed. "You can't have just normal days, can you?"

Weakly I answered. "Watch out or I'll become a wolverine just for your benefit." But I got in and lay my head back against the cool leather headrest while everyone else got in and buckled up.

I missed the whole ride home.

An hour later we were back home and the men began unloading packages. I was carried up the stairs and to bed immediately. I don't even know by whom. I just remember my head hitting the pillow. My eyes had closed well before we reached the neighborhood.

The next thing I know, Jonathan is in the room with me and giving me an injection. The nausea swept over me with a vengeance. I wanted to die. I pulled my hands tight around my stomach and tried to will it away. I was not going to make it the customary thirty to forty minutes without puking this time.

Jonathan pulled the trash can over and I bent down over the edge of the bed. My guts emptying into the trash can. He handed me a damp towel and I gratefully took it and wiped my mouth. I chewed on the opposite end of it in an effort to fight down the nausea.

I was relieved to finally have that second injection. "Bria, this is not the knock out punch you want, because I don't want you asphyxiating on me."

"Huh?" I said, too nauseated to care. Any relief was better than none.

"I don't want you choking to death on whatever might come back up." He explained.

"Oh, asphyxiating. Yeah, you're right. Wouldn't want that."

James came into the room, with a cup of mouthwash in his hand and a bottled water. I swished it gratefully and spit it into the trash can. I sipped the water, and handed it back to James.

"I'll be back in a minute." He said as he grabbed the trash can. He took it to the bathroom and he flushed the contents and then rinsed it before returning to my side. "You've done this before." It dawned on me that this was exactly what chemo patients went through. That's why this part was so hard.

Thank goodness I was nearing the end. Less than two weeks or so now and it would finally be over. I rolled away from the dreaded trash can and turned towards the opposite side of the bed. At least I didn't still have that taste in my mouth.

They were all watching for the signs of a final sickness and eventually a withdrawal. Now I understood why they were so in tune. How could I have not been thinking of it? I sighed as I felt the warmth spread over me. "I love you guys." I said it to the air.

A few minutes later, James crawled into bed with me. His arm right where it should be. I loved that feeling.

I fell into the first really vivid nightmare since Jonathan had been giving me some 'help'. I found myself trapped with Warren; he was raping me and smiling, the whole time telling me that he loved me.

.   I fought him but could not scream. My mouth gagged again with the clown necktie. I pushed and pushed with my arms.

439

His strength was too much for me. "You promised you would remember always that I loved you." He said. "You must remember. I love you."

He removed my gag to kiss me and I screamed. "You don't love me. How could you do this to me? This isn't love!" He backhanded me and blood spurted from my lip as he placed the gag back over my mouth.

He was dragging me through the snow. My hair being pulled almost from my scalp and I was crying. "Why?" I kept asking. "Because I can." He answered only it wasn't really his voice. I didn't understand. And then his voice changed again, softer, pleading me to listen to him. "I love you Bria. I have always loved you." He kept saying the words. I didn't believe him.

I tossed and turned and James kept me safe in the bed, but in my nightmares, I fought a valiant battle against his words and his actions. I cried when again the last scene in my nightmare was my body, now crumpled on the white snow, blood surrounding me in a spray and my hand upturned with my wedding rings just sitting in the palm.

"Bria, I'm here, Bria." I knew it wasn't Warren. "Bria, come back to me. Bria, come on. I am here." My eyes slowly opened, and I realized that I was still under the protective arm of James. "I'm here." He said one last time. "Thanks." I closed my eyes again.

I know why people get hooked on drugs I thought. It was so easy not to have or maybe not to remember the nightmares with that extra medicine that Jonathan had been giving me. No wonder it was easy for good people to do. I understood it perfectly.

The next morning dawned bright again. More snow was due to fall and though it was light out now, by the afternoon, it would be hazardous. We all decided that we would just take some time just to sit around the fireplace, sip hot cocoa and eat left over cookies.

It was around six in the evening when the electricity went out. Thank goodness for the fireplace. While my home didn't have a generator like James' homes had, we had plenty to eat and a nice roaring fire to sit in front of. I wasn't really prepared for a long time without electricity, but we were sure that we would survive the night.

Daniel had taken to building up our wood supply whenever he could. He was that bored. The guys had made fun of him for it, but now they were thanking him and he teased. "Some of us do have survival instincts. I knew it would come in handy."

It was a quiet night when we all gathered up blankets and pillows and crowded together in front of the fireplace. We closed off the room as best as we could, taping down draperies that had hung loosely over the windows. We pulled a couple of recliners from the other rooms into this one and we all began to settle in for the night.

"Bria, you need your injections." Jonathan interrupted my cozy thoughts.

"I don't think that tonight would be good for that do you?" I asked in the vain hope that he would let it go.

"Sorry sweetie, we have to do this." I knew he was right but I still didn't want my dreams or nightmares broadcast to them. Case piped up. "Besides Bria, we've all experienced your nightmares before. It won't be any different now."

I mumbled. "The nightmares are different."

I reluctantly held out my arm. I waited on the nausea and the sleep to settle over me but fighting down the nausea was hard when others were so obviously affected by just the sound of it.

When that had finally quieted, I tried to fight away the sleep so that I would not dream. I was trying desperately not to let it take over. I kept pinching my arms. I wasn't in bed. I wasn't in the comfort of my room. I was on a couch in front of a fireplace with all of my friends surrounding me.

I didn't want to share my new nightmares with an audience. I kept them at bay for a very long time. Others were beginning to fall asleep where they sat or lay... I knew the nightmare was going to be a bad one. I had fought it off for so long already.

James' eyes were already closed, and most everyone else was halfway there themselves, as I continued to try and fight it off. I finally had no choice. Sleep gathered me in its clutches.

"Little one." He said as he pulled me into his embrace. "I love you."

I was not gagged or bound in any way. I wanted to yell at him but something in me wouldn't do it. I spoke the words calmly, "You didn't love me. You never really did. Warren, you don't rape people you love. You don't choke people you love. Why?"

I dropped to my knees; I saw the blood spray and I crumpled to the snow. My palm slowly opened upwards slowly, one finger at a time. My wedding rings were lying squarely in the middle of my hand. My tears were freezing as they dropped like crystals onto the fallen snow.

The scene changed and quite suddenly I was being dragged away by my hair. "Why are you doing this?" I screamed. The answer came. "Because I can." I couldn't see. I was sure that I was heading to my death. I was screaming and crying and pulling away from him. I could not escape his grasp.

"You should have been killed when we found out, but no, you couldn't just die like the others did. You had to survive."

"Who are you?"

I couldn't tell any more. I was screaming. The nightmare was fading away.

The voice boomed in the air, laughing.

"No one can hear your scream. You're dead."

James had his arms around me. He was doing his best to comfort me. Holding me. His eyes wide with concern. Once again I was back in the room with my friends and they were all watching me go through my worst nightmare yet. Every one of them now knew my fears. I shook my head and folded forward, burying my head in my lap, crying. No one said a word. There was nothing left to say.

Chapter Forty-Three
Once Upon a December

I cried. Nothing new for me, but for the first time, everyone else was a witness to the terror on my face at the same time. The hysterical screams so profound that they were each a part of the nightmare playing out before them. No visual effects were needed.

I was so mad at myself for having put them through my nightmare that I couldn't look at them. The night drew long and cold and no one wanted to go to sleep again, all of us afraid of what the night held.

When morning finally came, the electricity was back on. The house was warming up and we all began to rise just to have something to do so that we were not all just sitting here recalling the horrors of the night.

I had a hard time looking anyone in their eyes. The day was too long for me. We tried to keep busy with the hanging up of more Christmas lights and decorating the house. At least, I thought, tonight, I wouldn't have an audience. I dreaded when the evening came and everyone was waiting for my regular trek up the staircase. I couldn't take it.

I begged James not to be there but he insisted. The night was pretty much the same as the one before. Horrific.

.

Days passed, it was now the tenth of December. We needed to finish shopping. Missy and I decided that we would go out and look for something to present to Jonathan on Christmas that would let him know that he would soon be a father.

I figured that we should get something for every other male around so that they didn't feel left out.

"Something with 'Uncle' printed on it." I had said. Missy laughed. We were happy to be going.

James insisted that at least one of them had to go with us. Missy was angry with him.

"Suppose we want to get some surprises?" she asked him.

"We'll act surprised."

"That's not good enough."

Daniel volunteered. "I've been trained in secrecy." He said. "I can keep a secret with the best of them" I looked at Missy. She shrugged her shoulders.

"But when we are getting yours, you have to disappear for a few minutes. Is that a deal?"

He looked at James. James nodded his head. "I don't like this, but I guess we can't hold the two of you prisoners of the house forever."

Daniel got ready and both Missy and I bundled up for the cold weather. The drive to the mall was filled with nothing more than whispered conversation about what we could look for.

Everything went smoothly. We spent the day shopping with Daniel trailing behind us. Every once in a while, he would make the trek to the limo and store the packages in the trunk. We would sit dutifully and wait for his return. As predicted. Everything went well.

Dinner was ready and waiting when we arrived home and the Christmas lights were up and on and glowing brightly. I loved the look of it and exclaimed happily at how wonderful it looked.

We had planned to take the evening to go up to see the Christmas lights at the temple or "Cinderella's castle" as they all still called it. We ate dinner together and each of us got dressed up appropriately to go to see the lights and the presentations that they would have up the hill at the temple.

It was too cold to walk so we all once again piled in the SUV. Snow covered uphill roads were not to be driven through in a limo.

The parking lot was packed with people. As cold as it was, there were few parking spaces and we had to park on the street and walk up about four blocks anyway. By the time we reached the live nativity scene, we were frozen. We couldn't wait to get inside. "We'll stop back by it on the way back down to the car."

The beauty of the building and the property was again stunning and I felt so at peace here. There was a serenity that I couldn't describe. I didn't want to have to leave.

It was great to see the faces of the others as they experienced the atmosphere for the first time. None of the others had really been there before and while Nick had driven by it during the holiday seasons before, this was his first time stopping. It was great to share it with them all.

This was everyone's first time actually walking through so we all separated, taking our time and really enjoying it. James took my hand and we walked slowly towards the benches in front of the temple.

We sat down, like so many others had and just looked up at the beautiful white structure. Its luminescence was beyond any common beauty. I didn't know much about this church, but it was easy to see that this was a very sacred and lovely place. I was completely at peace.

James put his hand over mine and I leaned into his arms and I knew that I was ready to be in his arms forever.

We were basking in the glow of the bright white building and its incredible warmth when I saw him.

I was sure it was Warren. He was walking away from the live nativity. I didn't want anything to spoil the moment and so I asked James if he would go and get the car so that none of the rest of us had to walk. "I'm sorry. I just don't think I can make it."

"Are you sure?" I was sure that I didn't want to have any incident spoil this for the thousands of people that were here.

"Yeah, I'm sure."

"I'll look for the others. We'll meet you near the nativity." I figured that if Warren was walking away from it, that I could easily get to it without being noticed by him and then James and I would call the others on their cells to get them back to the Pilot.

He kissed me on the cheek and walked me up to the stairs. I hoped that if I did happen to run into the others, that I would still be able to get them quickly to the car.

I climbed up the stairs and started to walk towards the building and the Nativity beside it. I turned and he saw me. He quickly closed the gap between us.

"I knew that you would be here. One night, you would be here. You can't seem to stay away from your Christmas castle."

He was talking to me like we were having a friendly conversation.

"Please don't Warren. I'll scream and all these people will react and you'll get caught. He reached for my arm and took it in his.

"Smile and enjoy this. If you don't it may be the last time you see it."

He walked me as fast as he could to the huge dark green Hummer, the one from the afternoon of the Halloween party. It was parked just at the front near the exit and I had noticed the tinted windows before, but now they meant more. James would never see me. He would never know. I started to cry.

"Don't make a sound." He opened the door and pushed me up and into it in front of him. I should have told James. I should have told him. I was berating myself.

The Hummer roared to life and I said good-bye to mine.

This was the moment that I knew that this was the nightmare becoming a reality. It was just as I had feared. I would be dead and no one would be the wiser. I cried into my gloves as he held me next to him. "Please Warren, just get it over with. Just kill me already. Just let me die quickly, please."

His face was contorted, injured.

"No, my little one, my little Bria. I love you. I have always loved you. You promised me you would love me forever."

I still cried.

He pulled me closer as if he couldn't get me close enough to him. It reminded me of that first night when we made love in the new house. I remembered it with fondness and suddenly, I asked. "Why haven't you killed me yet?"

"Because I don't want you dead. I love you." He was relaxing as we pulled farther and farther away from our home.

"Bria, I'll explain everything when we can get as far away from them as possible. I promise." He said, looking in the rearview mirror and both side mirrors.

Through my broken heart, I said, "James and Jonathan, none of them would ever hurt me."

"Not intentionally." He sneered. "They don't realize they're doing it. I have had a hell of a time trying to keep ahead of you all. You just kept disappearing and dropping out of sight. It was maddening."

He looked at me. "You'd make a great spy. You disappear so easily." I was shaking my head. "What are you talking about?"

"Bria, I never wanted any of this. I fell in love with you and I was trapped. I couldn't get out of the mess I had made of things. I wasn't supposed to fall in love with you. I wasn't, but I did."

"I know all about that. Mr. Hudgeson set it up right?"

I stopped talking. His voice suddenly took on that scary tone.

"Mr. Hudgeson is a stone cold killer. He would kill anyone that got in his way. He killed the guard that night at the house in Virginia. And though I can't prove it, I know he killed Annalisa." He stopped, choked up with emotion.

"He's been trying to kill you all along. Not me." He finally sobbed the tears all too real.

"Not me, Bria. Not me."

I tried taking in all that he was telling me.

"I think I knew it. I kept dreaming."

I knew that this was our end. I was no longer in love with him. I couldn't be. But I did still love him. Why? I couldn't even begin to explain. He had raped me in spite of all he said. That was not an act of love. But if my nightmare was coming true, we would both be dead by the morning.

I began to shake, cold and fear both contributing. I was cold. So very cold and very afraid. He pulled me close again.

"I'm trying to save your life." He realized that I was shaking. "Sorry." And he reached up and turned the heat on full blast.

We had been driving for over an hour when I noticed that he was becoming annoyed. He kept looking up in the mirrors. I tried to look back but he wouldn't let me turn around. I had no choice but to sit still. I knew we were headed north. North, where? I didn't know.

We were still on I-95 but it is a top to bottom of the east coast highway. Then everything changed. We were exiting and re-entering highways. Quickly. Moving faster than I had ever been before. His ability to make the Hummer move safely was at least a little comforting to me, but I was completely lost.

The snow began to fall. Fast and furious, coating the roads quickly. I wasn't even sure that we were still in Maryland.

I saw the restaurant and it was a marker for me. We had traveled long but not so far. I knew Sandy Pointe and Hemmingway's restaurant well. This was where we had eaten many delicious crab cakes. It was a fond memory, but I couldn't think about it as I was sure we were on our way to die.

The roads were becoming icy. I prayed silently that we would be safe, wherever he was taking me to, but I was resigned to our fate. We made it to an exit that was only slightly familiar. I couldn't really be sure about it though since it looked so different in the night snow.

We turned off the main road, following a two lane road when out of nowhere, we were hit from behind. A large car slammed into us on Warren's side.

His arm jarred and the wheel turned. He put both hands on the wheel.

"Hold on Bria. They're going to try to kill us together." He held the wheel with all of his might. I could tell for the first time that he *was* as scared as I was.

The Hummer skidded to the side and slid down an embankment. It never rolled, but it slid down the long way and slammed into the bottom. Warren grabbed me and pulled me out his open door. He jumped down onto the ground and pulled me into his arms. We were running as fast as he could get me to run.

"Warren, just leave me, please, just leave me." I was still crying.

"Bria, be quiet." He whispered. "It's dark, they might not see us if we're quiet."

I stumbled and fell. I was already so weak and now only adrenaline was pushing me beyond my limits. Instead of pulling me along by my hair like I had seen in my nightmare, he picked me up and ran with me over his shoulder, his speed picking up as he found familiar territory.

I suddenly understood that he knew where he was going. We ran for a long time. When he couldn't go any further, we huddled underneath trees in the hope that no one would see us.

We could hear several others running through the woods. I held my breath and Warren did too. I was shivering and even though Warren had expended so very much energy in getting us hidden, he too was shaking beside me.

We were both thankful that the snow was fast covering our tracks. When we could no longer hear those chasing us, I whispered as close to his ear as possible.

"Warren? We can't stay here. We'll both freeze to death." He put his hand over my mouth. He whispered back to me in my ear. "They're still here. Shhh. They're still too close. We'll move soon though. Try to stop chattering." He rubbed my arms up and down, trying to warm me.

I waited with him, his arms folded around me, his coat open and adding a layer to mine, trying to keep me warm. My emotions worn and frazzled, I kept thinking. I am in love with James. His family was my family.

There was no excuse for any of the things that Warren had done to me, and yet I couldn't run from him. I couldn't *see* the reason for his actions and no matter what I might feel at this moment, I could never be in love with him again. I didn't understand why I was still sitting in the cold and snow, hidden away from some supposed common enemy while he told me his fantastic tale.

A few minutes passed. We heard a vehicle start; revving its engines as if stuck in the snow and then finally driving away. Warren breathed easier. He pulled me to my feet. "Come on, Bria. We've got a ways to go just to get to a safe place." I wanted to run but something in me told me to stay with Warren. I was sure that if I didn't, my horrible adventure would never end.

Chapter Forty-Four
Discovery

The snow was piling up deeper and deeper and I didn't think that I could carry on much farther when we came quite suddenly to a hunter's cabin. I realized immediately that this was where Warren had intended on taking me all along. That was why we had turned off of the highway and traveled down such a treacherous road in the first place.

Warren picked up the lock that hung on the door. It was one of those big steel locks on a hinge like padlock. He inserted the key and unlocked it.

We rushed in; Warren turned and locked the door with the same kind of padlock on the inside. Then Warren immediately went over to the front window. He lifted it silently and climbed out. He locked the door back from the outside and climbed back in through that same window.

When he had climbed back in the window, he went to every window and closed wooden shutters on the inside locking them with the same type of steel locks and hinges. . I was happy he was being extra precautious. I had seen what had happened to us. Not only in my dreams, but now in reality.

I wasn't ready to believe all he had said to me, but I wasn't ready not to believe it either. He stood in front of the fireplace without moving, thinking. I jumped as my cell phone vibrated in my coat pocket. I was sure that he had heard it. I reached in and pressed the answer button. I hoped that they wouldn't say anything.

"Warren, I'm really cold. Can we start a fire here?" Warren carefully went to the fireplace and started a fire. "I'm sorry that this is all I've got for us. It was meant to be able to keep us safe in better weather."

He shook his head. I listened for my phone. I heard nothing. I knew they were listening.

"Where are we at, Warren? He looked at me. He shook his head and then said. "Why don't you grab that blanket on the couch? Of course, I'll understand if you don't want to sit beside me." I didn't say any thing as I grabbed the blanket and sat down beside him at the fire. I wanted him to be heard.

"You know, he didn't count on you being so adorable. And to be honest, neither did I. I was prepared to just go in and do my job."

He sighed. "All I had to do was record everything." I was taken by just how wonderful he looked. That goofy quality that made me say yes to that first date was easy to see as we sat huddled together in front of the rustic fire. "Instead, I was completely taken by you."

His face seemed resigned to his fate but he continued. "I wanted to just do my job. I fell so in love with you that it was impossible."

"Just what was your job, Warren? What were you supposed to do?"

"Watch you die." He said it quickly. "All I was told was that you were part of a cancer trial and that you were already going to die. I was to watch you and record your failing health and the side effects of the trial drug."

He looked down at his hands. They were shaking. I took my gloves off, and put them on him. Mine were thankfully warm. "Bria, they know that their drug doesn't work. They knew that people were going to die. I found out quite by accident that you were the only person that didn't really have cancer. But for the study, they had to have someone. They thought you were dispensable. It's about the almighty dollar. You were supposed to die. Most of the backers were happy to have you involved. Hudgeson picked you because you were genetically pre-disposed to cancer. The others were happy. After all, if they could have a break through, you were the most likely success story."

He stopped, remembering. I pulled slightly away from him,

"How could you sign on to watch someone die?"

He became defensive, "I didn't know at the time that you were not really a cancer patient on the verge of death already. Mr. Hudgeson kept giving excuses as to why you weren't dying. By the time I discovered he was lying to all of us, I was in love with you and only wanted to save you."

He was quiet again.

"Bria, we're really in trouble. They want to kill me. They want to kill you. Especially now."

"Why, especially now?" I was curious. I had been through hell already, what would make the difference. "Besides the fact that they are so close to the end with one survivor, it's all about money. But even that's not the worst of it. If we get out of this, I'll tell you. But for right now, just know that everything I did, I did to save your life. I was desperate. I never meant to hurt you. I just had to make it look like I was trying."

I began to feel really tired. I had cried so much and I really felt like crying now. I didn't want him to see how this affected me. I reached into my pocket and tapped on the phone lightly. I pulled my coat tighter. "Really, Warren, where are we?" I waited.

He took a deep breath and exhaled slowly. "Somewhere past Elkton. It's private property. I don't know all the particulars, I came upon this quite by accident and it seemed heaven sent. I was exploring while hiding out when you headed up to PA."

I gasped. "You followed me up there?"

"Yes. I did. I was always closer than any of your new friends could have imagined. In fact, do you remember the night that you died? It was the night after your frolicking little swim." His voice broke, "I was the reason you lived, even after you broke my heart by kissing him."

"Case saved me. And Jonathan." I said. "I saw them do it."

"What do you mean, you saw them?"

"I had this out of body experience, I guess. I saw them all."

"Well, Case, as you call him, was sleeping. If I hadn't woke him up, you would have stayed dead. You were turning blue," he clinched his fists, "and he was sleeping when he should have been watching you. But I was watching you. I was always watching you."

I tried to take it all in.

457

"You're not easy to keep alive when Mr. Hudgeson is trying to kill you. You were running from me and I was trying desperately to prevent him from poisoning you to death."

I finally had enough, I began to sob.

"Warren, why? Why did you try to kill me at the party?"

"Mr. Hudgeson had planned to kill you then. He was already angry at me for marrying you. But he was furious because I got you the house. He had paid me well to watch you die. When I spent that much of it on a house, he knew that I had changed the way I looked at you. You were no longer someone I would watch die. I was in love with you."

His voice quivered as he continued. "They were going to offer you a drink. Over and over you were to be poisoned. There were several there to make sure, but no one knew you didn't drink. You would have died in front of many witnesses in less than thirty minutes, but I recognized Annalisa immediately. I had turned into a spy and I knew what was happening. I would not let you die, even if I had to drink every drink that she carried. I noticed that one particular glass kept being switched over and over and I knew that it was the one they were using. When I reached and took it from her, she said that it didn't matter, one way or another you were not leaving the party alive."

I looked at him. His pain was etched on his face. I dumped the drink, but she was arguing with me. She was dressed as hired help and that was why no one recognized her. When she was about to make her move, you came to me and wanted to leave. I thought you might be dead any second, and so I pretended to choke you. I tried to keep my pressure light, but you needed to leave in someone else's care. I choked you just to the point of passing out." He looked at me. "You would leave in the safe confines of the ambulance and I would try and sneak out." His story was unfolding now with very reasonable explanations. Everything he was saying was turning my insides into a jumble of nervous confusion.

"Annalisa came to the room they had taken me to and I begged her, I pleaded with her. I told her that Mr. Hudgeson was wrong, that you didn't have cancer and that I was in love with you. That you weren't going to die of cancer anyway. When she saw me seriously in love with you, she decided then to help me get you out of my life and away from Mr. Hudgeson. I figured that if we got a divorce you would quit the trial and go home to your parents." He rolled his eyes.

"Then in court, when Annalisa saw another one of Hudgeson's cohorts, we knew that he planned to kill you there. Again I needed you to be transported safely away from the courthouse. If I used the same tactic, they would just assume that I was trying to kill you like I did before. And you would once more be taken to a safe place. I had tried to talk to you on several occasions but you were so frightened by the sight of me that I kept losing my cool with you. I began to take a different tactic. I thought I could make Hudgeson believe that I was trying to kill you off."

The wind was picking up outside and I could hear noises that I didn't think were sounds of the forest. I wasn't sure. I shivered and he pulled me back in close to him.

"If only you could have stayed hidden, but no, James told Hudgeson where you were staying. Oh Bria, why couldn't you stay hidden? It would have been over with if James hadn't told him. I didn't know what to do."

"Why didn't you just tell me?"

"Because I didn't want you to hate me for the work I do."

"Warren, I loved you so much, that I don't think I could have hated you. No matter what you do for a living. I was happy not knowing."

"Don't you see, Bria? It's now about making sure that you die. Even though I sabotaged every thing they did." He was remembering now, talking more to himself. "I switched out all the vials every time I could get into the house. Several times you were given poison in those injections and you almost died. I tried, but you kept running. And when you stole some from the physicians' room with the young kid, I thought you were dead again. All along, you were defeating me almost as much as Hudgeson was. It was maddening. You were maddening. And then the last time, when you ran away again, and went home, I was only able to switch out some of the vials. When I watched you Halloween day, I knew that you were going to die. You were so pale. Your color was so off, and when I saw you in that costume, your features so gaunt, I knew you would not make it once you were given another injection of poison. I couldn't be sure. And if you wound down at all, well the results would have been the same. Edward had said once to Annalisa that 'a mellow mood makes miserable death.'"

He stopped remembering it with pain. "And if you got another poisoned injection you would be dead before the morning. Before coming in the clown costume, I switched out all of the vials the doctor had left and then, I thought that if I could get you fighting me, that you would live, the adrenaline would push the remaining poison out of your system.

You were so lovely and so frail and I was way too aggressive. I was mixed with all the feelings of rage at what was happening and the romance I remembered of our first night in our home, and I couldn't seem to control myself. You were fighting me so valiantly." He laughed a little. "You are stronger than you look when you get scared." I put my finger over his lips. "Okay. Just stop. I need to catch my breath."

So here I was, face to face with the man I loved and the man I hated and the man I thought had tried to kill me for the past year. I didn't want to feel the change of feelings that was going on in me. I was in love with James. He and his family were now my family.

Warren was my first true love and I would love him forever. But I didn't know what to do. I knew what my dreams had foretold and I knew what was coming.

"Bria, there's more." I took a deep breath. "Please don't hate me even more."

"What else could there be, Warren, you've told me that someone else is trying to kill me and that I've been wrong all along, how much more could you tell me to shock me?"

461

"Bria, I was going to save this 'til we were safe, but since we may not be, you deserve to know." He swallowed hard. "Bria, that last bit of blood work came back. You're pregnant."

"That's not true. I'm not. I can't be." I was breathless. I was too sure that I wasn't.

"Bria is it mine or is it James?"

I began to sob. I couldn't breathe.

"Bria talk to me. Breathe, damn you Bria, breathe. I can't lose you now. We're almost home free. Breathe!" He hit me on the back and the air escaped from my lips.

"Don't do that to me!" he was shouting. "I have died a little inside every time you've suffered, whether at my hands or someone else's. Please, just tell me if it's my child or not."

"James and I haven't been intimate. You know how I am about those things."

"You're having my baby." He seemed happy, but I was not sure how I was feeling. Now what do I do?

"Oh Warren, how did this happen?" It was the first time tonight that he actually laughed. "Well Bria, sex equals baby."

He sighed. "I forced myself on you remember?"

"No Warren, that's called rape. We were divorced. We are divorced."

"But it saved your life. And together, by some miracle that I never expected, we have created another one."

I thought about it again. I'm going to have a baby.

"Oh, if there is a God in heaven, please let us survive this." He was so happy.

I listened as he began to cry again. "Bria, I need help getting you back to safety. If they find us here, we're all three dead."

All three. I was pregnant.

"Wait, why didn't Jonathan know? Why didn't they tell him?" "He was never in the loop, Bria. He was probably the only honest physician in the group. When they found out he was James' brother, they kept everything else from him. They will go after them all if we don't stop them."

He stopped. His emotions carefully in check. "They'll all be dead if they get any of this information. I tried to make sure that they were kept out of it. Edward even tried to have me killed in the beginning but I escaped him. I knew that if I didn't you would be dead. Poisoned, and no one would be the wiser, you would be just another death of a patient in an experimental drug trial. You know you are the only participant left alive? Right?"

"No."

"Did they even have a chance at survival?" I asked him, suddenly aware of the scope of the danger to more people than just me.

"No."

They never had a chance. It had all been false hope.

"They do know some things that may be useful to future trials. But if you were to die, then you were just a number. Your reports and my reports prove success but it was also tainted information because Edward was trying to kill you. He poisoned so many vials meant for you. I changed out the vials so many times trying to keep you alive. His poison was meant to kill you slowly. When I found out that everything about you was a lie, I dug deeper. You were only a part of it because honest physicians wanted someone with your genetic predisposition to be a candidate for an actual vaccine and not just a cure. Success would have come. I realized what was happening, and my own reports as well as the proof that I have gathered would have shown them all that the whole thing was a fake."

"What do we do now, Warren? What can we do?"

"Try and get some sleep, Bria. For now, that's all we can do."

He pulled me close to him. "Sleep. Gain your strength. I need you to be very strong for tomorrows escape."

"I don't think I can sleep. I am too frightened. I am too excited. I am too worried about all the people I love." I reached out and took his hand. I leaned in against his shoulder and was quiet.

"I love you Bria. I always have. I always will."

Chapter Forty-Five
Nightmare In Reality

The nightmares began almost as soon as I fell asleep. I had tried so desperately not to. I knew that tonight would be horrible. The new knowledge would flow into my dreams and I would see the complete picture of my death and Warren's.

I knew I had had the nightmares because Warren's face was the picture of pain as he shook me. "Bria, my love, Bria, its okay, I'll protect you as best as I can while I'm here. And when I'm gone…. well…. Bria, je m'appelle ange guardian." He whispered to me in his attempt at French. I am your guardian angel or something like that it meant. He held me so close. I had to pull slightly away from him just to breathe again.

I did not want to believe that my nightmare was coming true. I closed my eyes again as he held me. Wishing that the events that had unfolded so many times in my nights would never become our reality didn't make it so. The hours passed slowly as I drifted in and out of sleep, getting colder by the minute.

The room was cold and the breath frosted in the air as I stood waiting on Warren to make sure that the 'coast was clear' for us to step out into the cold and try to make it back to civilization. The Hummer had GPS on it as well and we were going to try and get back to it and somehow get help.

The door blew open as he pushed against it. He grabbed my hand and pulled me out into the even colder and bitter wind. The blowing snow began covering our tracks almost as soon as we left them, we both walked hunched over as we trekked through the snow towards what we hoped was safety.

A crack behind us startled both of us and Warren and I turned around, looking like scared rabbits. He looked back for several seconds but then pushed me in front of him. He put one hand on my back between my shoulder blades, directing me as a dancer would. I went where he directed me, all the while he would look behind him, sure we were being followed.

I turned around to ask Warren if he was sure that we were going in the right direction. I moved closer so that I didn't have to shout, but my question was interrupted.

The shot rang out like lightning hitting a tree. Warren stopped and fell forward blood spraying over me. He grabbed my hand as he fell and looked in my eyes. "I love you my little Bria, I love you." He was failing fast.

"I'm …….. sorry……. I've…… failed…. you..." I saw the hole through his upper left chest. I couldn't scream. I picked up handfuls of snow and packed it tight on the bleeding hole, talking to him all the while. "Please don't die. Please don't leave me. I don't know what to do. I don't know where to go. Please don't leave me." His eyes began to roll back in his head. I kissed him. "I love you too, I love you Warren. I love you." He turned my hand over and lay my wedding rings in my palm. Then, he was still. I sat crumpled in the snow, blood sprayed all over me and sobbed, my head falling into my lap in the snow. My hand upturned with my wedding rings in the center of my palm. Blood mingled with the gold and diamonds that glittered against the snow.

I heard the laugh behind me. "Well, he did take the bullet for you after all." The voice was wicked. Jovial in its mocking contempt for us. "Why didn't you just die like the rest of them?" he laughed. "Because Warren loved you? Love is for the weak. Not good enough. We had to traipse up and down the east coast to find you. Fortunately, you will never be found again."

He grabbed me by my hair and began to drag me away. "Why are you doing this? Why?"

"Because I can." He sneered. "Because I make the rules. Because my money makes me more powerful than God!" He was steaming, moving with each word as if to make his point.

"Because we had to show success with a patient who did not yet have cancer to meet the guidelines. You failed us with your first report. We saw that you were surviving. That would have meant that we would have to produce the product for bigger trials. My money would be spent and not the governments."

I wanted to fight back, but I couldn't get my footing as he dragged me through the snow. He stopped and jerked my head back and forced me to look at Warren lying in the snow, blood sprayed out in front of him except in the space where I had stood. It was the perfect scene for a movie.

He moved his face close to mine, speaking next to my ear. "Warren saved you the first time quite by accident and he continued to save you over and over again." He looked at me with disgust. You gave him a conscience. You took my star pupil and turned him against me. You took two star pupils. And even when we put a bug in the PI's ear that Warren knew where you were, neither he nor his men seemed capable of catching Warren for us. It would have ended then." He put the gun to my head. "YOU! You cost me millions and millions!" He waved the gun. "If you had died, we could have continued. 'Just another casualty', we would say, 'so close', we would say, as we showed them your successful reports. Surely more funding would be needed since we were 'so close', but no! You survived!" He was screaming at me. "Every damn time, you survived!"

I didn't understand. "You could make more if it succeeded." I screamed it at him. He backhanded me with the gun in his hand.

"It also would have cost me more you stupid bitch! There is no immediate profit made in production. It only costs money. I'd have been broke for years and years pouring funds into it. But get close and they would fund us with millions again."

He began to troop away again, dragging me behind. I dug my heels into the snow to try and slow him down. Deep trenches that no matter what would be covered up in a matter of hours. I didn't know if I would be alive that long. I began to grab at small twigs and rocks and anything else that I could with my hands. Drops of blood were becoming a faint trail to wherever he was taking me to die. They were being covered up almost instantly, disappearing as I soon would.

I heard what sounded like the crunch of footsteps in the snow behind me. I searched the white behind me but could see no one. Were there others? Were his accomplices watching his back or on their way to dispose of Warren's body?

Mr. Hudgeson did not seem to notice and was still fuming as he talked to the wind in front of him. I concentrated hard on my efforts to slow him down.

I saw the truck as he threw my head down on the ground. I propped myself up on my elbows and felt the blood gushing down over my eyebrow and over my eye. As he walked over to the truck, I looked around for any means of escape.

I looked back at him as he pulled down the tailgate. I noticed the huge dead buck in the back of it. The animal's underbelly was slit, internal organs hanging out. Blood had at one time been oozing and dripping from the bed of the truck into the snow. He reached beside the back wheel well and pulled out a large hunting knife, the blade stained dark with blood.

I instantly knew my fate. My blood mixed with that of the animal would probably never be detected. My body could more easily be done away with. I watched as he turned toward me, his face contorted in its fury.

"Now, you'll pay for everything you have cost me." He took a step towards me. I began to scramble backwards in my attempt to get away from him.

"Where can you go?" he asked. "I have you cornered here" he spread his hands wide, the gun in one hand and the knife in the other, "where wild animals live," he looked back at the buck and pointing with the knife, continued his sentence, "and die."

He laughed. "You have already cost me millions. But with you gone, we'll get new funding. No one will hesitate to fund us.

Your reports were all positive but inconclusive since your disappearance." He was weaving the story that he would tell. "She was just hiding from her abusive ex-husband and dropped out of the trial and off of the face of the earth. You're going to be famous, Bria Stone. I can see the headlines now, 'Man's ex-wife missing, man suspected in disappearance. Man disappears.'" He laughed even louder as he progressed towards me. "What a pity that our results were inconclusive? Had she continued, with more funding…well you get the idea." He took another step forward. "It's time for you to die, Mrs. Stone."

I screamed.
"NO!"

Knowing my death was imminent, he was thoroughly enjoying his opportunity to torture me with the facts of his betrayal to so many helpless people.

"Go ahead and scream. No one will hear you. You're dead."

The echo of the gun sent chills through me. I couldn't look down at my body; all I could do was look up at the face of evil that was Mr. Hudgeson.

His face was frozen in mid laugh. The knife was still in his raised hand as he fell to the ground just two feet in front of me.

My screams echoed off the trees around me. Louder and louder, over and over I screamed as the figure in all white ran to me. He closed the gap swiftly and knelt in front of me. The rifle slung over his shoulder, he removed his ski mask.

Daniel's features were clear, but my screams wouldn't stop.

"Bria, snap out of it. It's me, Daniel. We've got to move, there are too many others out here."

He reached in his pocket and spoke into a two-way radio. "He's dead but there are other tracks all around here. I'm sure you know that I've got her but follow the signal, we'll meet you back at the shack."

I didn't understand. I couldn't move. He helped me to my feet and we began to trudge back the way we had come, my blood trails just drops fading under the blowing snow. My dragging heels had left a trail that was still lightly visible.

Daniel was now holding the rifle in front of him, ready for any danger.

"Warren," I whispered. Where was he?

"We know." He said. "We'll try to get to him first and do what we can." I looked down at the rings still clutched in my hands.

"He was trying to save me."

"Yes." He said and he repeated, "We know."

I couldn't think. I was following Daniel's footprints in the snow. My head was spinning with the pain and I kept wiping the blood that was still dripping from above my eye. The ground loomed in front of me as I fell forward into the snow just as Daniel's footprints began to spin. Though he was a couple of yards ahead of me, he heard me fall.

In two running steps, he was by my side and he said, "We can't stop, Bria, if we have any hope of saving ourselves, or Warren."

"I'm sorry." I was instantly up in his arms. He didn't answer. He was focused on his destination. I watched for Warren from his arms though it was hard to with the blood blurring my vision.

I saw where he had lain. He was no longer there. There were footprints around and leading away from where he had fallen.

Blood had pooled in one spot but it was turning pink in the newly falling snow. Daniel looked at the different footprints around where he had lain in the snow. He shook his head.

"Warren!" I screamed. "Warren!" but there was no answer. Daniel began to follow the footprints as best he could but they were slowly being filled with the still falling snow. Soon, they disappeared altogether after turning into the denser trees in the forest.

I dropped my head against the white ski suit of Daniel's shoulder, blood staining it, but I didn't care. The tears were freely falling. My heart aching for all that I had lost. I wrapped my hand across my stomach, suddenly remembering that a piece of Warren grew inside me. The tears began to drop more earnestly and I closed my eyes trying to remember everything he had said to me.

Daniel picked up the pace and in several more minutes made it to the cabin where Warren and I had spent most of the night. Footprints were all around it as if it had been searched. Fear filled me again.

Daniel walked up onto the porch and kicked open the door and James and Jonathan jumped to their feet. I was sobbing by this point, fear and pain adding to the terrorizing fear of what might have been done to Warren under Mr. Hudgeson's orders.

Daniel put me down on the couch. I tried to turn towards the back of it. I couldn't look at the two men. I couldn't rectify my feelings.

James moved to sit on one side of me and reached into my pocket pulling two cell phones. I looked down at the two cell phones. Mine and Warren's. Mine was dead, but Warren's was on and working sending back every word that had been said and every sound.

I knew then that Warren had, in desperation at the end, saved my life one final time. James flipped it off and slipped it into his pocket. He put his arm around me and held me tight. Jonathan put his arms around both of us.

Blood pooled on Jonathan's shoulder as he held us protectively. Daniel stood, rifle at the ready, at the front door of the little cabin.

After moments of sobbing into the arms of two of the men in my life, I wanted to go and find Warren. I looked at the three men and said, "We have to find Warren." I was trying to calm my fears and quit sobbing. "I don't know what else they could do to him, but we have to find him." I looked up at Daniel. "Please?"

Daniel looked from me to James and he shook his head.

"Darling," James said, "it will be too difficult with the snowstorm raging so hard outside. Without help from others, *we* are stuck here till the storm lets up."

"No, no, no." I cried, but I knew. I stood up and walked to where Daniel stood. "Please, please, Daniel." My heart so heavy with pain that I lost all sight of reason.

Just as Daniel and I had lost sight of all tracks no more than a hundred yards from where Warren had fallen, there was ho hope now. We would have to wait out the rest of the day and the night.

"Bria, I'm not going to allow it. We will do no good for Warren if we are lost too. The storm will clear, and we will find him." He took my hand and pulled me back to where Jonathan and James sat taking in the scene of my distress.

Daniel walked back to his station at the door. He locked and bolted the door from the inside, determined not to be surprised by anyone else lurking in the woods. "This is private property and even though we have permission, others often trespass here. We'll wait here until help is close enough to lead in."

We sat for quite a while, noting the sound of the howling wind. I sat with my head in my hands crying. I could not get the picture of Warren on the ground out of my head.

Frost began to form in the room from the cold and Daniel handed the rifle to James. James followed him as he walked over to the back door and opened it up, bringing in several logs of broken soaked wood. He bolted it back before going to the fireplace. He wrapped the wet logs with the old sheets that were on a small military like bunk in another room. I hadn't even noticed any other rooms. The fire started more easily then and soon the chill on the room was much less. He sat back on his heels, watching it quietly build in strength.

When the flames were higher, Daniel went once more out the back door with James behind him guarding his activities with the rifle in front of him. I couldn't watch it all. I was tired. Too tired.

The new small pile of snow soaked wood sat beside the now roaring fire. It would have to do.

I had tried to avoid eye contact with Jonathan all together. The blood that still flowed from above my eye was slowing down.

We all sat mesmerized by the flames and the heat that had finally began to fill the cabin. Finally, James took me over to the tattered and worn couch and lay me down on it. It was exactly what Jonathan had been waiting for. Not having his backpack of supplies, he tore cloth from the bottom of his shirt, wet it in the sink and mopped at the blood above my eye. Cleaning the blood that was beginning to clot, he washed my face as best as he could and left the gash alone. He knew it would leave a scar in my left eyebrow but there was nothing he could do.

We were all pretty silent for a long time before I spoke. "Warren was never trying to kill me. All he did was try and save my life." I began to cry again.

"We know." James said. "We heard it all."

Jonathan added, "When Warren called this morning after your phone died, he told us your approximate location. He led us to you by keeping his phone on and placing it in your pocket. He said his good byes to us and apologized for all of his tactics that failed to save you. He told us to take care of you and his baby."

"Oh," I could say no more. I couldn't stop the tears.

The long night was harder than any nightmare ever was. Reality had set in and I was now firmly planted in shock. I lay on the couch, and I prayed that Warren could be found.

I closed down. I could not talk. I could not think. I would not respond. Blood loss and complete and utter sadness overwhelmed me. I loved Warren. And our child would only know of how much he loved us both. One day, when the time is right, I would show our child his grave and tell them of his bravery. I could do that for him. I would do that for him. He would be a hero in their eyes. And….. in mine.

Chapter Forty-Six
No Fairytale Ending

The chill within the room was nothing compared to the chill within my heart. I was lost in nightmares that had come true. All that I believed had been a lie. From the beginning to the end, it was all a lie.

The crackle of a two-way radio in Daniel's pocket shattered the silence, bringing with it the dawning of a new day. Each of us had been dozing or silently reviewing the past few hours and our own parts in it. All the revelations from Warren put us ill at ease with all the events of the past year. Everything, both good and bad, was now turned upside down and it was hard to know who the enemy was.

During the night, I had stayed sick, violently ill. Throwing up over and over again as the scenes kept playing in my mind. Blood, the stained knife, the hole in Warren's chest, my hands bloody from packing it with the snow, it was all real. No longer was it a troublesome nightmare with unanswered questions. Some of the questions had been answered, but not all. I guessed that the important ones had been answered in some way, but not fully. In fact, it opened up a whole new set of questions.

Daniel's whispered conversation had us all awake now. The snowmobiles could be heard in the snow as they made their way to the little cabin in the woods. Barely conscious, I was strapped behind a rescuer as we all made our way back to the highway. I had barely the strength or the will to cling to him, not caring if I lived or died any more. I was sure that my ordeal wasn't over. The night had been long but it was one fraught with every possible scenario scrolling through my mind.

The snow had stopped and it covered the floor of the woods like a thick plush carpet among the evergreens. Small animal tracks and glistening new snow belied the tragedy that had happened amongst them. No sign of blood and no terrifying scream echoed off of the trees to tell the tale.

Daniel had contacted authorities. They would "muster", as he had said, and they would be out looking for the bodies of both Warren and Edward Hudgeson. He had specifically made them aware that if Warren was found alive, that he was not to be treated as a criminal and he was to be cared for at Jonathan's expense. I knew he had added the 'if' in the sentence for my benefit. I also knew that it would be awhile before we heard anything, but my heart was heavier now than it ever had been. As comforting as that thought was meant to be to me, it only made me hurt me more.

When we arrived at the highway, rescue vehicles, police and detectives were waiting. Daniel made plans to go back out with them and direct them to Mr. Hudgeson's truck and his body. He would take them to where Warren had been shot and some of them; himself included, would begin to track him from there.

My eyes were swollen and glazed over and one look at me was enough for Jonathan to declare that I was in shock. The paramedics immediately began to try and help me. When they tried to put me onto a stretcher, I begin to cry in earnest and pleaded that I not be taken to a hospital.

Jonathan wouldn't hear of it. "No, Bria, just the shock alone is enough, but look at your hands," and he pried one open showing me my bleeding fingertips and palms where I had tried to stop Mr. Hudgeson from dragging me. My blood mingled with Warren's suddenly made me sick. I leaned into Jonathan and he guided me into the paramedic's hands. I closed my eyes and sobbed.

I wanted to go home. To my home. To our home. Letting everything happen around me. I didn't know how to say it, but some part of me wanted to be where Warren and I had been the happiest. Even though my love for him had changed, there was still a part of me that would always be his.

When Jonathan and James climbed into the ambulance with me, we rode in silence to the hospital. I needed to be alone with my thoughts and they both could feel that.

My heart was aching as I realized that they too must be hurting. They knew everything now, too. I slowly opened up my eyes and slowly reached over to James. I took his hand in mine and not looking up at him, I asked;

"Could you love Warren's child?"

"Oh, Bria." He said. But he bit back the tears and did not continue. The ride to the hospital seemed so very long.

Missy, Nick, and Case met us at the hospital where Jonathan immediately took over my care. He called each of them into the room to reassure everyone that we all had made it out pretty much unscathed.

Those words haunted me. How could he say we got away unscathed? I was bruised and battered emotionally forever. I was never going to be okay with any of the things that had taken place. I would live the nightmare over and over every night now as I had before. I would wait by the phone until they found Warren's body and we could make all the necessary arrangements.

I turned away from the rest of them. I didn't want to give away my feelings. I was sad. Devastatingly sad. I knew that the words Warren had said were true and I knew that the only reason I was alive, was because he had given up everything for me.

I suddenly felt very unworthy of the sacrifice that he had made for me. His love for me was perfect and I had failed his one request of me.

*"I will never love any one or any thing as much as I love you. No matter what happens, no matter how many fights we may have, **promise me** that you will always remember that I love you. Please, Bria, remember that one thing."*

"Promise me" he had said. And I had promised. But I broke that promise that very night. I had made the decision to file the charges of abuse against him. I shook my head trying not to remember, but his words hung in my heart. "Promise me." Why hadn't I paid attention then? "No matter what happens," he had said. And yet, I had failed him. In so many ways I had failed him.

I clenched my fists in anger at myself and in my hands I could feel the rings that he had placed there. They still were right where he had placed them in spite of all the grasping and grabbing at things in the woods. He had given them to me with his last breath. I closed my eyes again. *His last breath.* I sobbed, hiccupping it back inside.

James made his way to stand in front of me. He took my hands and opened them, not realizing the symbols of love that were held in them. He stared at them for a moment then reached over to take several pieces of gauze that were being prepared to clean up the gash above my eye and took the rings from me. He cleaned them almost tenderly and put them both on his pinky finger as he cleaned the rest of my hand of the blood that had stained it. Once more it came to me. Warren's blood and my blood.

He took my right hand and placed the rings on my right ring finger and said, "Because he deserves his place in your heart, too." I looked up at him, tears blurring my vision and whispered softly. "I love you James. I'm so sorry." I knew his own heart was once again breaking.

He reached into his pocket and pulled out a handkerchief and dabbed my eyes with it. "I meant to give this to you the next time you cried in my arms, but now seems to be the right time." I didn't understand until he lifted the handkerchief. Tied to the bottom point of it was the most beautiful engagement ring I had ever seen. I drew in my breath and he took my left hand in his and placed the ring on my left ring finger. I was overwhelmed. My tears began to flow easily and he pulled me into his arms.

I wrapped my arms around his neck and looked over his shoulder. His ring sparkled as I looked at it on my left hand knowing it meant a new future. I intertwined my hands, and as I did so the two ring fingers were clasped together crossing and meeting in the middle. I cried unabashedly. My sobs coming from deep in the deepest parts of my soul and they were uncontrollable.

It took quite a while before I was able to stop the intense sobbing. My friends all stood by me, watching, suffering in their own way. Jonathan waited patiently until I was ready to have James release me to work on my injuries.

Nick was the first to say anything of the three of them that had not been with us during the night.

He cleared his throat, "So you just couldn't wait on the rest of us? You had to go camping alone." He chuckled and shook his head as if scolding me, but I knew that he was hiding his disappointment that he hadn't been involved in my rescue. I looked at him and smiled.

"Well, I'll go back and wait on you to rescue me if you like."

He rolled his eyes.

"He's right, you know. Do we have to put a tracking device on you to keep you safe?" Case added.

"Not any more." I whispered, and my voice cracked with the emotion that was getting impossible to control.

"Actually, I won't be convinced of that until they find everyone that was involved." James said. "It took more than just Edward and Warren to pull off everything that Warren spoke of."

"Not to mention that we still have a little over a week more of the trial injections. You are almost there." Jonathan said.

I was already shaking my head. "No, I don't. Warren was making changes to the vials all along. I shouldn't have to take any more."

Missy touched my shoulder, speaking for the first time. "Actually, we don't know what he substituted it with. Your blood work has always come back within the normal parameters so you have to continue just in case. And we don't know how much of the paperwork is real so…" Jonathan added, "We can't let you get really sick. Especially now."

"We'll go shopping for things together, won't that be fun. Almost like twins." Suddenly Missy's voice choked up as well, realizing that I hadn't mentioned it in front of them. "I'm sorry, we…, well, we all heard everything and so I told them about our little secret."

The room got quiet, Jonathan began performing his duties as a doctor and pretty soon he had me bandaged and ready for a trip home. We had been in the hospital ER for several hours when Jonathan finally cleared it for us to leave. We were all a little subdued but very ready to go home and rest. We just wanted to be somewhere warm and relatively safe.

James said, "I'll go get the car." We were all more than willing to wait in the warmth of the hospital, while he drove around to pick us up.

James turned to leave when Daniel walked through the electronic entrance doors. We all knew that something wasn't right. Something was missing from the expression on his face. He nodded to James. James turned to Nick and Case and said, "Wait here and take care of them both for a minute." I knew that this meant that we were not to follow. Both Jonathan and James walked quickly to where Daniel stood waiting.

I saw the look of shock on James face and I wondered if they had found Warren's body. My imagination was working overtime. Had it been destroyed by wild animals or… had men done even worse? We watched as the three men talked quietly amongst themselves. I didn't like what I was witnessing. It all seemed too different than I had imagined delivery of the news of what had happened to Warren would be. I was not prepared. Even though I had witnessed it, I was not ready for it.

After several minutes, Daniel turned and walked back out through those electronic doors. I stared at him as he left and continued to stare as James and Jonathan walked slowly back to where we all stood waiting. "Let's get going." James said. I didn't hear any urgency in his voice and so I let things go for the moment. I wasn't sure I could handle it anyway.

We walked slowly out to the waiting vehicle. Nick had the keys since he had driven here with Case and Missy. Daniel had whatever car had been driven to the road by the cabin, so we all climbed into the Pilot and James pulled my hand into his as we drove down the highway towards my home.

No one spoke. Each one of us in our own thoughts. I turned in the seat, releasing the seat only a little to lay it down by about half way. I pulled my bruised legs up underneath me, leaned my head back against the seat. My eyes slowly closed and in minutes I was in that semi-sleep that had you only partially paying attention to the things around you. Bumps in the road, roused me. Turns roused me, and finally I just let go. My head dropping almost to my chest in shear exhaustion.

James felt my hand let go and completely relax and he knew that I would be out of it for a while. My body was "sleeping" even when my mind was not. James reached up and pushed my blood sticky hair away from my eyes and whispered "I love you." I could not whisper back. My body was too tired to even make the effort.

Jonathan spoke first, I heard him whisper to the others, but I wasn't sure what he was saying. I wanted to tell him not to talk, that I could hear him and that I was trying to rest, but I couldn't make my mouth open past the slight open mouth breathing that I was now doing in my half sleep.

The voices quickly became much clearer and louder. "What do you mean they didn't find either body?" Missy was too frightened to be really quiet. "Edward's body was gone, the truck was gone and the only thing any where near that area was a bullet proof vest with a bullet hole in the left shoulder tossed over a tree limb. There was very little blood, so it didn't go through him, or hit vital organs." Jonathan was whispering so that both Nick and Case could hear.

"Oh, and it gets even better. Warren's tracks were followed and Daniel said that someone had him. By the amount of blood on Bria's hand and clothing, he must have been bleeding heavily, but there is no trace of it anywhere. Someone got to him, which would explain why Edward was able to disappear so quickly. If Warren is alive, he's badly injured. It would make sense that if Edward was alone when Daniel shot him that he had already sent someone or left them there to do whatever he had in mind to finish off Warren."

They were all quiet while they took in what Jonathan had told them. James whispered back to them, "They're not sure what to think, but they have two scenarios. If they think Warren is alive, they think he's a prisoner. He may be near death or going to be put to death.

Their second scenario is that he is dead and they were just doing away with the body. Either way, Bria is still not safe. Until Warren or his body is found, she still needs us to protect her. The same goes for Edward. We know that he is dangerous. If we believe Warren, he has already killed, and we know from Daniel and Bria and from listening ourselves that he is more than willing to kill again. Of course we already know that he wants Bria dead."

Jonathan added, "So we can't let our guard down. But, we can't let Bria get overly upset either. Her body is not strong enough now to carry a baby to term. If she wants to keep this baby, then we have to help her do it. That doesn't even include what any of the poisons have done to her."

"You know that we're here to do just that, but I think we really should think about that tracking device Case talked about." Nick said. Then as if he thought about what he said. "Do they make such a thing?"

"I don't think so, Nick." But you could hear in Jonathan's voice, he wished there was.

The ride home seemed to take forever and I decided to not let them know just yet how much I knew. I continued to listen to their quiet conversation until I finally let my mind understand what I had learned.

Warren could possibly still be alive, but for how long? Edward was still alive, and he would, most likely, still be trying to kill me. He couldn't have been working alone. Others had to be involved. That meant that I and my little family were still in danger. And more importantly, my unborn child, Warren's unborn child, was in danger, too. Not only from outside forces, but possibly from my own weakened body.

I silently made up my mind. I would do everything I could to find Warren, to keep him alive, and to finally get out from under the threat that Edward represented, not just to me, but to all of us. There had to be a way. There had to be. And I would find it.

To be continued……

With

A Hidden Heart